ONE PIECE

Ace's Story

THE MANGA

2

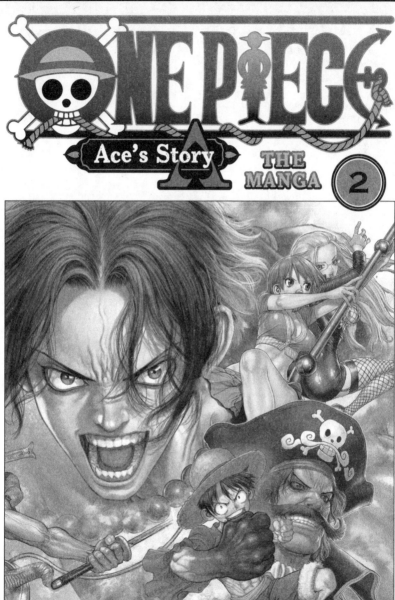

Art by **Boichi**　　Storyboards by **Ryo Ishiyama**　　Created by **Eiichiro Oda**

Based on *One Piece: Ace's Story* by Sho Hinata & Tatsuya Hamazaki

CONTENTS

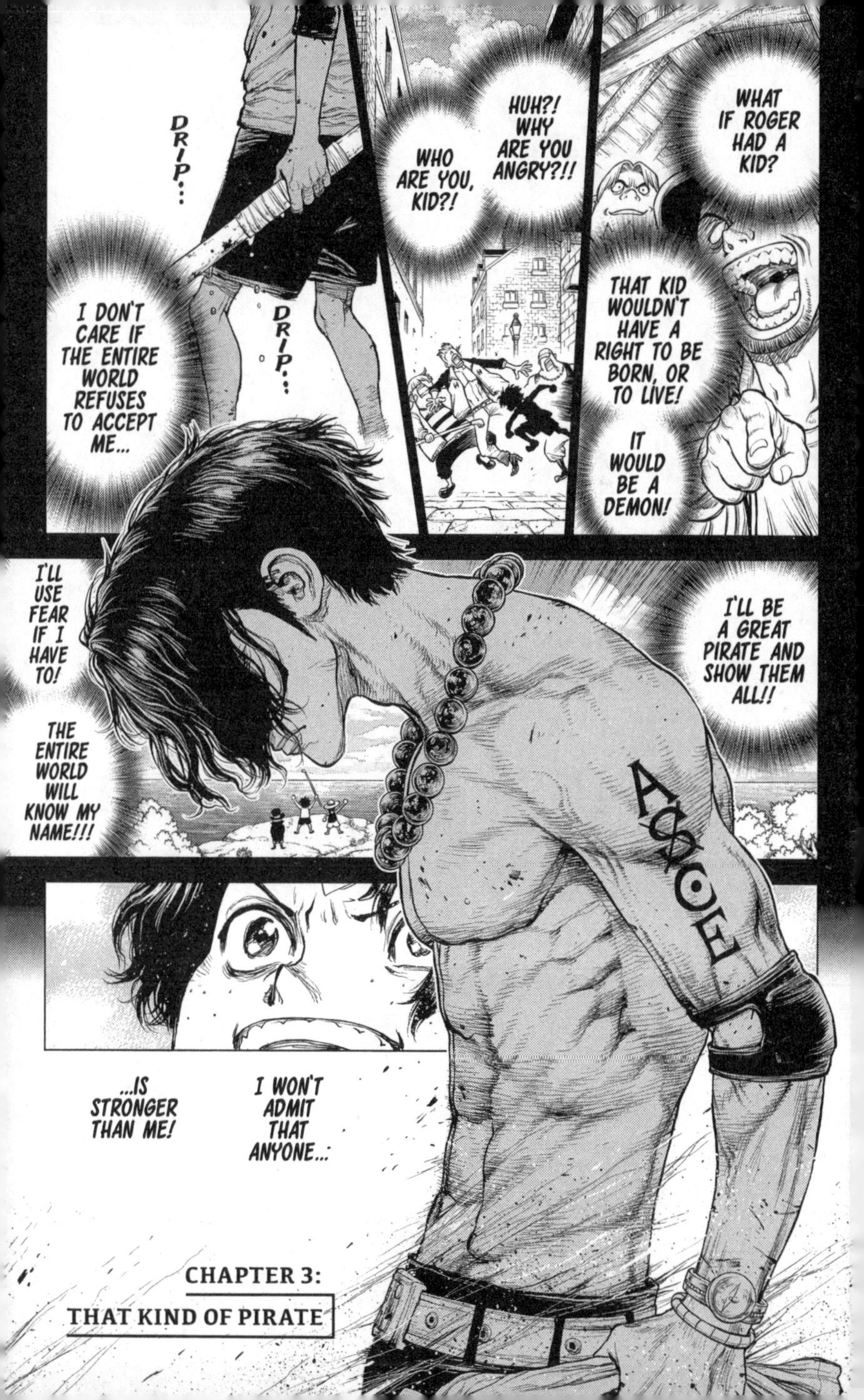
WHAT IF ROGER HAD A KID?
THAT KID WOULDN'T HAVE A RIGHT TO BE BORN, OR TO LIVE!
IT WOULD BE A DEMON!
HUH?! WHY ARE YOU ANGRY?!!
WHO ARE YOU, KID?!
DRIP...
DRIP...
I DON'T CARE IF THE ENTIRE WORLD REFUSES TO ACCEPT ME...
I'LL BE A GREAT PIRATE AND SHOW THEM ALL!!
I'LL USE FEAR IF I HAVE TO!
THE ENTIRE WORLD WILL KNOW MY NAME!!!
I WON'T ADMIT THAT ANYONE...
...IS STRONGER THAN ME!
ACE
CHAPTER 3:
THAT KIND OF PIRATE

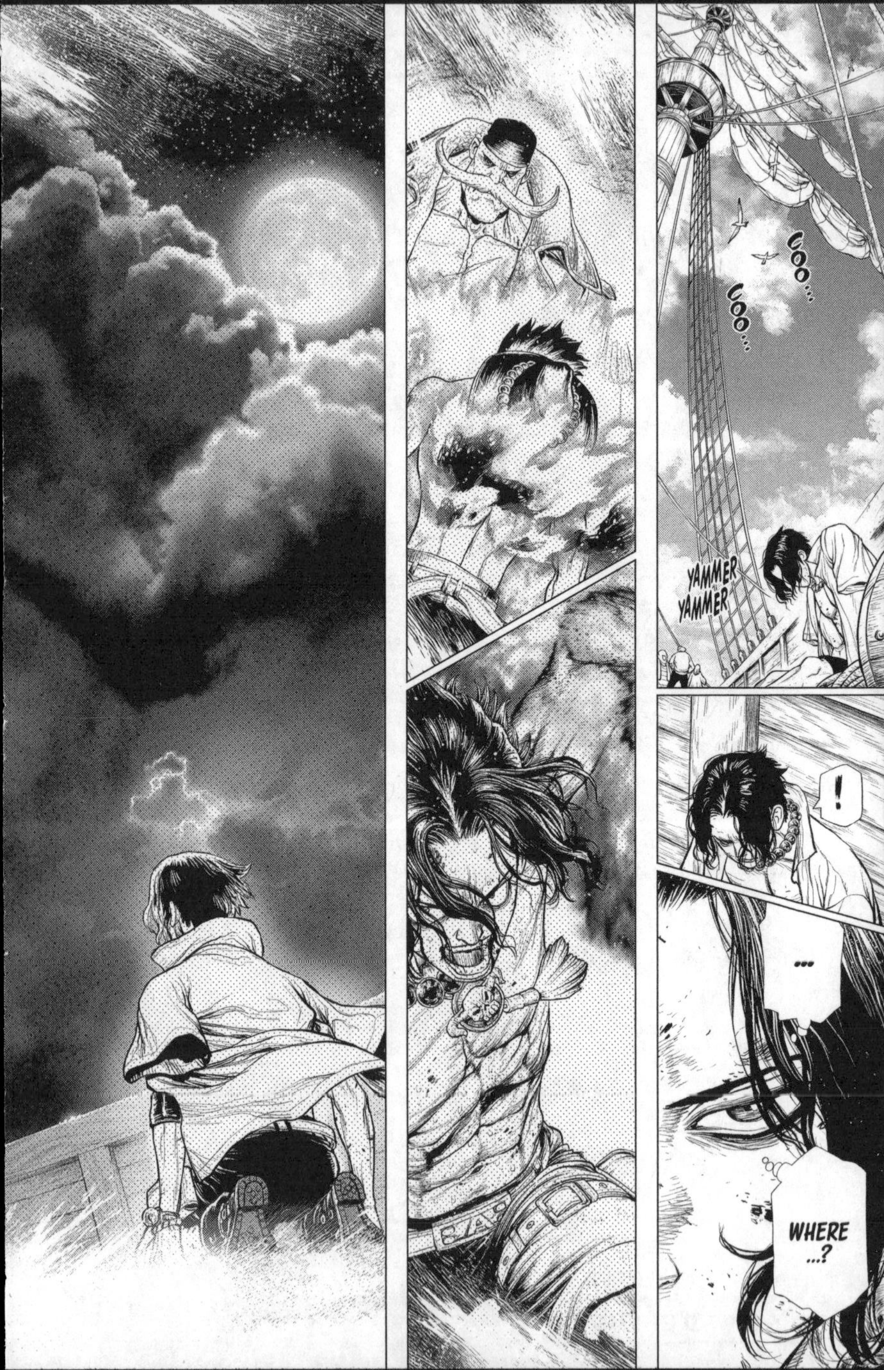
COO...
COO...
YAMMER YAMMER
!
...
WHERE ...?

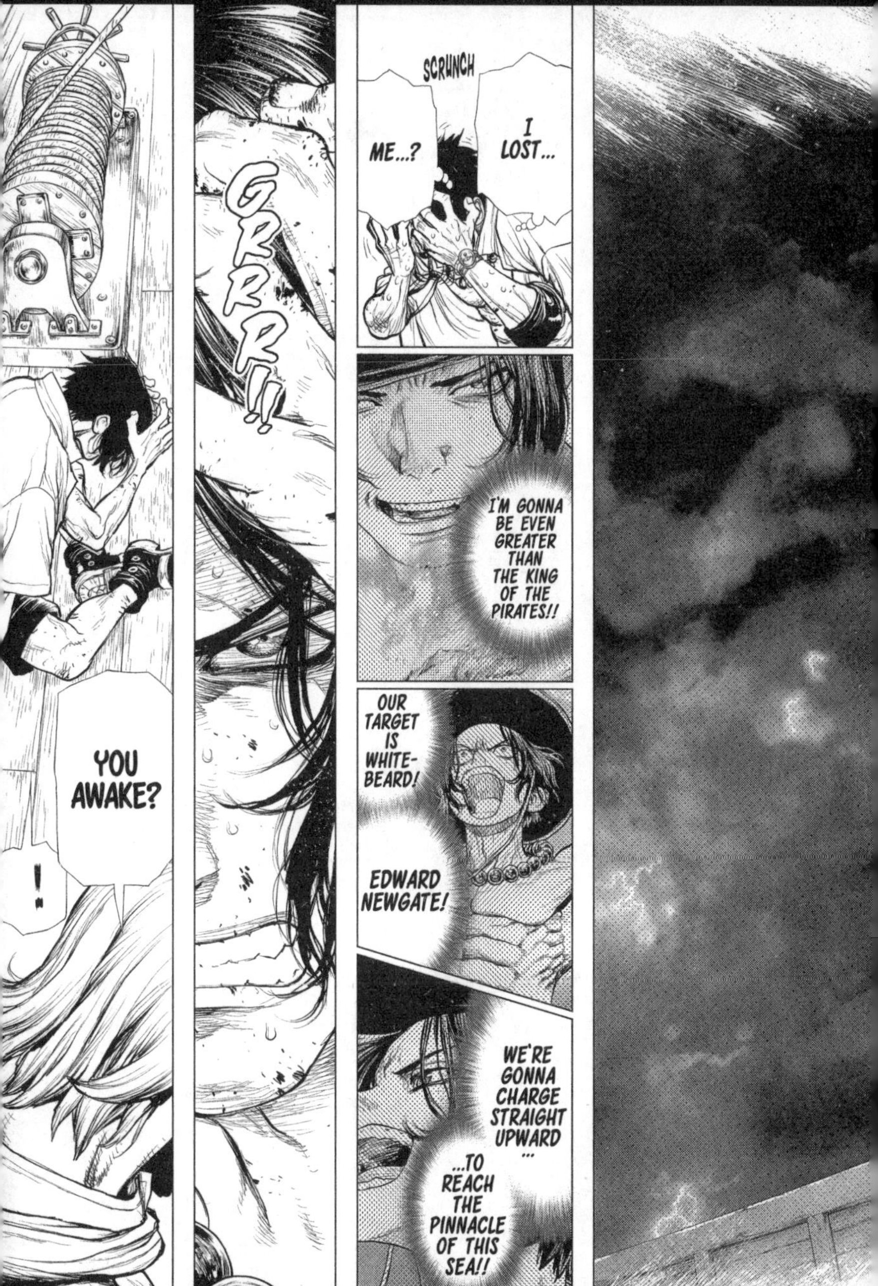
SCRUNCH
I LOST...
ME...?
I'M GONNA BE EVEN GREATER THAN THE KING OF THE PIRATES!!
OUR TARGET IS WHITE-BEARD!
EDWARD NEWGATE!
WE'RE GONNA CHARGE STRAIGHT UPWARD...
...TO REACH THE PINNACLE OF THIS SEA!!
GRRR!!
YOU AWAKE?
!

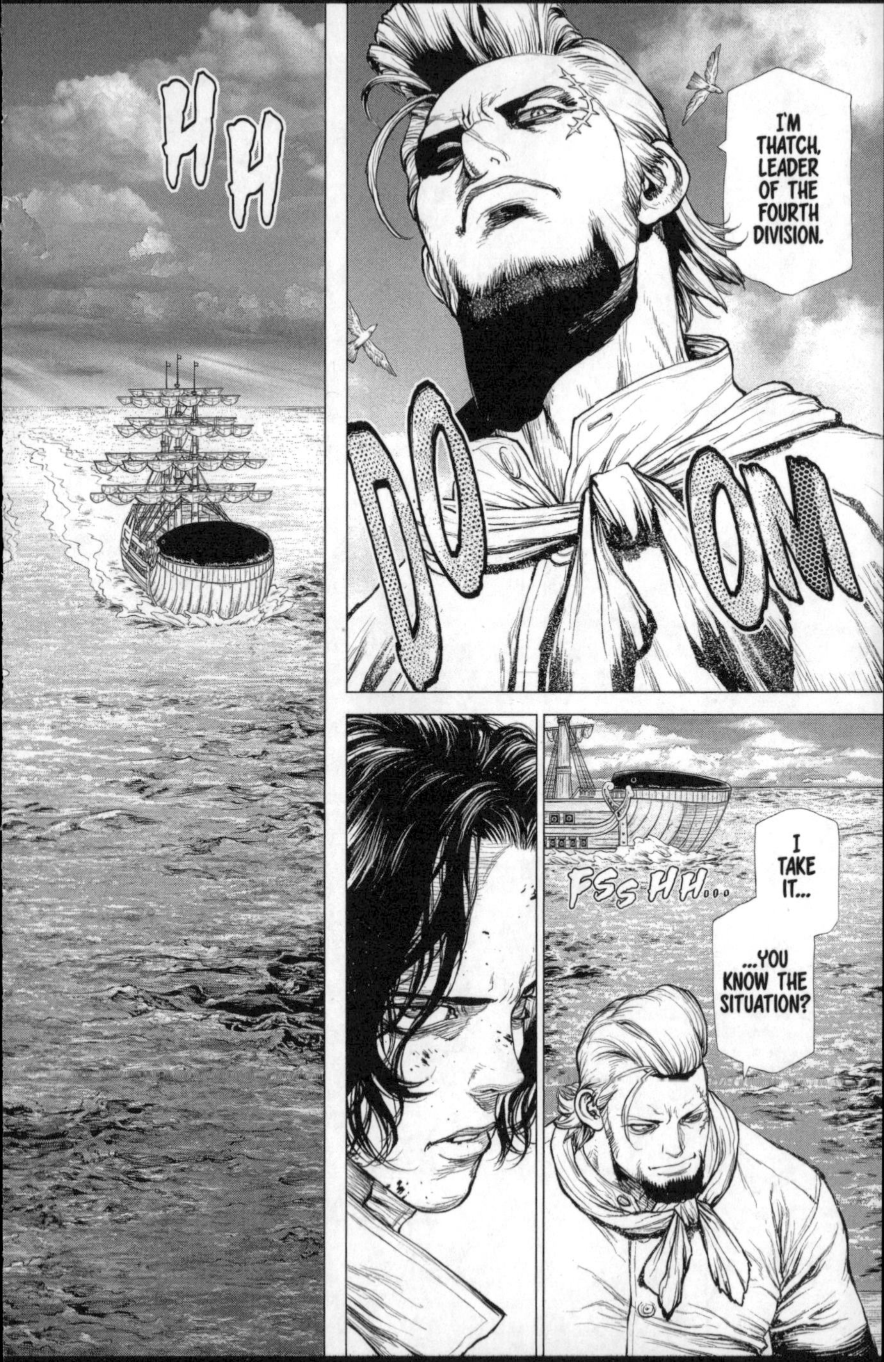
I'M THATCH, LEADER OF THE FOURTH DIVISION.
DOOOM
I TAKE IT...
FSSHH...
...YOU KNOW THE SITUATION?
HH

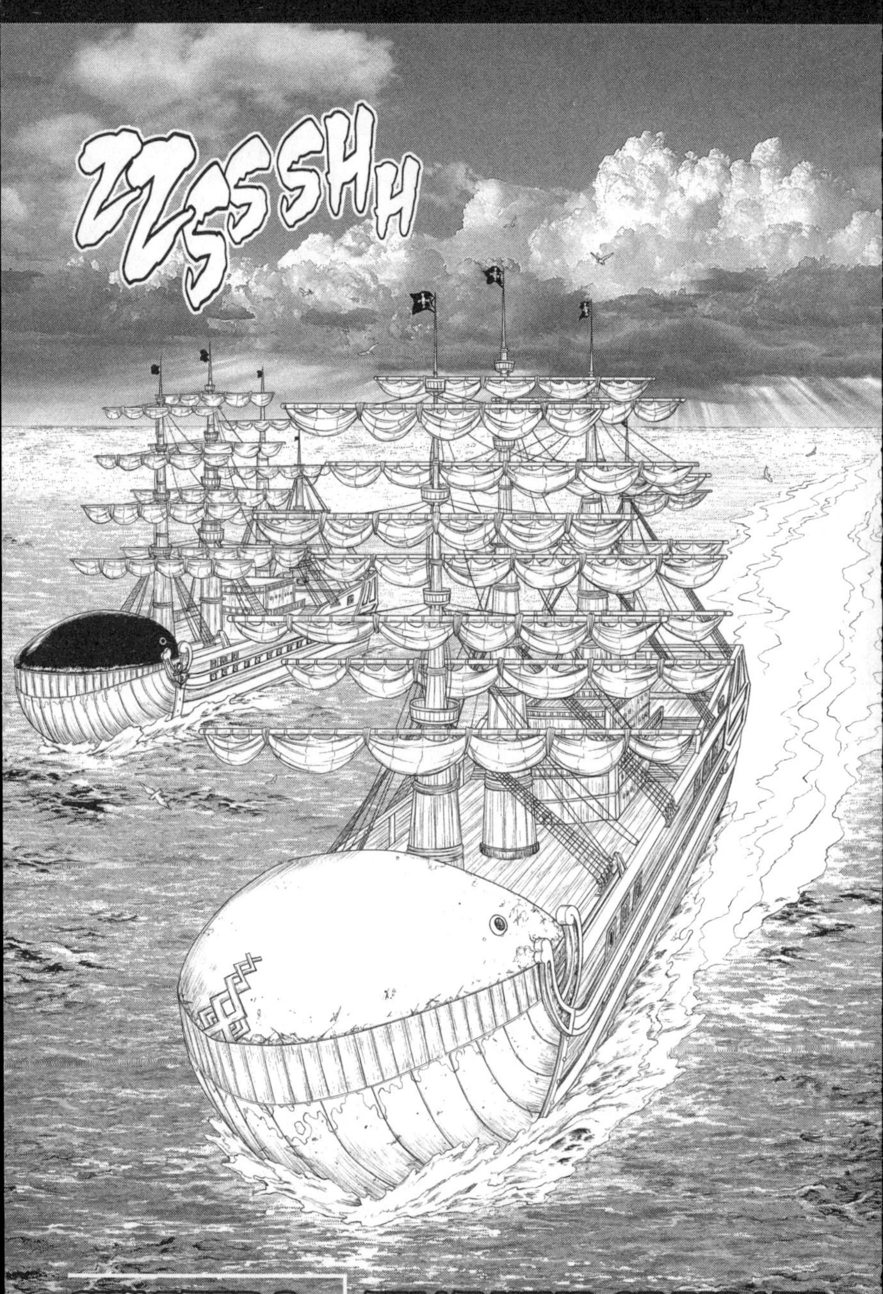
ZZSSSHH

CHAPTER 3: THAT KIND OF PIRATE

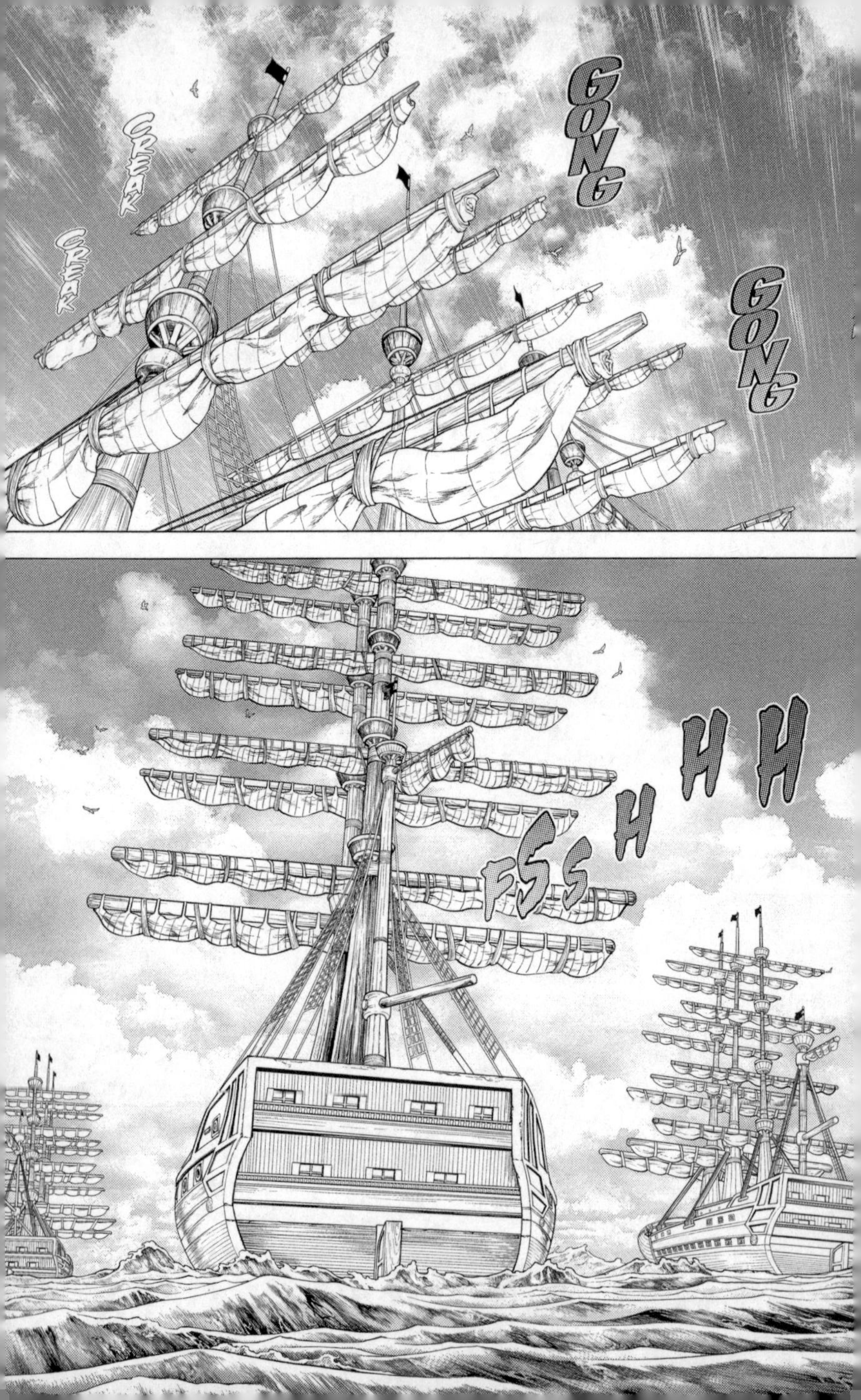
GONG
GONG
CREAK
CREAK
FSSHHH

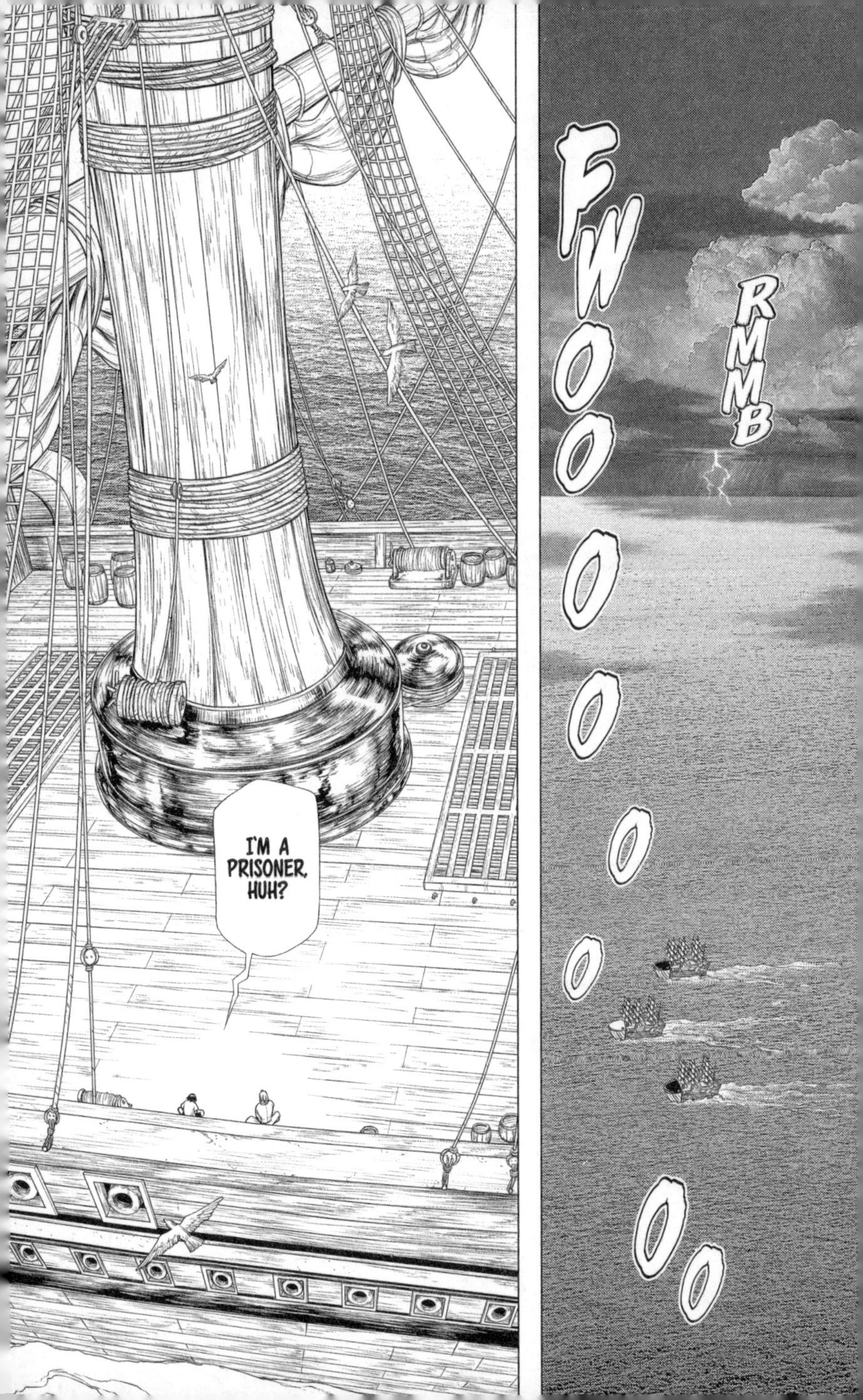

FWOOOOOOOO
RMMB
I'M A PRISONER, HUH?

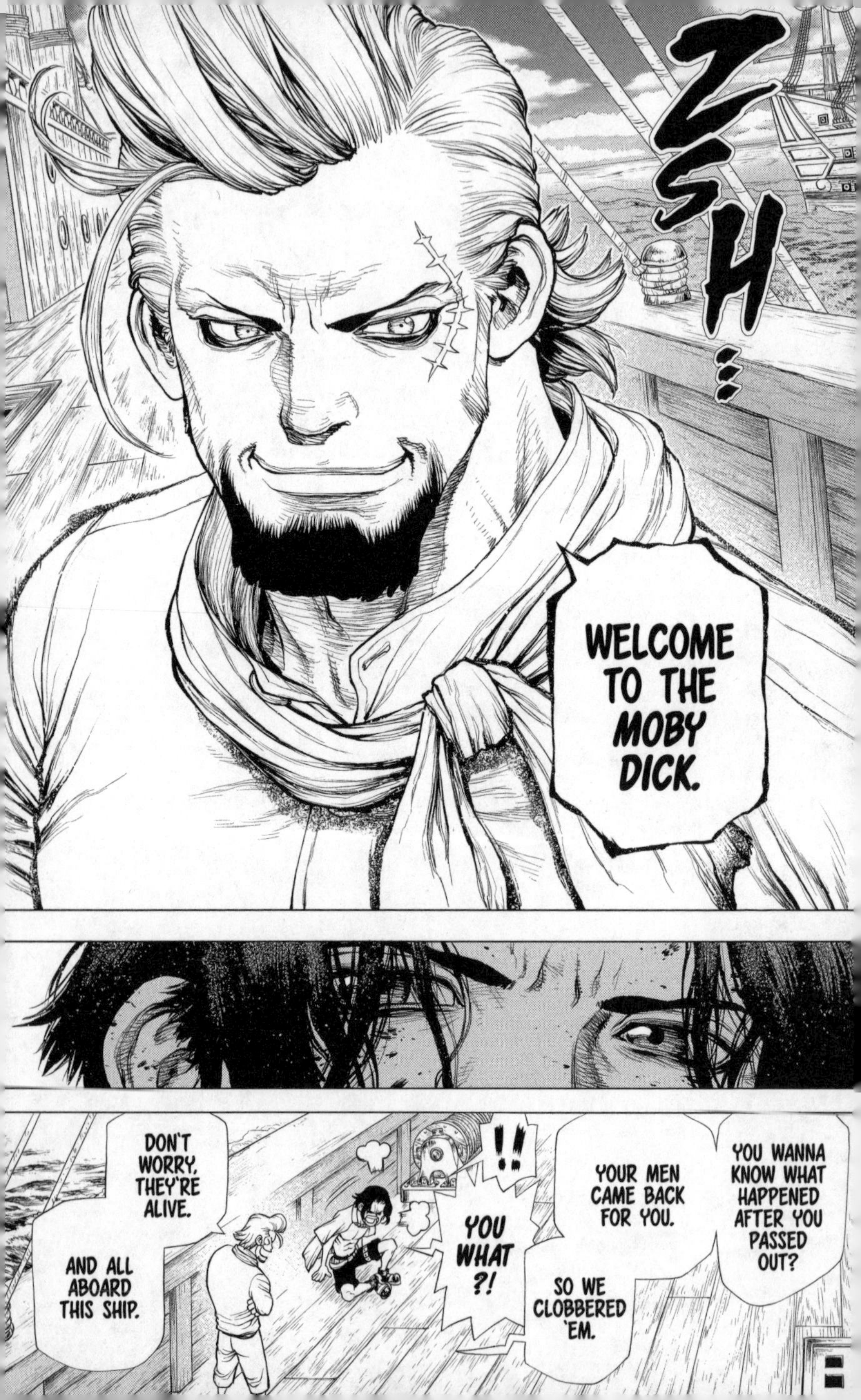
ZSH...
WELCOME TO THE MOBY DICK.
YOU WANNA KNOW WHAT HAPPENED AFTER YOU PASSED OUT?
YOUR MEN CAME BACK FOR YOU.
SO WE CLOBBERED 'EM.
!!
YOU WHAT?!
DON'T WORRY, THEY'RE ALIVE.
AND ALL ABOARD THIS SHIP.

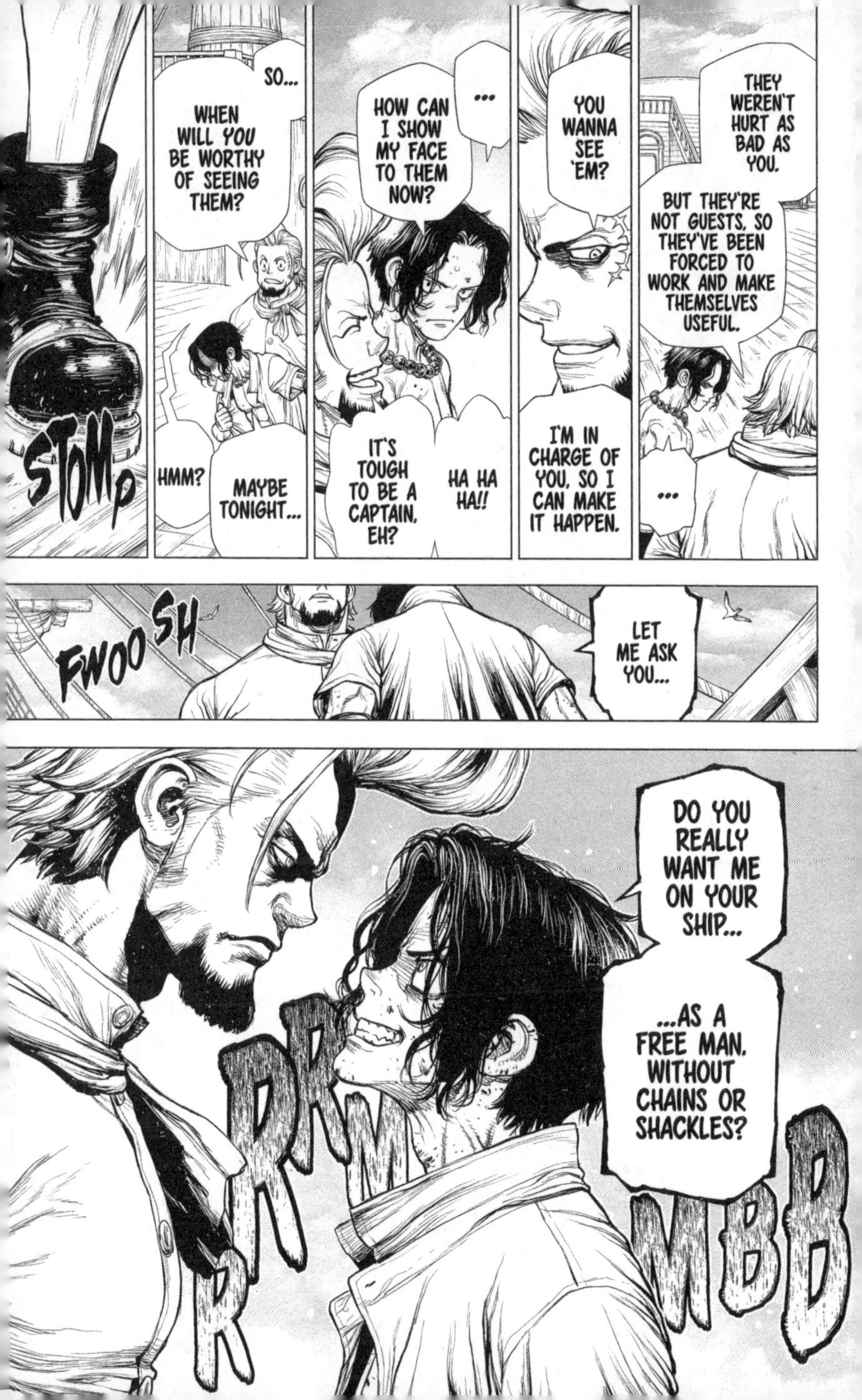
THEY WEREN'T HURT AS BAD AS YOU.
BUT THEY'RE NOT GUESTS, SO THEY'VE BEEN FORCED TO WORK AND MAKE THEMSELVES USEFUL.
...
YOU WANNA SEE 'EM?
I'M IN CHARGE OF YOU, SO I CAN MAKE IT HAPPEN.
...
HOW CAN I SHOW MY FACE TO THEM NOW?
HA HA HA!!
IT'S TOUGH TO BE A CAPTAIN, EH?
SO...
WHEN WILL YOU BE WORTHY OF SEEING THEM?
MAYBE TONIGHT...
HMM?
STOMP
LET ME ASK YOU...
FWOOSH
DO YOU REALLY WANT ME ON YOUR SHIP...
...AS A FREE MAN, WITHOUT CHAINS OR SHACKLES?
DRRRMBB

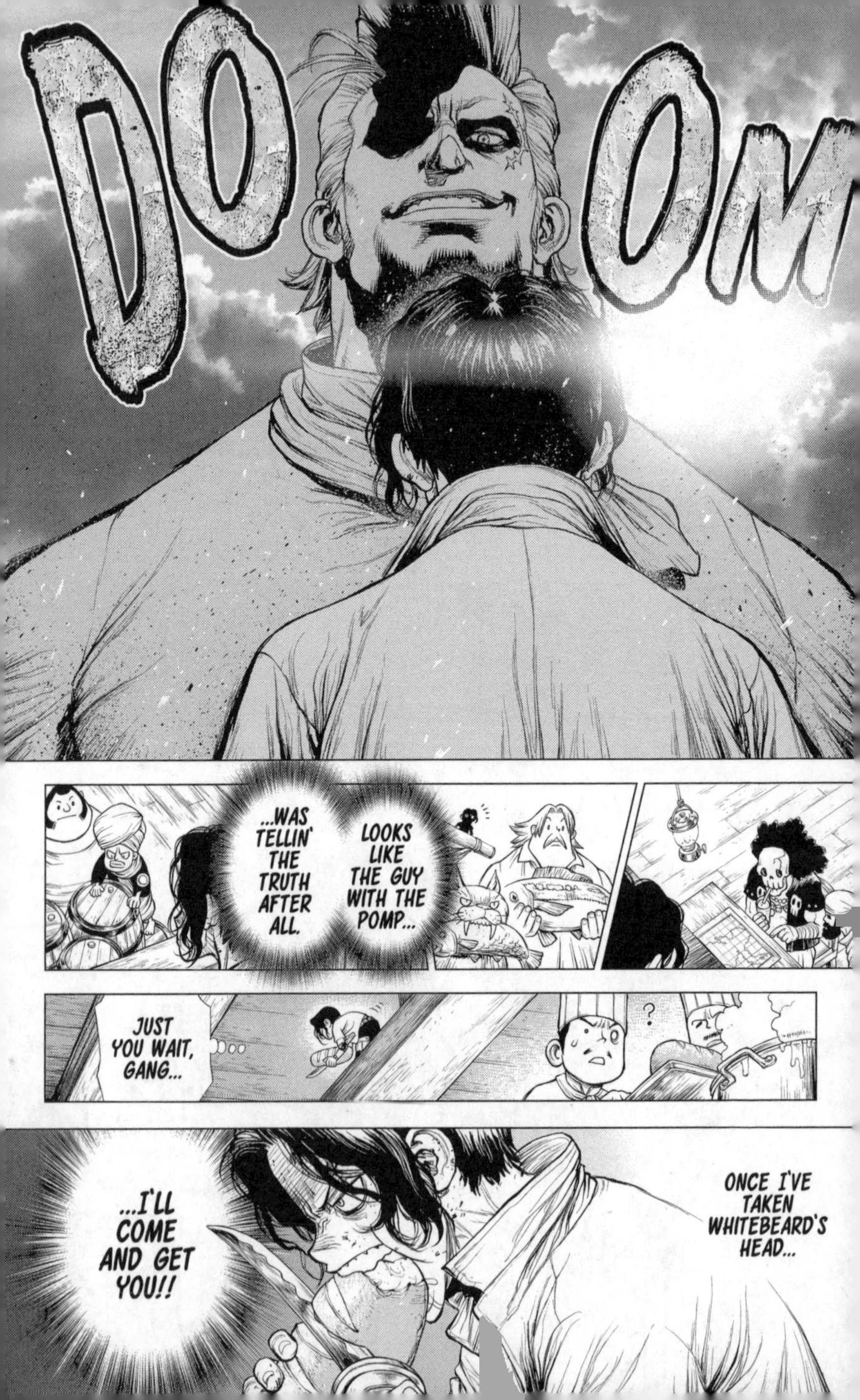
DO OM
LOOKS LIKE THE GUY WITH THE POMP...
...WAS TELLIN' THE TRUTH AFTER ALL.
?
JUST YOU WAIT, GANG...
ONCE I'VE TAKEN WHITEBEARD'S HEAD...
...I'LL COME AND GET YOU!!

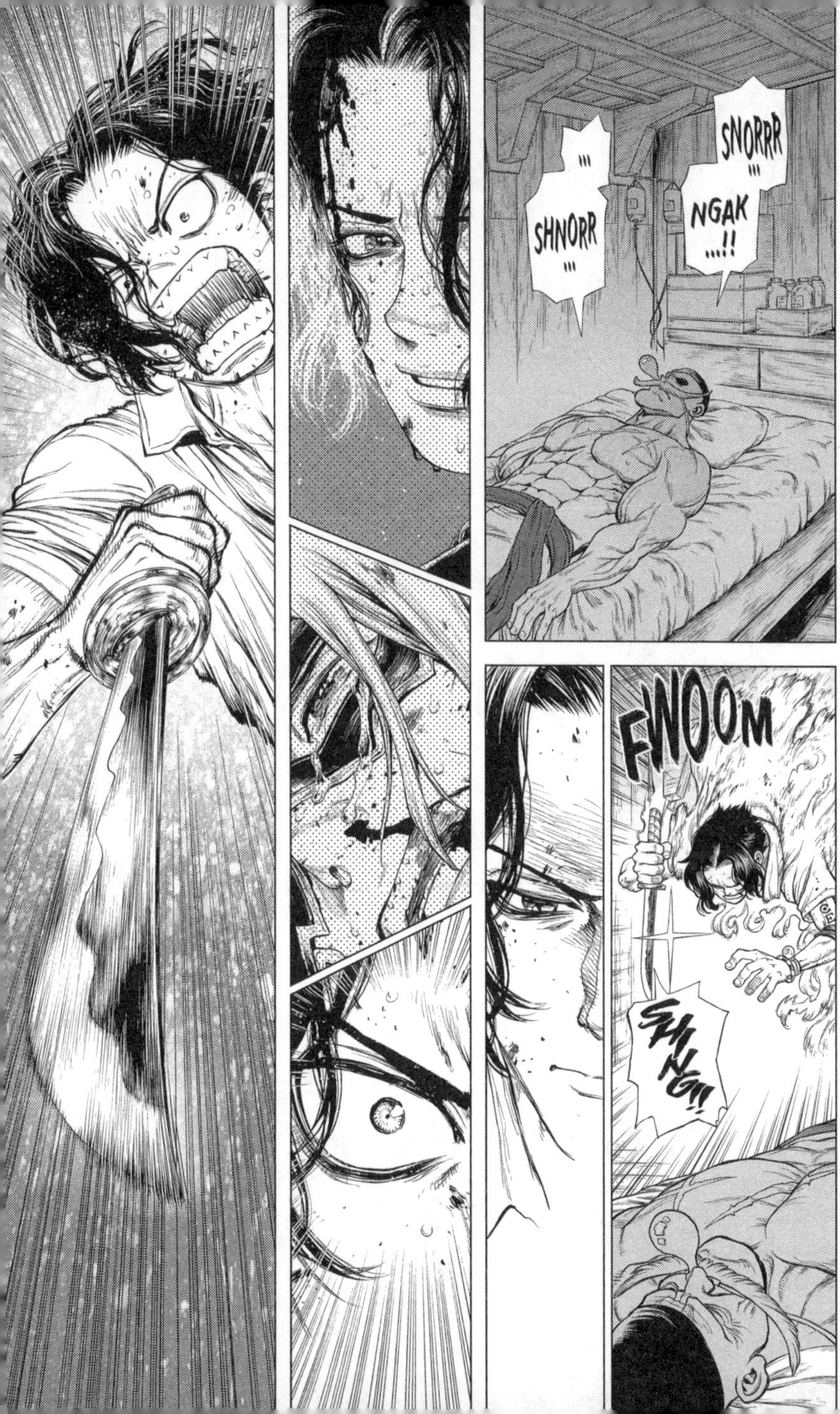
SNORRR...
NGAK
...!!
...
SHNORR...
FWOOM
SHING!!

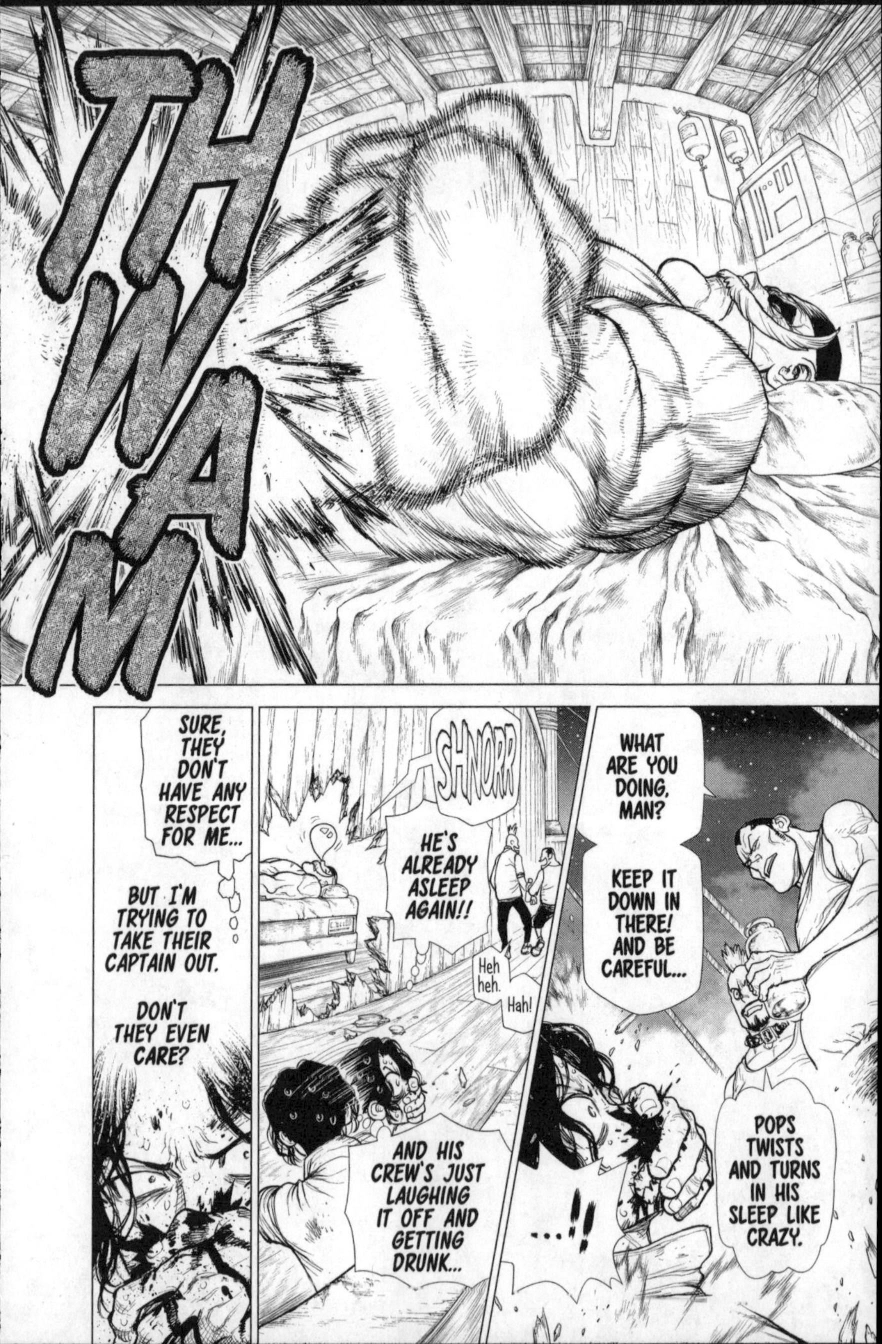
THWAM
WHAT ARE YOU DOING, MAN?
KEEP IT DOWN IN THERE! AND BE CAREFUL...
POPS TWISTS AND TURNS IN HIS SLEEP LIKE CRAZY.
...!!
SHNORR
HE'S ALREADY ASLEEP AGAIN!!
Heh heh.
Hah!
AND HIS CREW'S JUST LAUGHING IT OFF AND GETTING DRUNK...
SURE, THEY DON'T HAVE ANY RESPECT FOR ME...
BUT I'M TRYING TO TAKE THEIR CAPTAIN OUT.
DON'T THEY EVEN CARE?

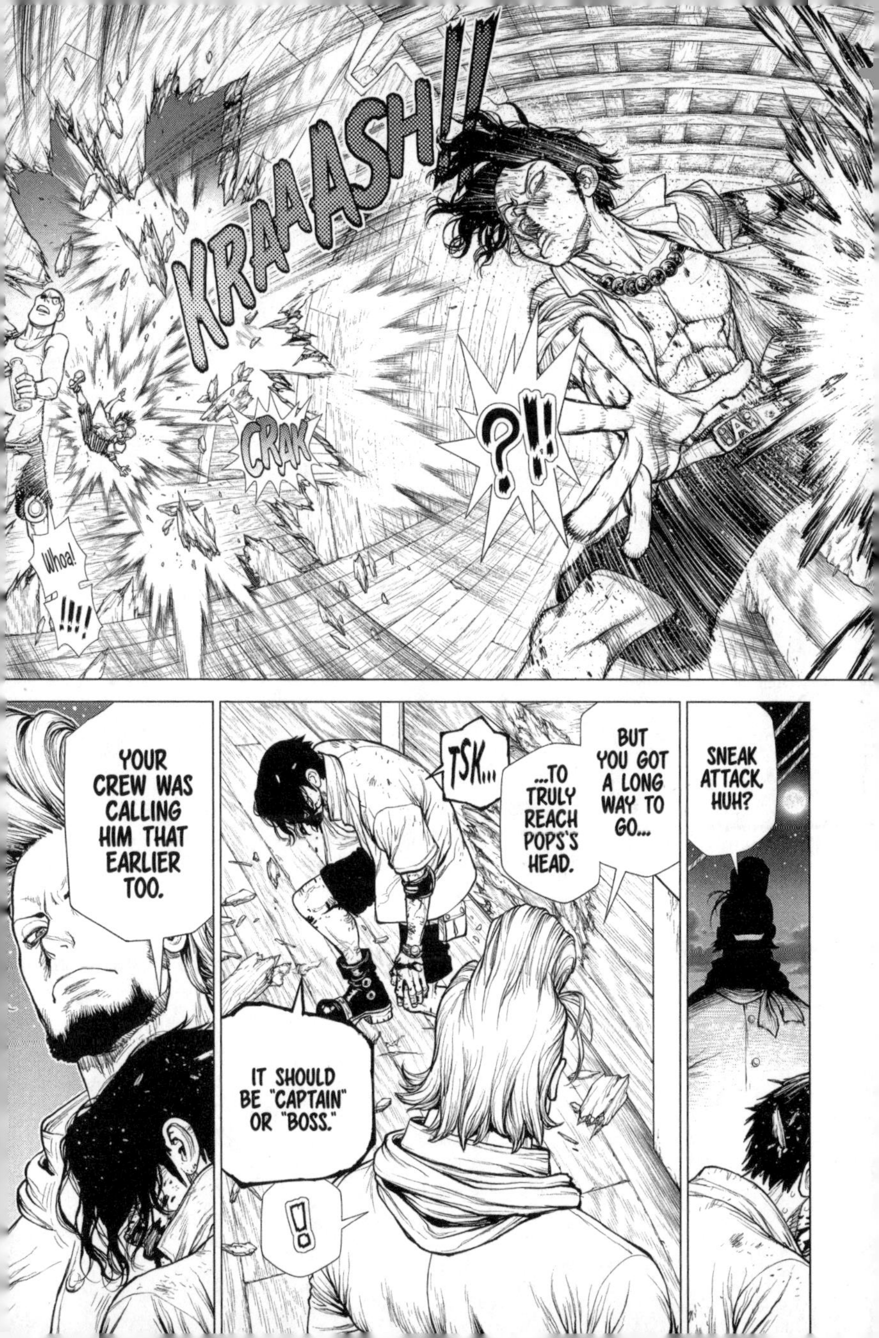
KRAAASH!!
?!!
CRAK
Whoa!
!!!!
SNEAK ATTACK, HUH?
BUT YOU GOT A LONG WAY TO GO...
...TO TRULY REACH POPS'S HEAD.
TSK...
IT SHOULD BE "CAPTAIN" OR "BOSS."
!
YOUR CREW WAS CALLING HIM THAT EARLIER TOO.

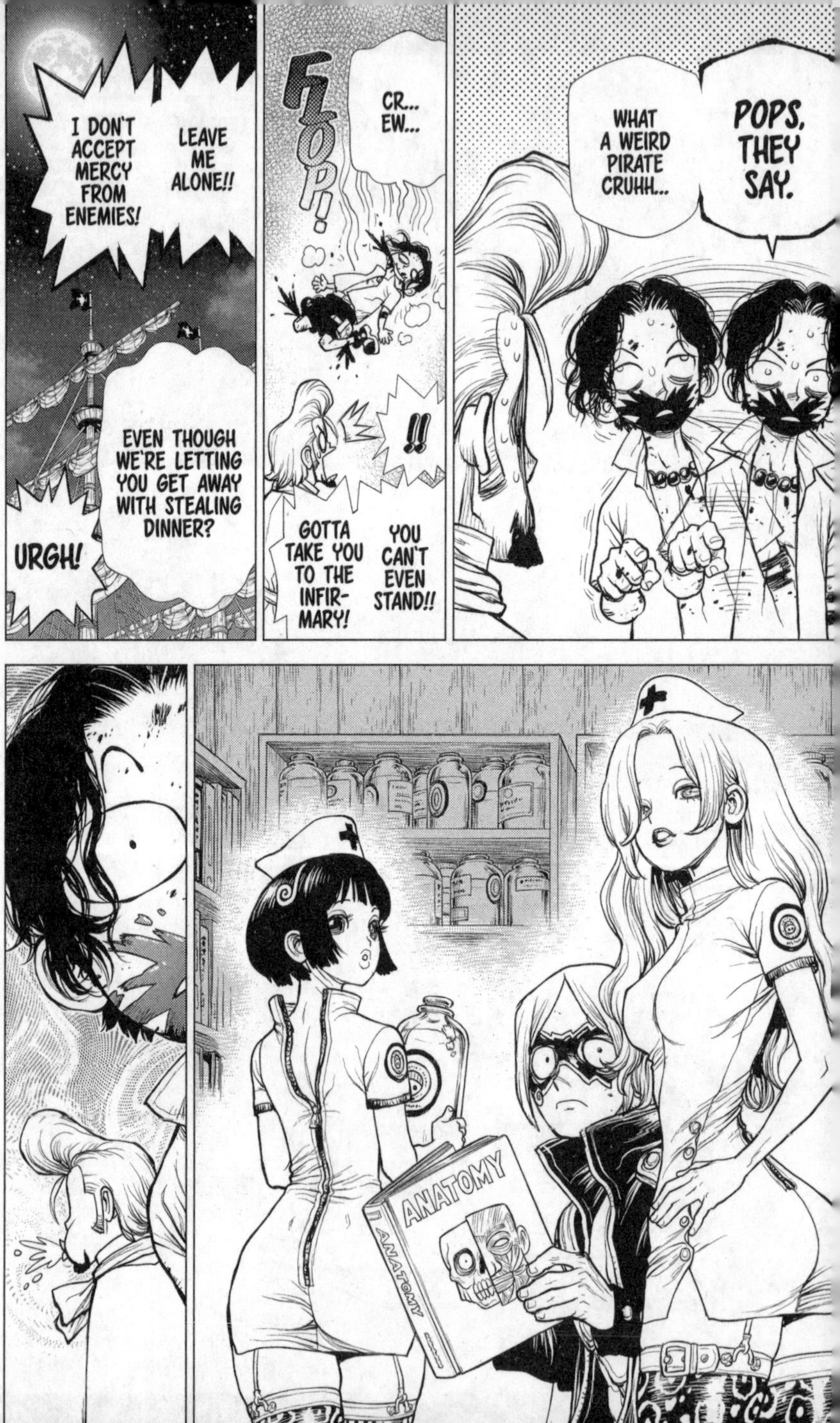
POPS, THEY SAY.
WHAT A WEIRD PIRATE CRUHH...
FLOP!!
CR... EW...
!!
YOU CAN'T EVEN STAND!!
GOTTA TAKE YOU TO THE INFIRMARY!
LEAVE ME ALONE!!
I DON'T ACCEPT MERCY FROM ENEMIES!
EVEN THOUGH WE'RE LETTING YOU GET AWAY WITH STEALING DINNER?
URGH!
ANATOMY
ANATOMY

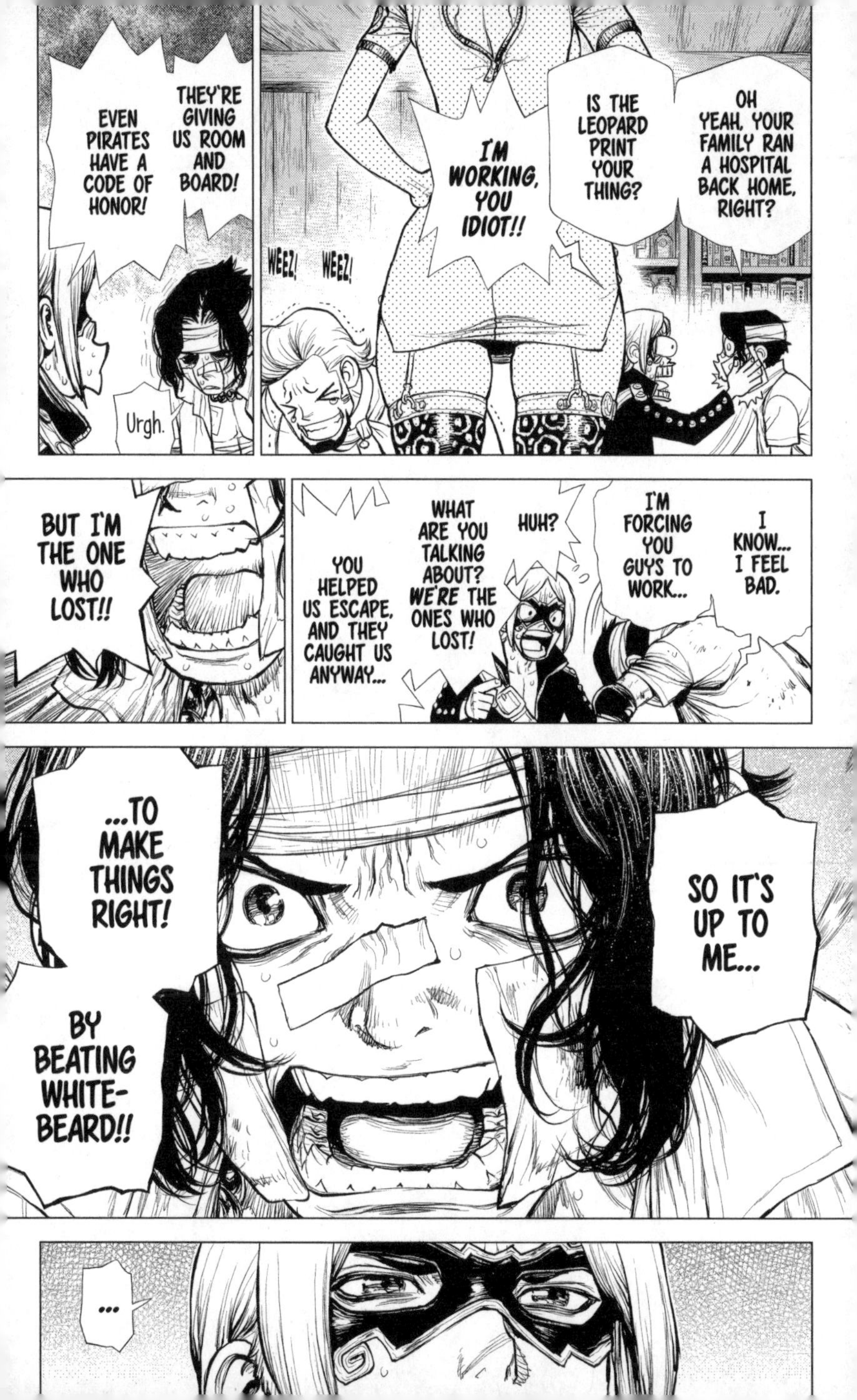
OH YEAH, YOUR FAMILY RAN A HOSPITAL BACK HOME, RIGHT?
IS THE LEOPARD PRINT YOUR THING?
I'M WORKING, YOU IDIOT!!
WEEZ!
WEEZ!
THEY'RE GIVING US ROOM AND BOARD!
EVEN PIRATES HAVE A CODE OF HONOR!
Urgh.
I KNOW... I FEEL BAD.
I'M FORCING YOU GUYS TO WORK...
HUH?
WHAT ARE YOU TALKING ABOUT? WE'RE THE ONES WHO LOST!
YOU HELPED US ESCAPE, AND THEY CAUGHT US ANYWAY...
BUT I'M THE ONE WHO LOST!!
SO IT'S UP TO ME...
...TO MAKE THINGS RIGHT!
BY BEATING WHITE-BEARD!!
...

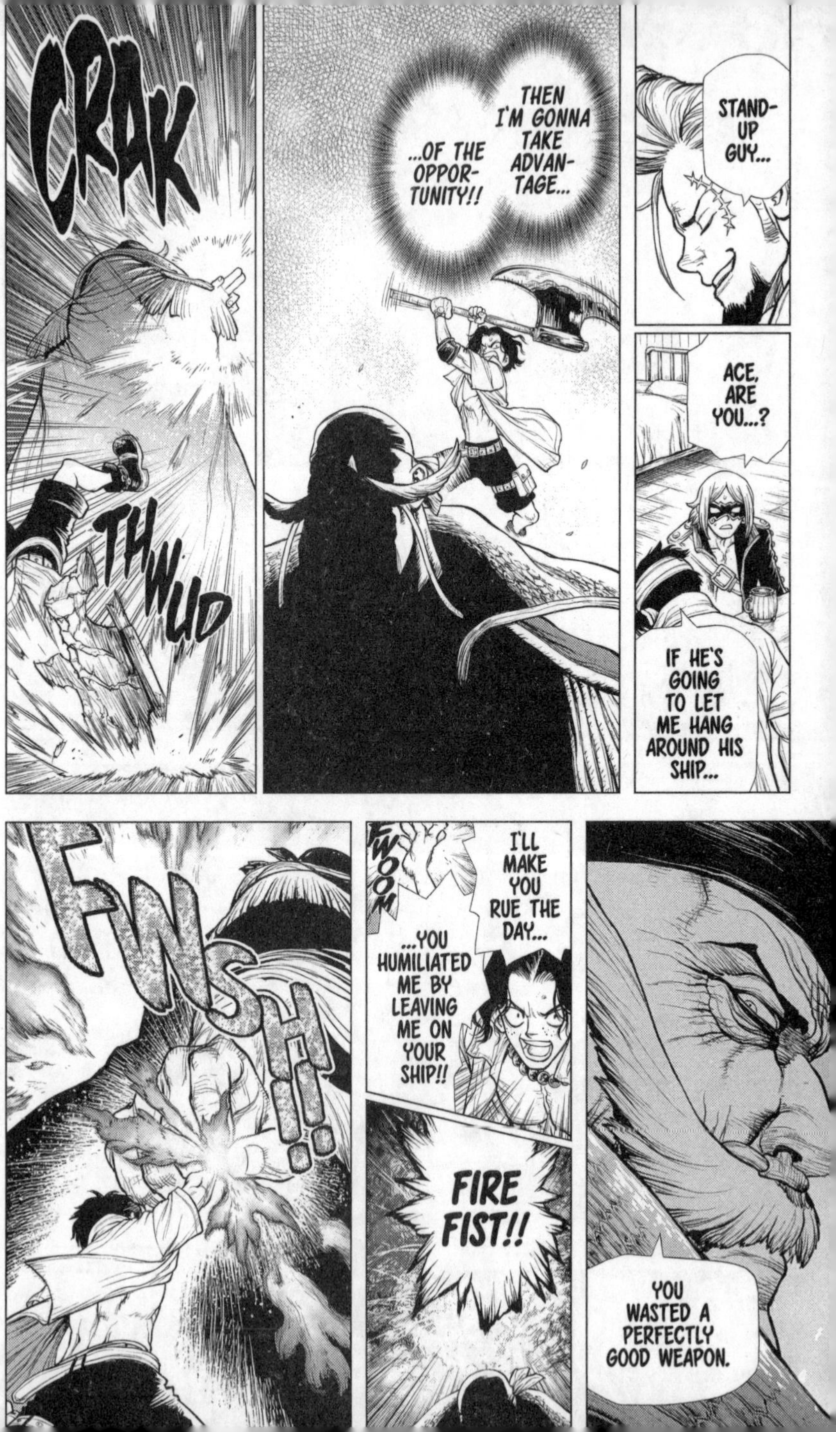
STAND-UP GUY...
ACE, ARE YOU...?
IF HE'S GOING TO LET ME HANG AROUND HIS SHIP...
THEN I'M GONNA TAKE ADVANTAGE...
...OF THE OPPORTUNITY!!
CRAK
THWUD
YOU WASTED A PERFECTLY GOOD WEAPON.
FWOOM
I'LL MAKE YOU RUE THE DAY...
...YOU HUMILIATED ME BY LEAVING ME ON YOUR SHIP!!
FIRE FIST!!
FWSH!!

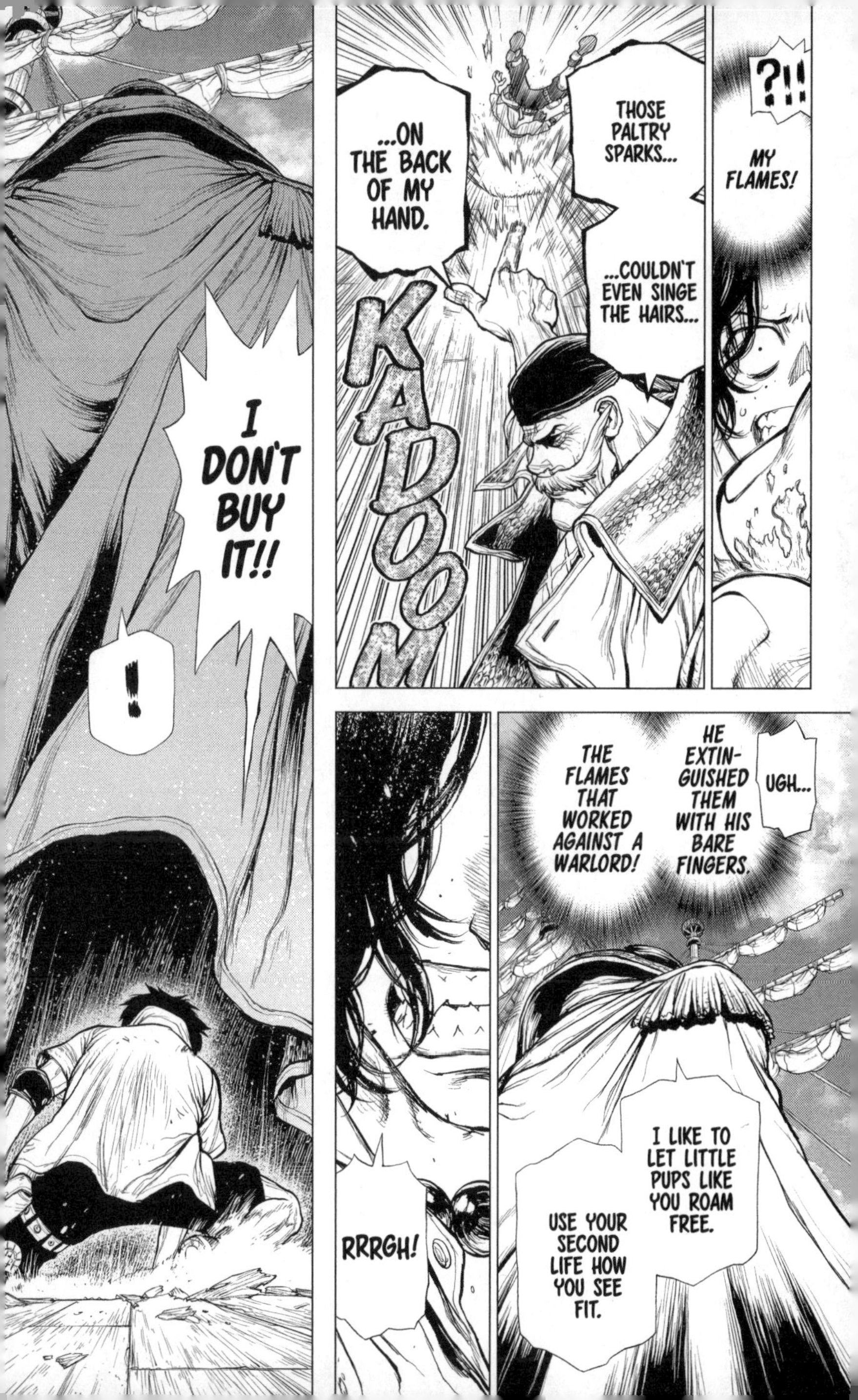
?!!
MY FLAMES!
THOSE PALTRY SPARKS...
...COULDN'T EVEN SINGE THE HAIRS...
...ON THE BACK OF MY HAND.
KADOOM
UGH...
HE EXTIN-GUISHED THEM WITH HIS BARE FINGERS.
THE FLAMES THAT WORKED AGAINST A WARLORD!
I LIKE TO LET LITTLE PUPS LIKE YOU ROAM FREE.
USE YOUR SECOND LIFE HOW YOU SEE FIT.
RRRGH!
I DON'T BUY IT!!
!

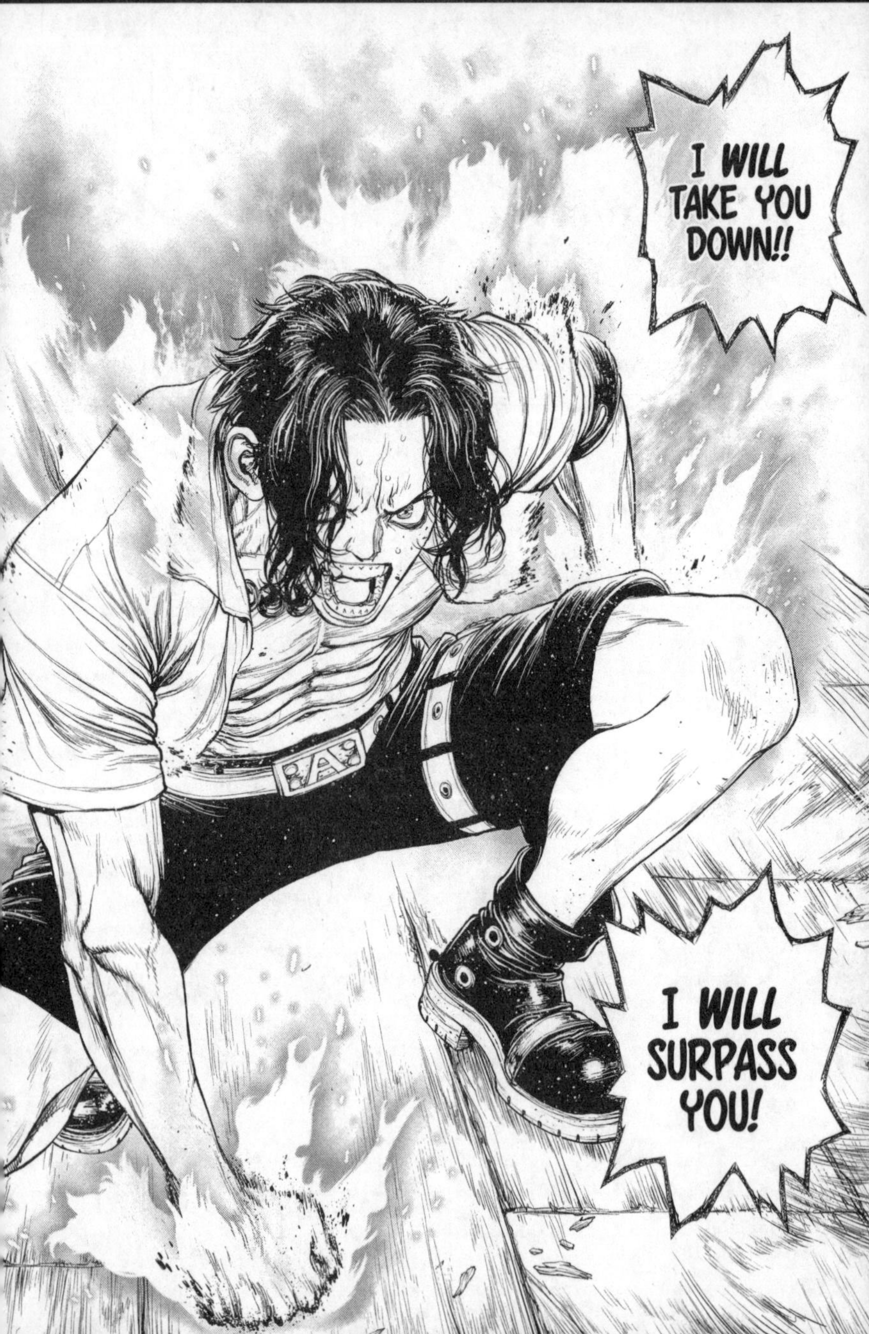
I WILL TAKE YOU DOWN!!
I WILL SURPASS YOU!

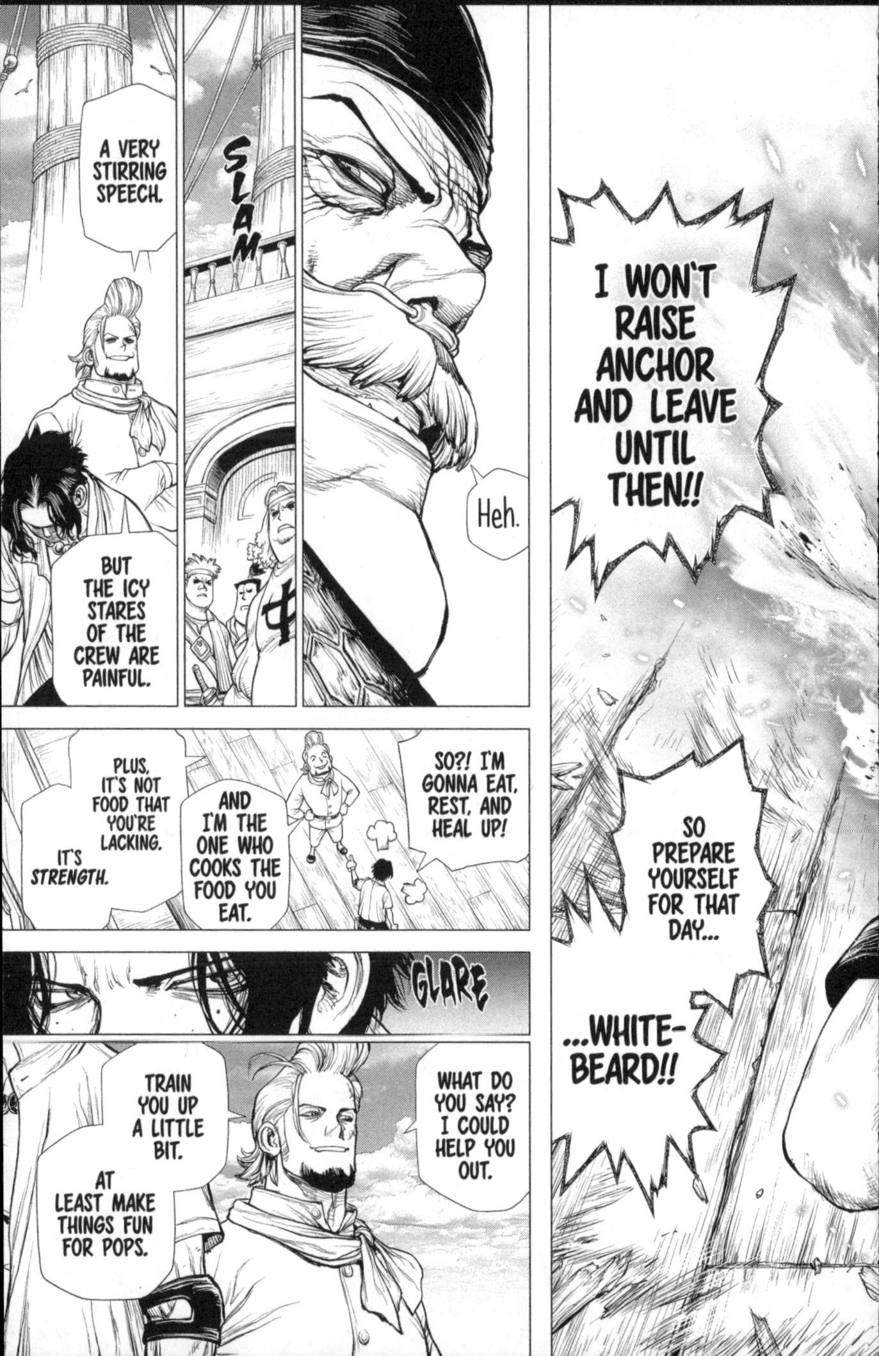
I WON'T RAISE ANCHOR AND LEAVE UNTIL THEN!!
SO PREPARE YOURSELF FOR THAT DAY...
...WHITE-BEARD!!
Heh.
SLAM
A VERY STIRRING SPEECH.
BUT THE ICY STARES OF THE CREW ARE PAINFUL.
SO?! I'M GONNA EAT, REST, AND HEAL UP!
AND I'M THE ONE WHO COOKS THE FOOD YOU EAT.
PLUS, IT'S NOT FOOD THAT YOU'RE LACKING.
IT'S STRENGTH.
GLARE
WHAT DO YOU SAY? I COULD HELP YOU OUT.
TRAIN YOU UP A LITTLE BIT.
AT LEAST MAKE THINGS FUN FOR POPS.

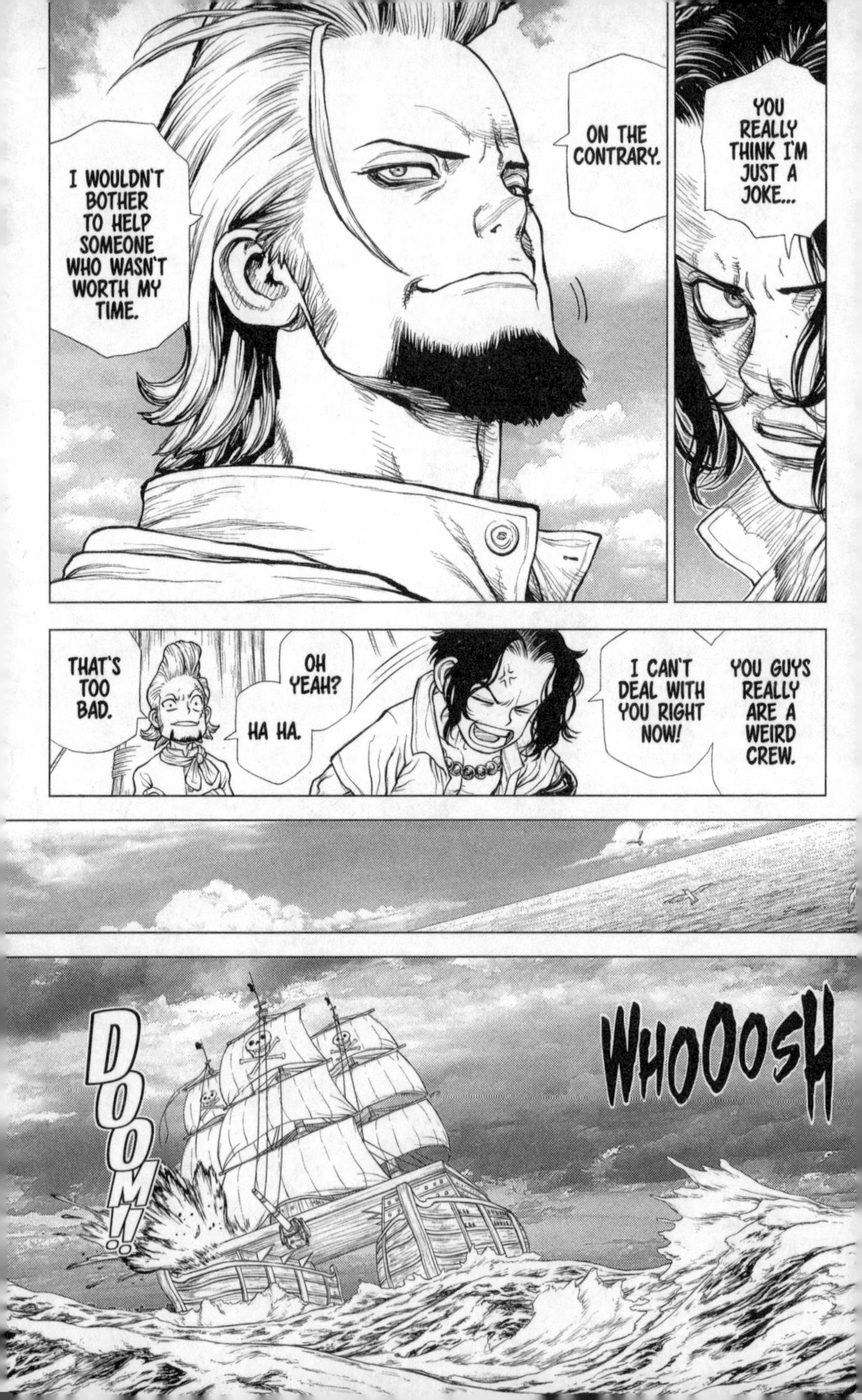
YOU REALLY THINK I'M JUST A JOKE...
ON THE CONTRARY.
I WOULDN'T BOTHER TO HELP SOMEONE WHO WASN'T WORTH MY TIME.
YOU GUYS REALLY ARE A WEIRD CREW.
I CAN'T DEAL WITH YOU RIGHT NOW!
OH YEAH?
HA HA.
THAT'S TOO BAD.
WHOOOSH
DOOOM!!

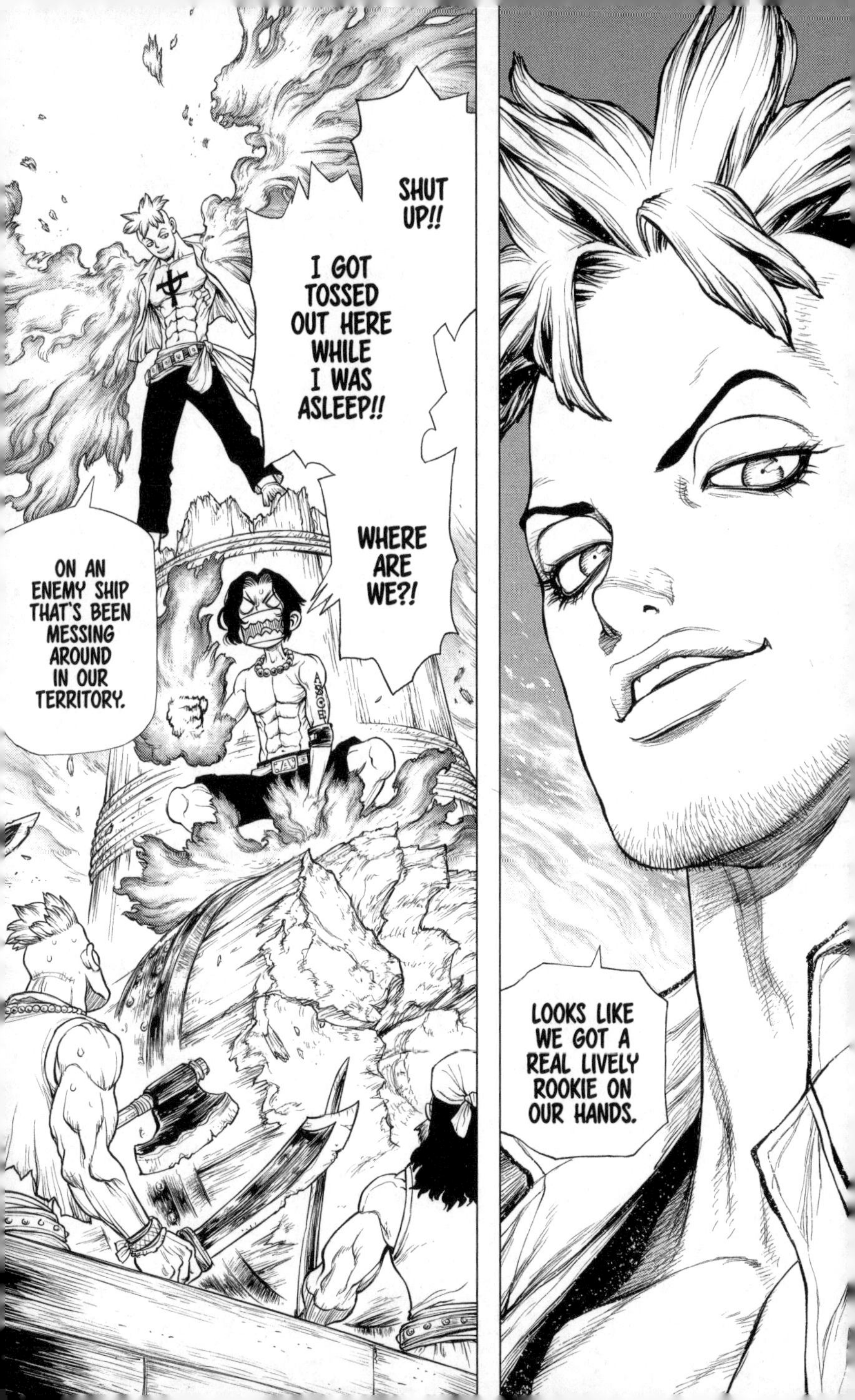
LOOKS LIKE WE GOT A REAL LIVELY ROOKIE ON OUR HANDS.
SHUT UP!!
I GOT TOSSED OUT HERE WHILE I WAS ASLEEP!!
WHERE ARE WE?!
ON AN ENEMY SHIP THAT'S BEEN MESSING AROUND IN OUR TERRITORY.

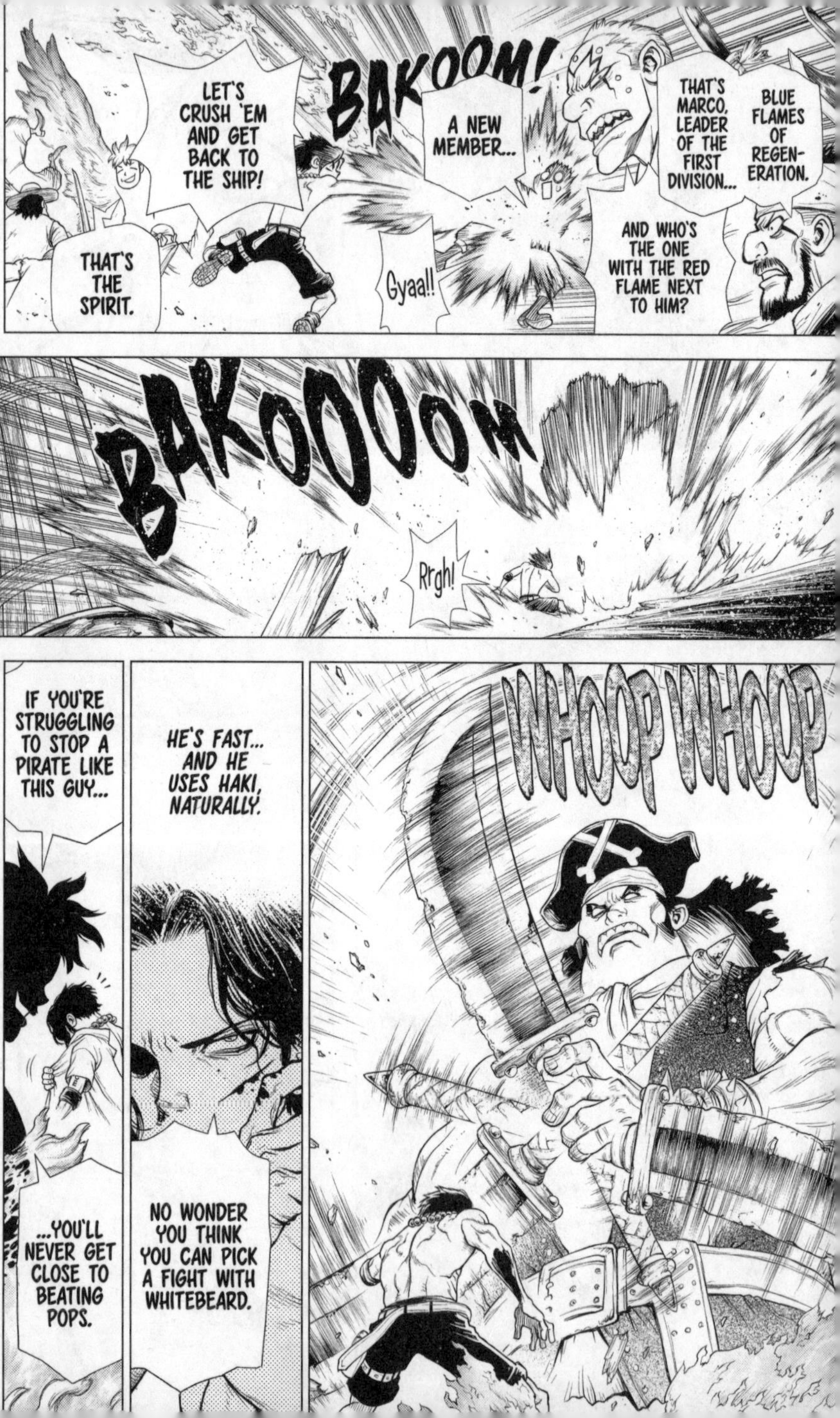
BLUE FLAMES OF REGENERATION.
THAT'S MARCO, LEADER OF THE FIRST DIVISION...
AND WHO'S THE ONE WITH THE RED FLAME NEXT TO HIM?
A NEW MEMBER...
BAKOOM!
Gyaa!!
LET'S CRUSH 'EM AND GET BACK TO THE SHIP!
THAT'S THE SPIRIT.
BAKOOOOM
Rrgh!
WHOOP WHOOP
HE'S FAST... AND HE USES HAKI, NATURALLY.
NO WONDER YOU THINK YOU CAN PICK A FIGHT WITH WHITEBEARD.
IF YOU'RE STRUGGLING TO STOP A PIRATE LIKE THIS GUY...
...YOU'LL NEVER GET CLOSE TO BEATING POPS.

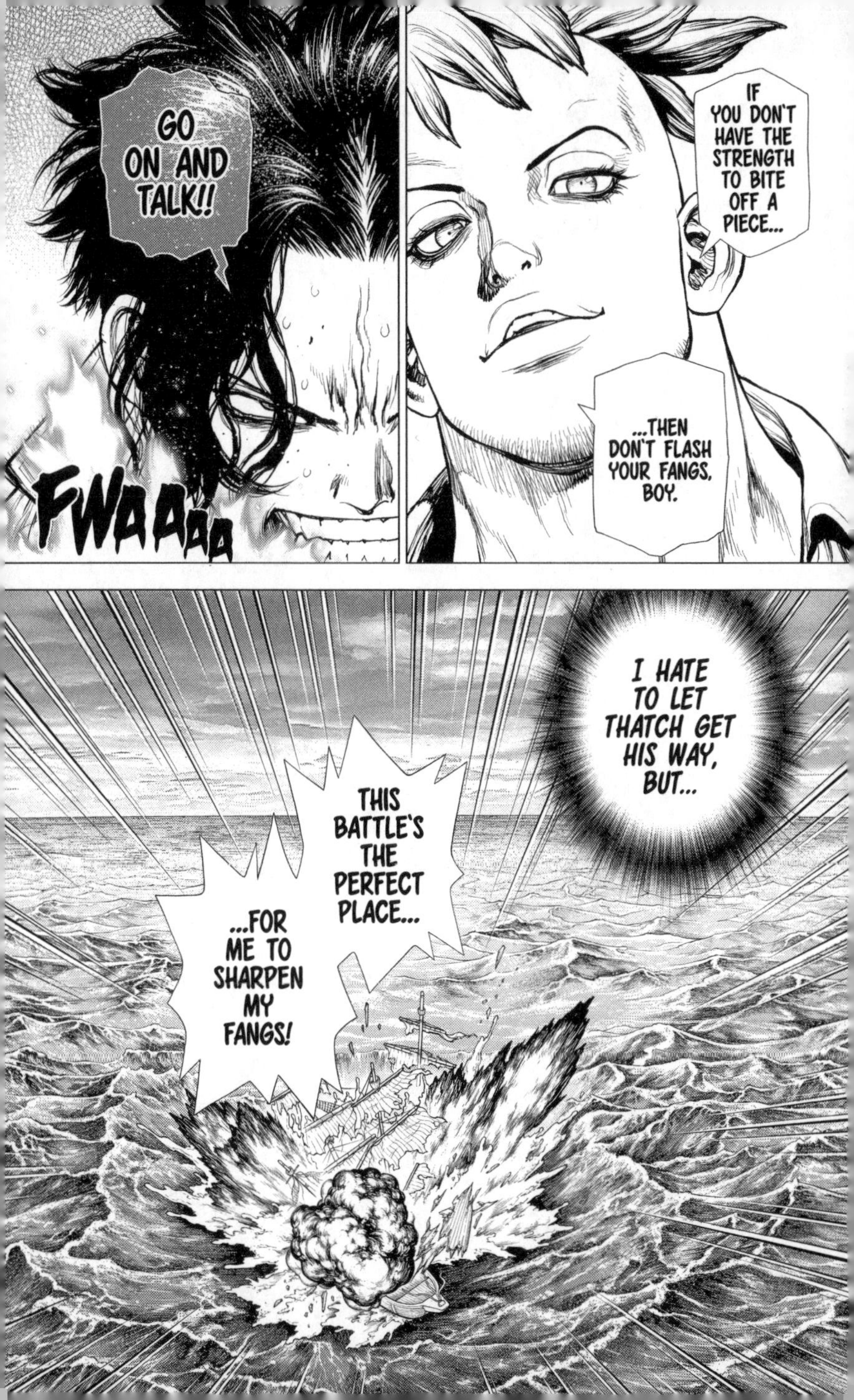
IF YOU DON'T HAVE THE STRENGTH TO BITE OFF A PIECE...
...THEN DON'T FLASH YOUR FANGS, BOY.
GO ON AND TALK!!
FWAAAA
I HATE TO LET THATCH GET HIS WAY, BUT...
THIS BATTLE'S THE PERFECT PLACE...
...FOR ME TO SHARPEN MY FANGS!

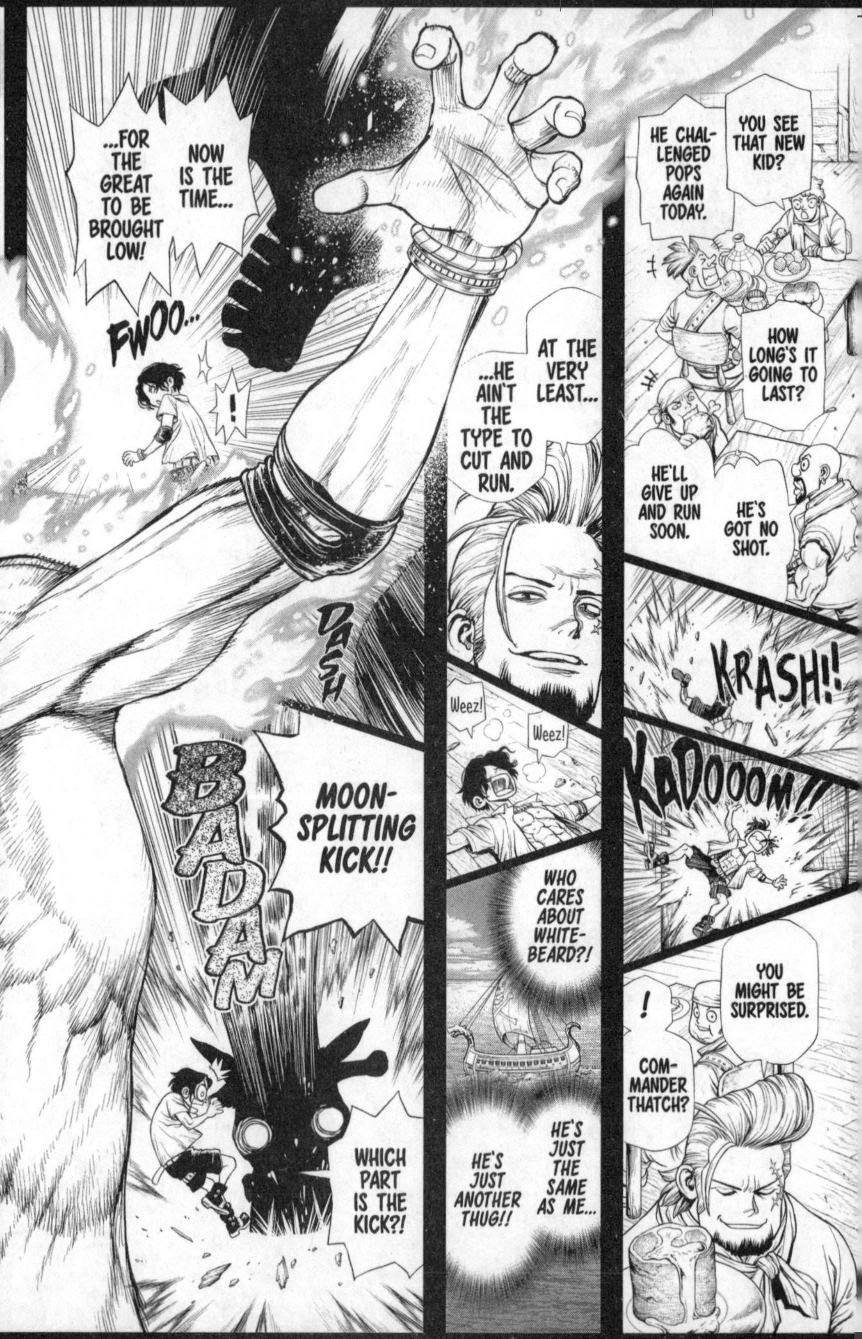
YOU SEE THAT NEW KID?
HE CHAL-LENGED POPS AGAIN TODAY.
HOW LONG'S IT GOING TO LAST?
HE'S GOT NO SHOT.
HE'LL GIVE UP AND RUN SOON.
KRASH!!
KADOOOM!!
YOU MIGHT BE SURPRISED.
!
COM-MANDER THATCH?
AT THE VERY LEAST...
...HE AIN'T THE TYPE TO CUT AND RUN.
Weez!
Weez!
WHO CARES ABOUT WHITE-BEARD?!
HE'S JUST THE SAME AS ME...
HE'S JUST ANOTHER THUG!!
NOW IS THE TIME...
...FOR THE GREAT TO BE BROUGHT LOW!
FWOO...
!
DASH
BADAM
MOON-SPLITTING KICK!!
WHICH PART IS THE KICK?!

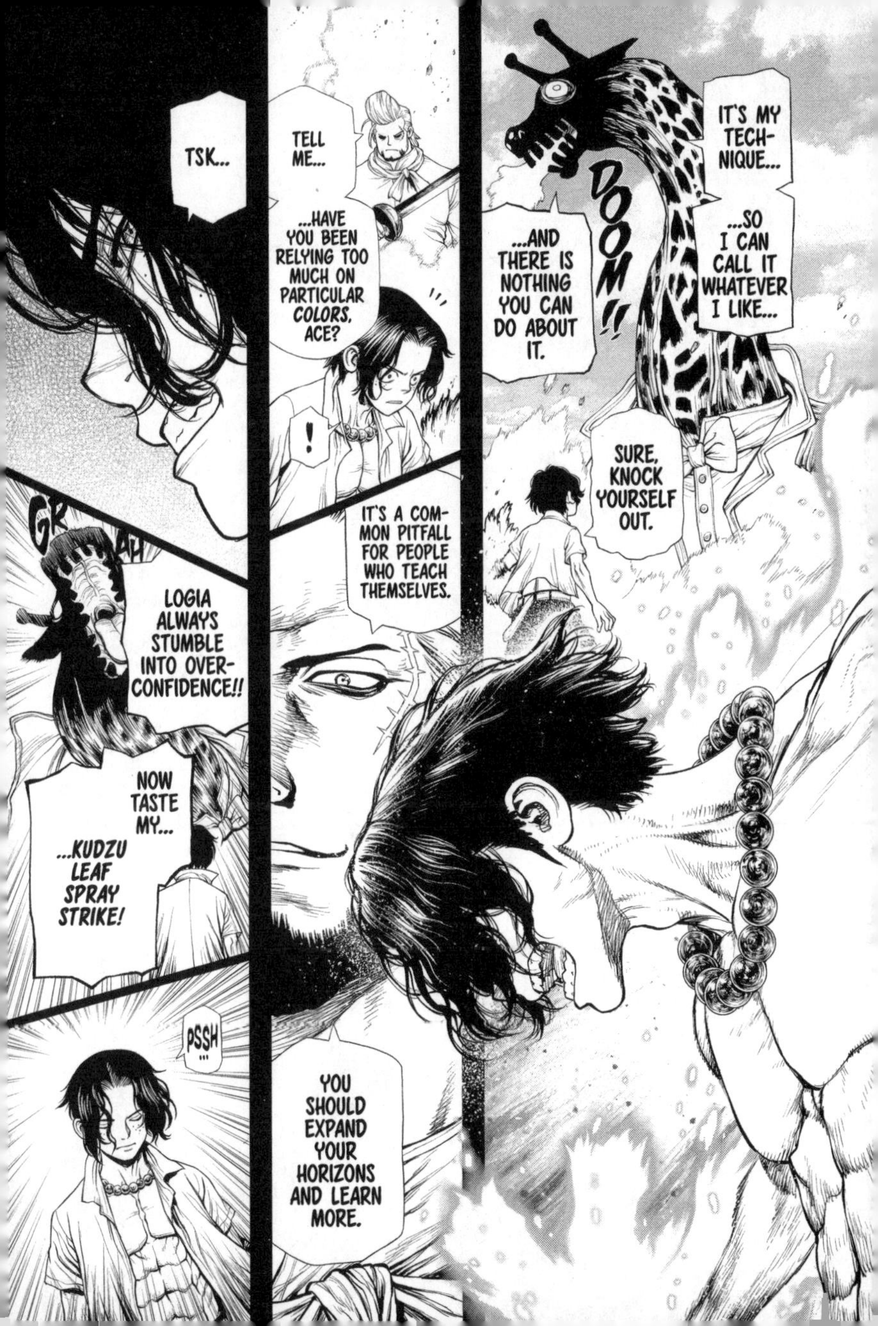
IT'S MY TECH-NIQUE...
...SO I CAN CALL IT WHATEVER I LIKE...
DOOM!!
...AND THERE IS NOTHING YOU CAN DO ABOUT IT.
SURE, KNOCK YOURSELF OUT.
TELL ME...
...HAVE YOU BEEN RELYING TOO MUCH ON PARTICULAR COLORS, ACE?
!
IT'S A COM-MON PITFALL FOR PEOPLE WHO TEACH THEMSELVES.
YOU SHOULD EXPAND YOUR HORIZONS AND LEARN MORE.
TSK...
LOGIA ALWAYS STUMBLE INTO OVER-CONFIDENCE!!
NOW TASTE MY...
...KUDZU LEAF SPRAY STRIKE!
PSSH...

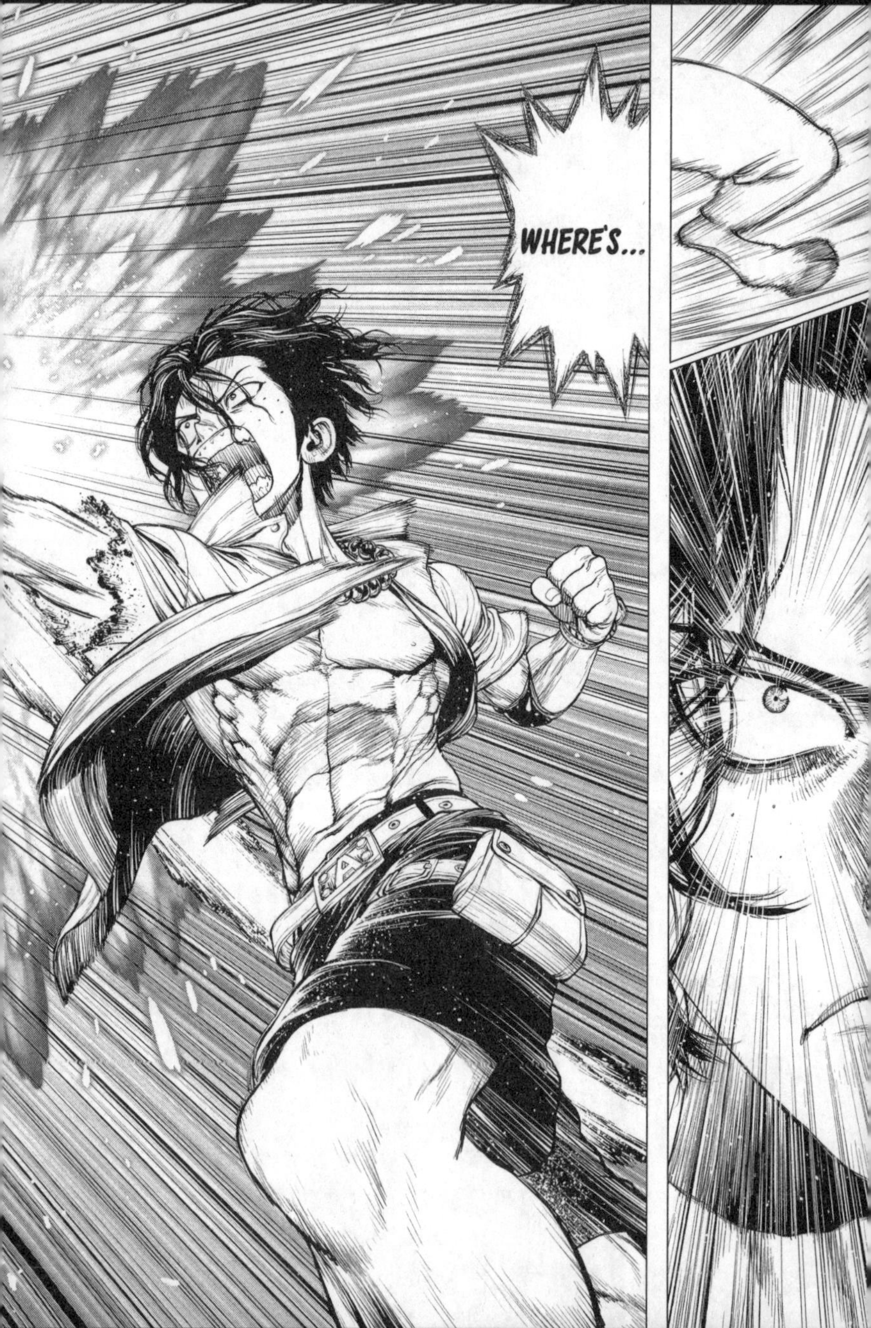
WHERE'S...

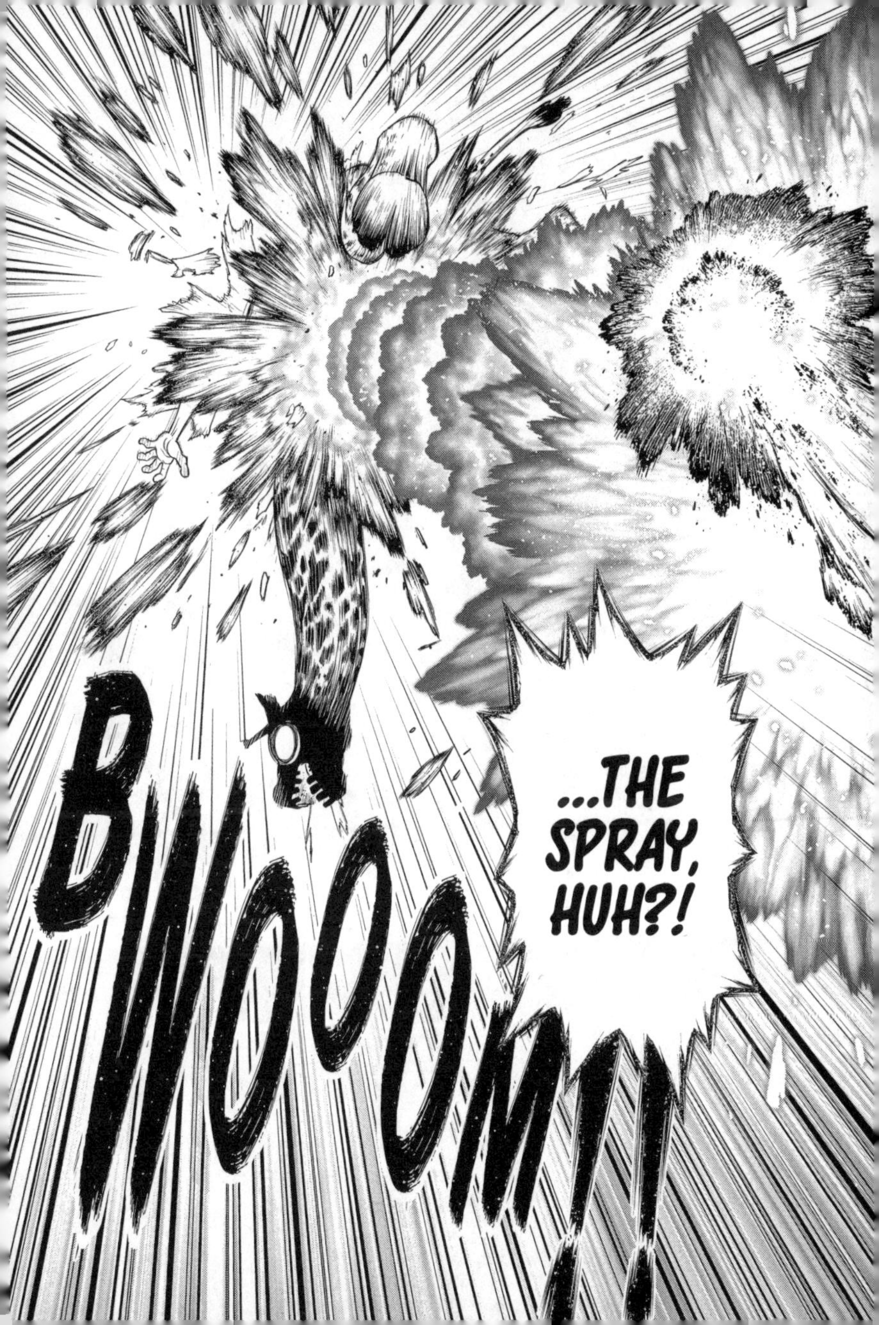
...THE SPRAY, HUH?!
BWOOOM!!

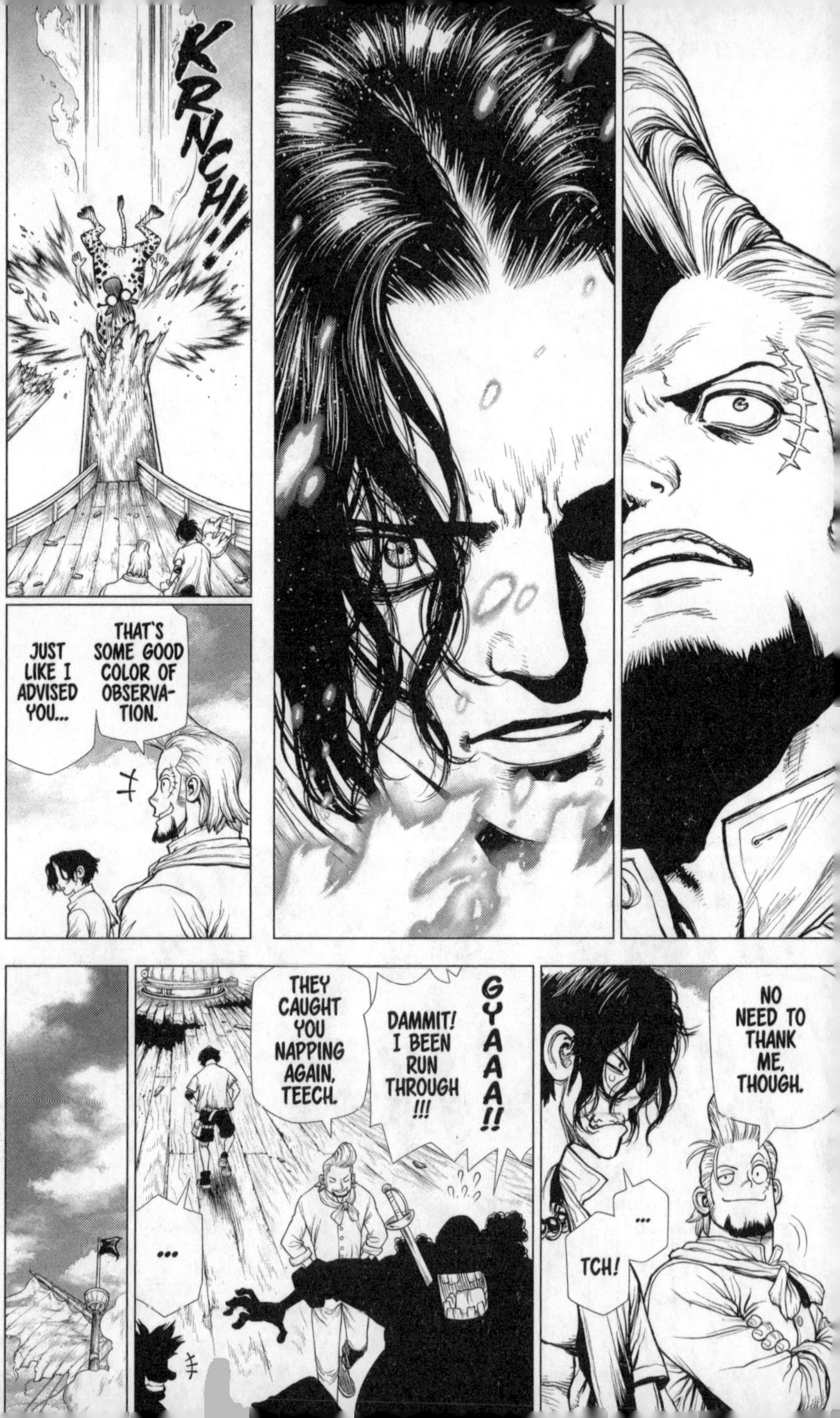
KRNCH!!!
THAT'S SOME GOOD COLOR OF OBSERVATION.
JUST LIKE I ADVISED YOU...
NO NEED TO THANK ME, THOUGH.
...
TCH!
GYAAAA!!
DAMMIT! I BEEN RUN THROUGH !!!
THEY CAUGHT YOU NAPPING AGAIN, TEECH.
...

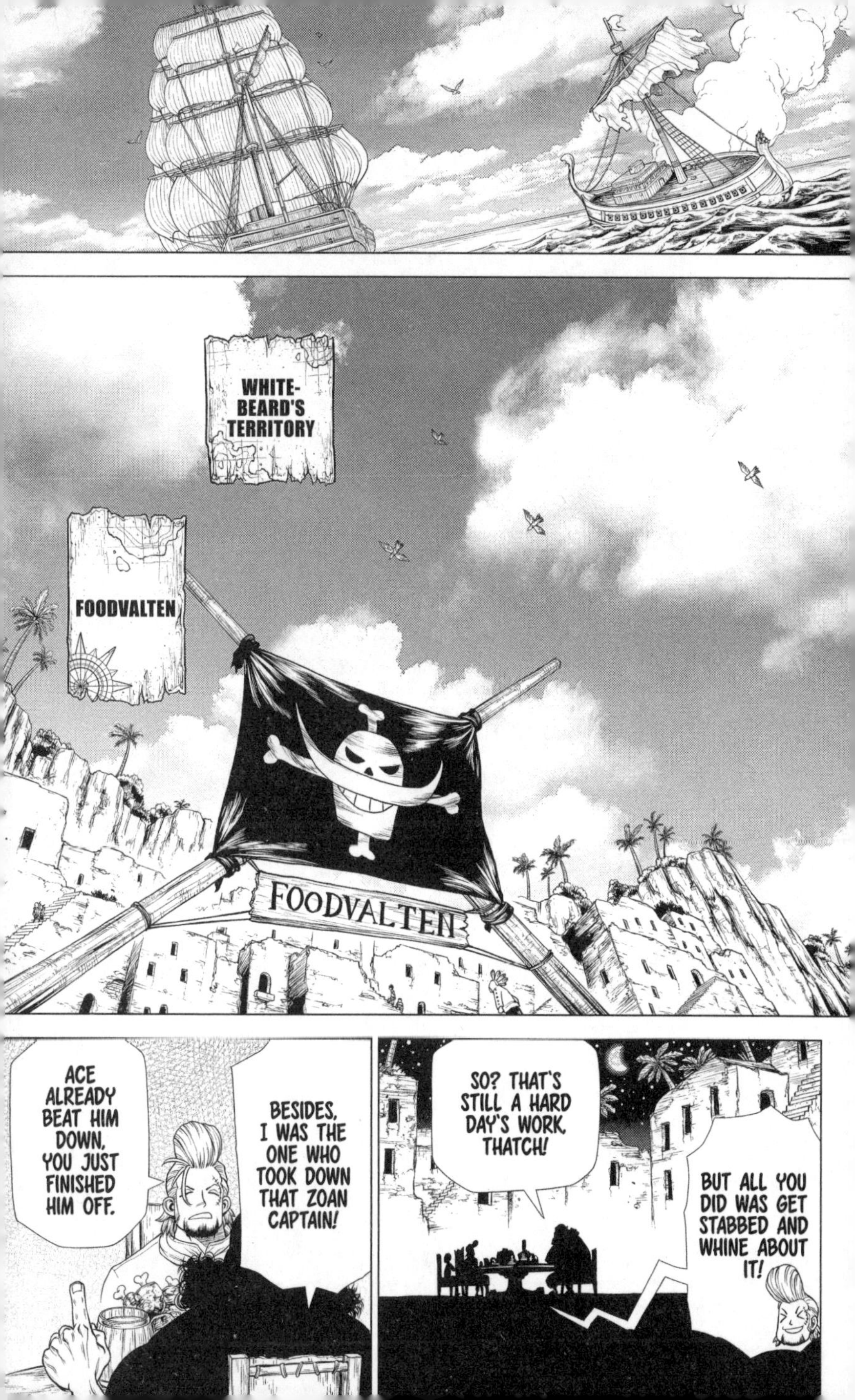
WHITE-BEARD'S TERRITORY
FOODVALTEN
FOODVALTEN
SO? THAT'S STILL A HARD DAY'S WORK, THATCH!
BUT ALL YOU DID WAS GET STABBED AND WHINE ABOUT IT!
BESIDES, I WAS THE ONE WHO TOOK DOWN THAT ZOAN CAPTAIN!
ACE ALREADY BEAT HIM DOWN, YOU JUST FINISHED HIM OFF.

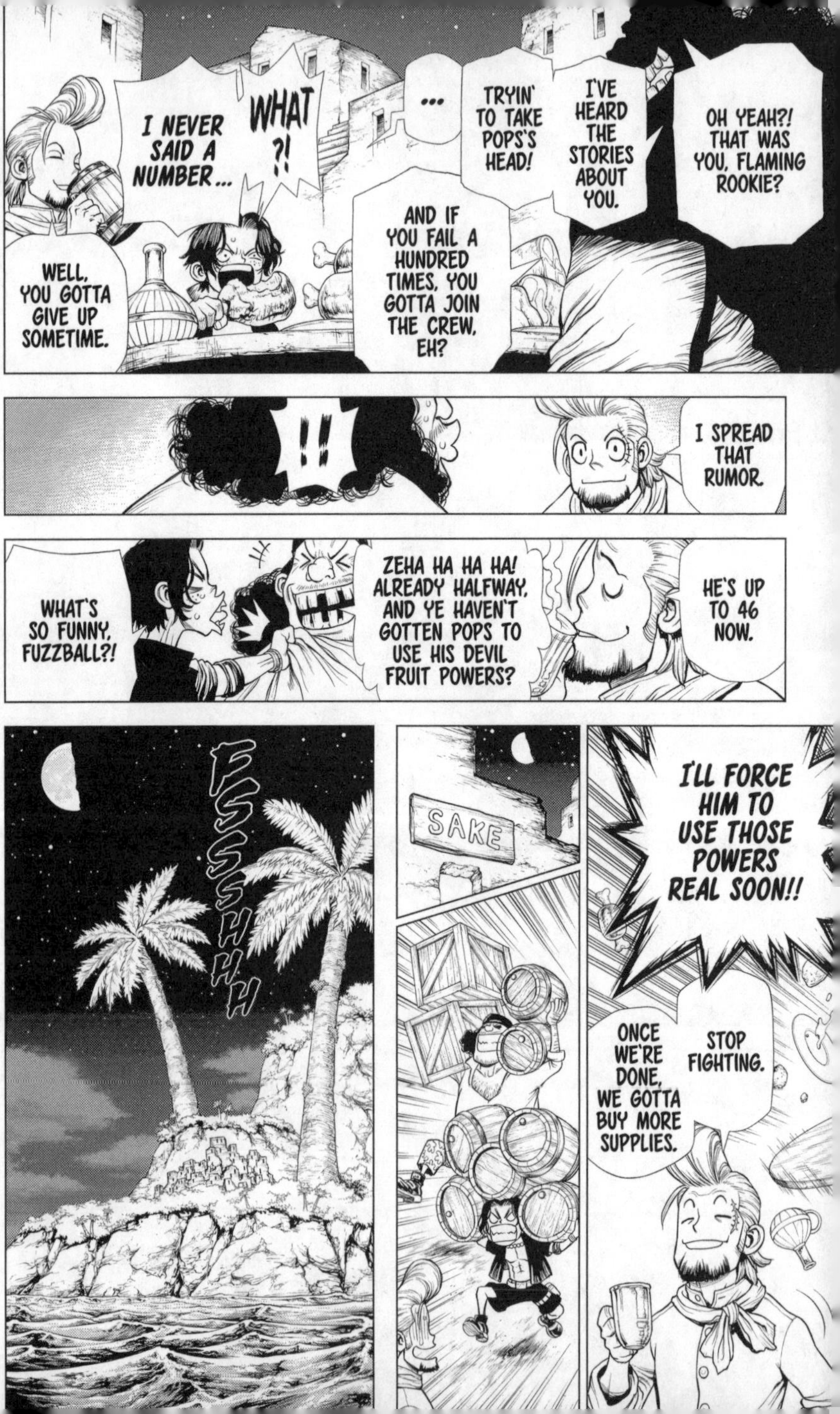
OH YEAH?! THAT WAS YOU, FLAMING ROOKIE?
I'VE HEARD THE STORIES ABOUT YOU.
TRYIN' TO TAKE POPS'S HEAD!
...
AND IF YOU FAIL A HUNDRED TIMES, YOU GOTTA JOIN THE CREW, EH?
WHAT?!
I NEVER SAID A NUMBER...
WELL, YOU GOTTA GIVE UP SOMETIME.
I SPREAD THAT RUMOR.
!!
HE'S UP TO 46 NOW.
ZEHA HA HA HA! ALREADY HALFWAY, AND YE HAVEN'T GOTTEN POPS TO USE HIS DEVIL FRUIT POWERS?
WHAT'S SO FUNNY, FUZZBALL?!
I'LL FORCE HIM TO USE THOSE POWERS REAL SOON!!
STOP FIGHTING.
ONCE WE'RE DONE, WE GOTTA BUY MORE SUPPLIES.
SAKE
FSSSHHH

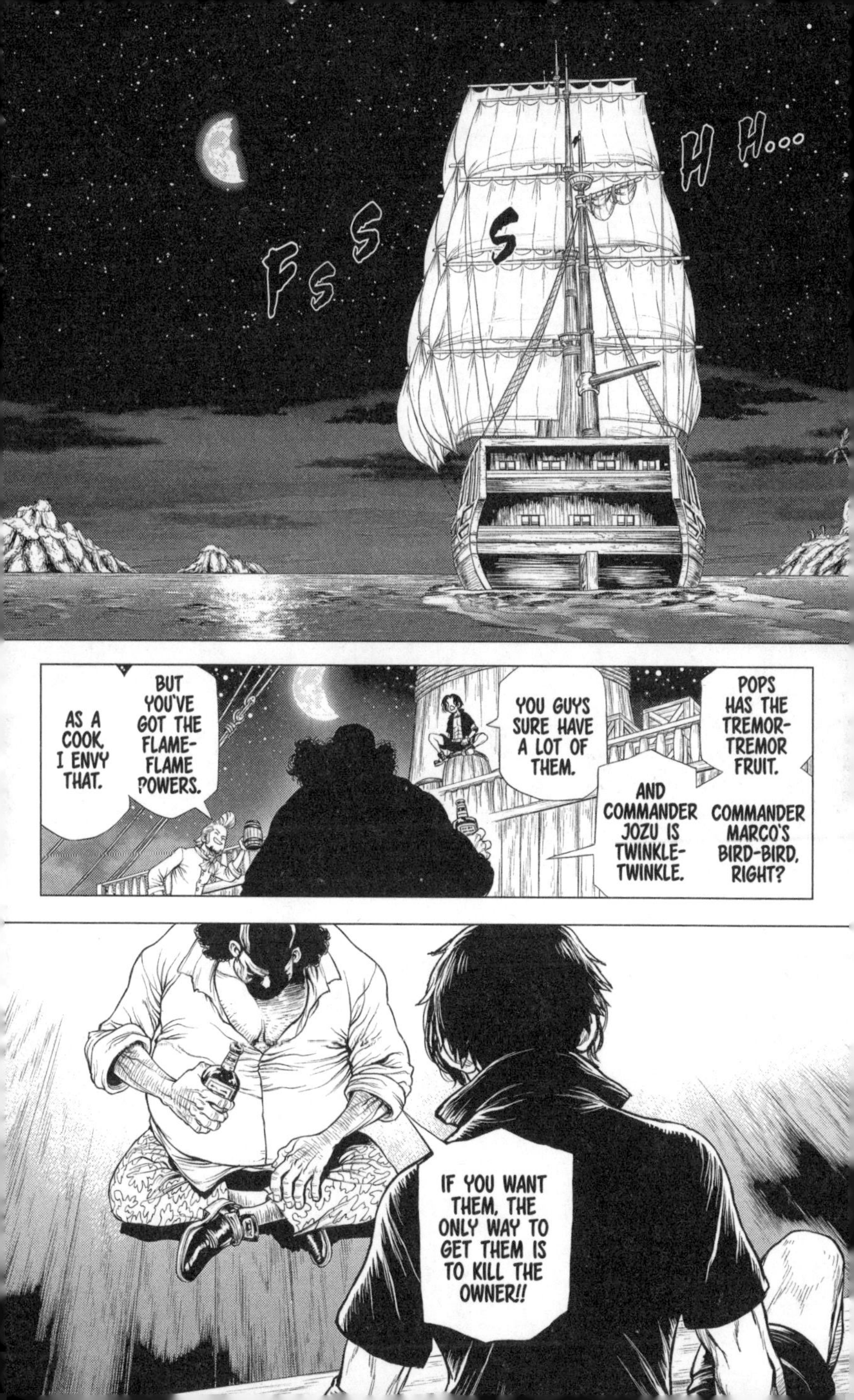
FsSSHH...
POPS HAS THE TREMOR-TREMOR FRUIT.
COMMANDER MARCO'S BIRD-BIRD, RIGHT?
AND COMMANDER JOZU IS TWINKLE-TWINKLE.
YOU GUYS SURE HAVE A LOT OF THEM.
BUT YOU'VE GOT THE FLAME-FLAME POWERS.
AS A COOK, I ENVY THAT.
IF YOU WANT THEM, THE ONLY WAY TO GET THEM IS TO KILL THE OWNER!!

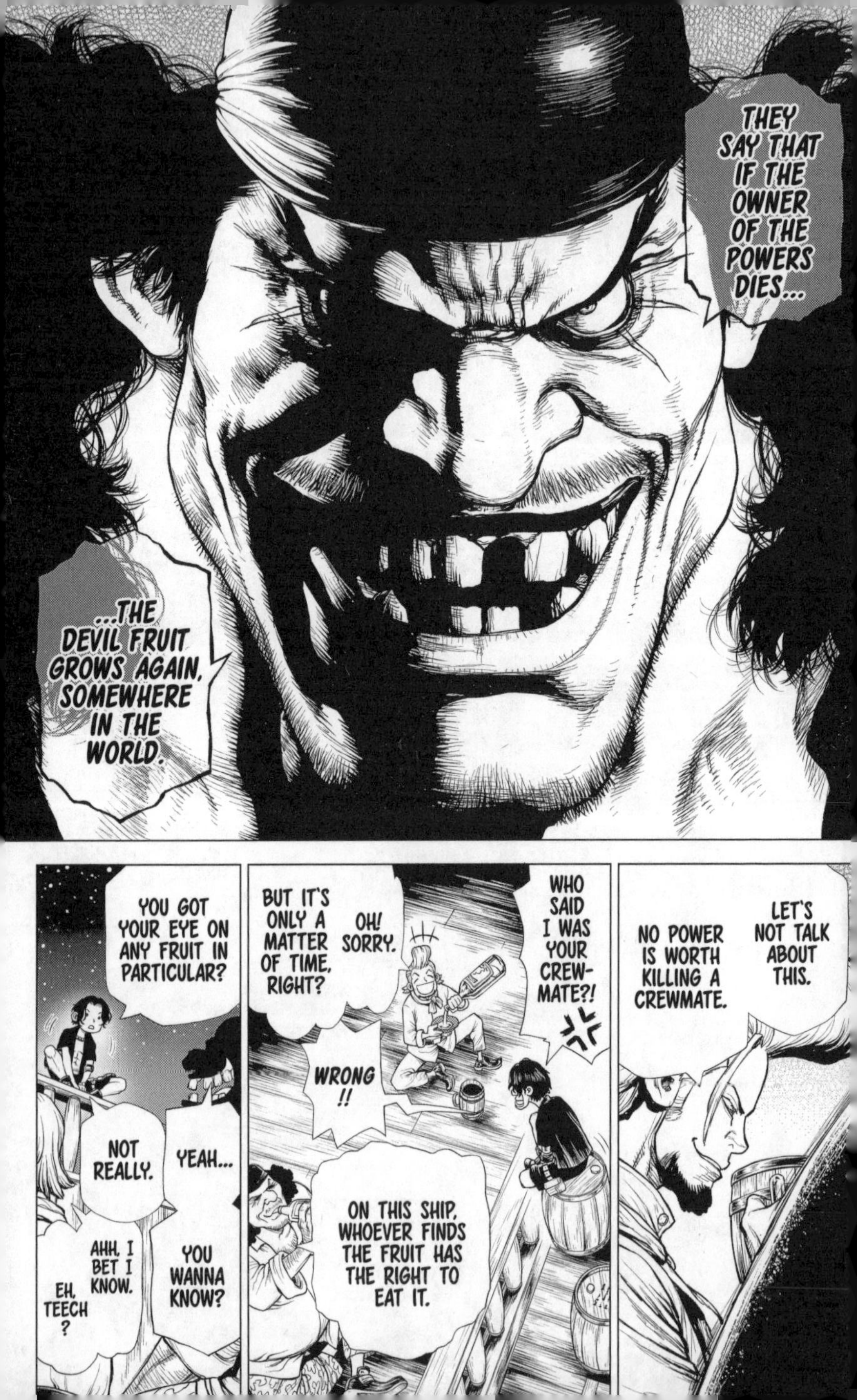
THEY SAY THAT IF THE OWNER OF THE POWERS DIES...
...THE DEVIL FRUIT GROWS AGAIN, SOMEWHERE IN THE WORLD.
LET'S NOT TALK ABOUT THIS.
NO POWER IS WORTH KILLING A CREWMATE.
WHO SAID I WAS YOUR CREW-MATE?!
OH! SORRY.
BUT IT'S ONLY A MATTER OF TIME, RIGHT?
WRONG!!
ON THIS SHIP, WHOEVER FINDS THE FRUIT HAS THE RIGHT TO EAT IT.
YOU GOT YOUR EYE ON ANY FRUIT IN PARTICULAR?
YEAH...
NOT REALLY.
YOU WANNA KNOW?
AHH, I BET I KNOW.
EH, TEECH?

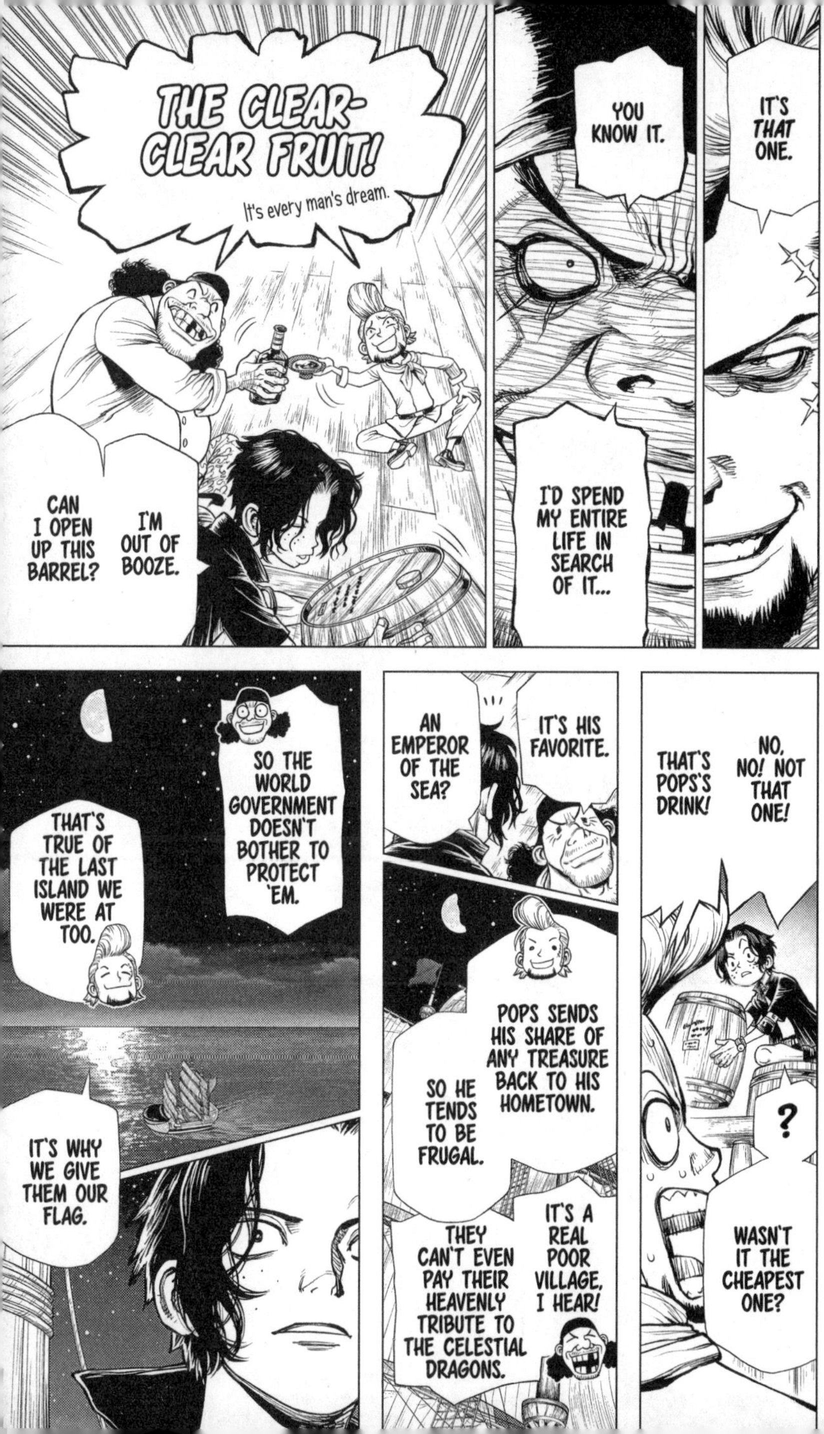
IT'S THAT ONE.
YOU KNOW IT.
I'D SPEND MY ENTIRE LIFE IN SEARCH OF IT...
THE CLEAR-CLEAR FRUIT!
It's every man's dream.
I'M OUT OF BOOZE.
CAN I OPEN UP THIS BARREL?
NO, NO! NOT THAT ONE!
THAT'S POPS'S DRINK!
?
WASN'T IT THE CHEAPEST ONE?
IT'S HIS FAVORITE.
AN EMPEROR OF THE SEA?
POPS SENDS HIS SHARE OF ANY TREASURE BACK TO HIS HOMETOWN.
SO HE TENDS TO BE FRUGAL.
IT'S A REAL POOR VILLAGE, I HEAR!
THEY CAN'T EVEN PAY THEIR HEAVENLY TRIBUTE TO THE CELESTIAL DRAGONS.
SO THE WORLD GOVERNMENT DOESN'T BOTHER TO PROTECT 'EM.
THAT'S TRUE OF THE LAST ISLAND WE WERE AT TOO.
IT'S WHY WE GIVE THEM OUR FLAG.

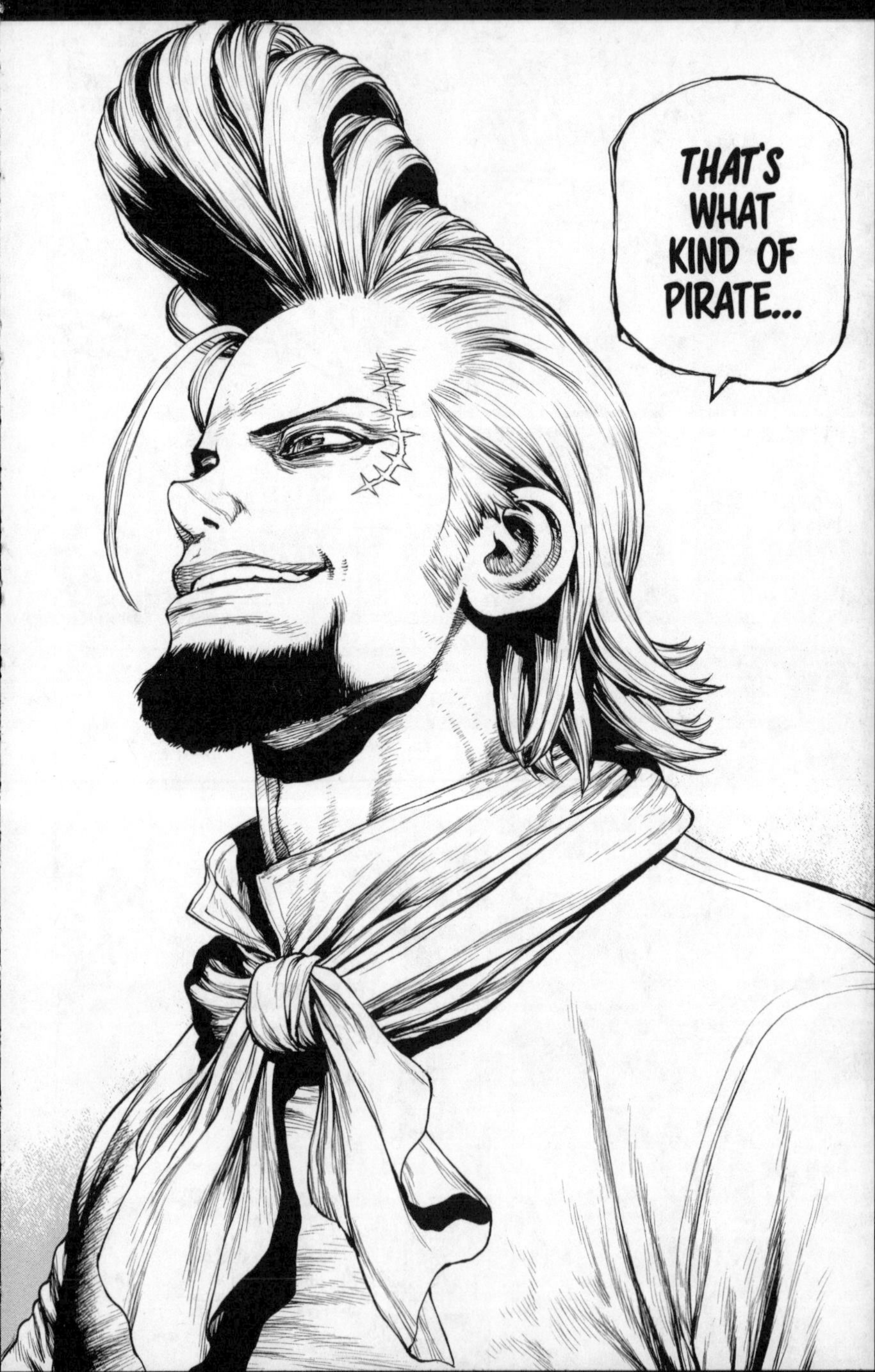
THAT'S WHAT KIND OF PIRATE...

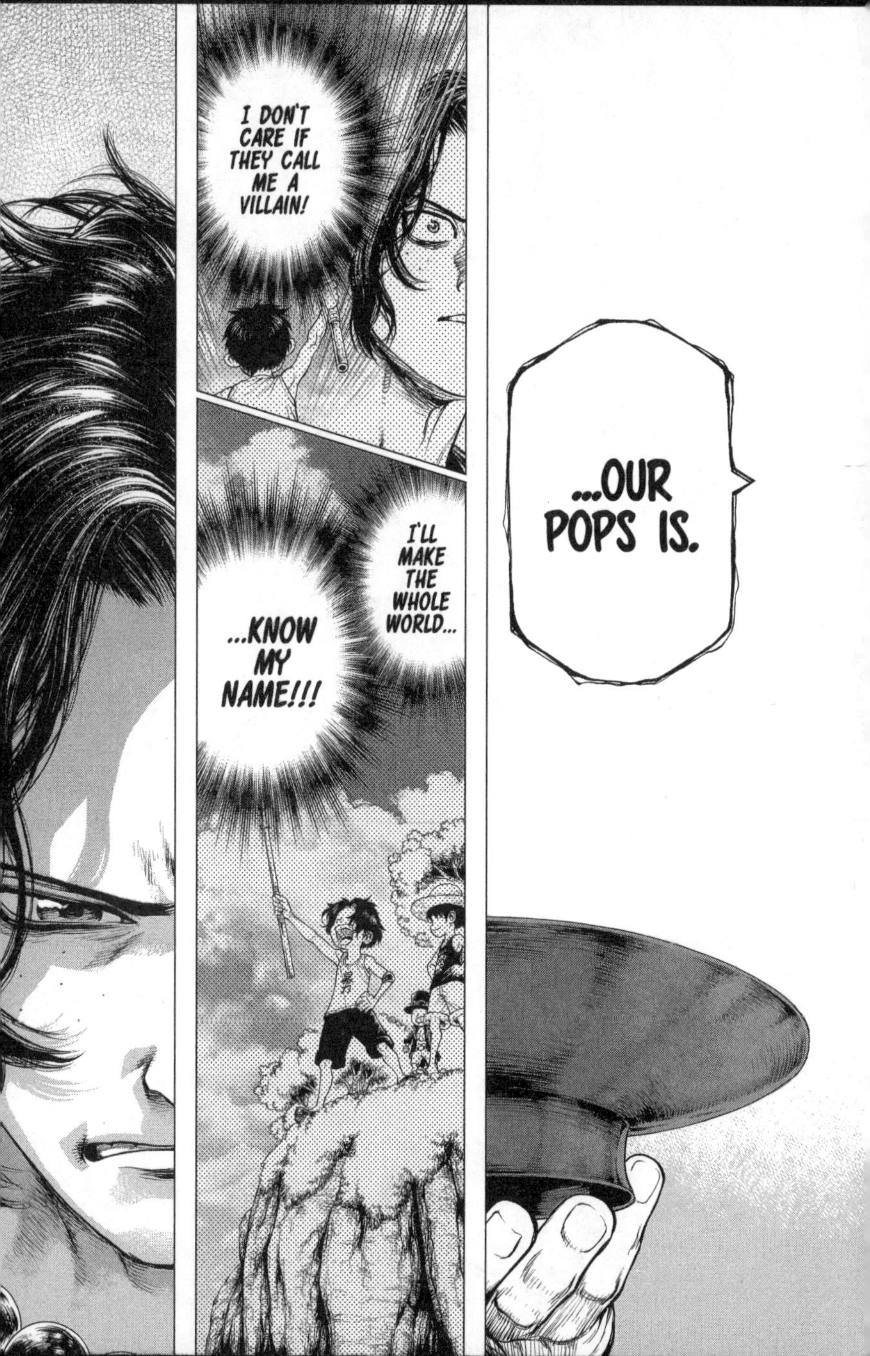
...OUR POPS IS.
I DON'T CARE IF THEY CALL ME A VILLAIN!
I'LL MAKE THE WHOLE WORLD...
...KNOW MY NAME!!!

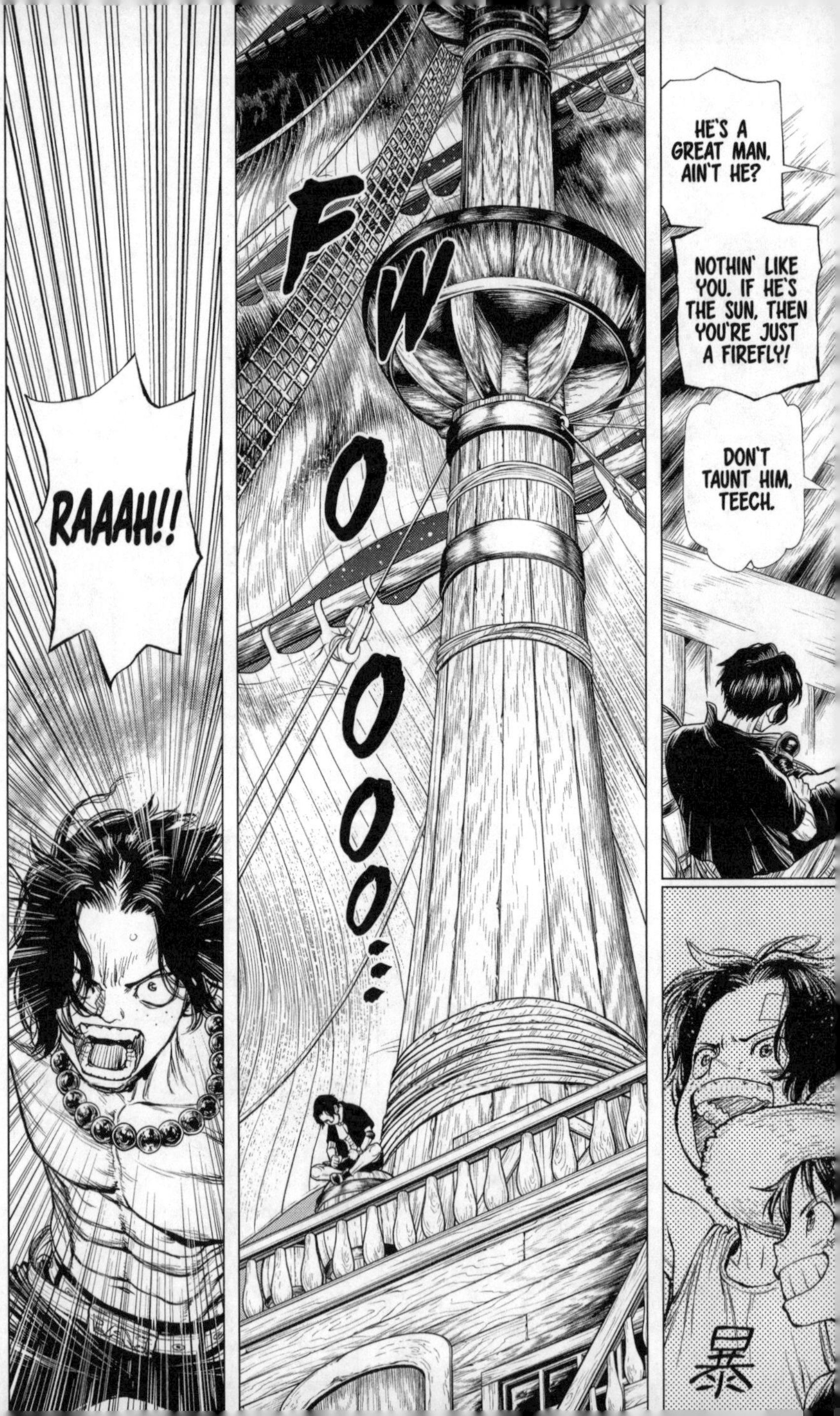
HE'S A GREAT MAN, AIN'T HE?
NOTHIN' LIKE YOU. IF HE'S THE SUN, THEN YOU'RE JUST A FIREFLY!
DON'T TAUNT HIM, TEECH.
暴
FWOOOO...
RAAAH!!

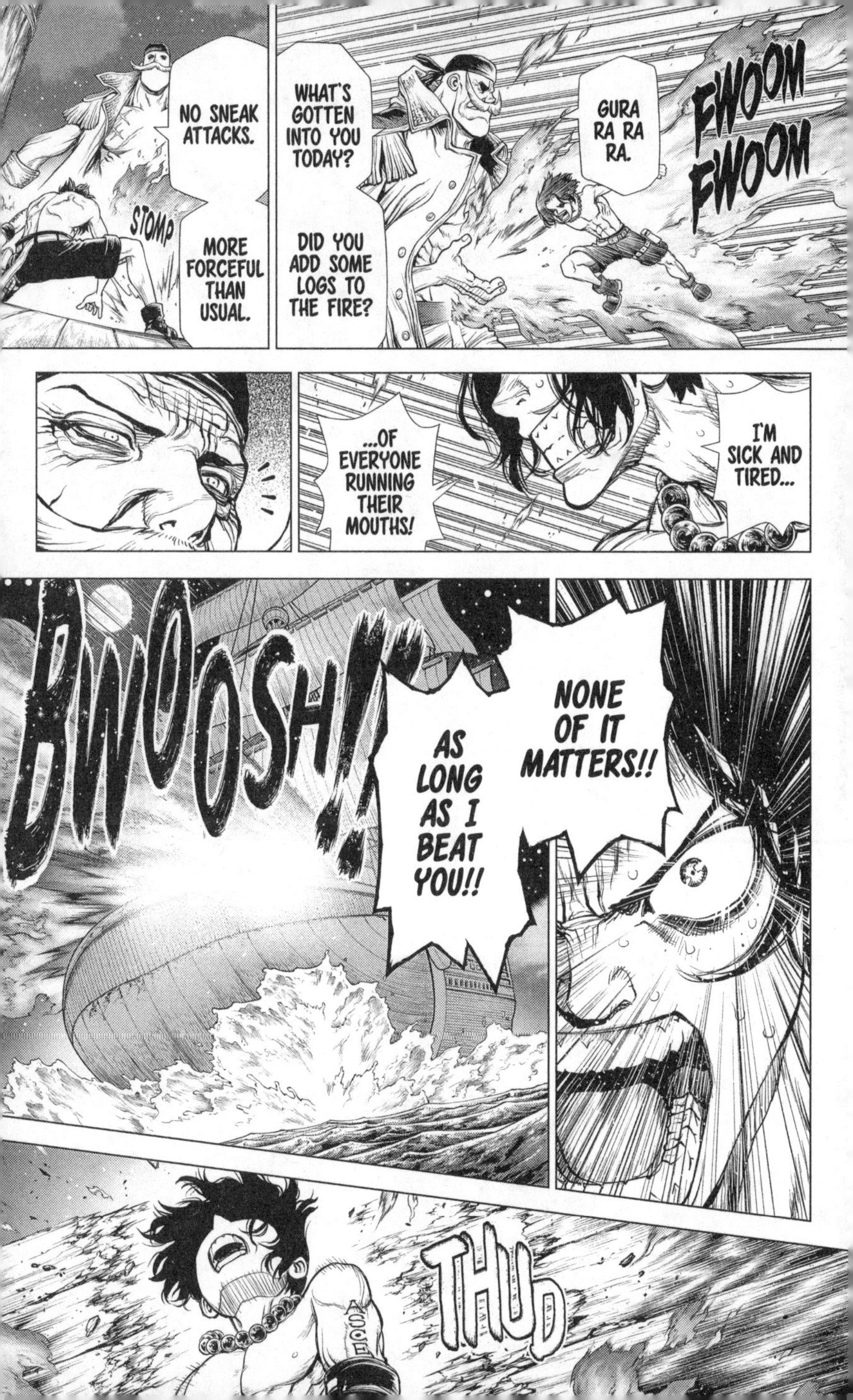
FWOOM FWOOM
GURA RA RA RA.
WHAT'S GOTTEN INTO YOU TODAY?
DID YOU ADD SOME LOGS TO THE FIRE?
NO SNEAK ATTACKS.
MORE FORCEFUL THAN USUAL.
STOMP
I'M SICK AND TIRED...
...OF EVERYONE RUNNING THEIR MOUTHS!
NONE OF IT MATTERS!!
AS LONG AS I BEAT YOU!!
BWOOSH!!
THUD

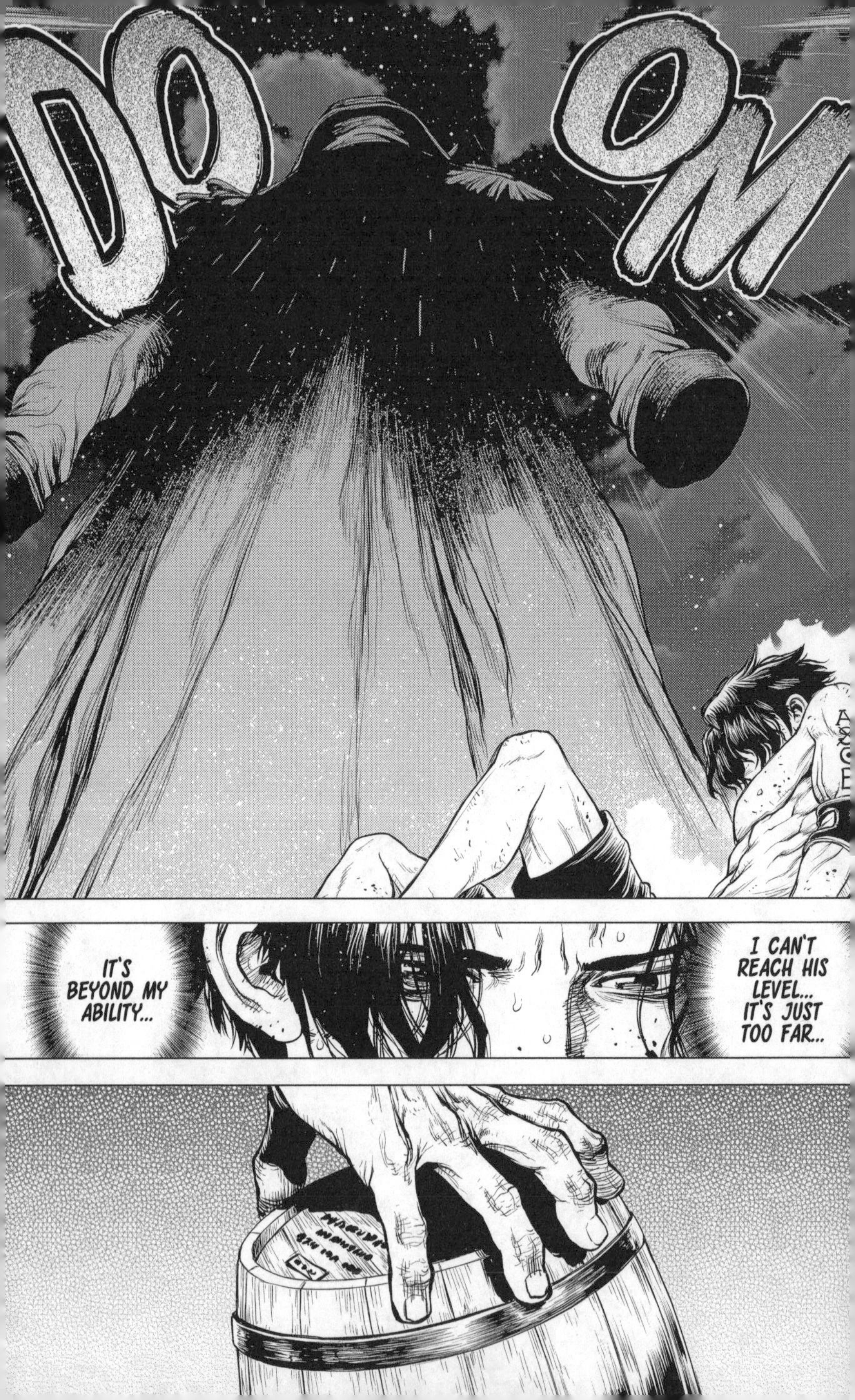
DOOM
I CAN'T REACH HIS LEVEL... IT'S JUST TOO FAR...
IT'S BEYOND MY ABILITY...

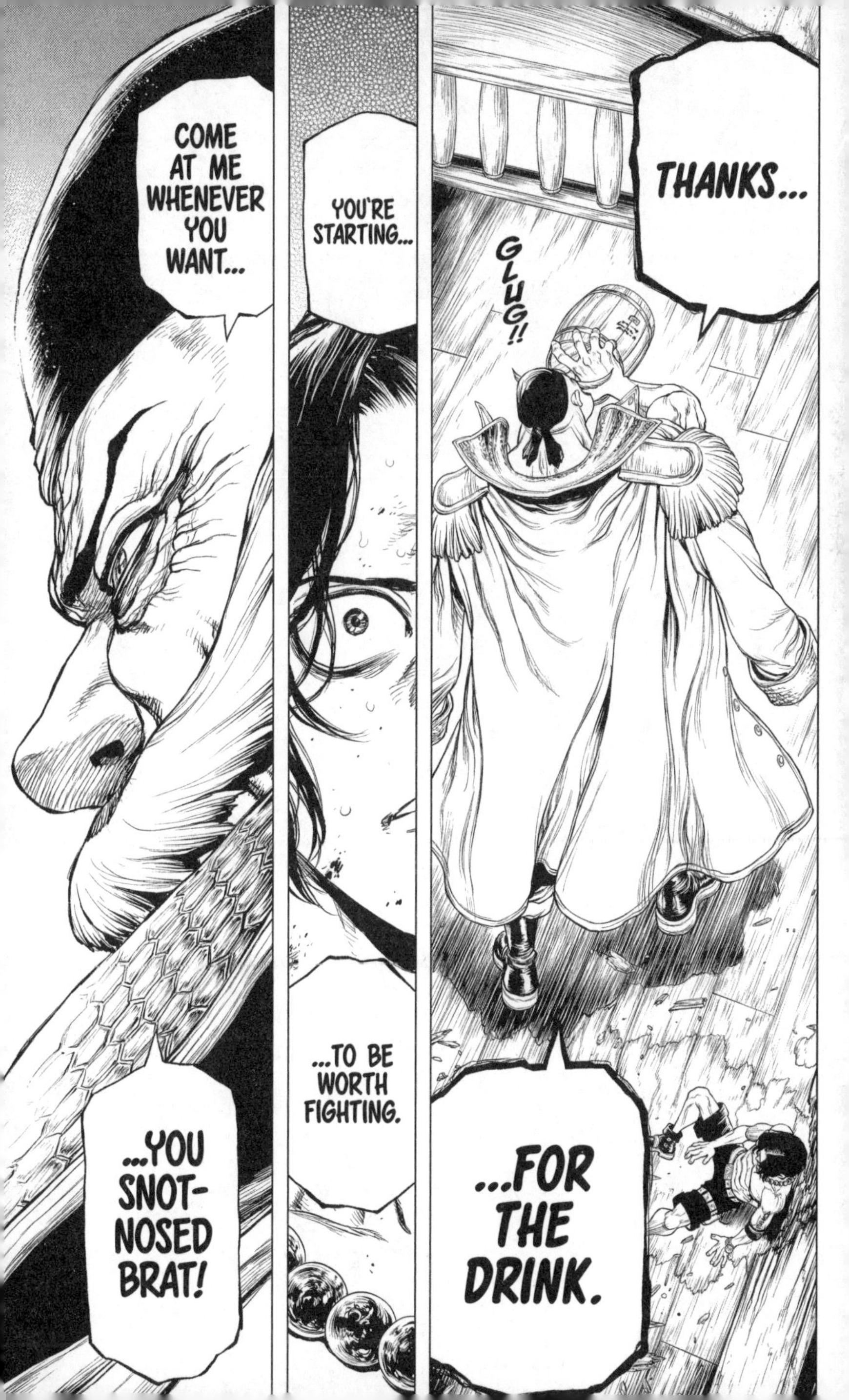
THANKS...
GLUG!!
...FOR THE DRINK.
YOU'RE STARTING...
...TO BE WORTH FIGHTING.
COME AT ME WHENEVER YOU WANT...
...YOU SNOT-NOSED BRAT!

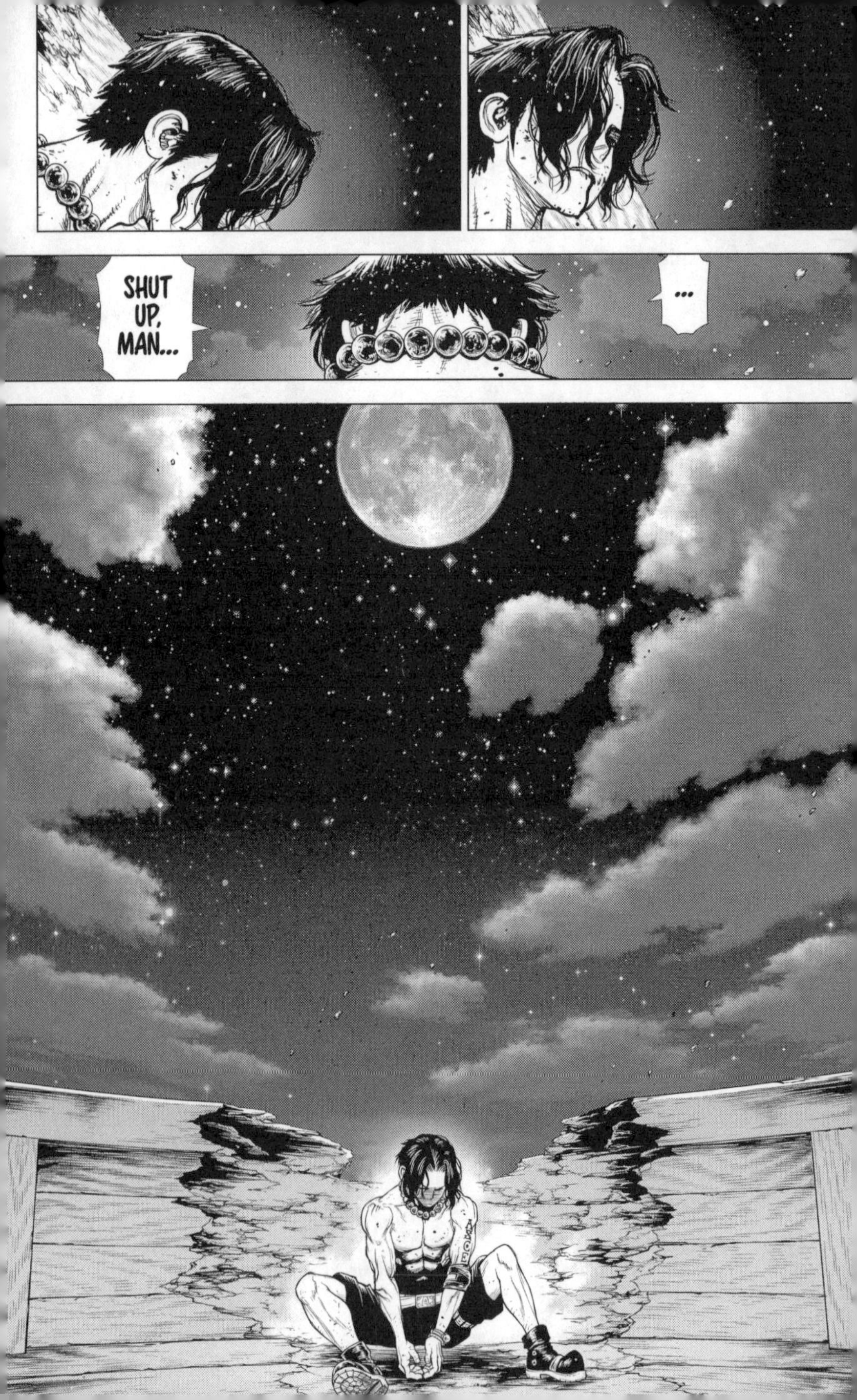
...
SHUT UP, MAN...

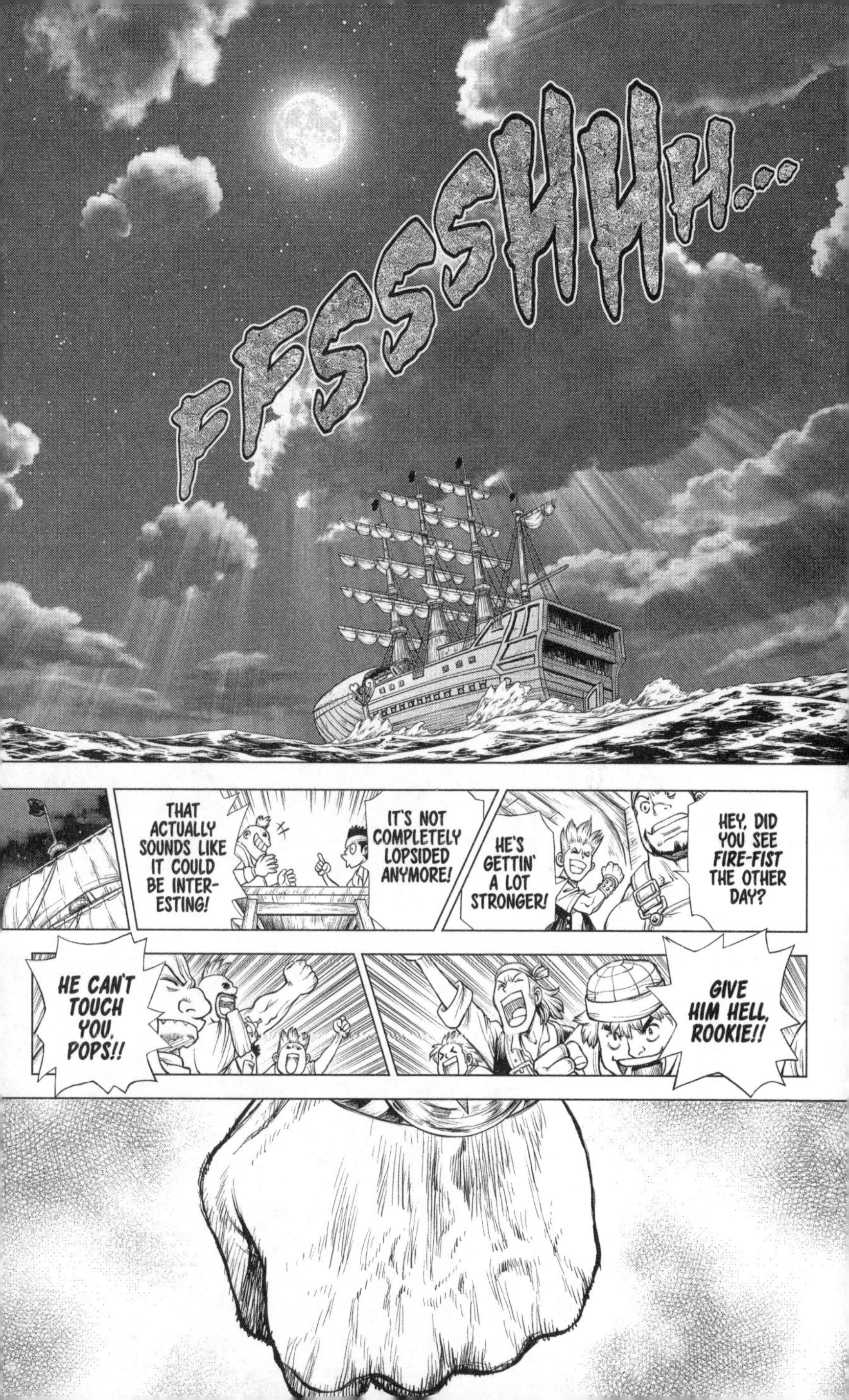
FSSSHHH...
HEY, DID YOU SEE FIRE-FIST THE OTHER DAY?
HE'S GETTIN' A LOT STRONGER!
IT'S NOT COMPLETELY LOPSIDED ANYMORE!
THAT ACTUALLY SOUNDS LIKE IT COULD BE INTER-ESTING!
GIVE HIM HELL, ROOKIE!!
HE CAN'T TOUCH YOU, POPS!!

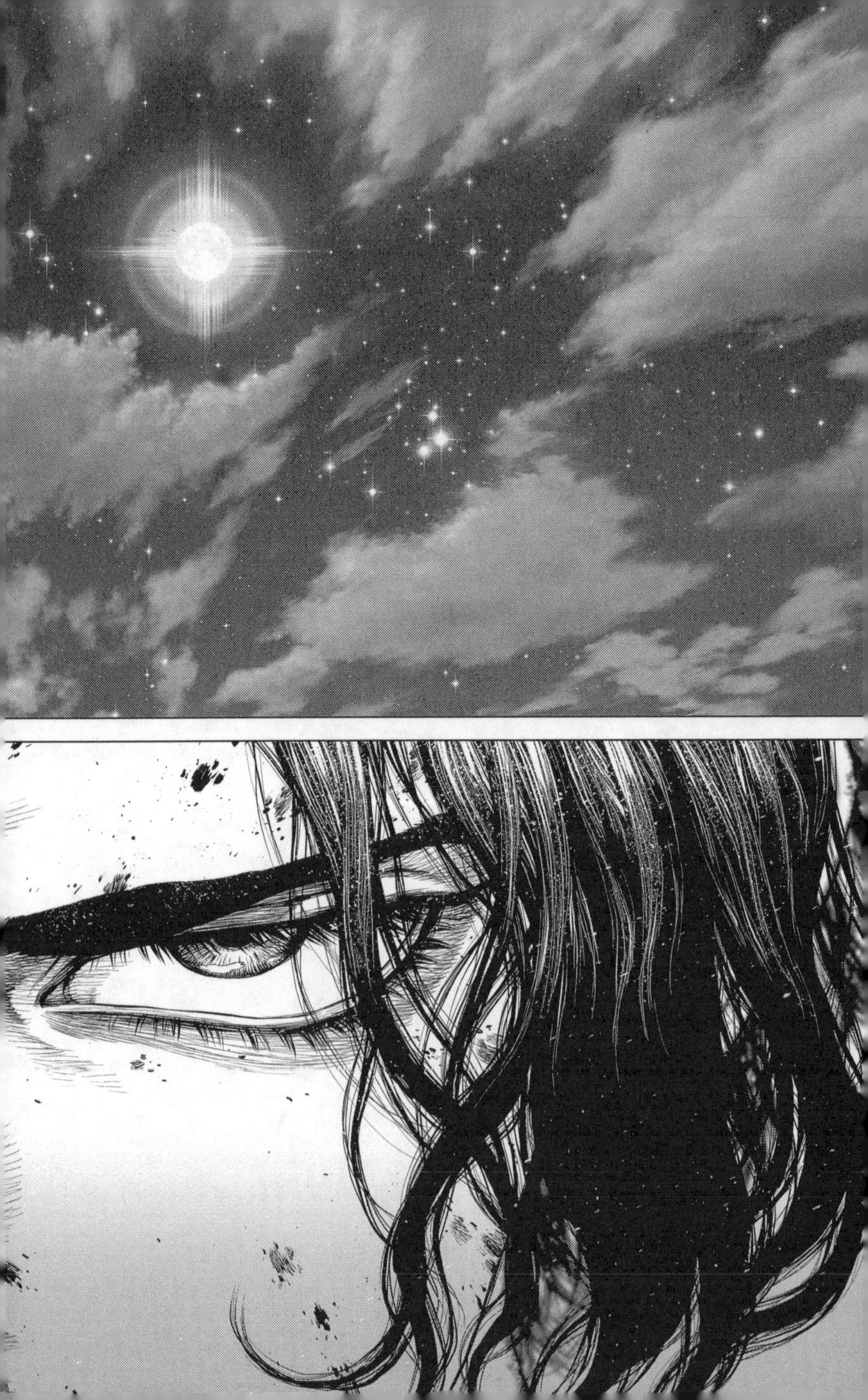

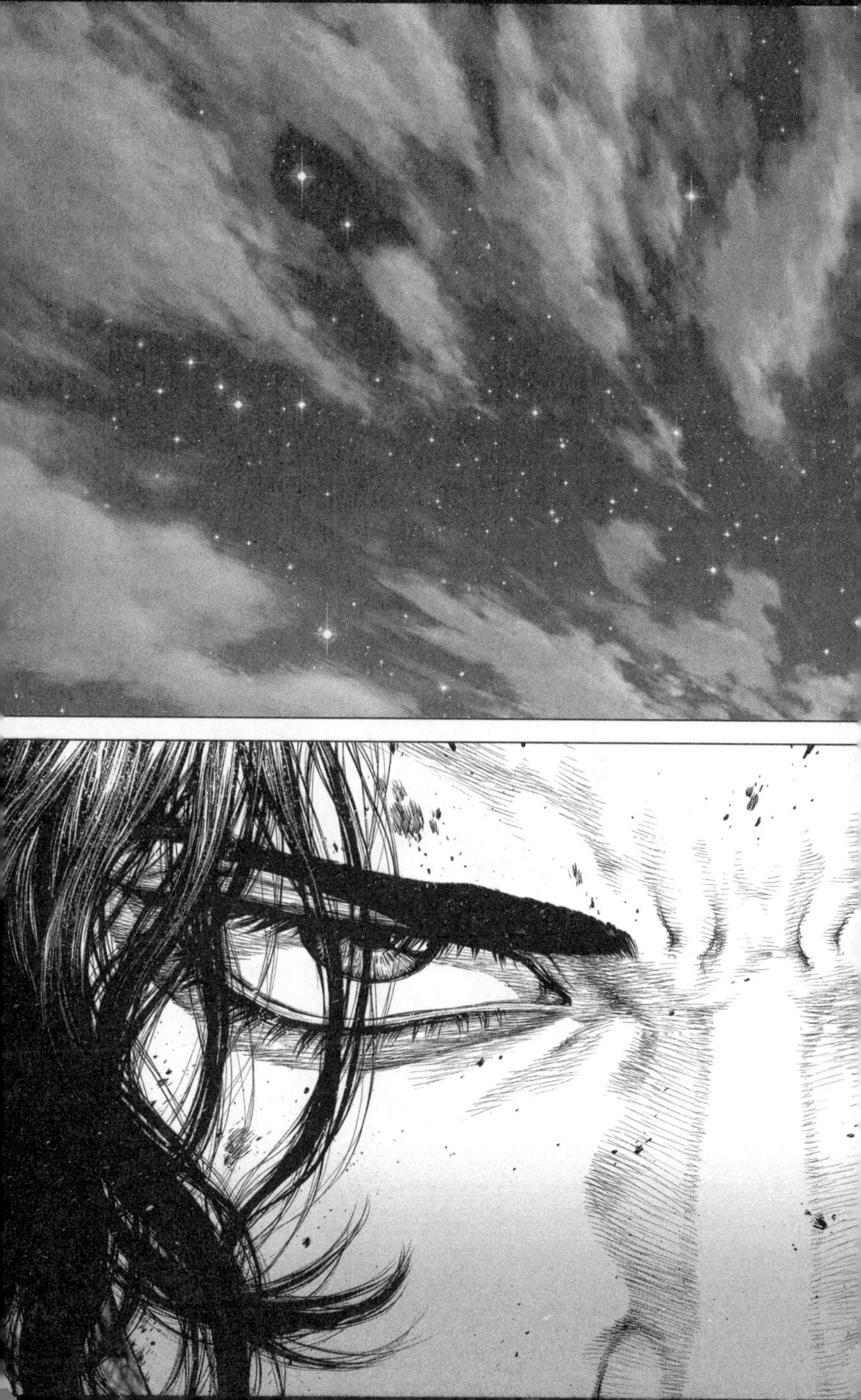

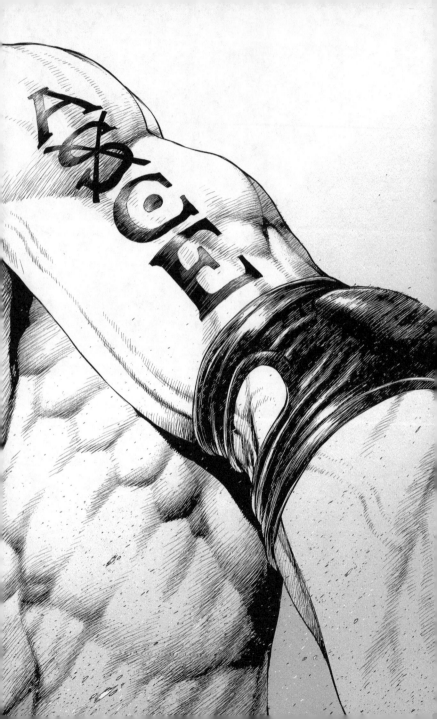

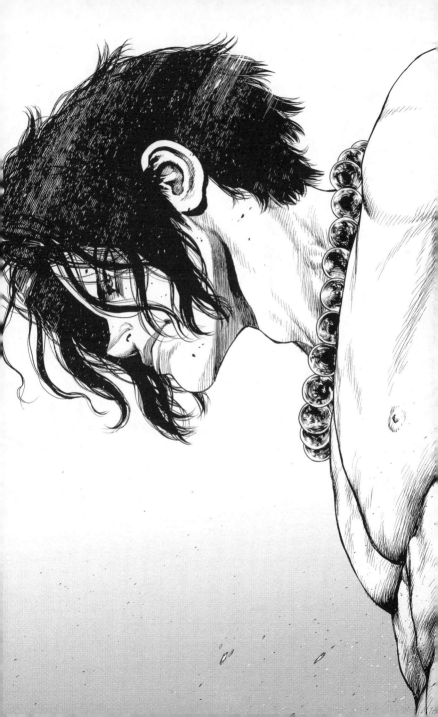

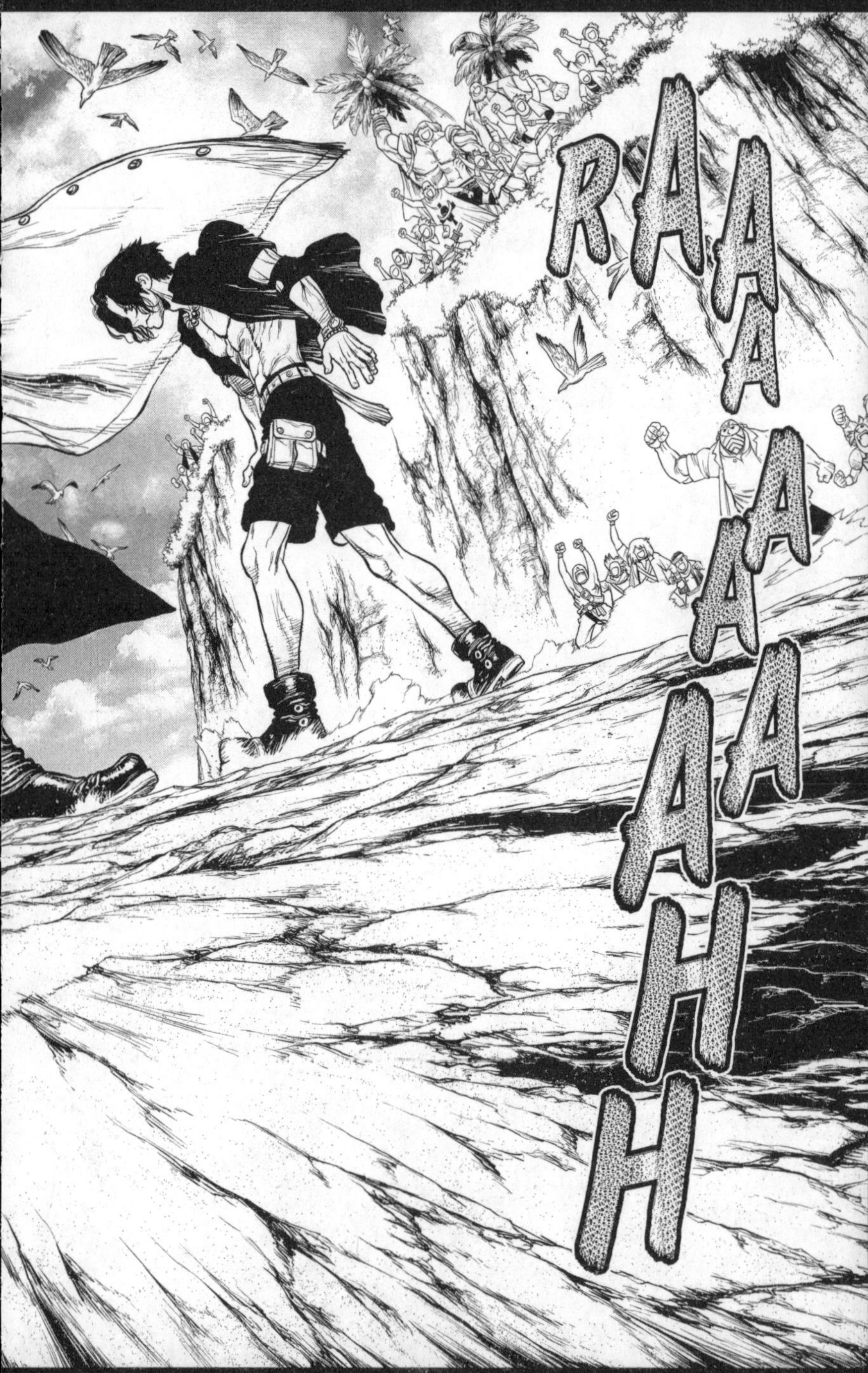
RAAAAAAAHH

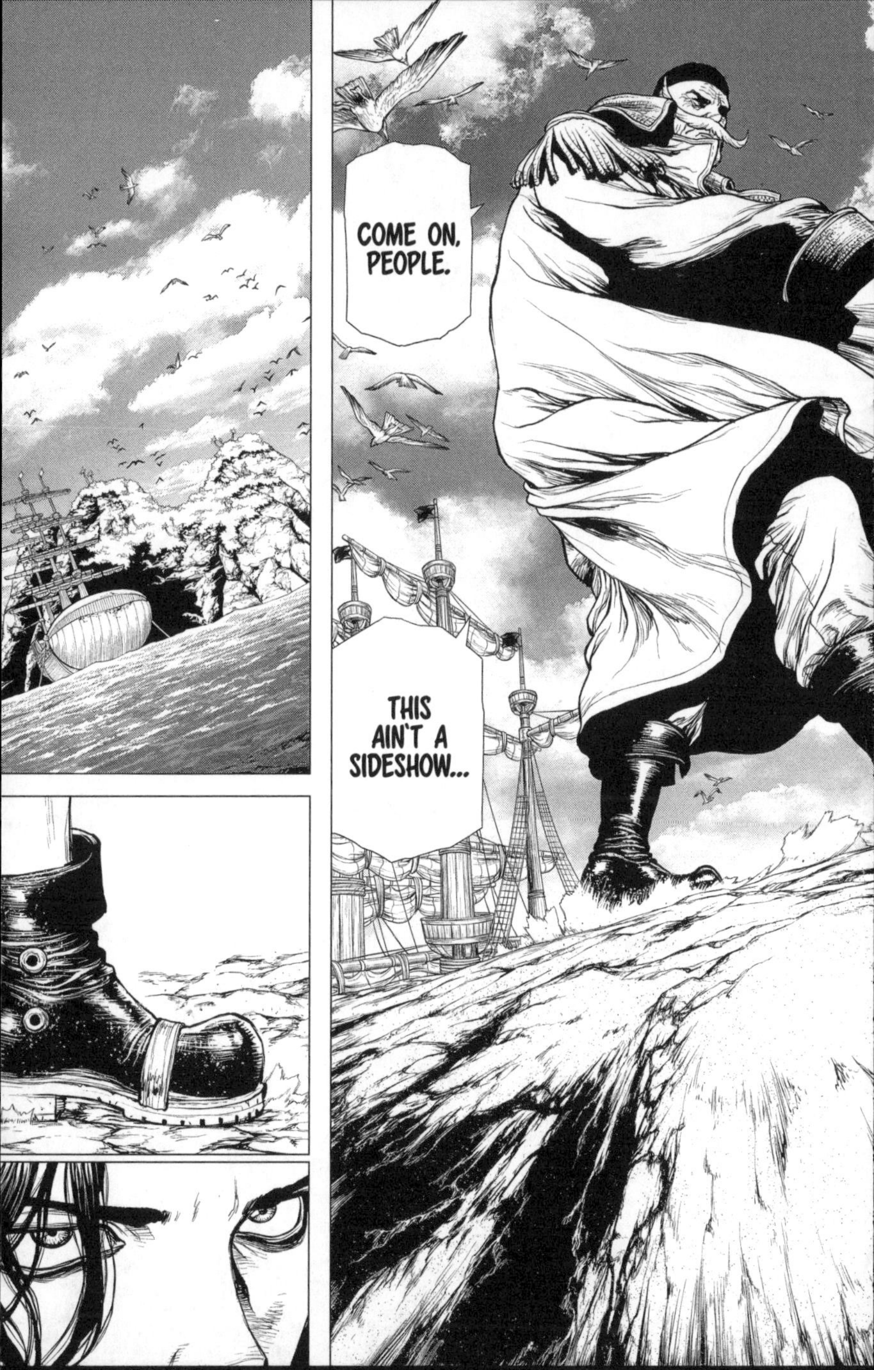
COME ON, PEOPLE.
THIS AIN'T A SIDESHOW...

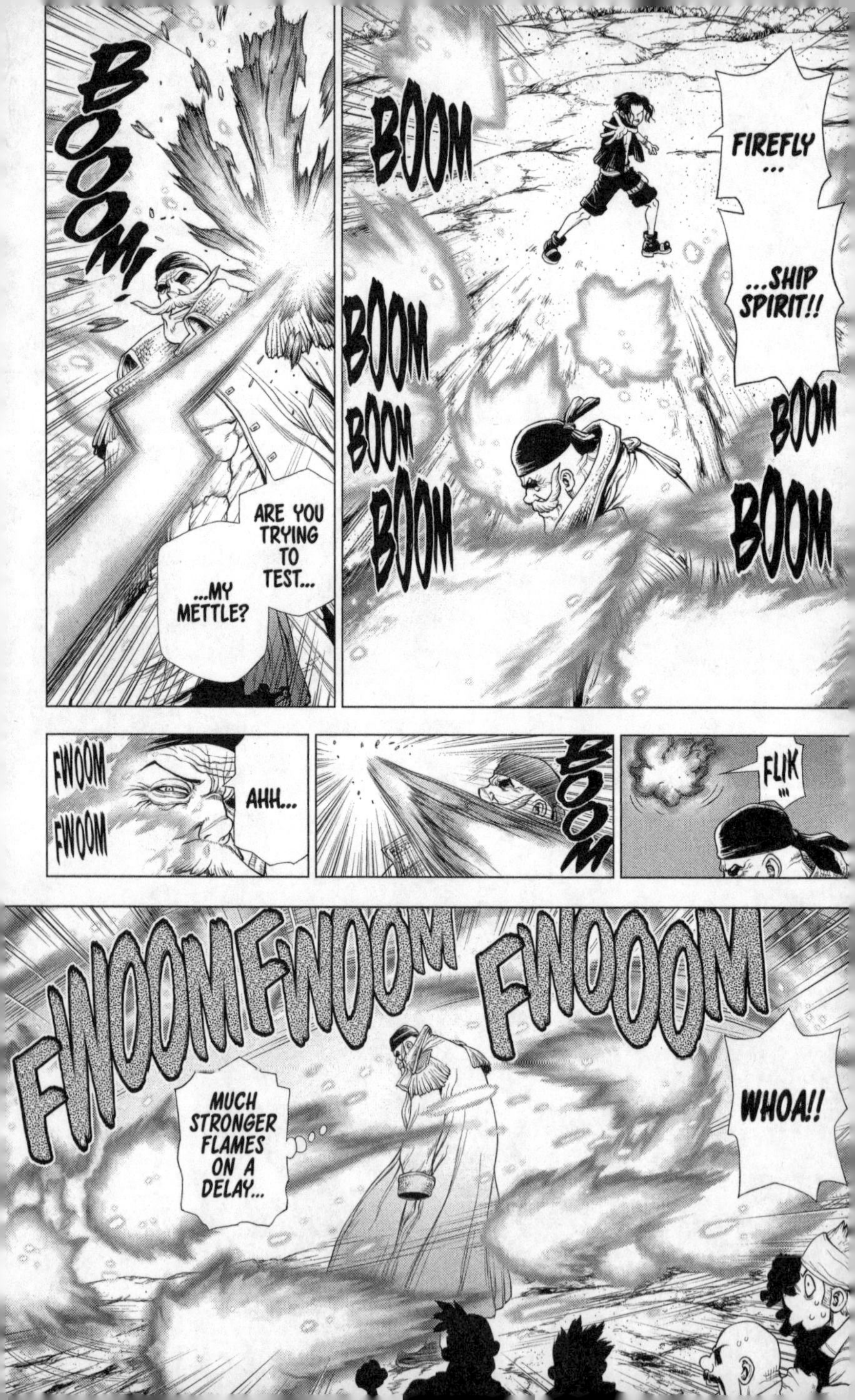
FIREFLY...
...SHIP SPIRIT!!
BOOM
BOOM
BOOM
BOOM
BOOM
BOOM
BOOM
BOOOOM!
ARE YOU TRYING TO TEST...
...MY METTLE?
FLIK...
BOOM
AHH...
FWOOM
FWOOM
FWOOOM
FWOOM
FWOOM
WHOA!!
MUCH STRONGER FLAMES ON A DELAY...

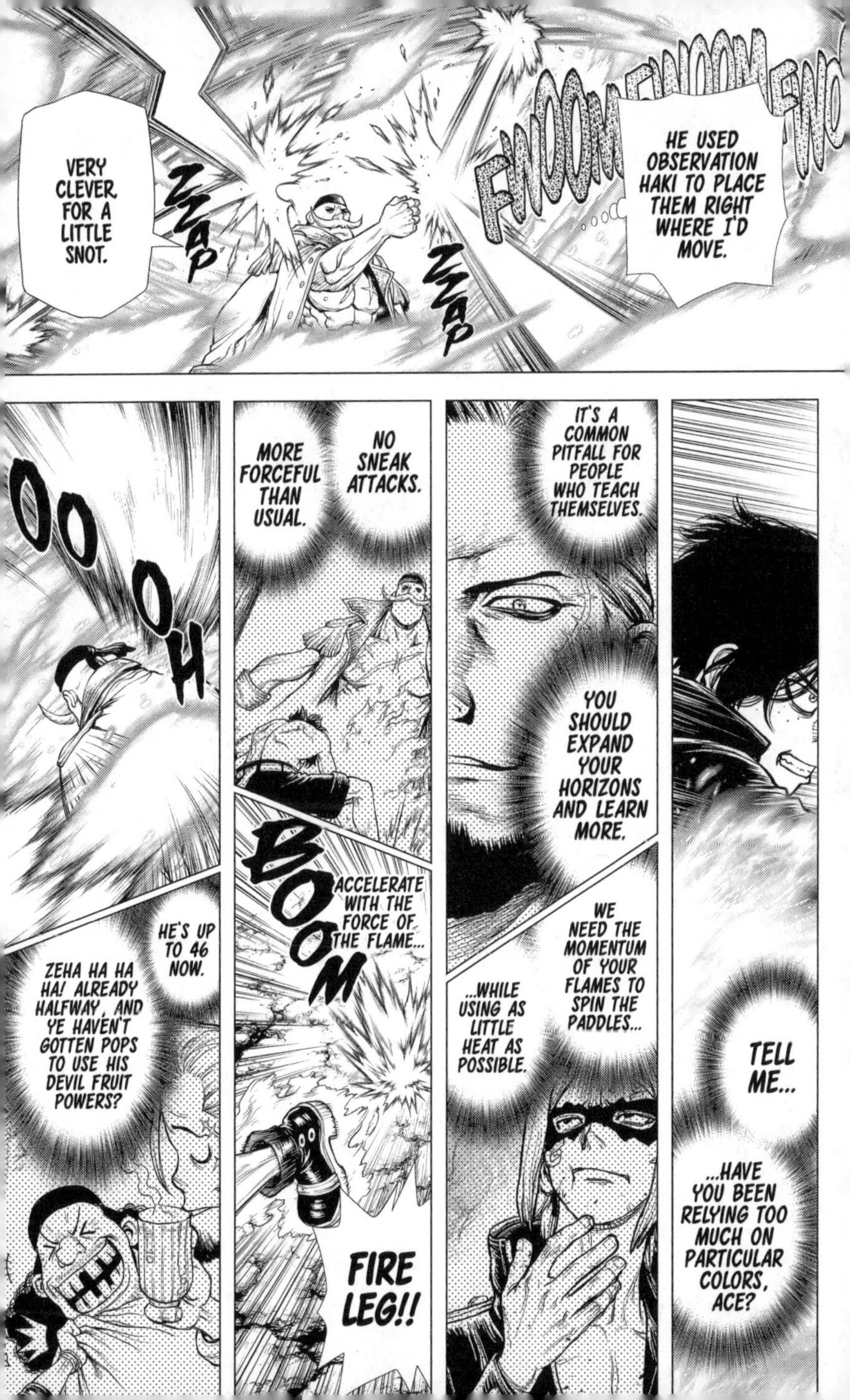
FNOOM FNOOM FNO
HE USED OBSERVATION HAKI TO PLACE THEM RIGHT WHERE I'D MOVE.
ZZAP
ZZAP
VERY CLEVER, FOR A LITTLE SNOT.
TELL ME...
...HAVE YOU BEEN RELYING TOO MUCH ON PARTICULAR COLORS, ACE?
IT'S A COMMON PITFALL FOR PEOPLE WHO TEACH THEMSELVES.
YOU SHOULD EXPAND YOUR HORIZONS AND LEARN MORE.
WE NEED THE MOMENTUM OF YOUR FLAMES TO SPIN THE PADDLES...
...WHILE USING AS LITTLE HEAT AS POSSIBLE.
NO SNEAK ATTACKS.
MORE FORCEFUL THAN USUAL.
BOOM
ACCELERATE WITH THE FORCE OF THE FLAME...
FIRE LEG!!
OOOOH
HE'S UP TO 46 NOW.
ZEHA HA HA HA! ALREADY HALFWAY, AND YE HAVEN'T GOTTEN POPS TO USE HIS DEVIL FRUIT POWERS?

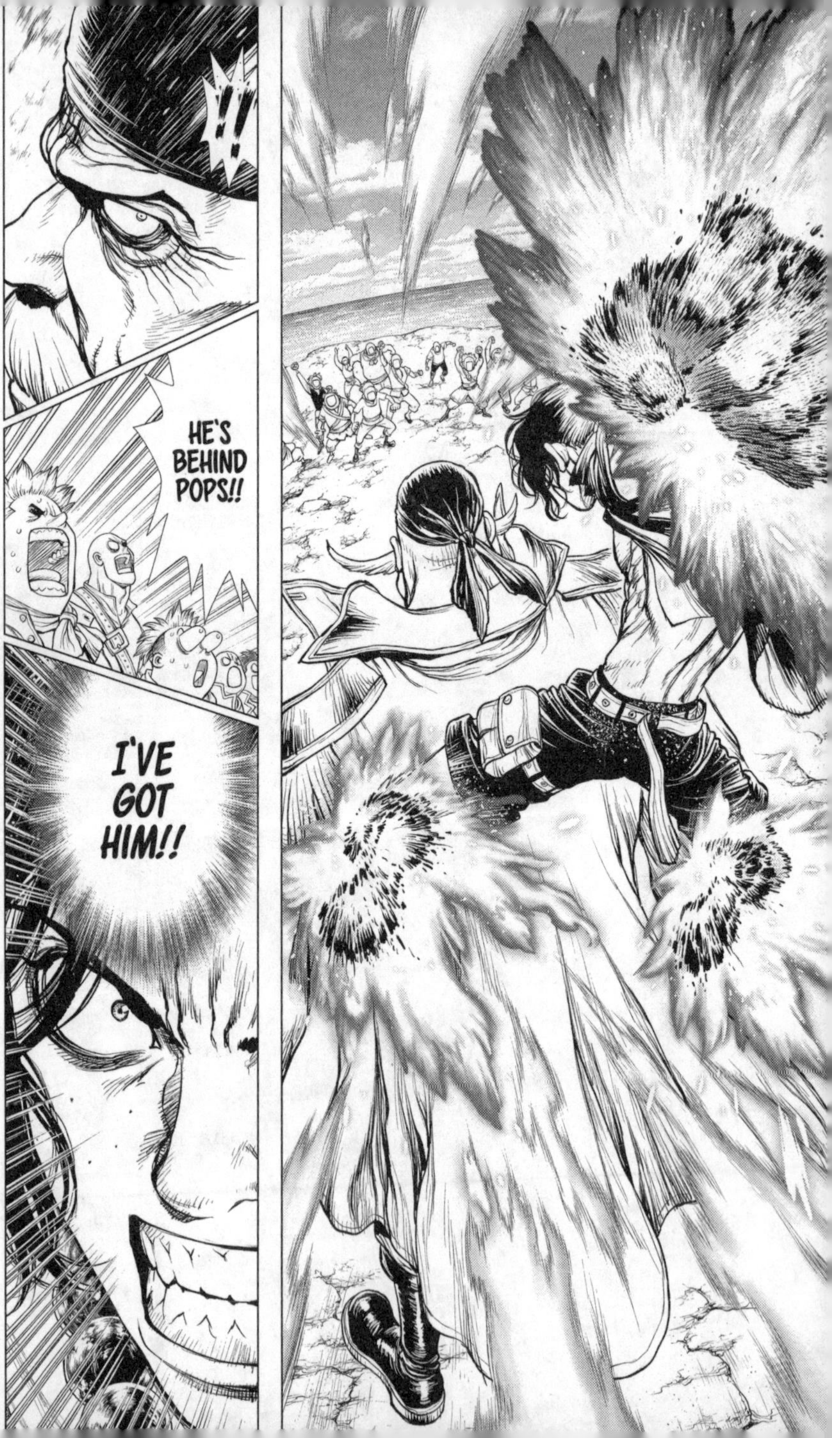
!!
HE'S BEHIND POPS!!
I'VE GOT HIM!!

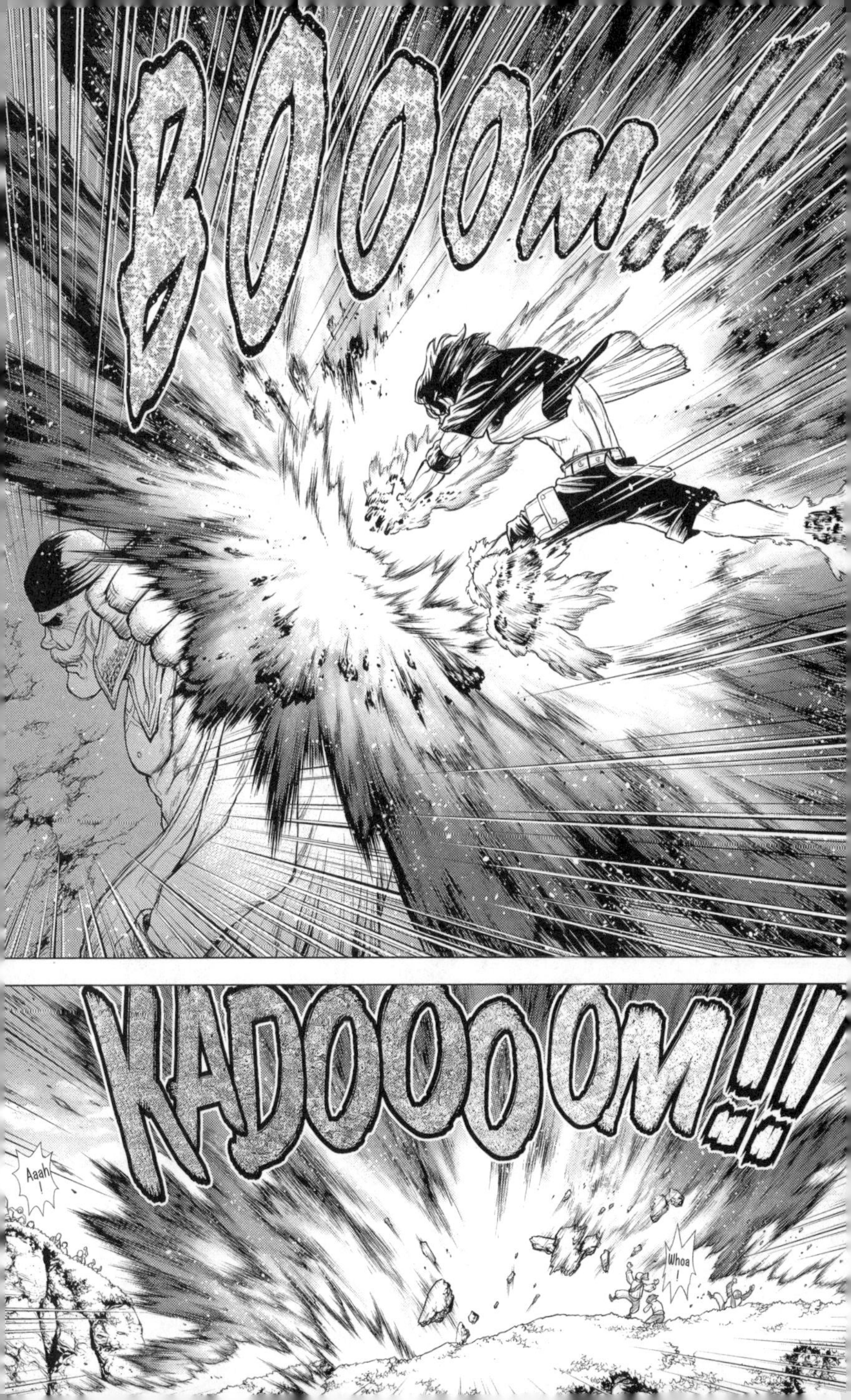
BOOOM!!
KADOOOOM!!
Whoa!
Aaah!

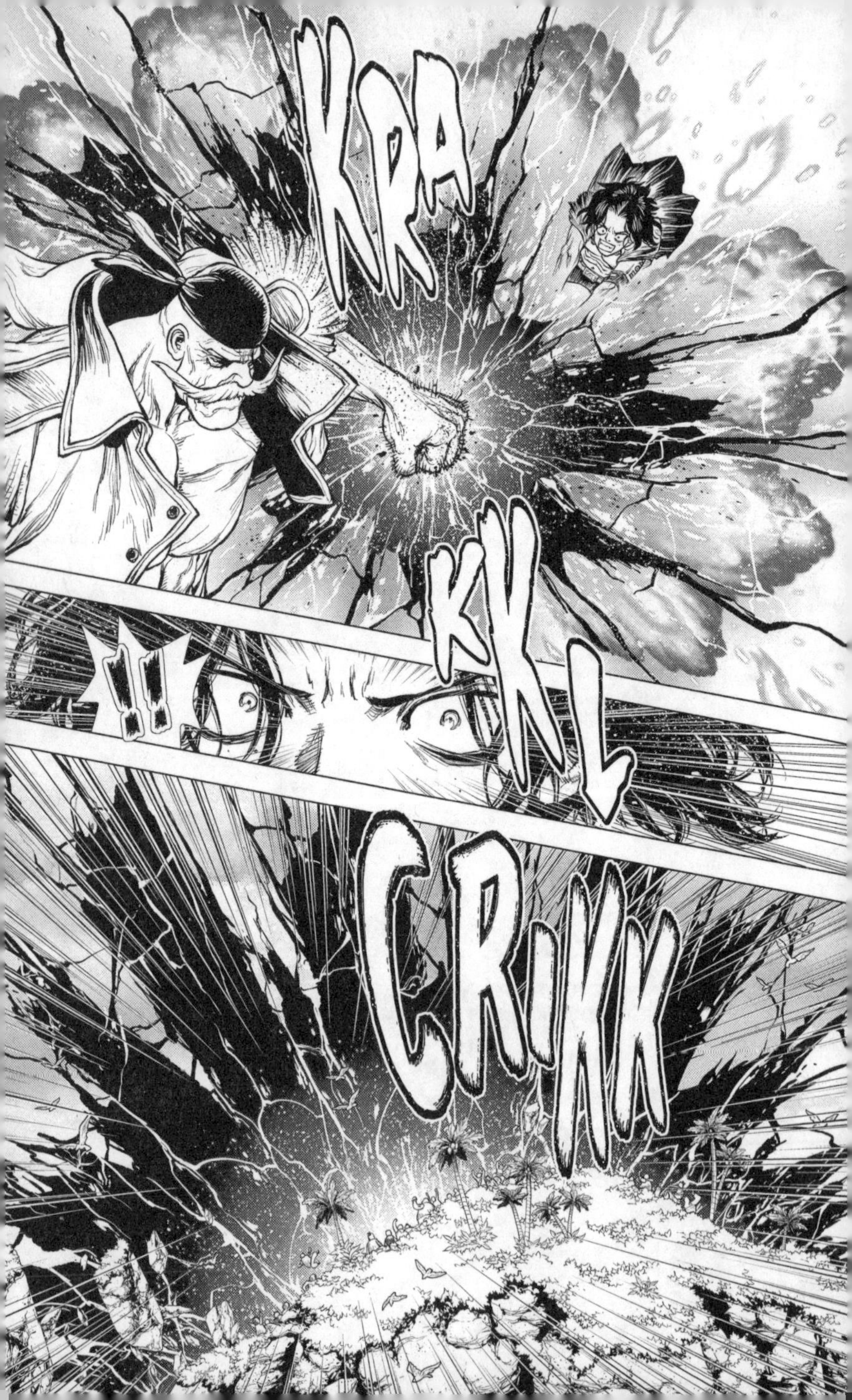
KRA
KKL
!!
CRIKK

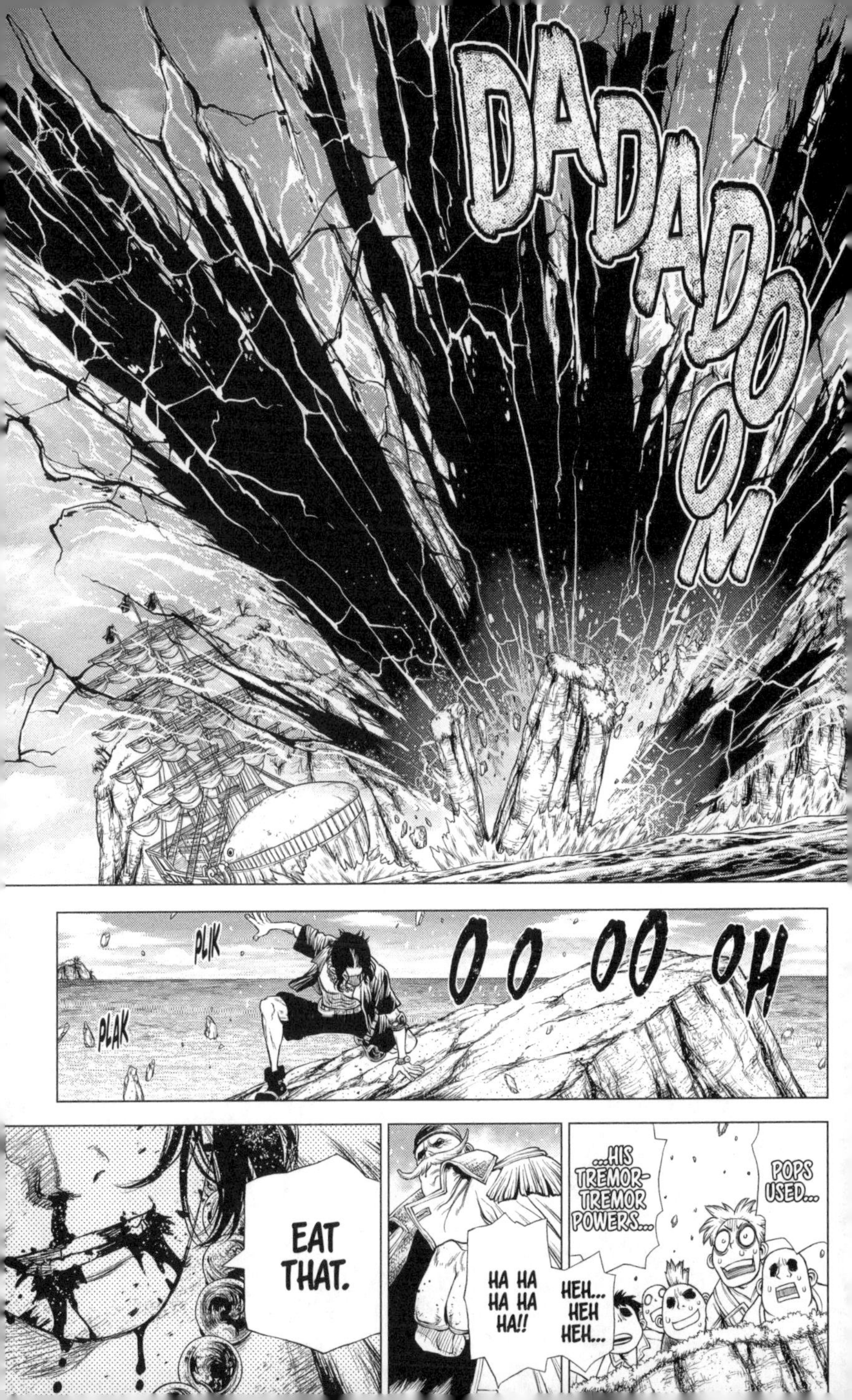
DADADOOOM
O O OO OH
PLIK
PLAK
POPS USED...
...HIS TREMOR-TREMOR POWERS...
HEH... HEH HEH...
HA HA HA HA HA!!
EAT THAT.

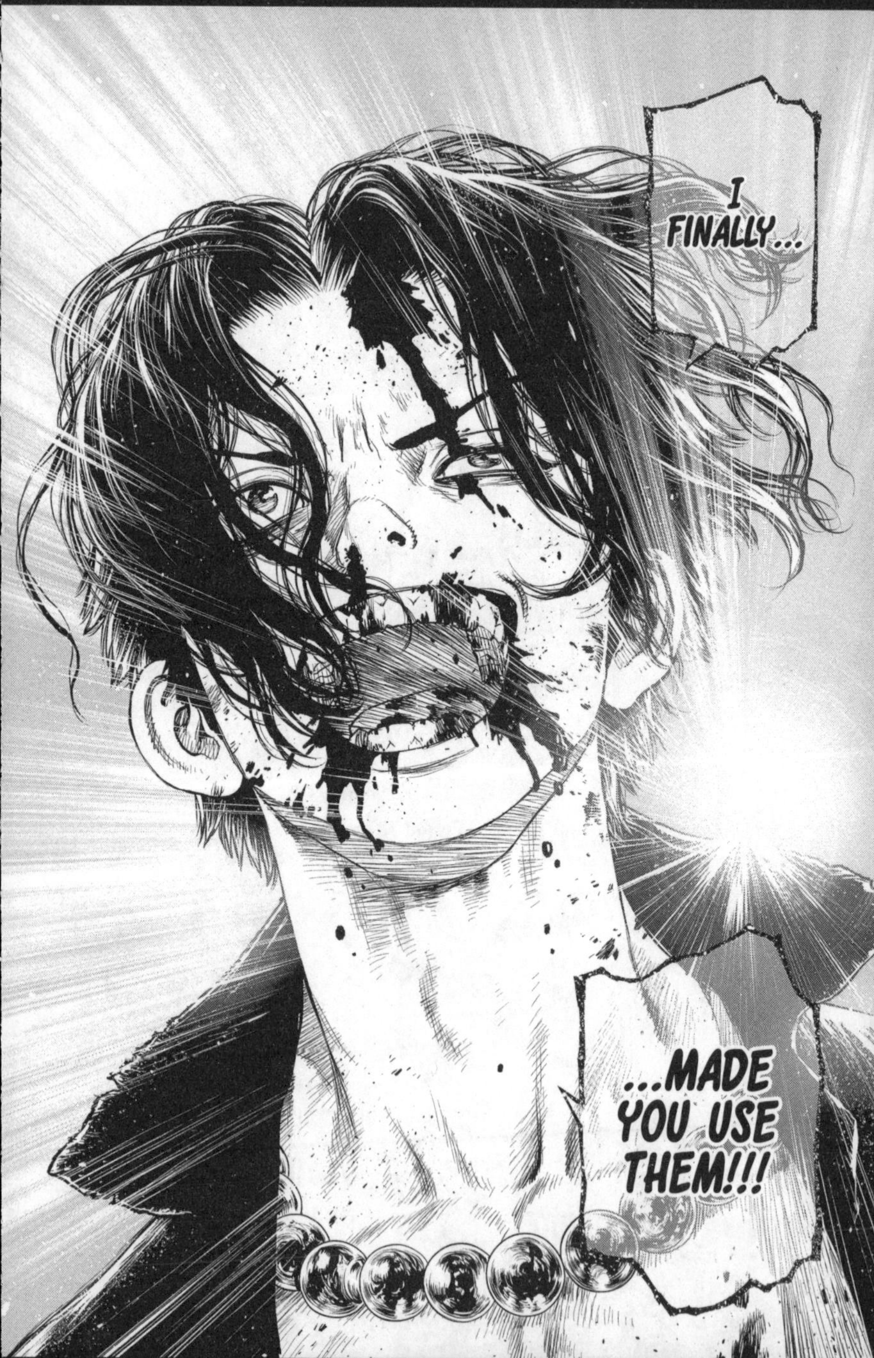
I FINALLY...
...MADE YOU USE THEM!!!

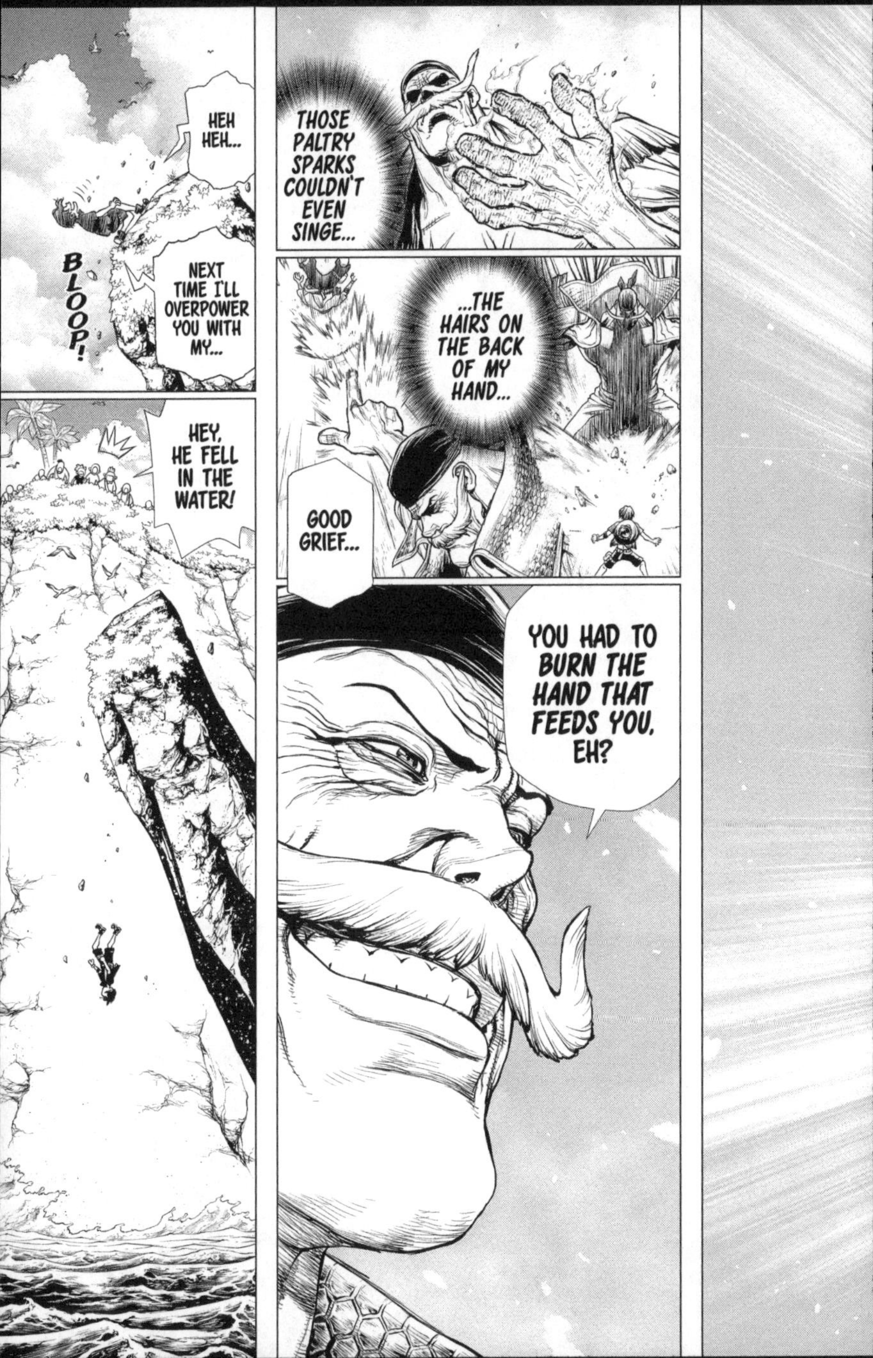
THOSE PALTRY SPARKS COULDN'T EVEN SINGE...
...THE HAIRS ON THE BACK OF MY HAND...
GOOD GRIEF...
YOU HAD TO BURN THE HAND THAT FEEDS YOU, EH?
HEH HEH...
NEXT TIME I'LL OVERPOWER YOU WITH MY...
BLOOOP!
HEY, HE FELL IN THE WATER!

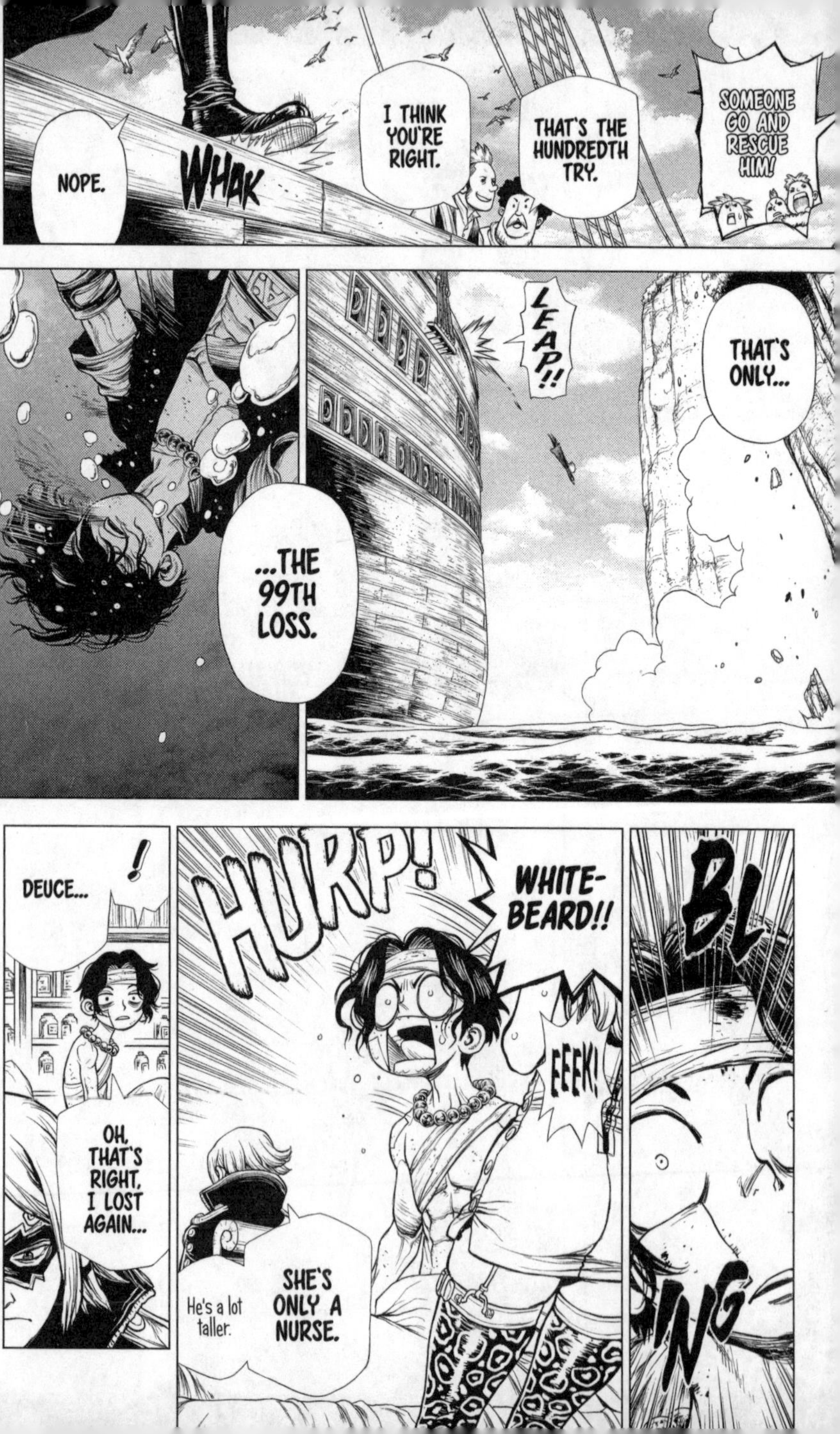
SOMEONE GO AND RESCUE HIM!
THAT'S THE HUNDREDTH TRY.
I THINK YOU'RE RIGHT.
WHAK
NOPE.
THAT'S ONLY...
LEAP!!
...THE 99TH LOSS.
BL
NG
HURP!
WHITE-BEARD!!
EEEK!
SHE'S ONLY A NURSE.
He's a lot taller.
!
DEUCE...
OH, THAT'S RIGHT, I LOST AGAIN...

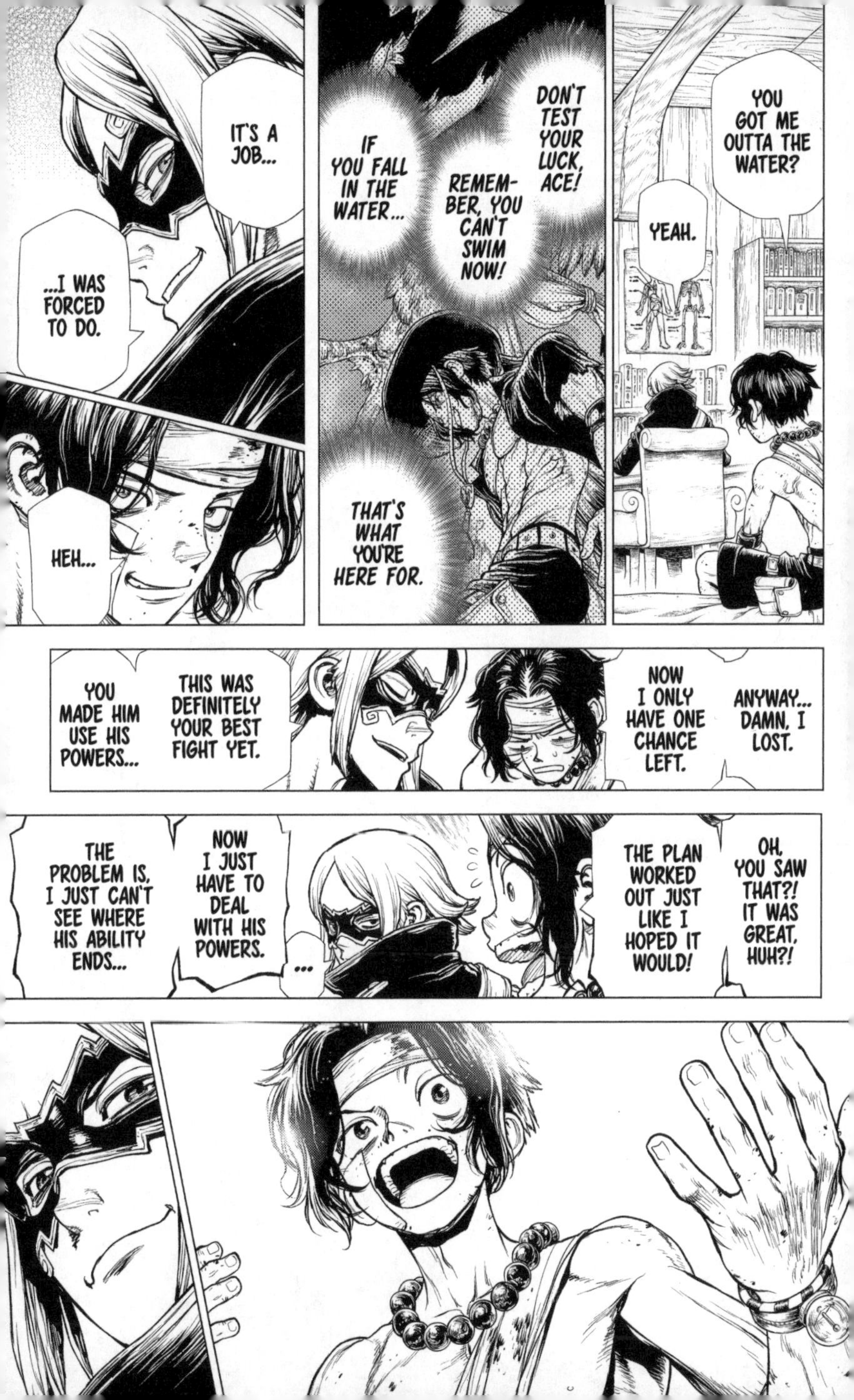
YOU GOT ME OUTTA THE WATER?
YEAH.
DON'T TEST YOUR LUCK, ACE!
REMEMBER, YOU CAN'T SWIM NOW!
IF YOU FALL IN THE WATER...
THAT'S WHAT YOU'RE HERE FOR.
IT'S A JOB...
...I WAS FORCED TO DO.
HEH...
ANYWAY... DAMN, I LOST.
NOW I ONLY HAVE ONE CHANCE LEFT.
THIS WAS DEFINITELY YOUR BEST FIGHT YET.
YOU MADE HIM USE HIS POWERS...
OH, YOU SAW THAT?! IT WAS GREAT, HUH?!
THE PLAN WORKED OUT JUST LIKE I HOPED IT WOULD!
...
NOW I JUST HAVE TO DEAL WITH HIS POWERS.
THE PROBLEM IS, I JUST CAN'T SEE WHERE HIS ABILITY ENDS...

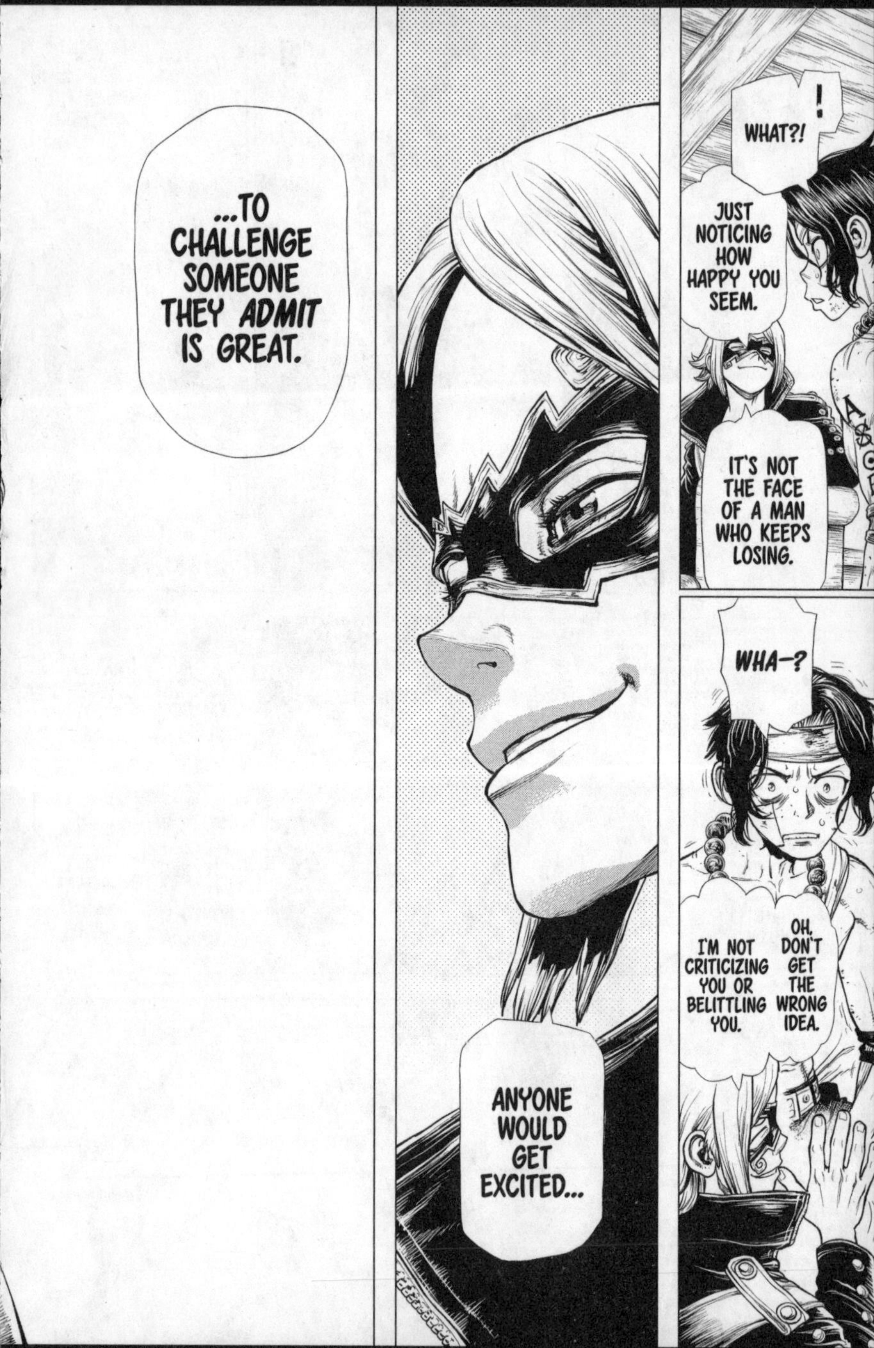
!
WHAT?!
JUST NOTICING HOW HAPPY YOU SEEM.
IT'S NOT THE FACE OF A MAN WHO KEEPS LOSING.
WHA-?
OH, DON'T GET THE WRONG IDEA.
I'M NOT CRITICIZING YOU OR BELITTLING YOU.
ANYONE WOULD GET EXCITED...
...TO CHALLENGE SOMEONE THEY ADMIT IS GREAT.

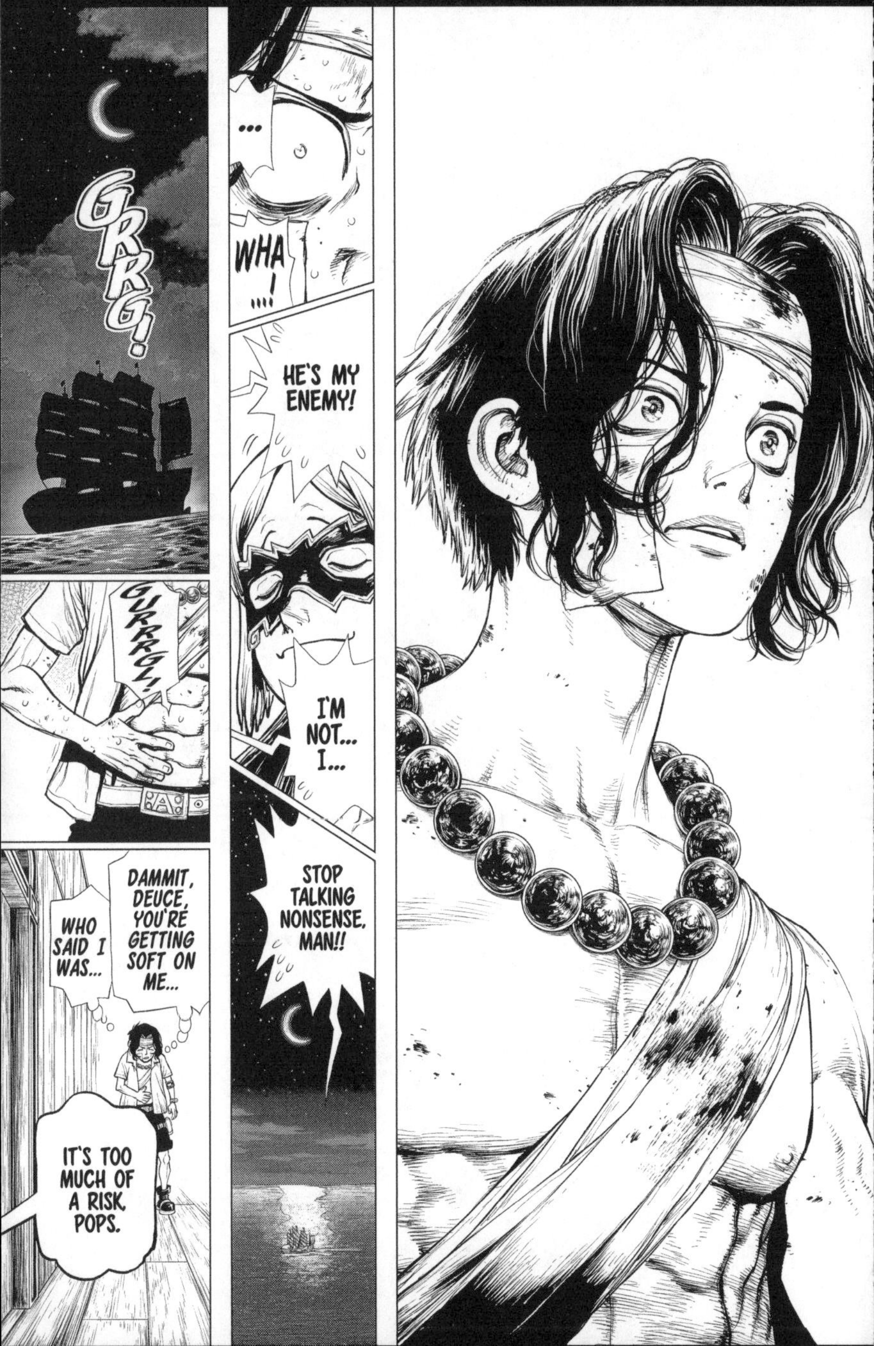
...
WHA! ....!
HE'S MY ENEMY!
I'M NOT... I...
STOP TALKING NONSENSE, MAN!!
GRRG!
GURRRGL!
DAMMIT, DEUCE, YOU'RE GETTING SOFT ON ME...
WHO SAID I WAS...
IT'S TOO MUCH OF A RISK, POPS.

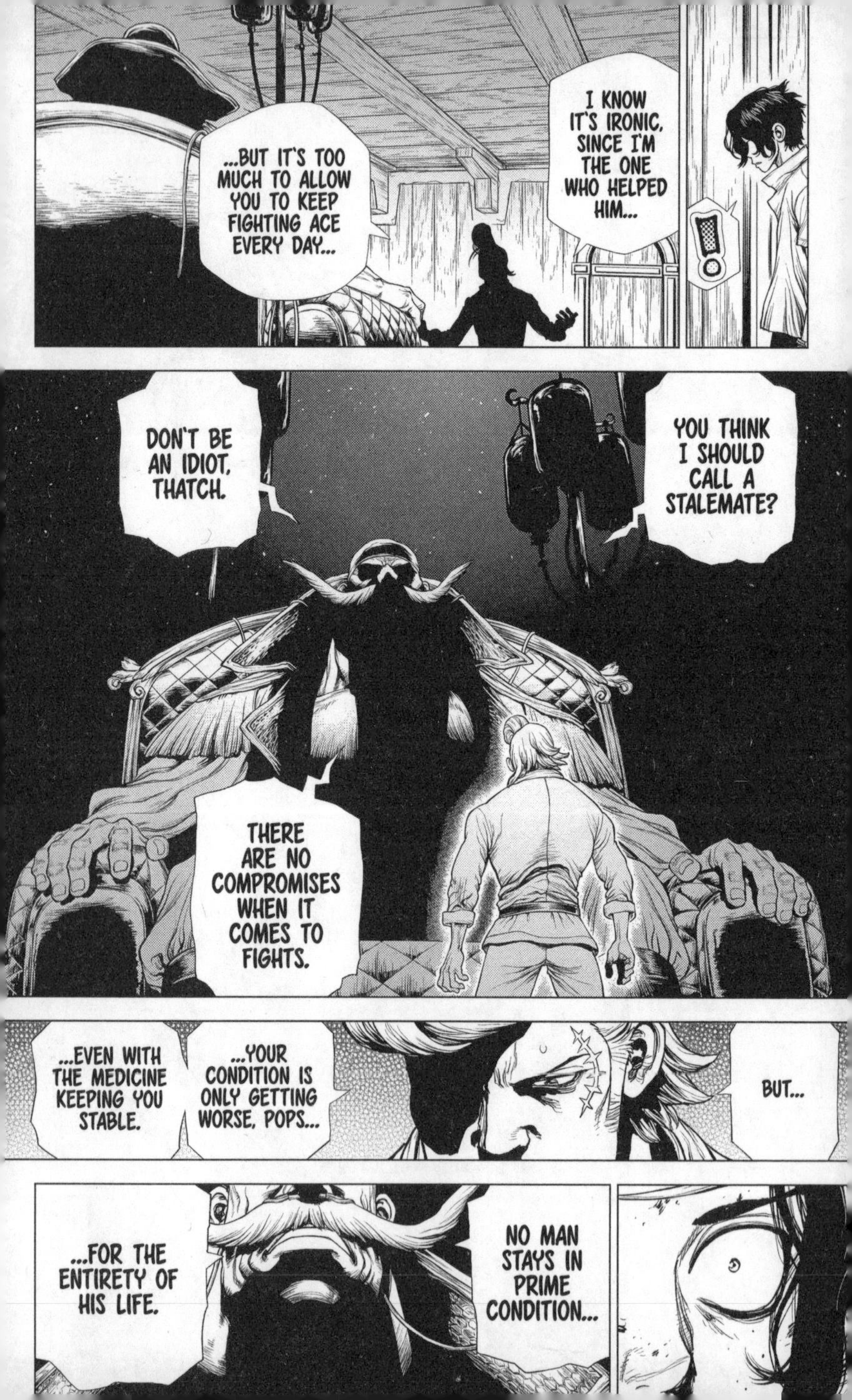
!
I KNOW IT'S IRONIC, SINCE I'M THE ONE WHO HELPED HIM...
...BUT IT'S TOO MUCH TO ALLOW YOU TO KEEP FIGHTING ACE EVERY DAY...
YOU THINK I SHOULD CALL A STALEMATE?
DON'T BE AN IDIOT, THATCH.
THERE ARE NO COMPROMISES WHEN IT COMES TO FIGHTS.
BUT...
...YOUR CONDITION IS ONLY GETTING WORSE, POPS...
...EVEN WITH THE MEDICINE KEEPING YOU STABLE.
NO MAN STAYS IN PRIME CONDITION...
...FOR THE ENTIRETY OF HIS LIFE.

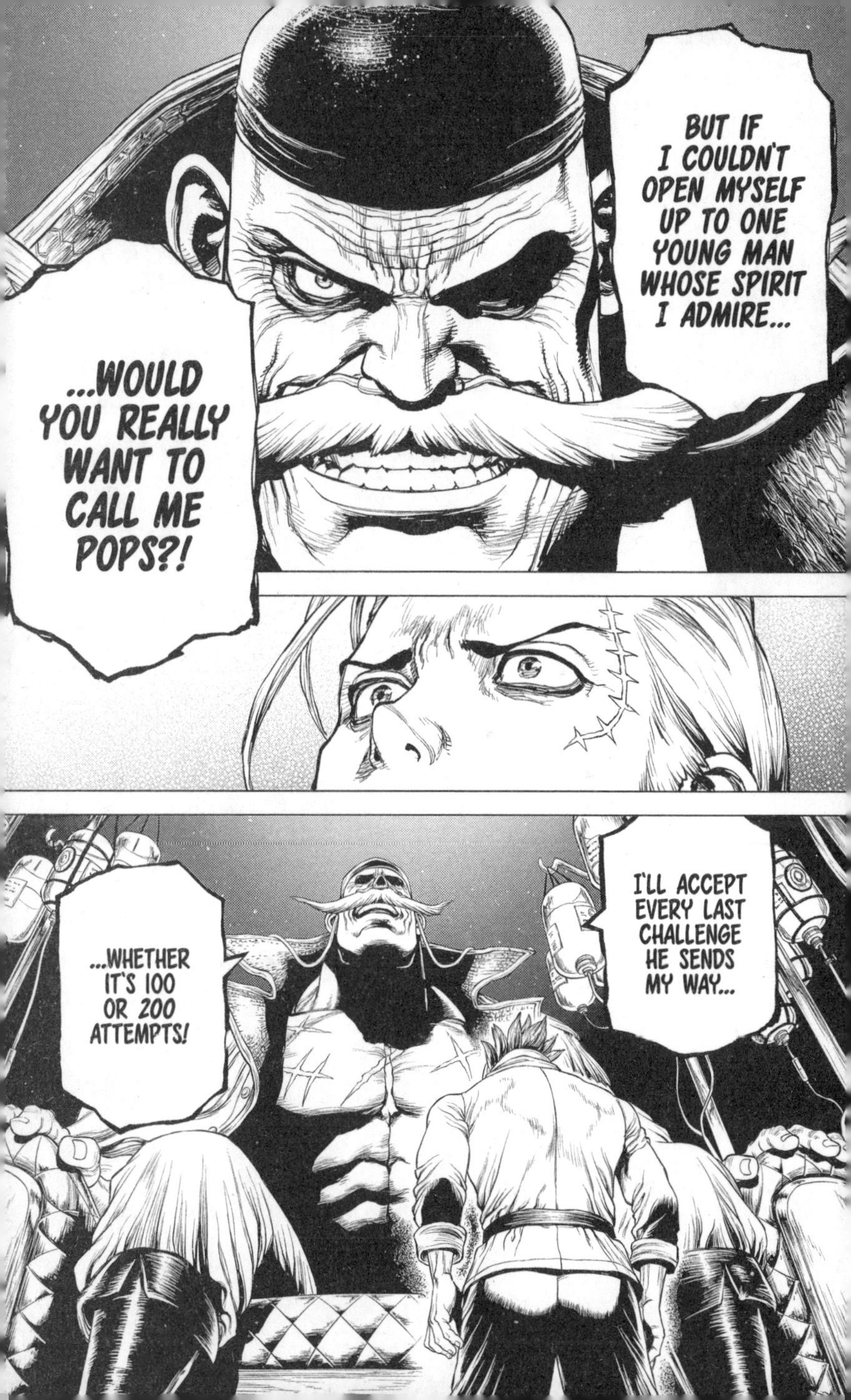
BUT IF I COULDN'T OPEN MYSELF UP TO ONE YOUNG MAN WHOSE SPIRIT I ADMIRE...
...WOULD YOU REALLY WANT TO CALL ME POPS?!
I'LL ACCEPT EVERY LAST CHALLENGE HE SENDS MY WAY...
...WHETHER IT'S 100 OR 200 ATTEMPTS!

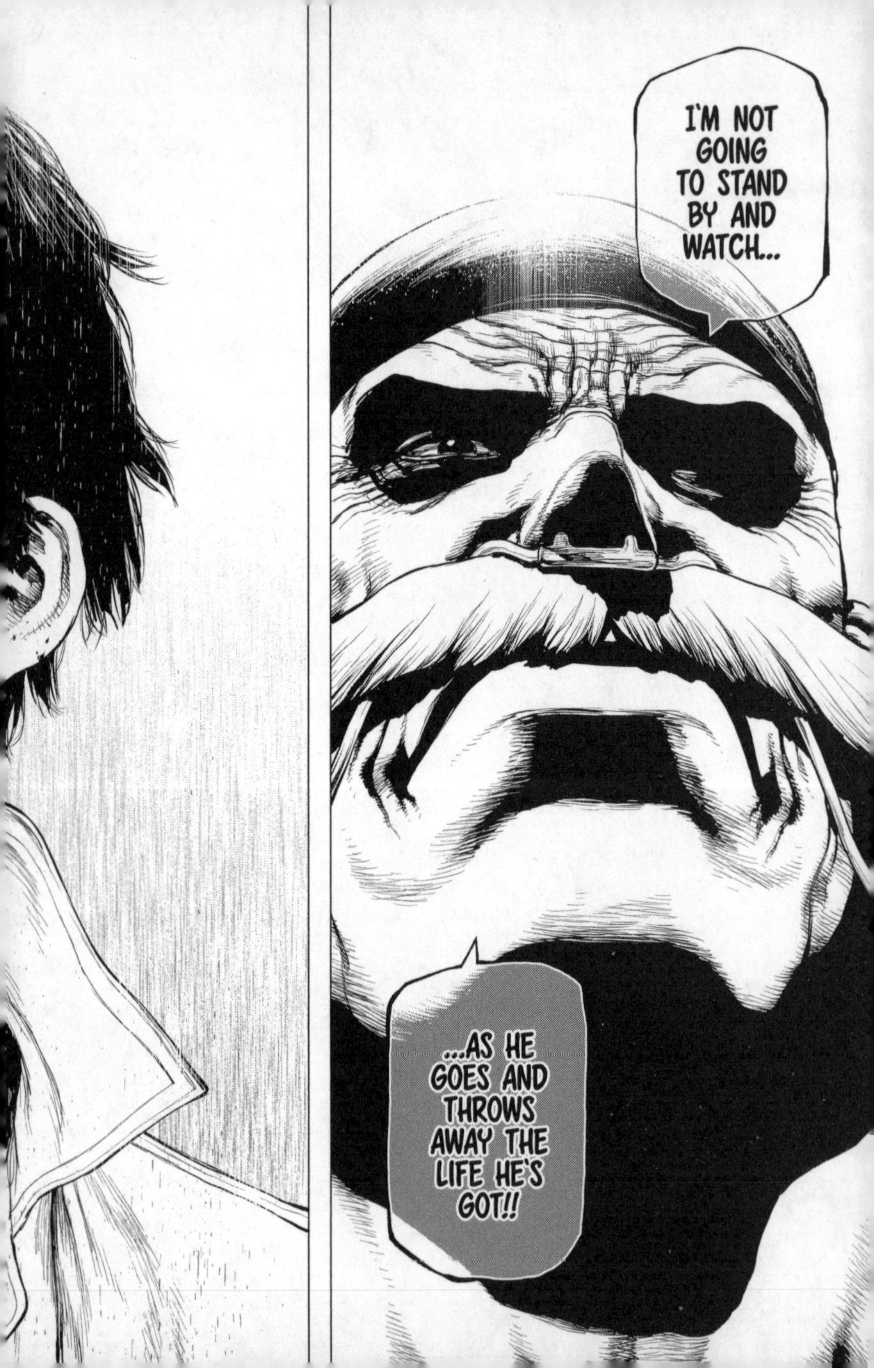
I'M NOT GOING TO STAND BY AND WATCH...
...AS HE GOES AND THROWS AWAY THE LIFE HE'S GOT!!

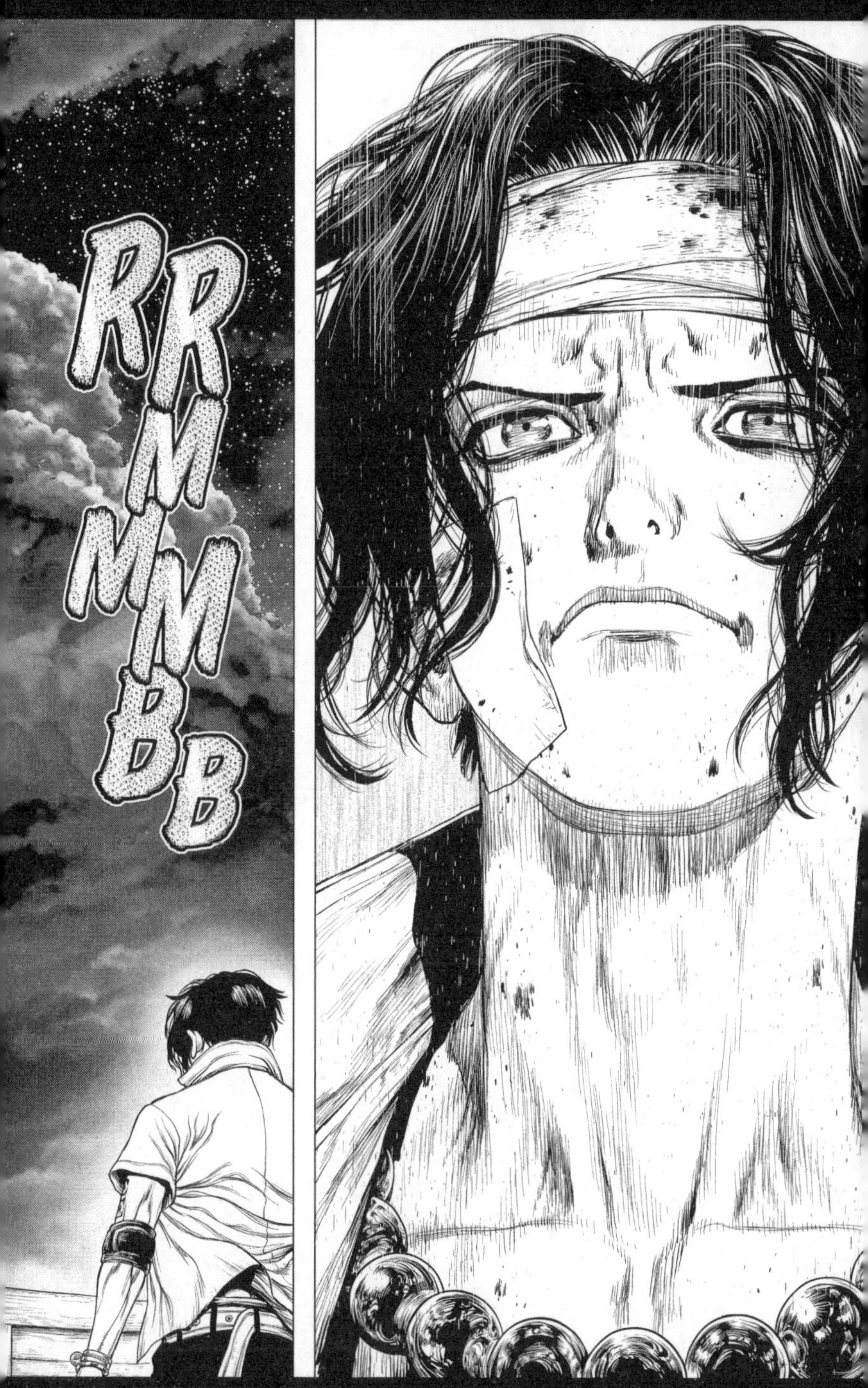
RRMMBB

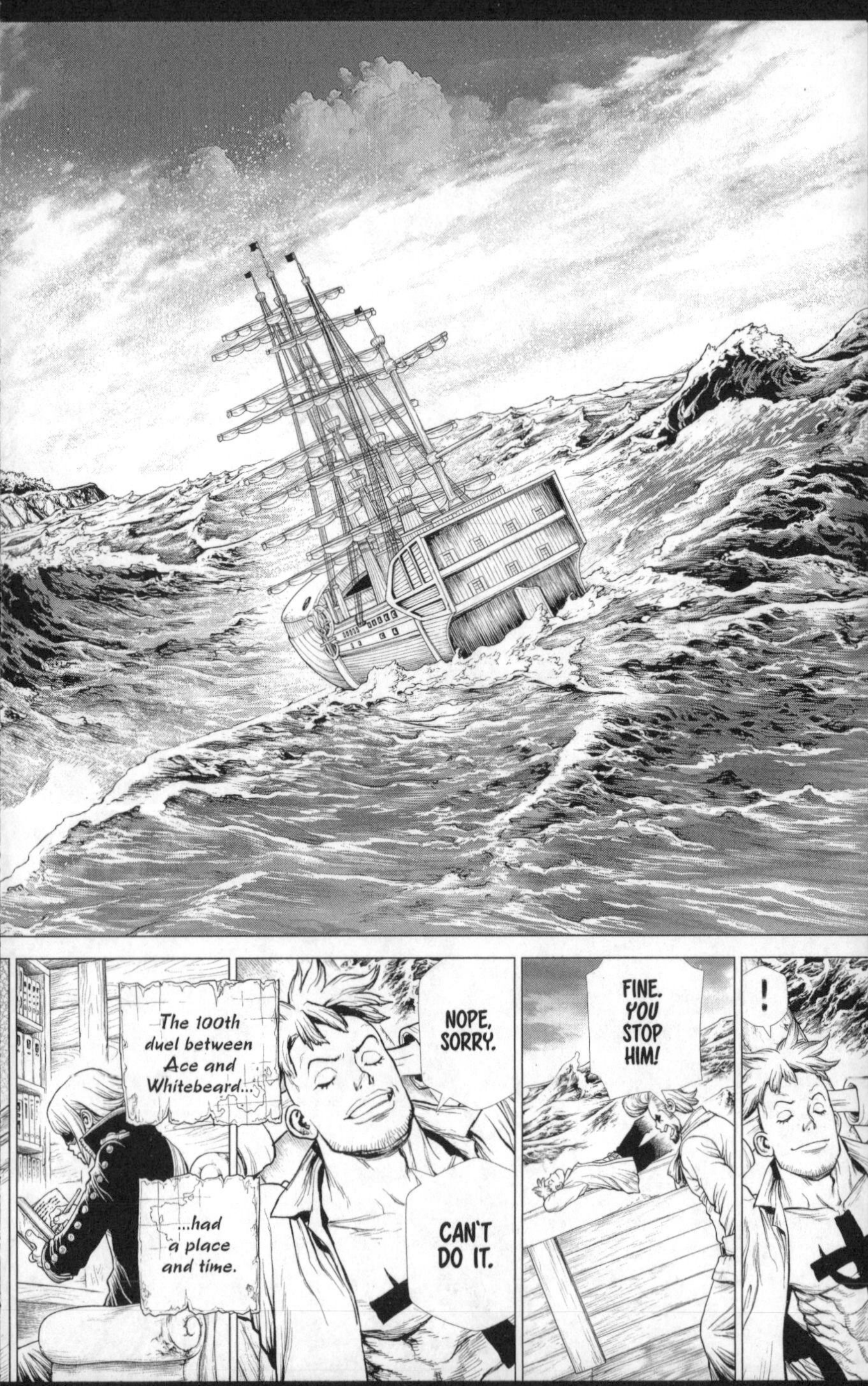
!
FINE. YOU STOP HIM!
NOPE, SORRY.
CAN'T DO IT.
The 100th duel between Ace and Whitebeard...
...had a place and time.

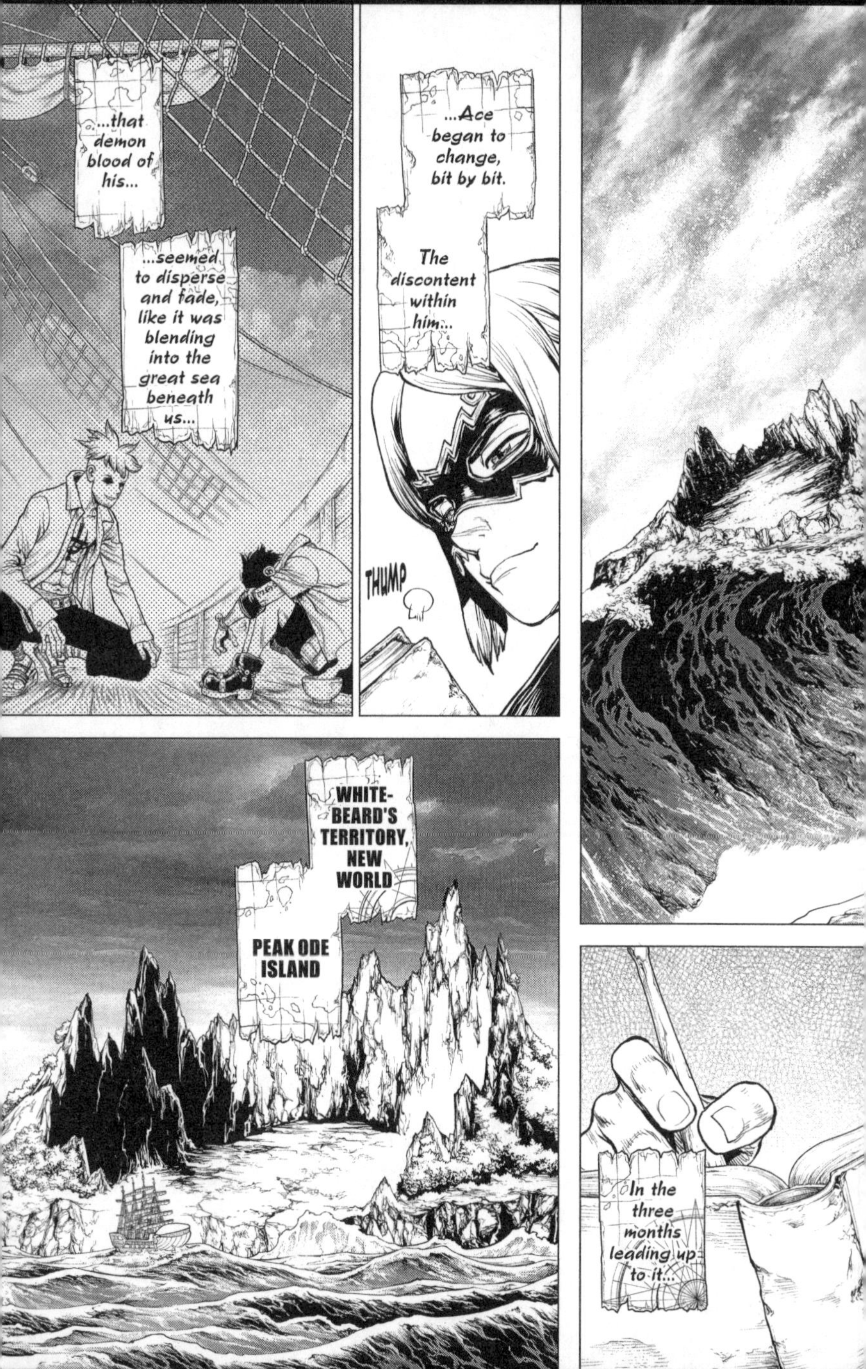

...Ace began to change, bit by bit.
The discontent within him...
THUMP
...that demon blood of his...
...seemed to disperse and fade, like it was blending into the great sea beneath us...
WHITEBEARD'S TERRITORY, NEW WORLD
PEAK ODE ISLAND
In the three months leading up to it...

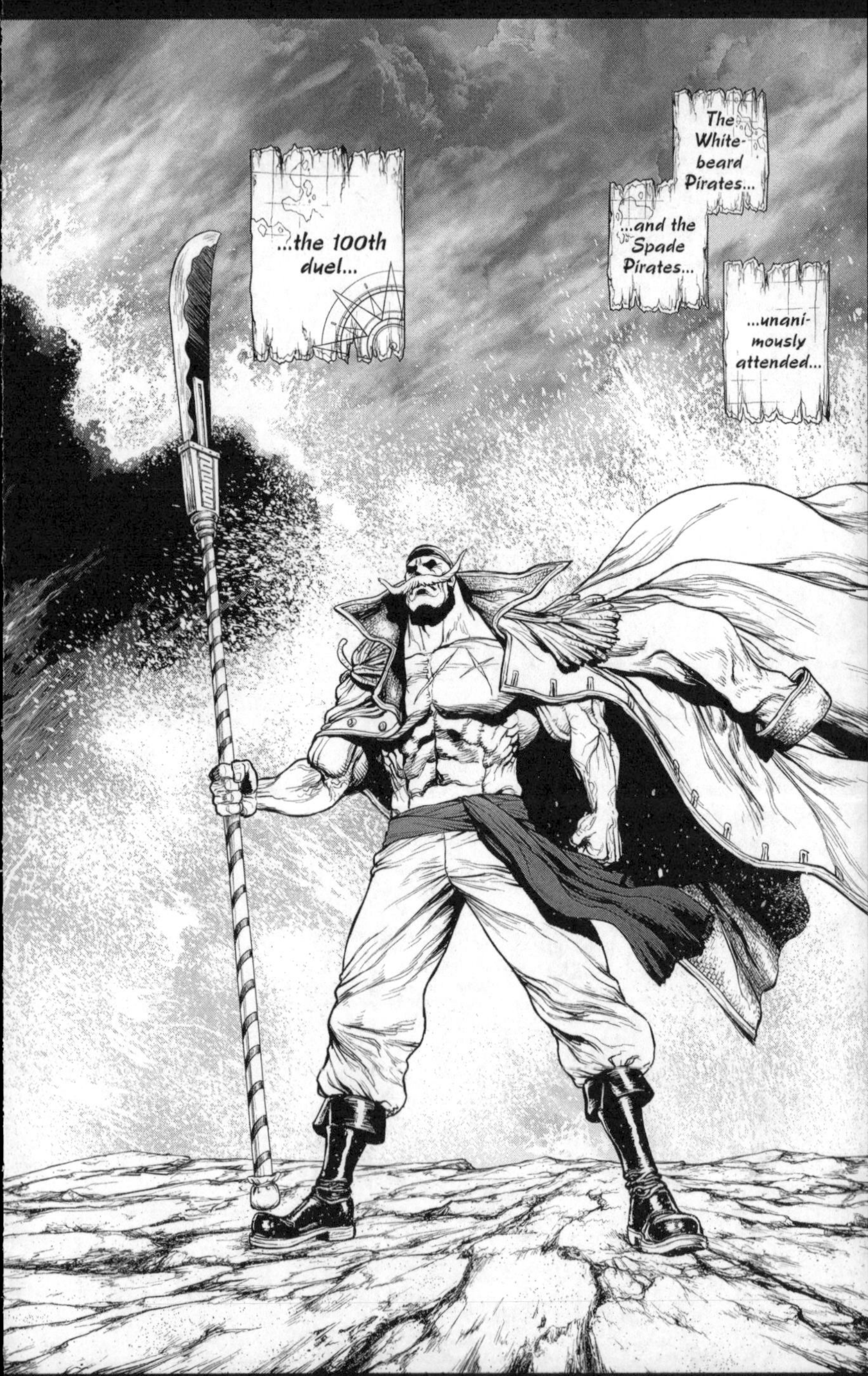
The White-
beard
Pirates...
...and the
Spade
Pirates...
...unani-
mously
attended...
...the 100th
duel...

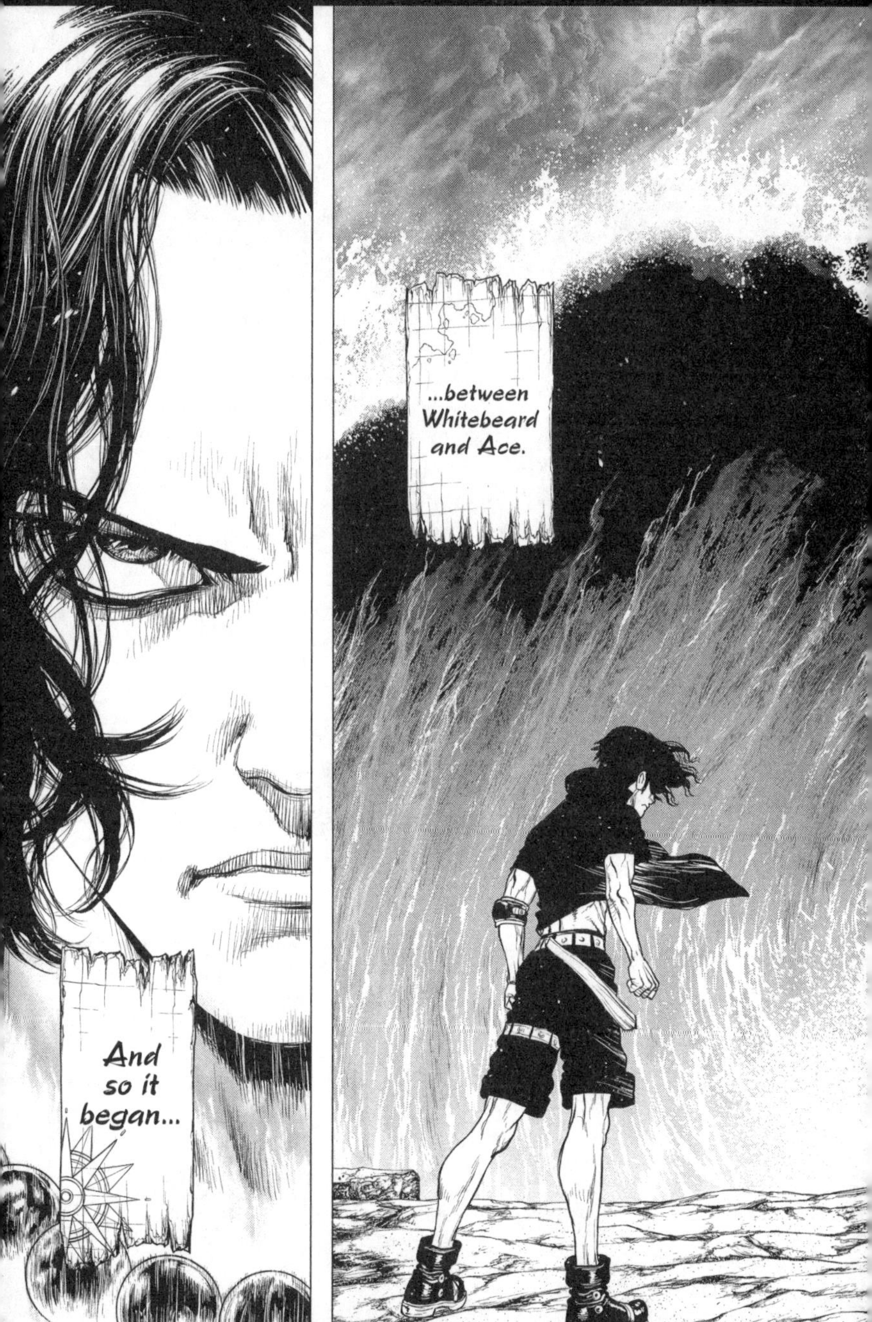
And so it began...
...between Whitebeard and Ace.

ONE PIECE

Ace's Story

THE MANGA

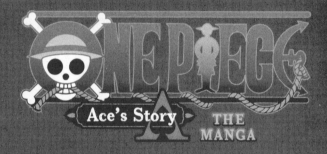

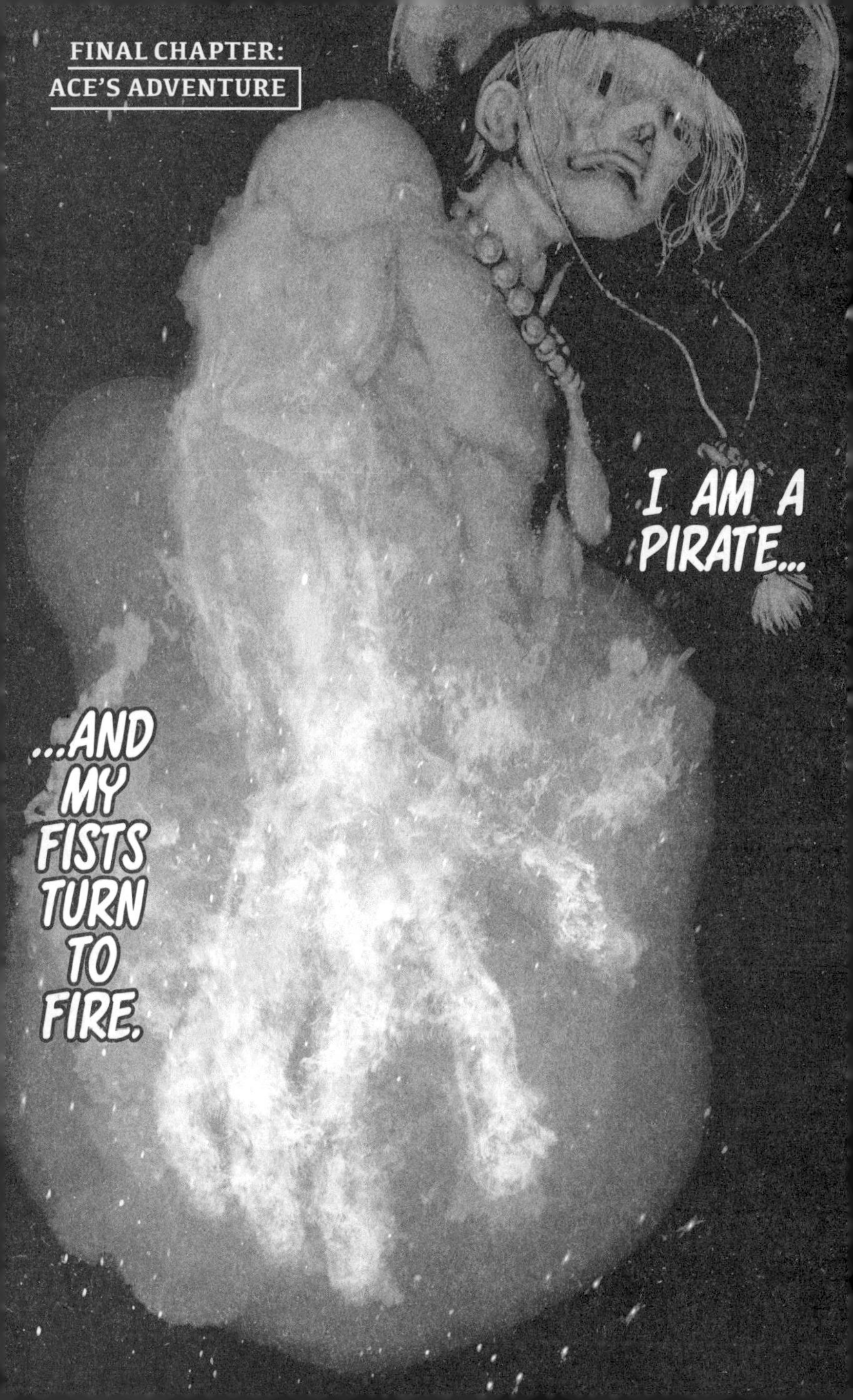
FINAL CHAPTER:
ACE'S ADVENTURE
I AM A PIRATE...
...AND MY FISTS TURN TO FIRE.

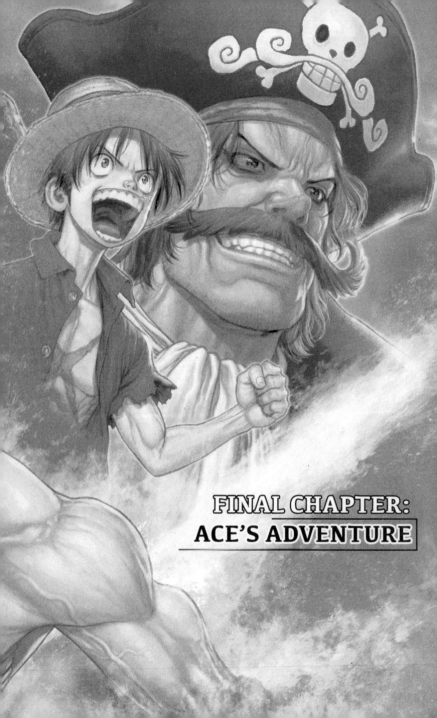

FINAL CHAPTER:
ACE'S ADVENTURE

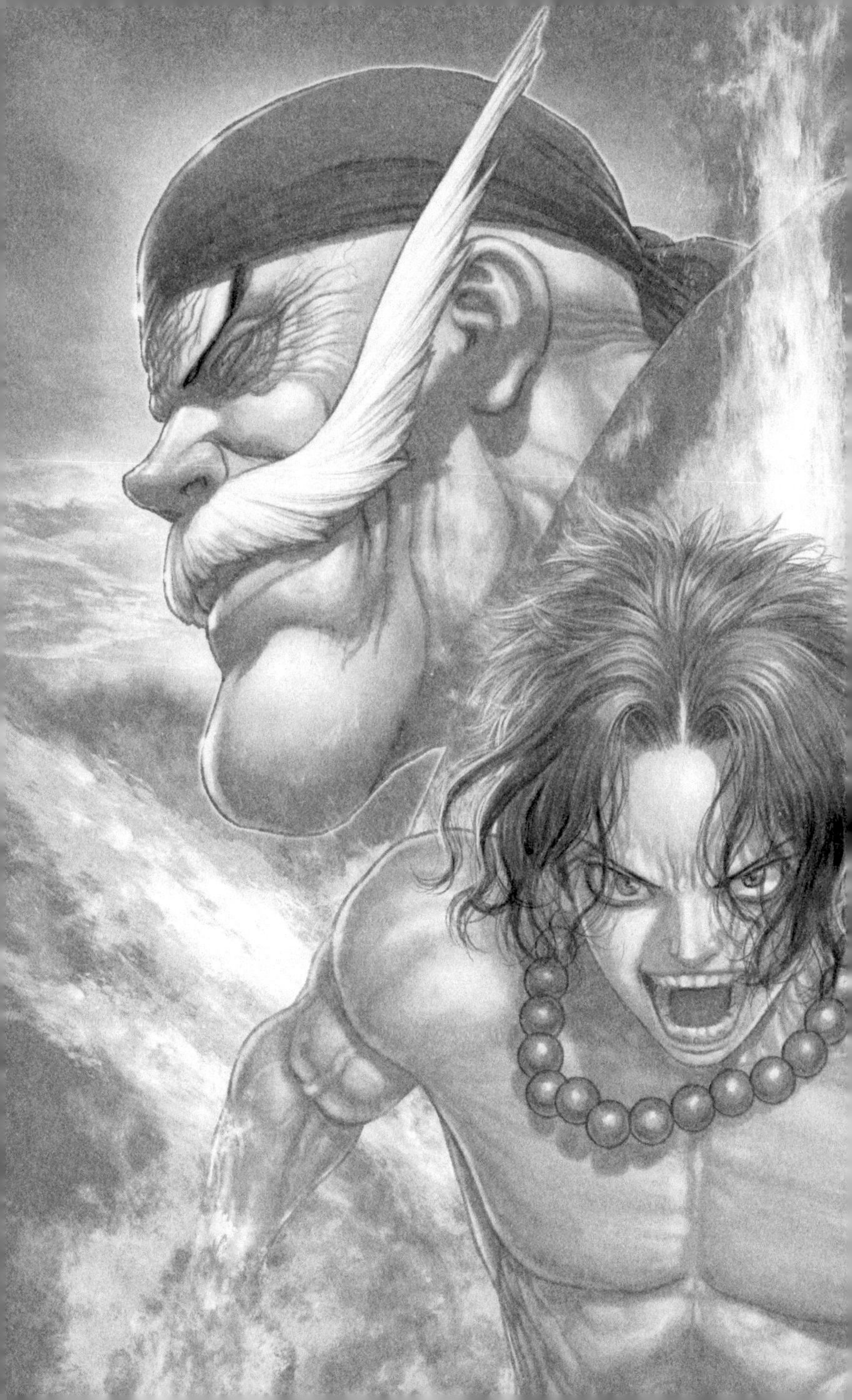

ONE PIECE

Ace's Story

THE MANGA

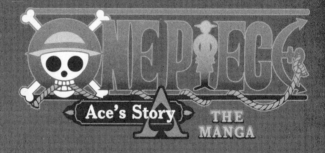

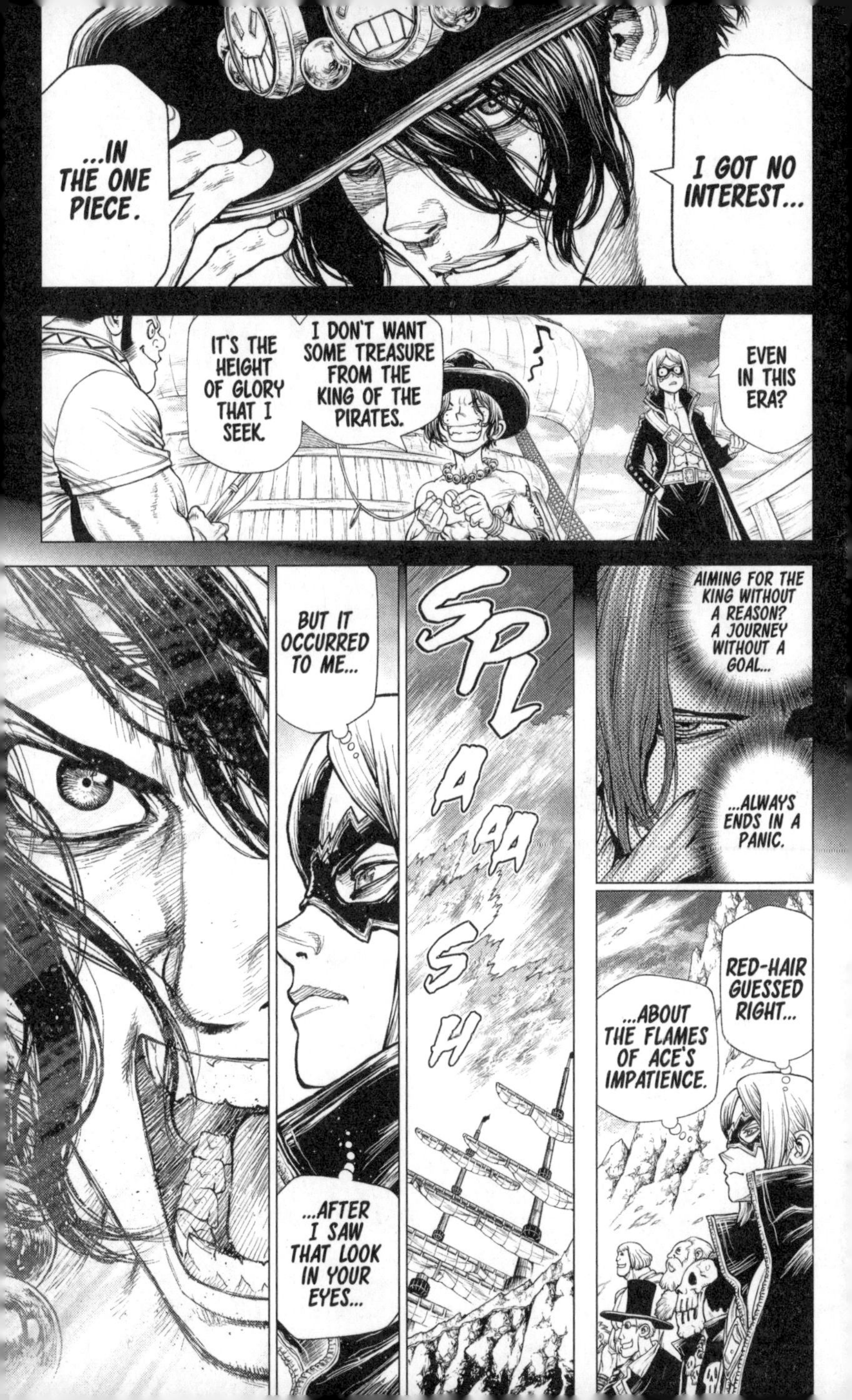
I GOT NO INTEREST...
...IN THE ONE PIECE.
EVEN IN THIS ERA?
I DON'T WANT SOME TREASURE FROM THE KING OF THE PIRATES.
IT'S THE HEIGHT OF GLORY THAT I SEEK.
AIMING FOR THE KING WITHOUT A REASON? A JOURNEY WITHOUT A GOAL...
...ALWAYS ENDS IN A PANIC.
RED-HAIR GUESSED RIGHT...
...ABOUT THE FLAMES OF ACE'S IMPATIENCE.
SPLAAAASH
BUT IT OCCURRED TO ME...
...AFTER I SAW THAT LOOK IN YOUR EYES...

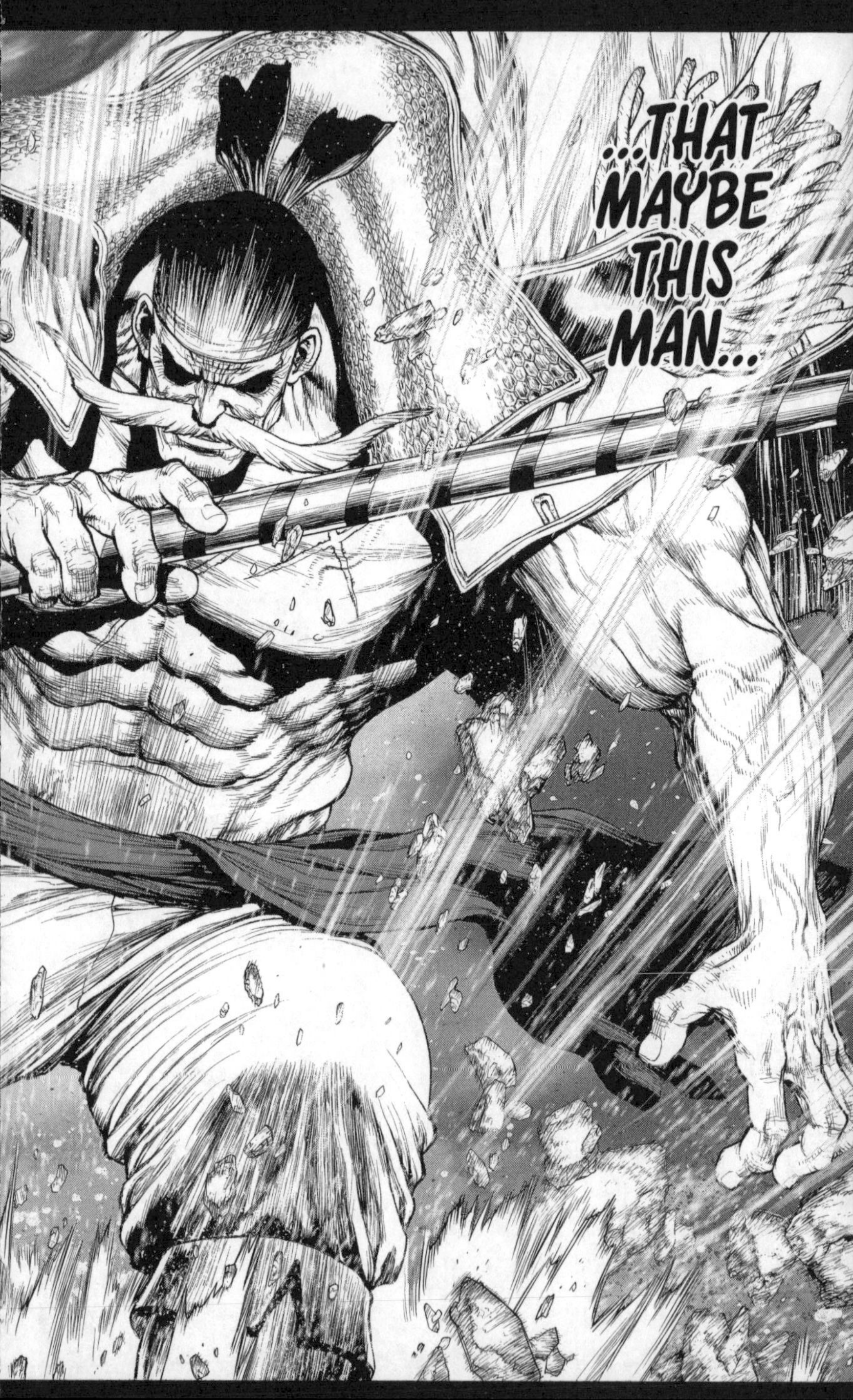
...THAT MAYBE THIS MAN...

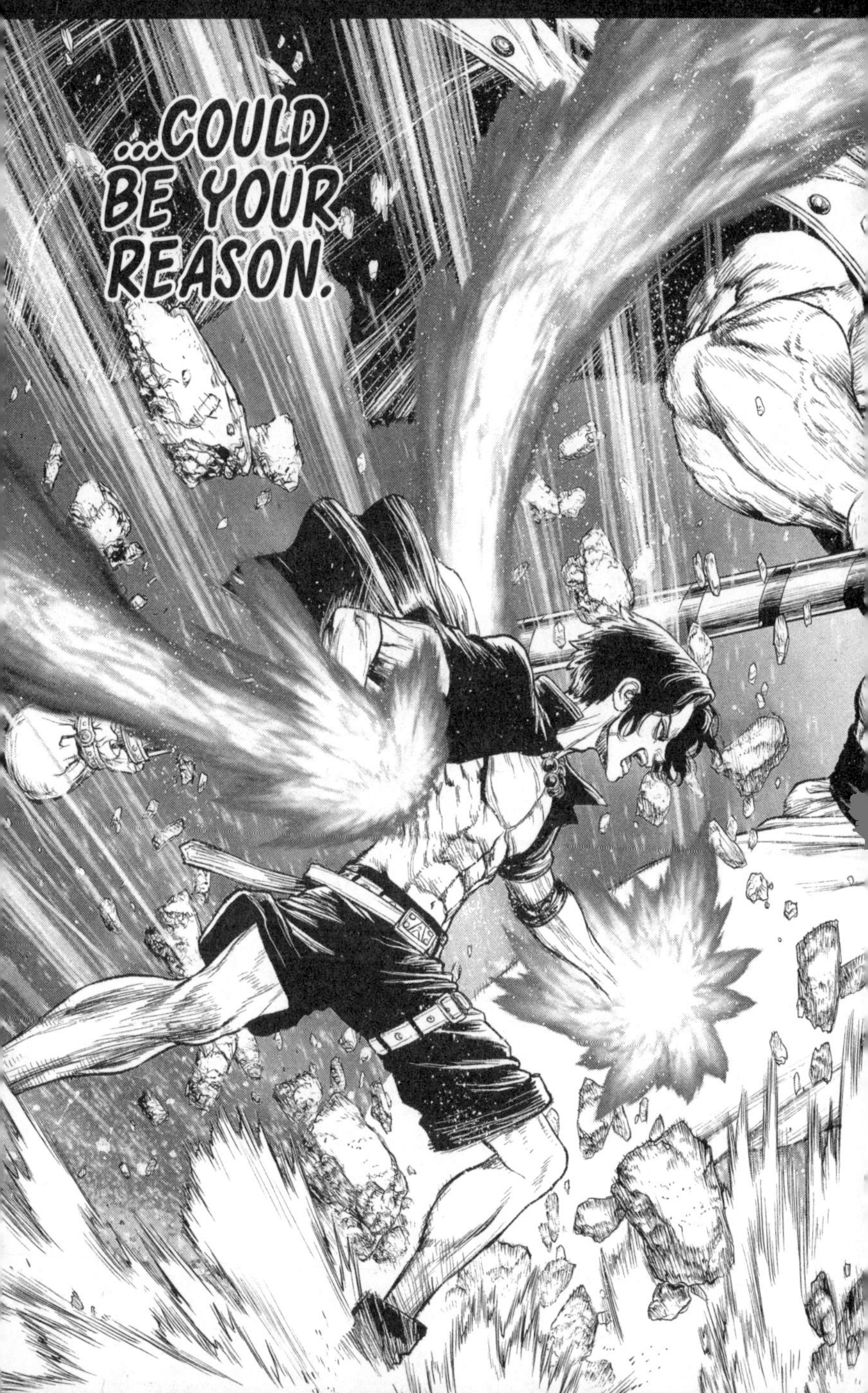
...COULD BE YOUR REASON.

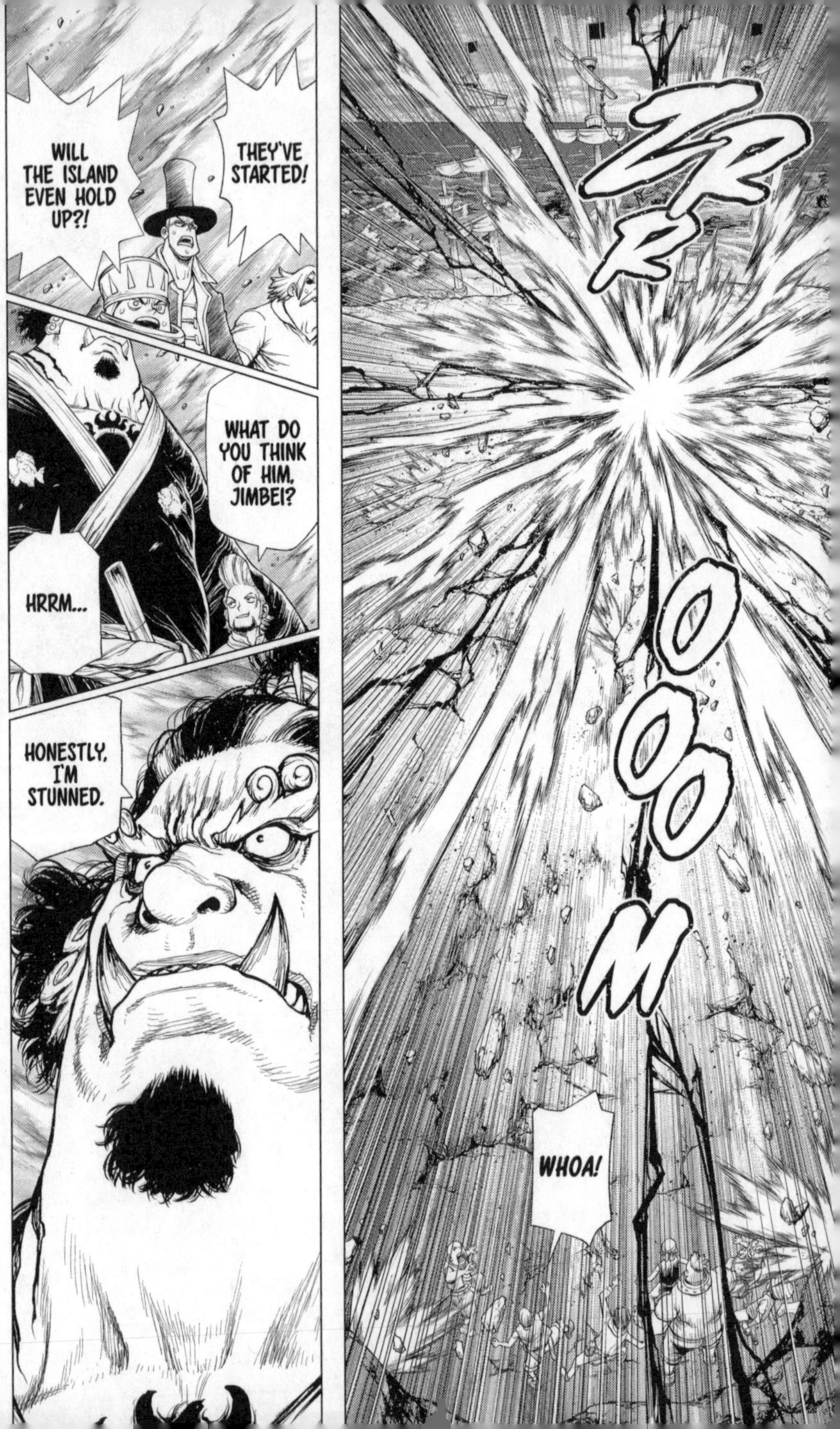
WHOA!
THEY'VE STARTED!
WILL THE ISLAND EVEN HOLD UP?!
WHAT DO YOU THINK OF HIM, JIMBEI?
HRRM...
HONESTLY, I'M STUNNED.

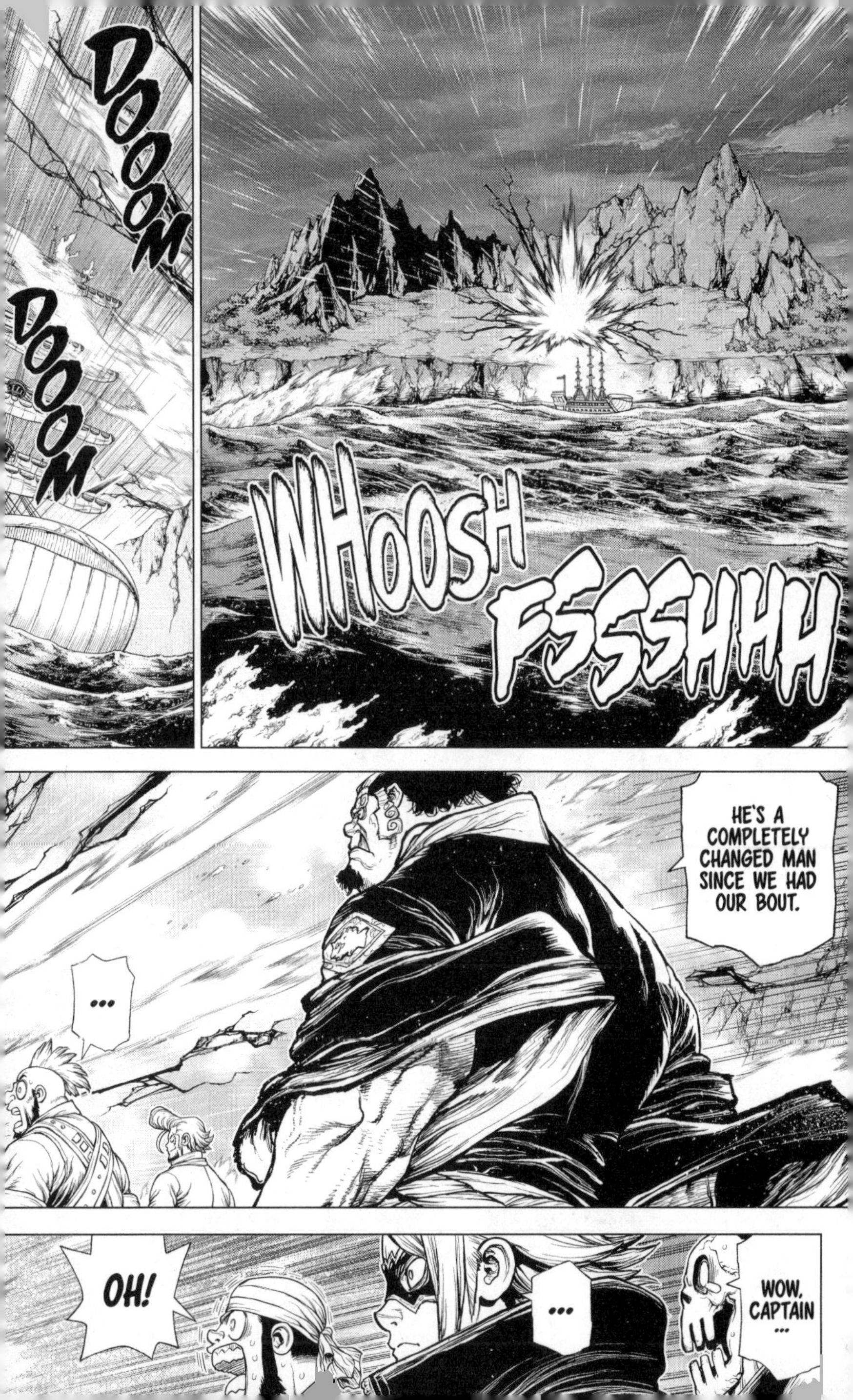
WHOOSH
FSSSHHH
DOOOOM
DOOOOM
HE'S A COMPLETELY CHANGED MAN SINCE WE HAD OUR BOUT.
...
WOW, CAPTAIN ...
...
OH!

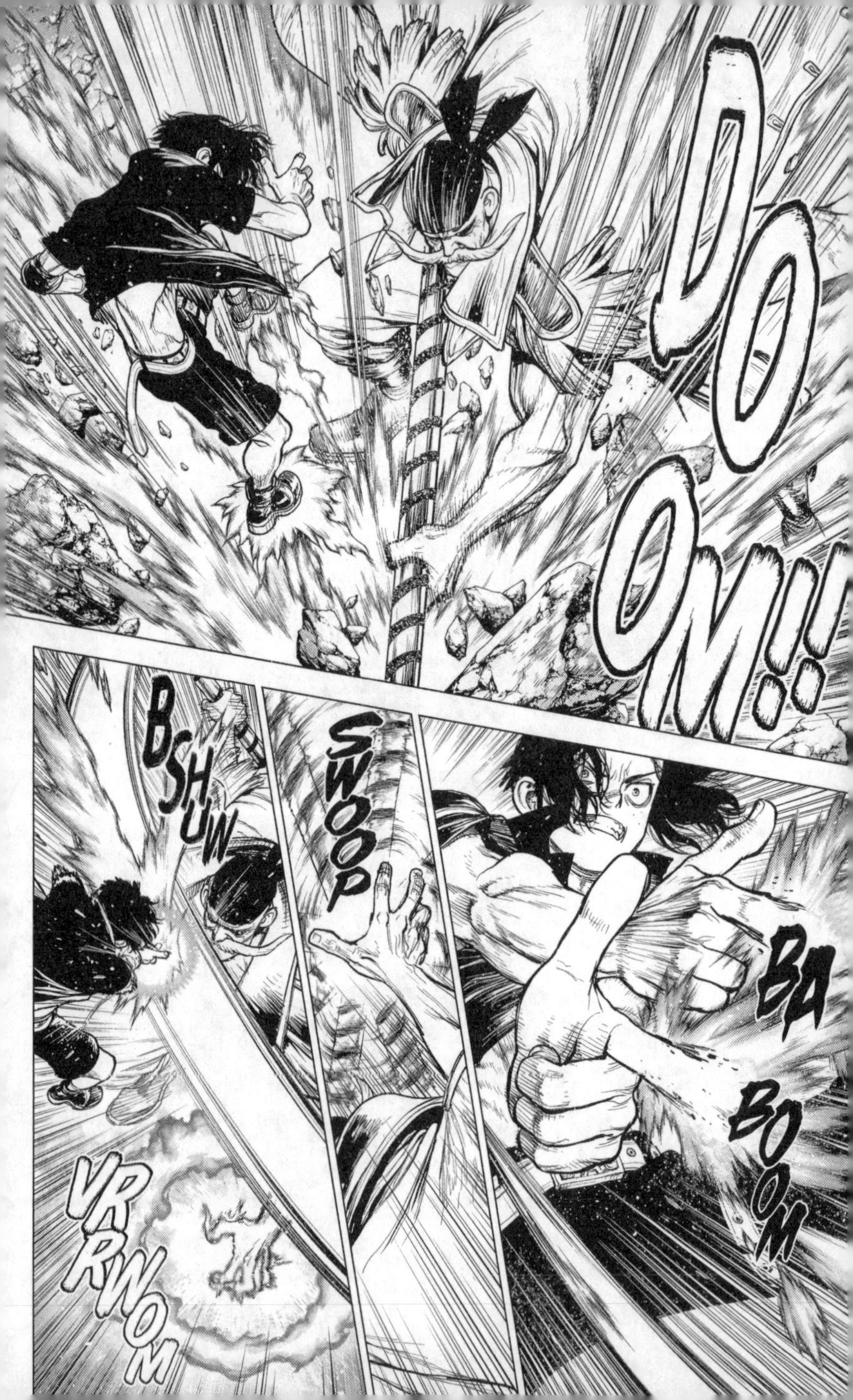
DOOM!!
BA BOOM
SWOOP
BSHUW
VRRWOM

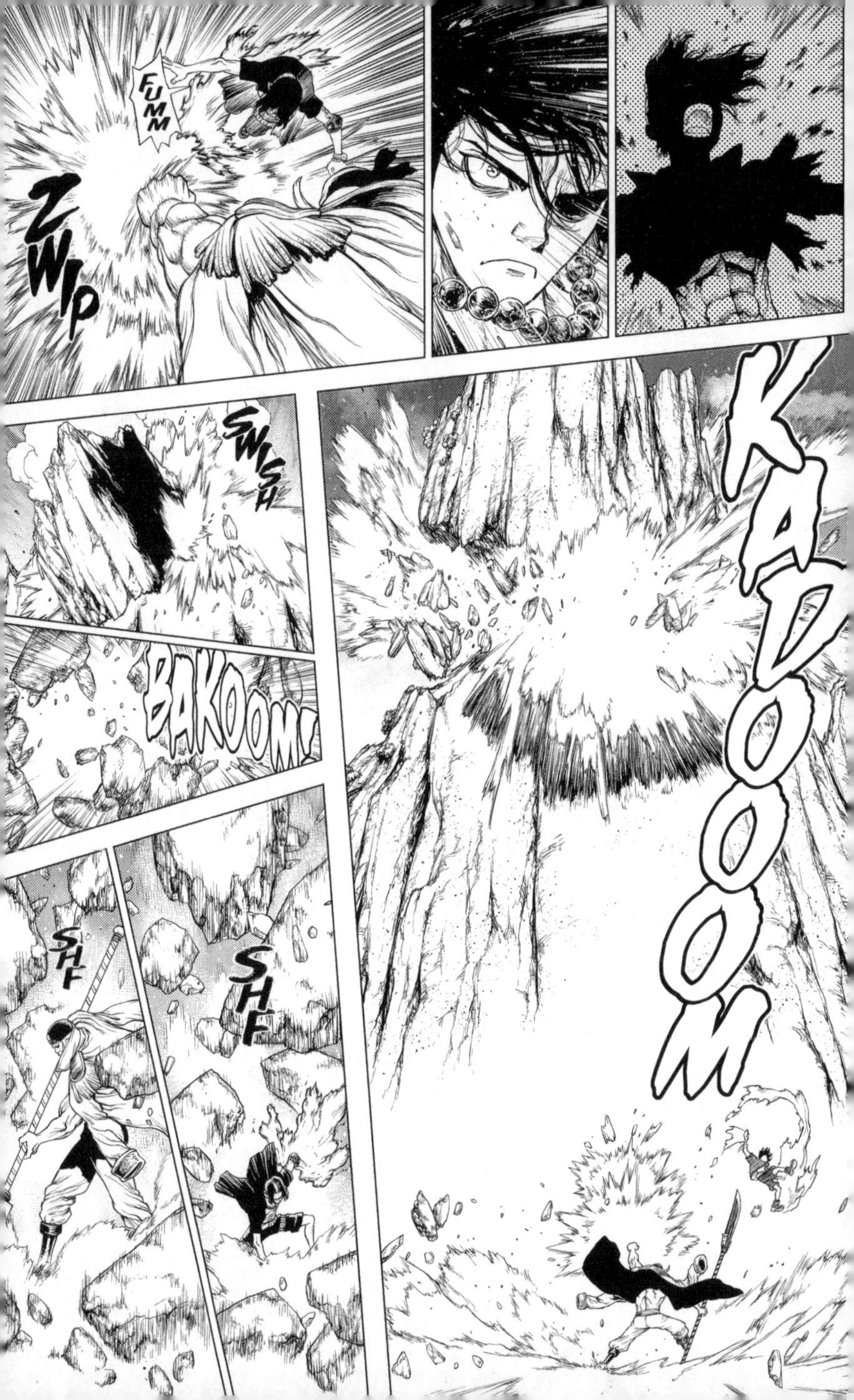
FUMM
ZWIP
KADOOOOM
SWISH
BAKOOM!
SHF
SHF

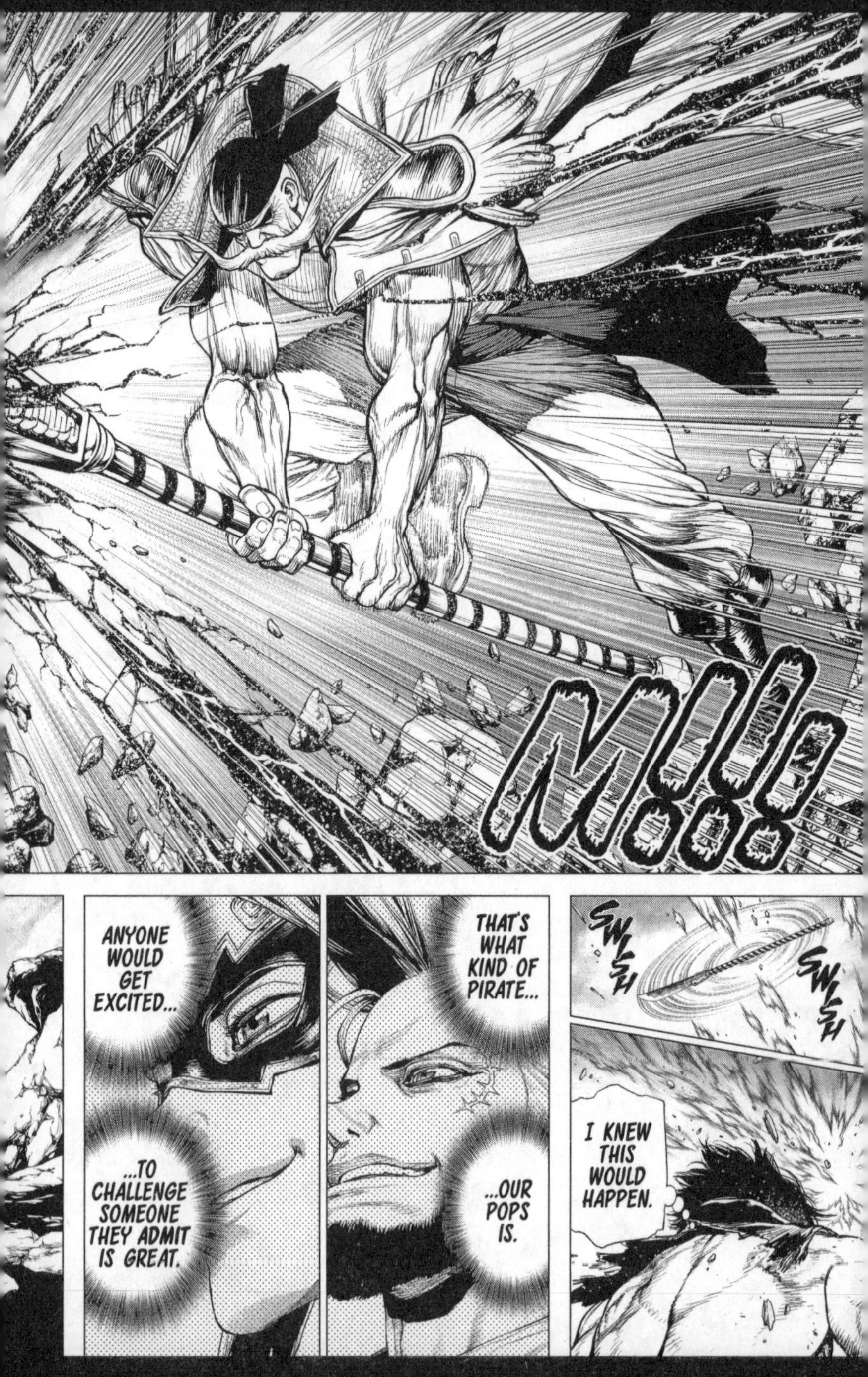
SWISH
SWISH
I KNEW THIS WOULD HAPPEN.
THAT'S WHAT KIND OF PIRATE...
...OUR POPS IS.
ANYONE WOULD GET EXCITED...
...TO CHALLENGE SOMEONE THEY ADMIT IS GREAT.

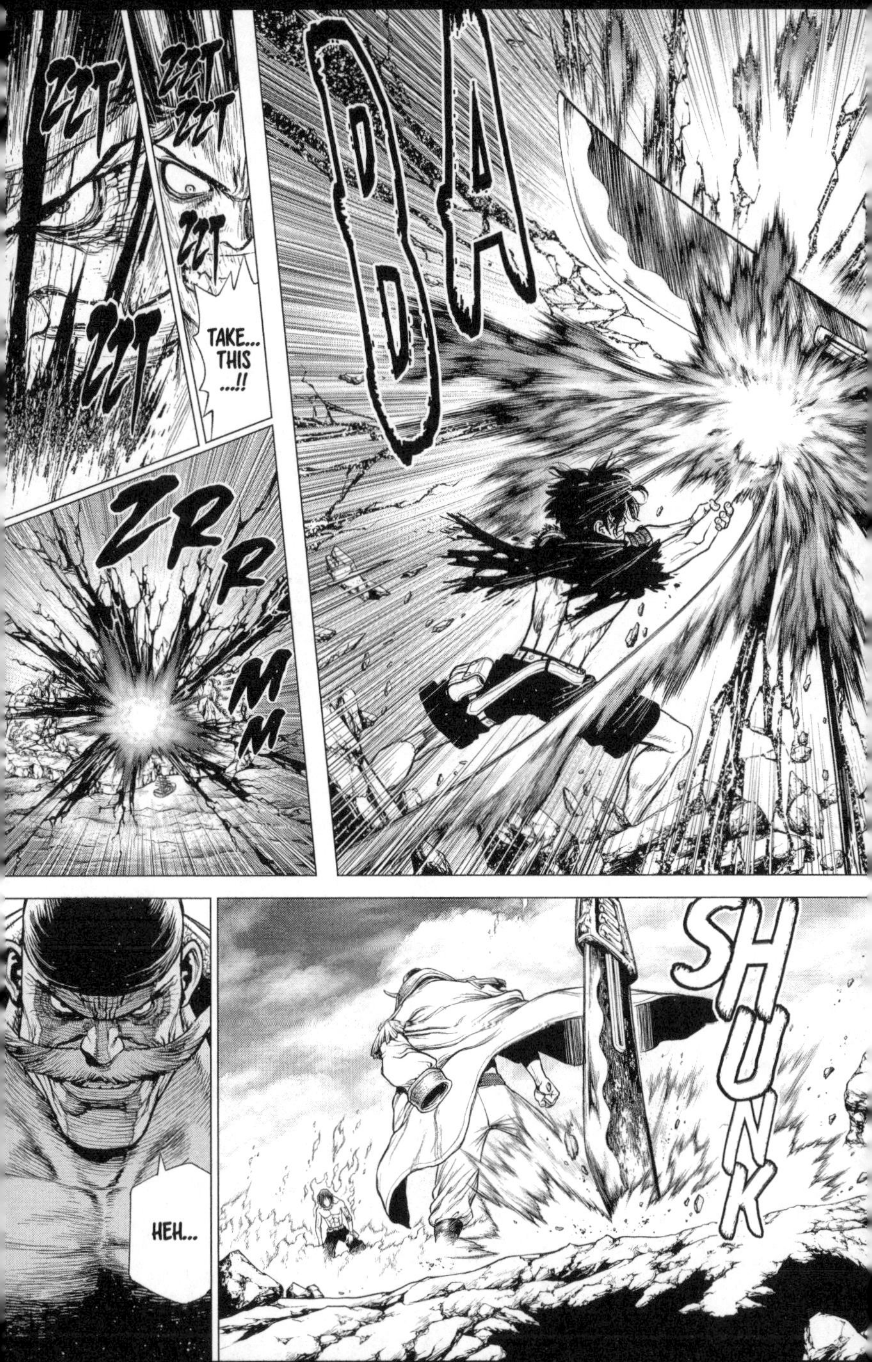
DDA
ZZT ZZT
ZZT
TAKE... THIS ...!!
ZZT
ZZT
ZRRMMM
SHUNK
HEH...

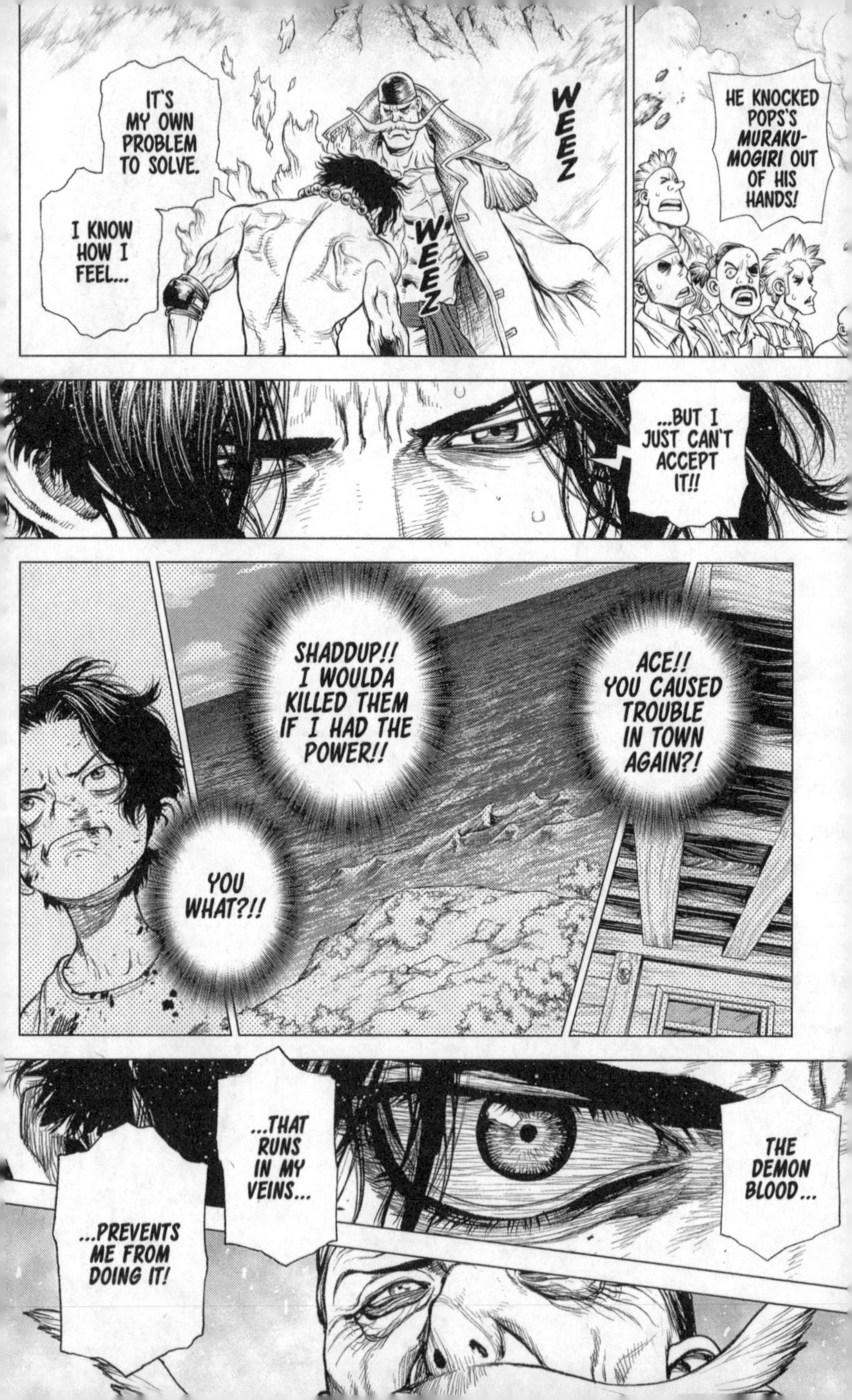
HE KNOCKED POPS'S MURAKU-MOGIRI OUT OF HIS HANDS!
WEEZ
IT'S MY OWN PROBLEM TO SOLVE.
WEEZ
I KNOW HOW I FEEL...
...BUT I JUST CAN'T ACCEPT IT!!
ACE!! YOU CAUSED TROUBLE IN TOWN AGAIN?!
SHADDUP!! I WOULDA KILLED THEM IF I HAD THE POWER!!
YOU WHAT?!!
THE DEMON BLOOD...
...THAT RUNS IN MY VEINS...
...PREVENTS ME FROM DOING IT!

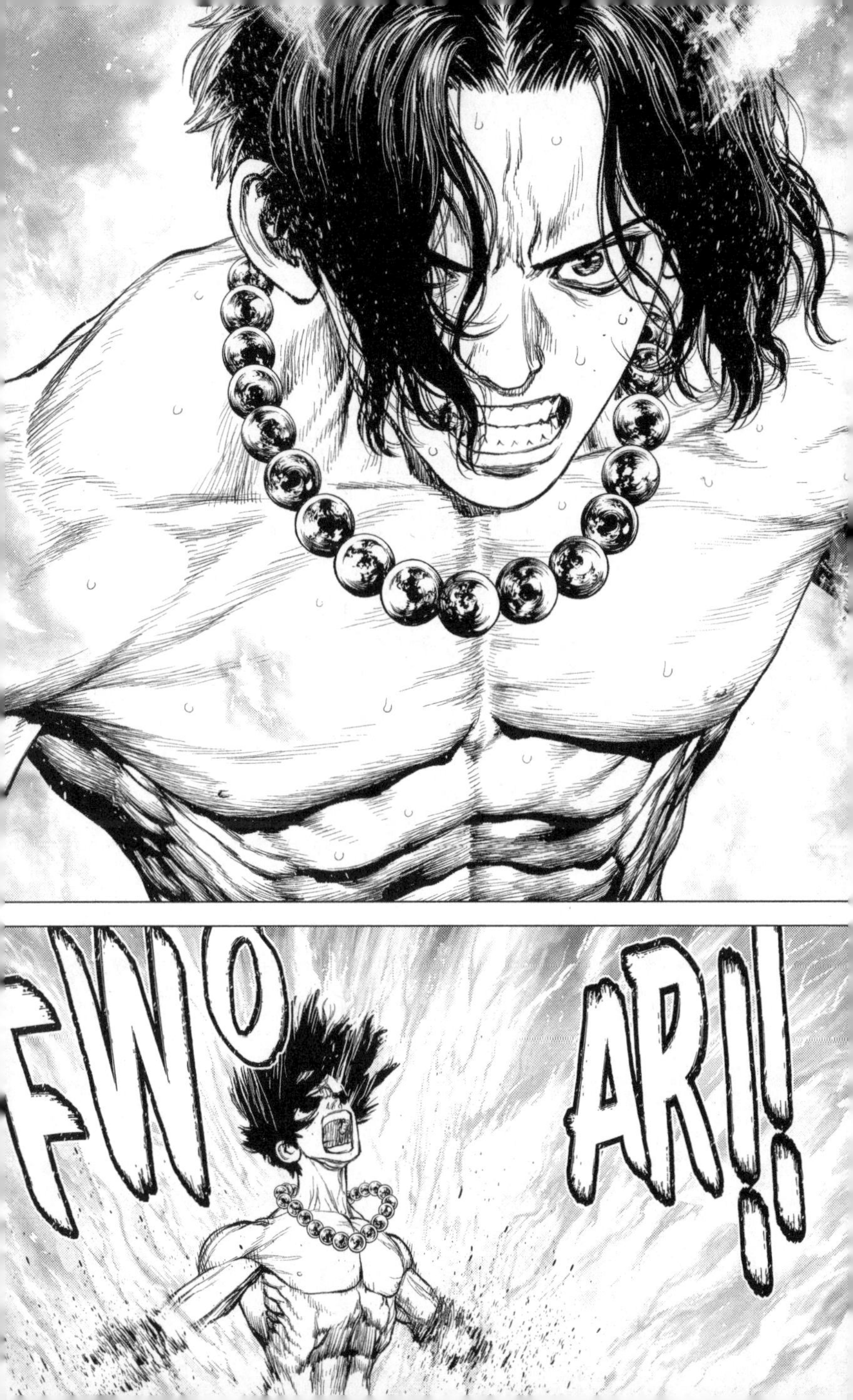
FWOOAR!!

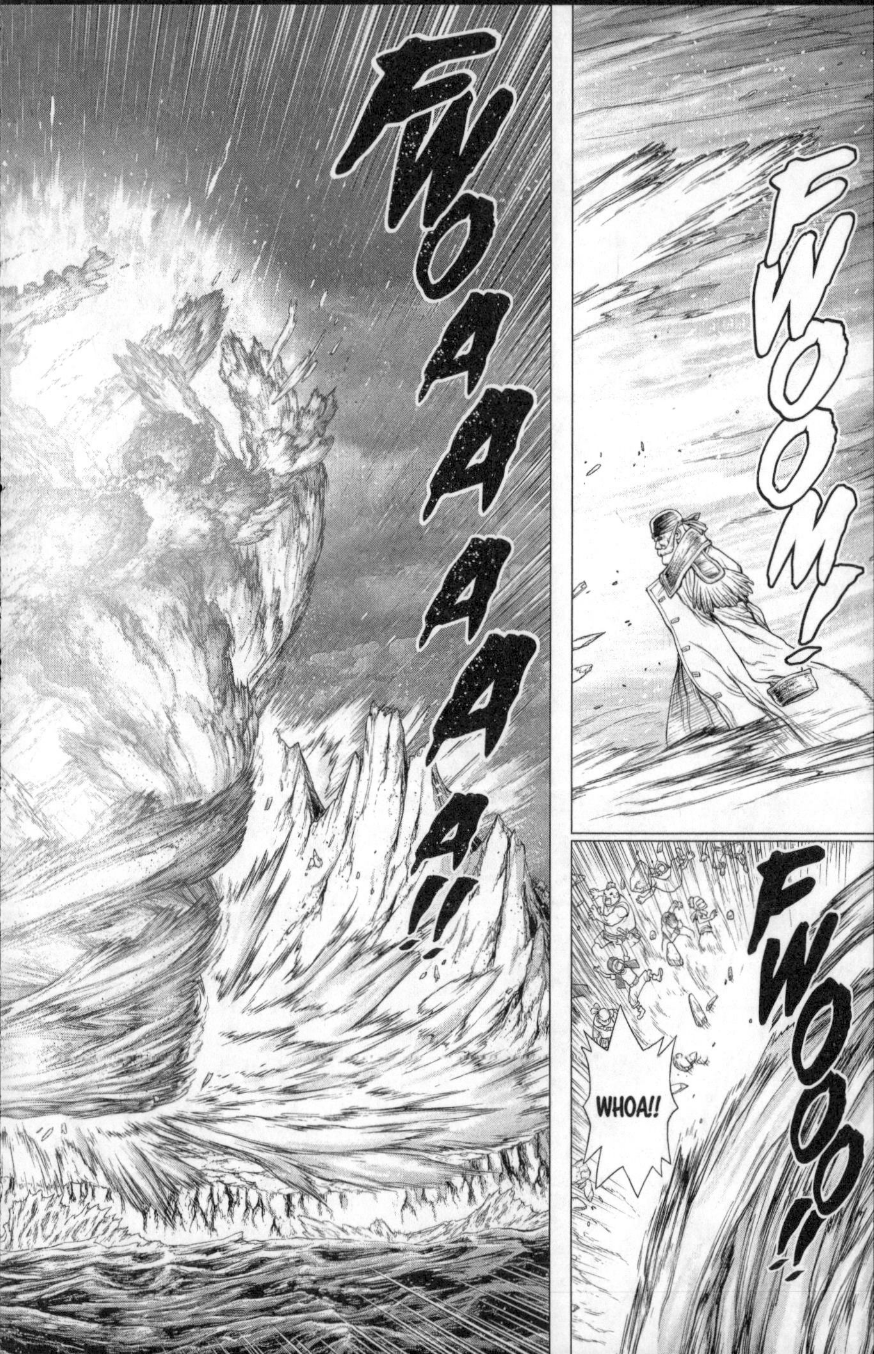
FWOOM!
FWOOO!!
WHOA!!
FWOAAAAA!!

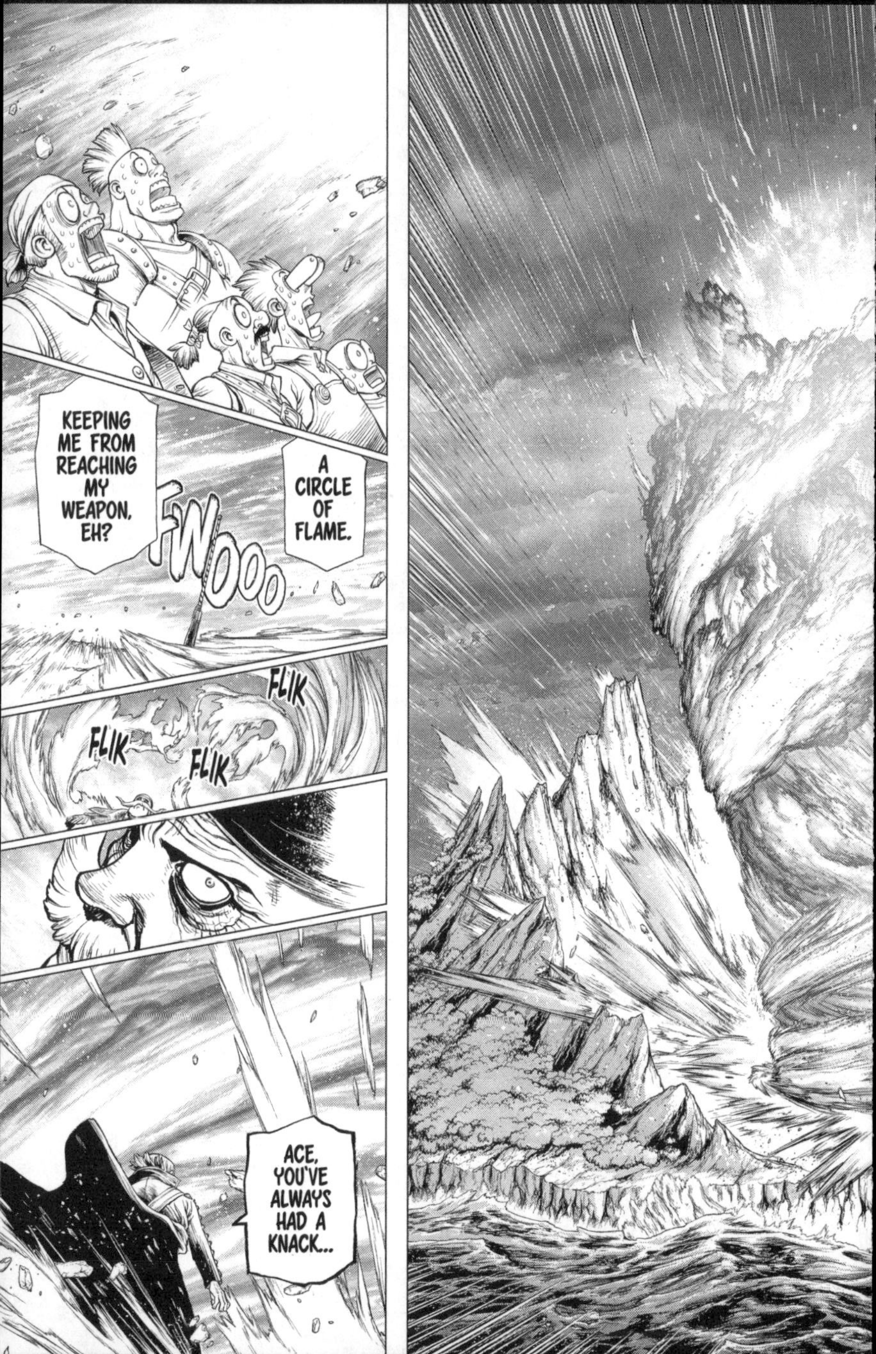
A CIRCLE OF FLAME.
KEEPING ME FROM REACHING MY WEAPON, EH?
FWOOO
FLIK
FLIK
FLIK
ACE, YOU'VE ALWAYS HAD A KNACK...

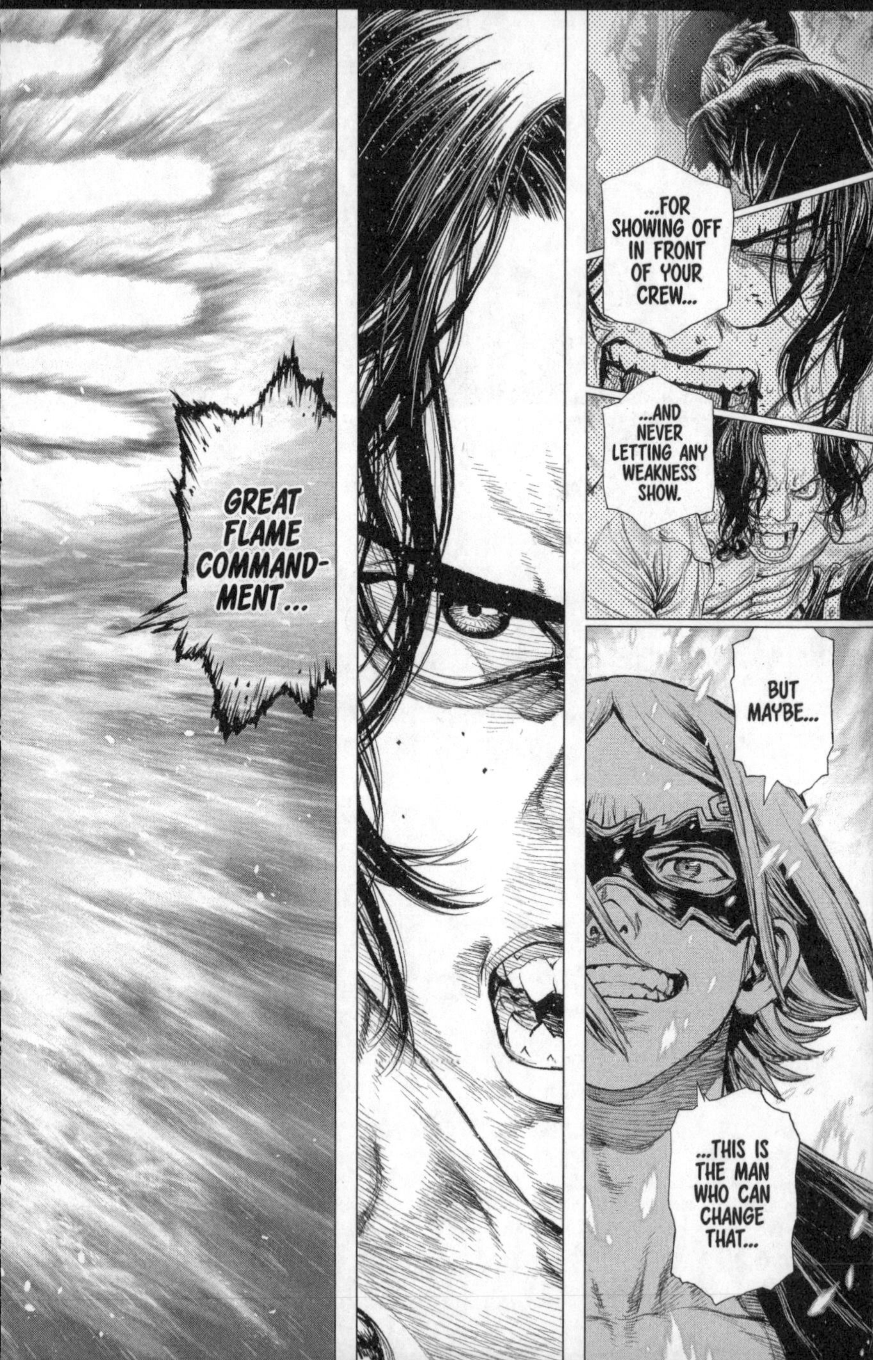
...FOR SHOWING OFF IN FRONT OF YOUR CREW...
...AND NEVER LETTING ANY WEAKNESS SHOW.
BUT MAYBE...
...THIS IS THE MAN WHO CAN CHANGE THAT...
GREAT FLAME COMMANDMENT...

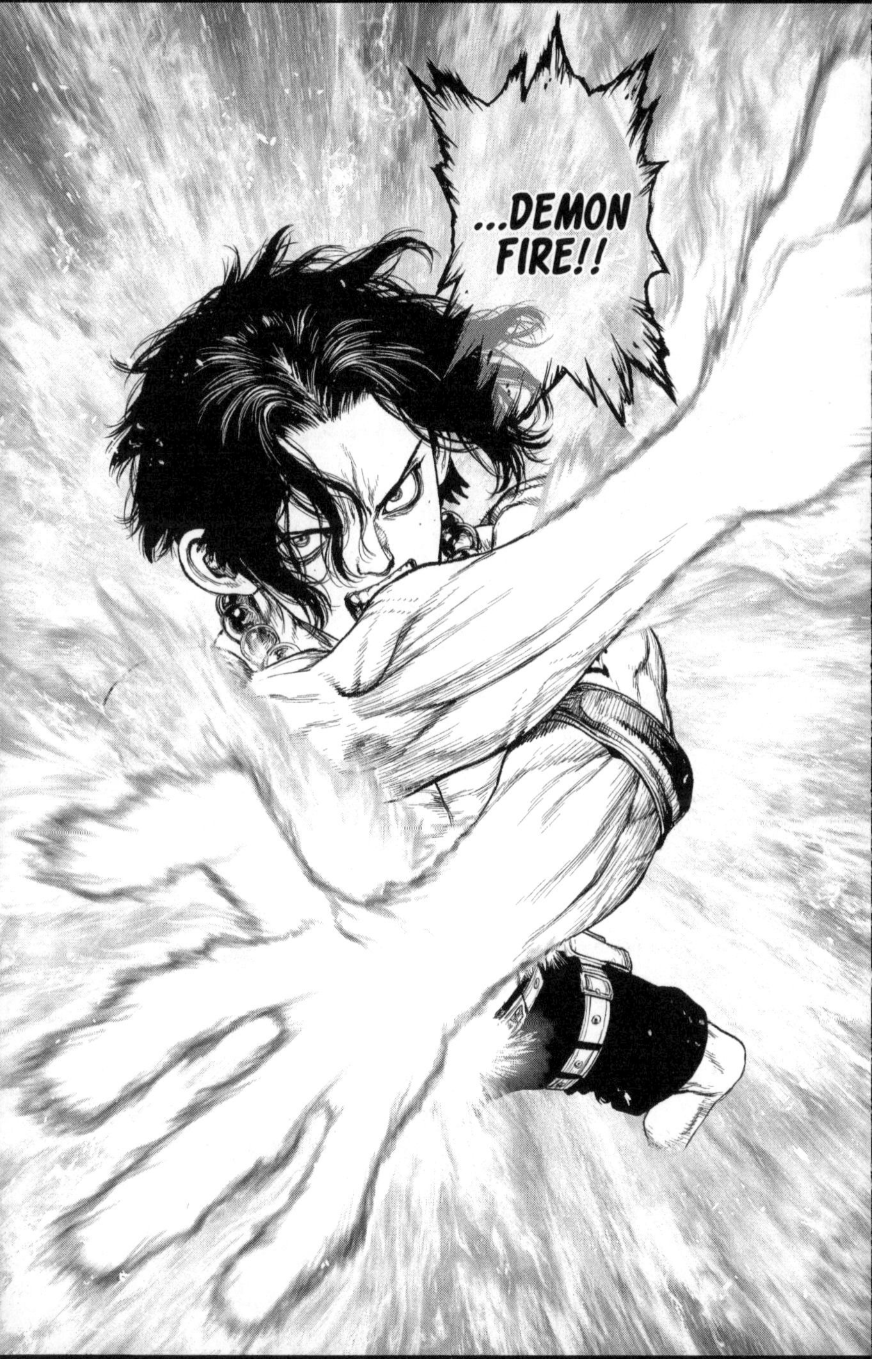
...DEMON FIRE!!

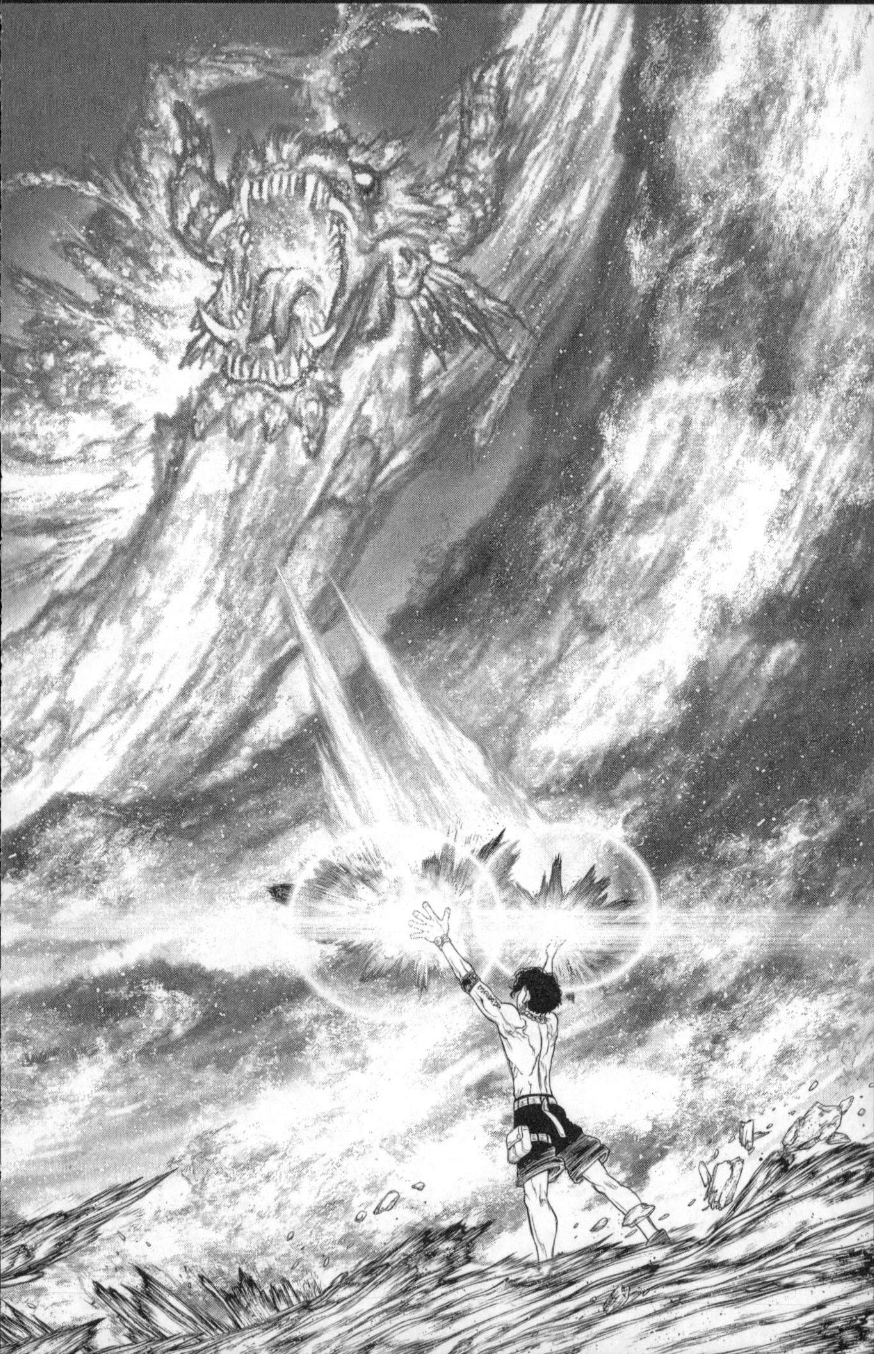

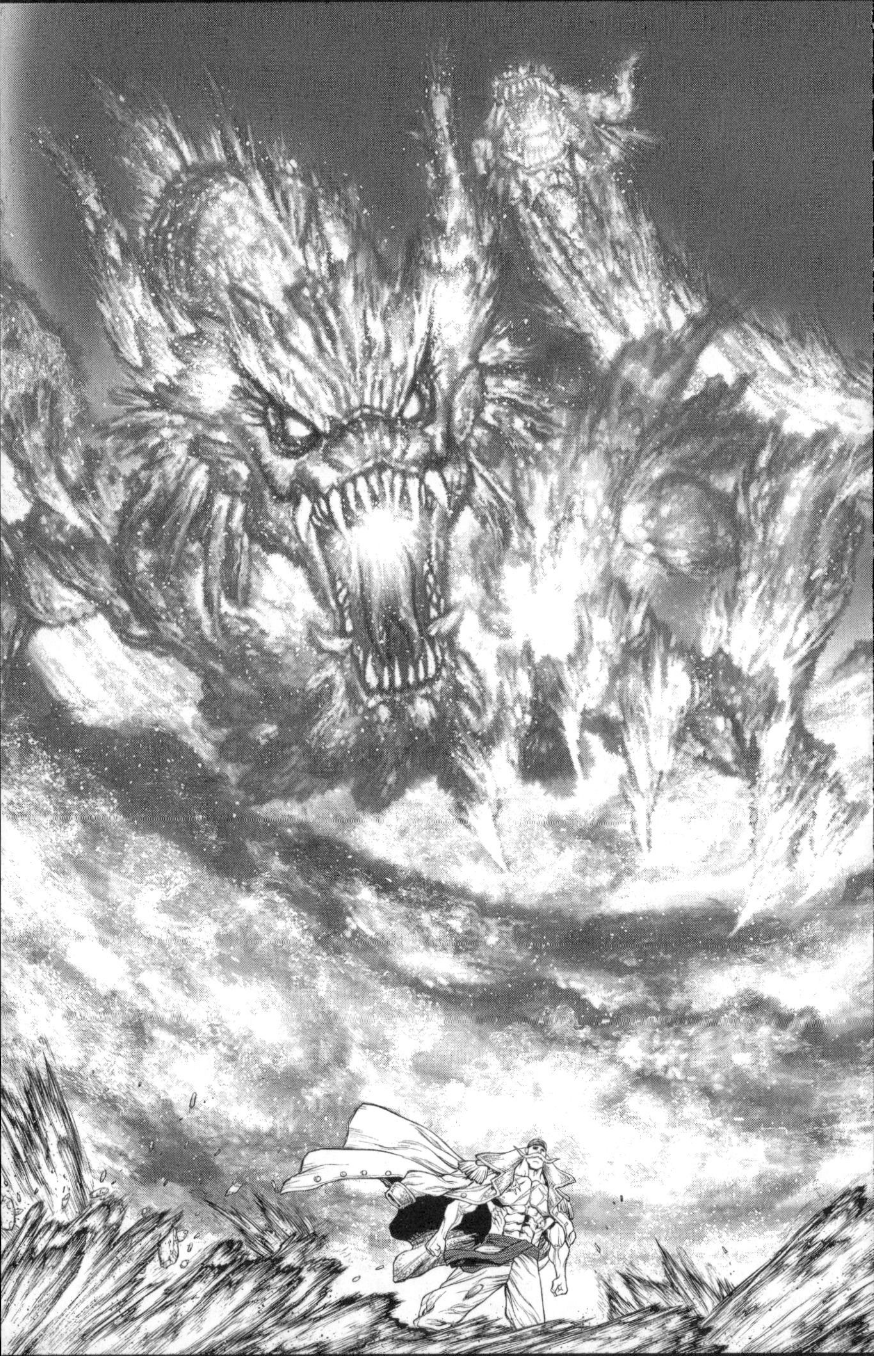

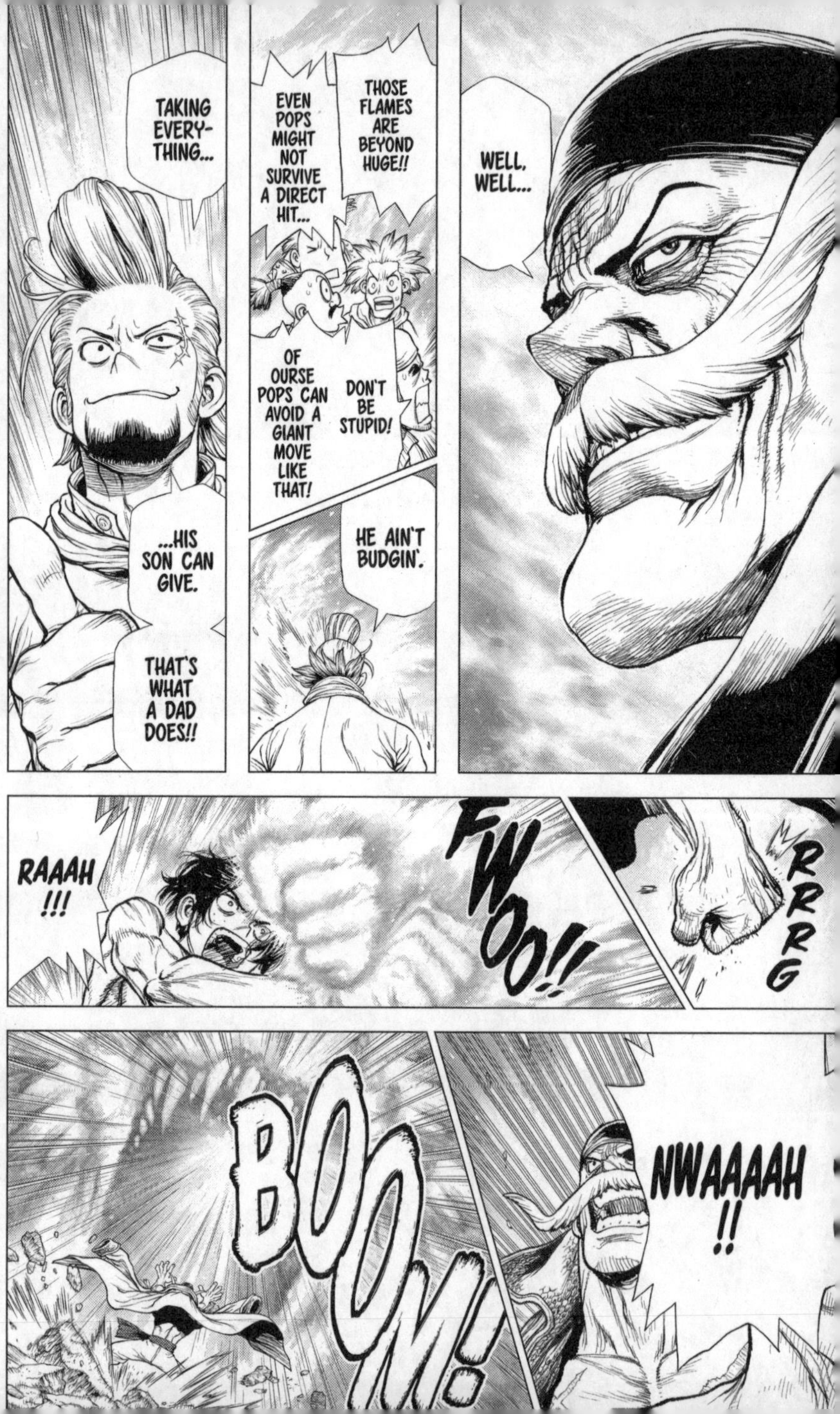
WELL, WELL...
THOSE FLAMES ARE BEYOND HUGE!!
EVEN POPS MIGHT NOT SURVIVE A DIRECT HIT...
DON'T BE STUPID!
OF OURSE POPS CAN AVOID A GIANT MOVE LIKE THAT!
HE AIN'T BUDGIN'.
TAKING EVERY-THING...
...HIS SON CAN GIVE.
THAT'S WHAT A DAD DOES!!
RRRG
FWOO!!
RAAAH!!!
NWAAAAH!!
BOOM!

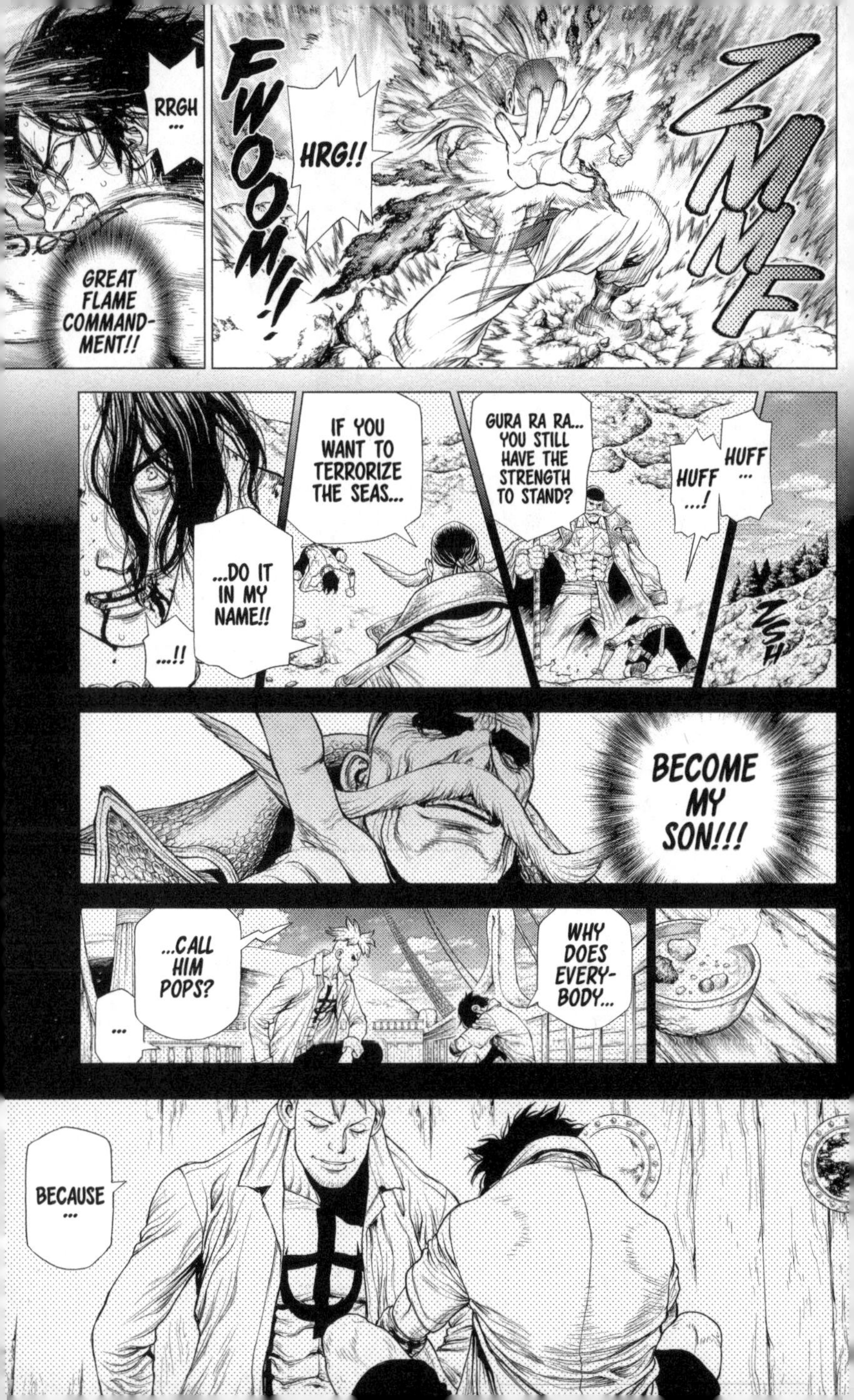
ZMMF
HRG!!
FWOOM!!
RRGH...
GREAT FLAME COMMAND-MENT!!
HUFF...
HUFF...!
ZSH
GURA RA RA... YOU STILL HAVE THE STRENGTH TO STAND?
IF YOU WANT TO TERRORIZE THE SEAS...
...DO IT IN MY NAME!!
...!!
BECOME MY SON!!!
WHY DOES EVERY-BODY...
...CALL HIM POPS?
...
BECAUSE...

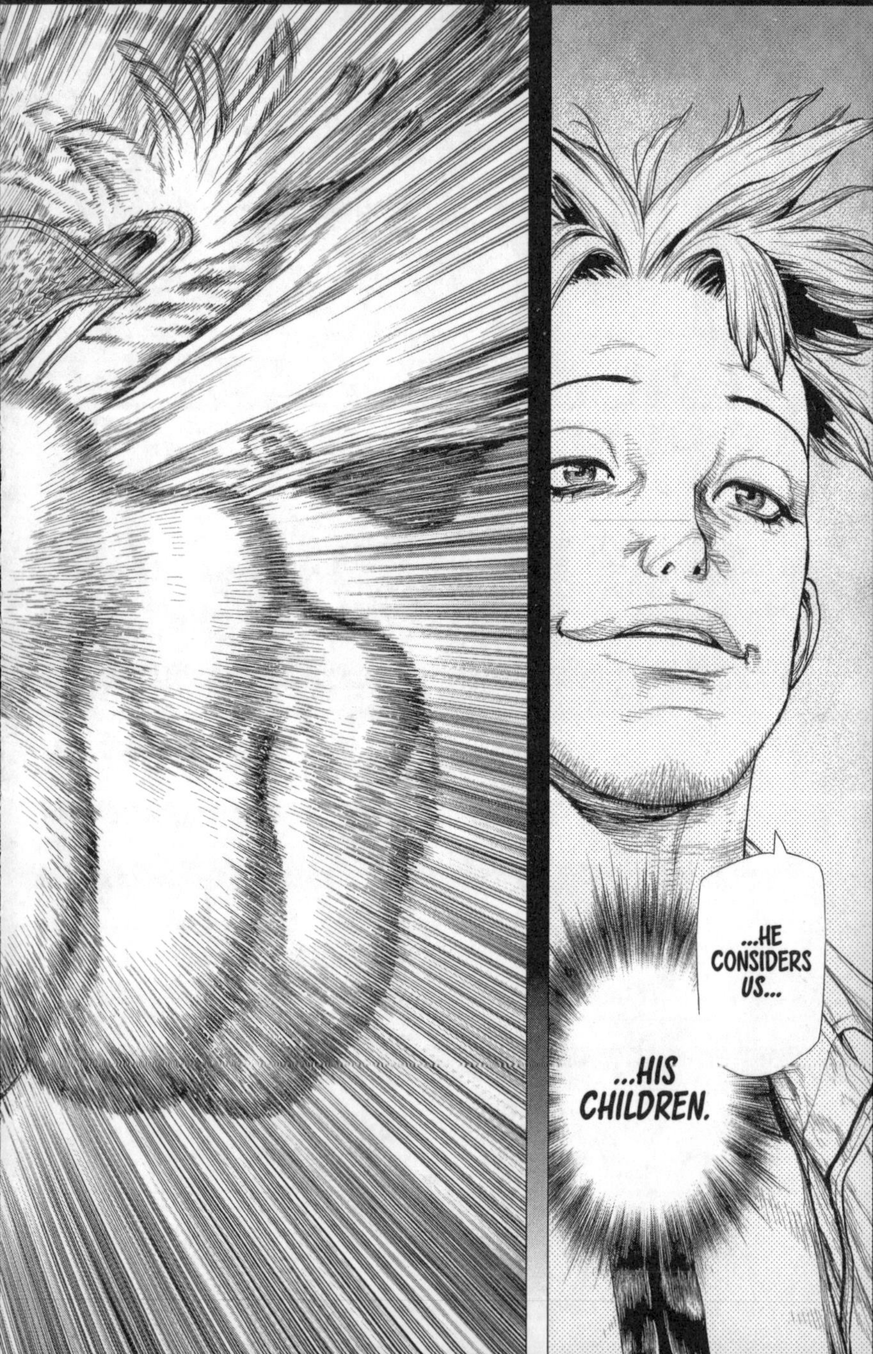
...HE CONSIDERS US...
...HIS CHILDREN.

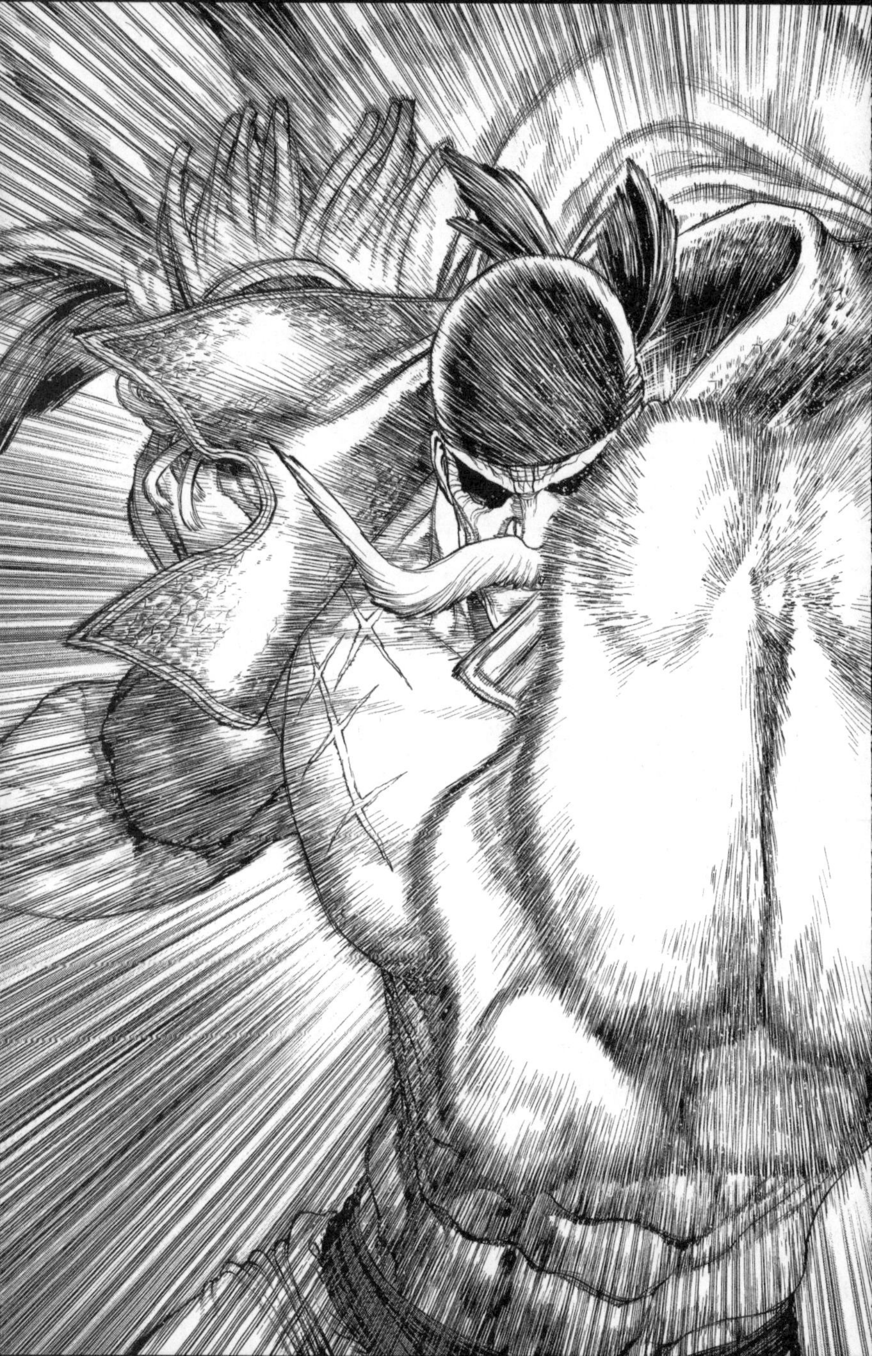

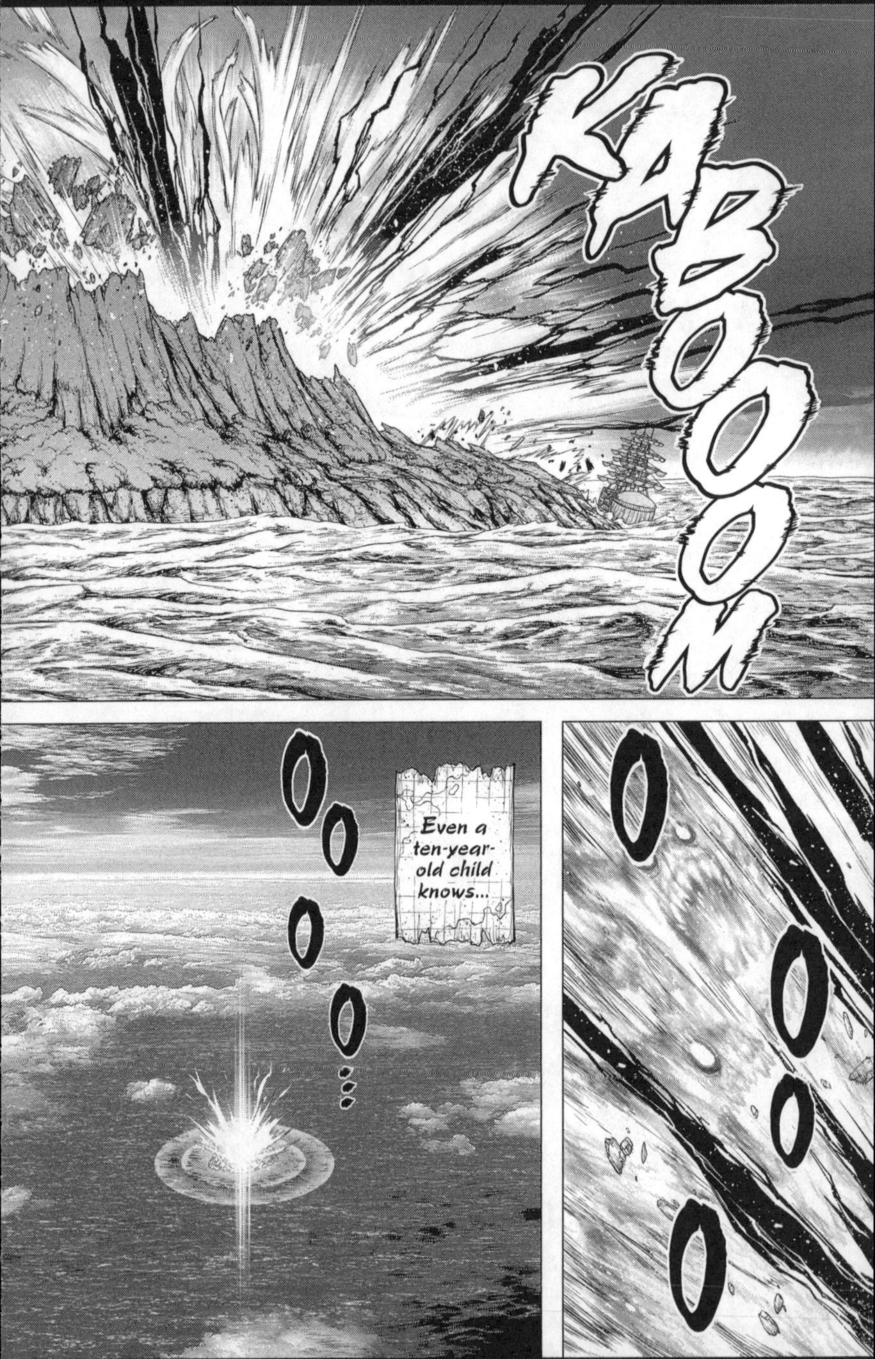
KABOOOOM
OOOOOO
OOOO...
Even a ten-year-old child knows...

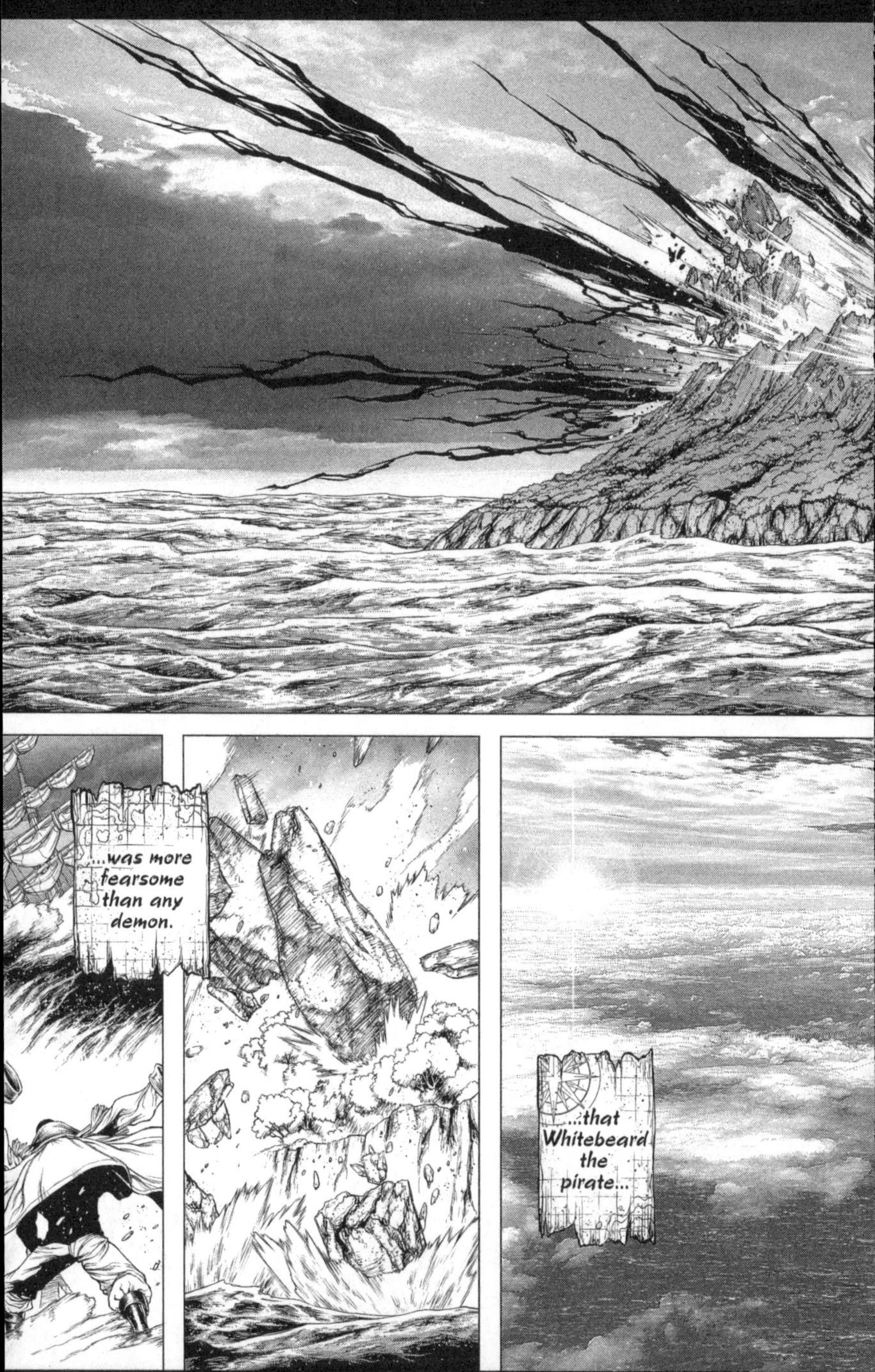
...that Whitebeard the pirate...
...was more fearsome than any demon.

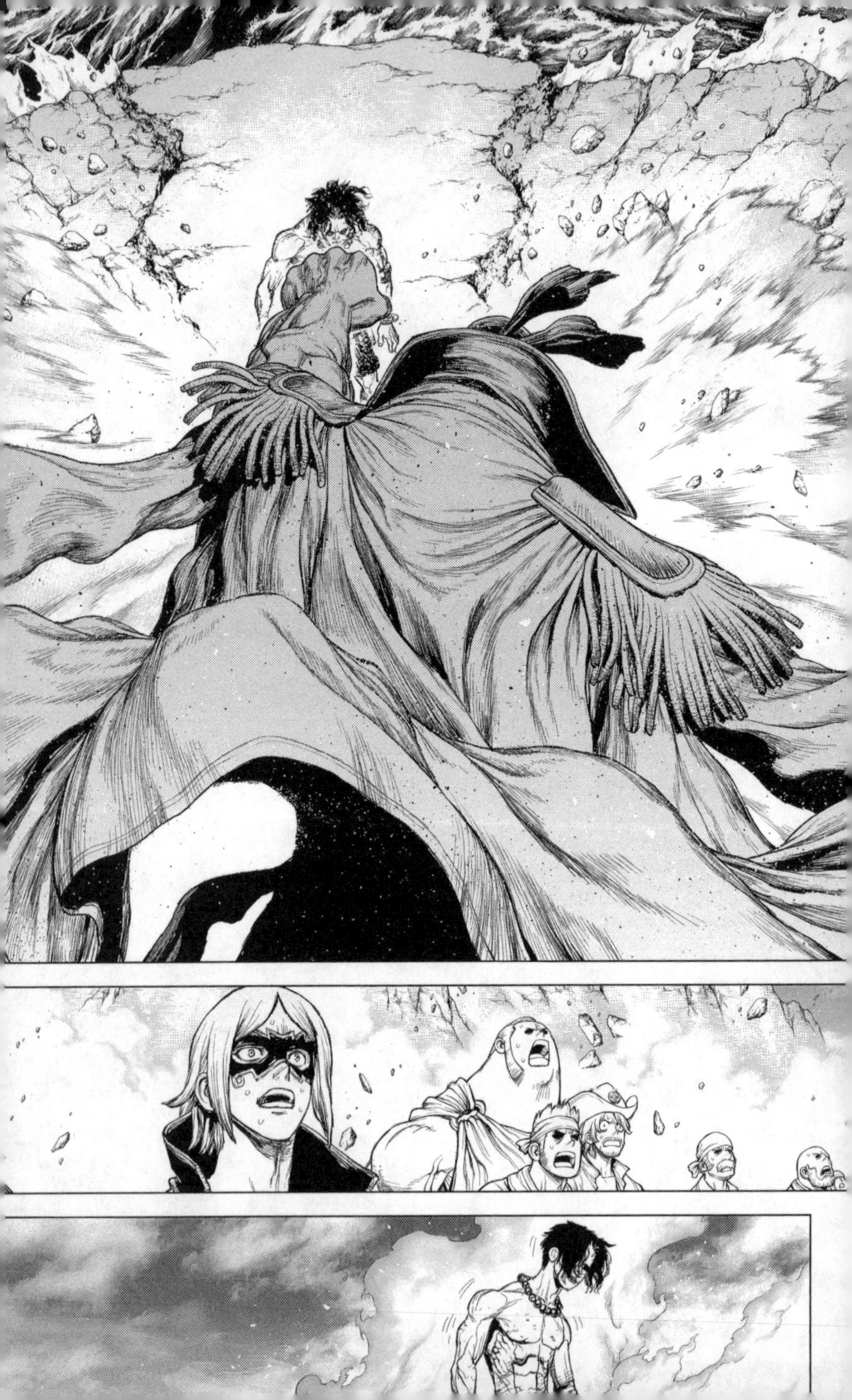

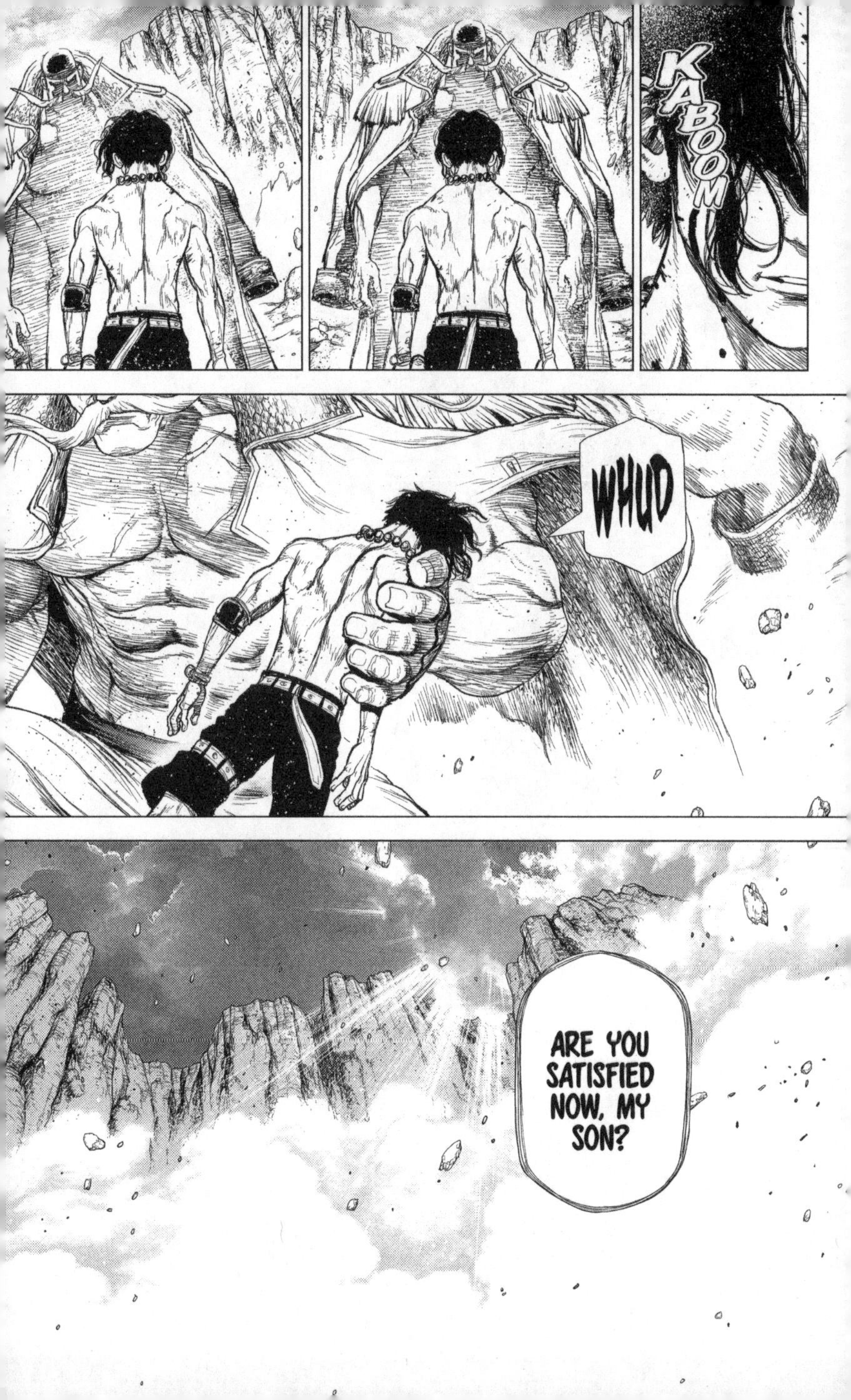
KABOOM
WHUD
ARE YOU SATISFIED NOW, MY SON?

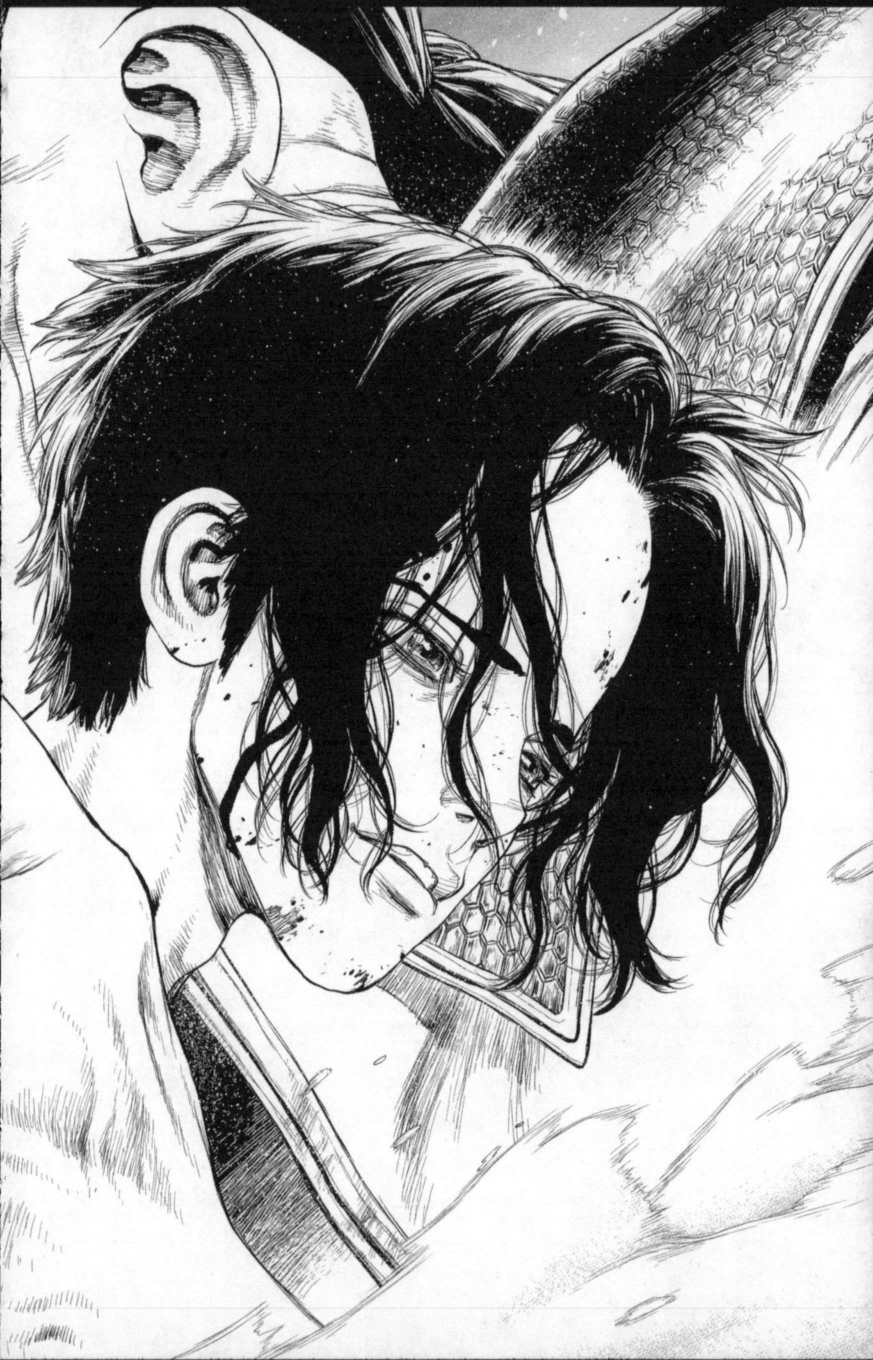

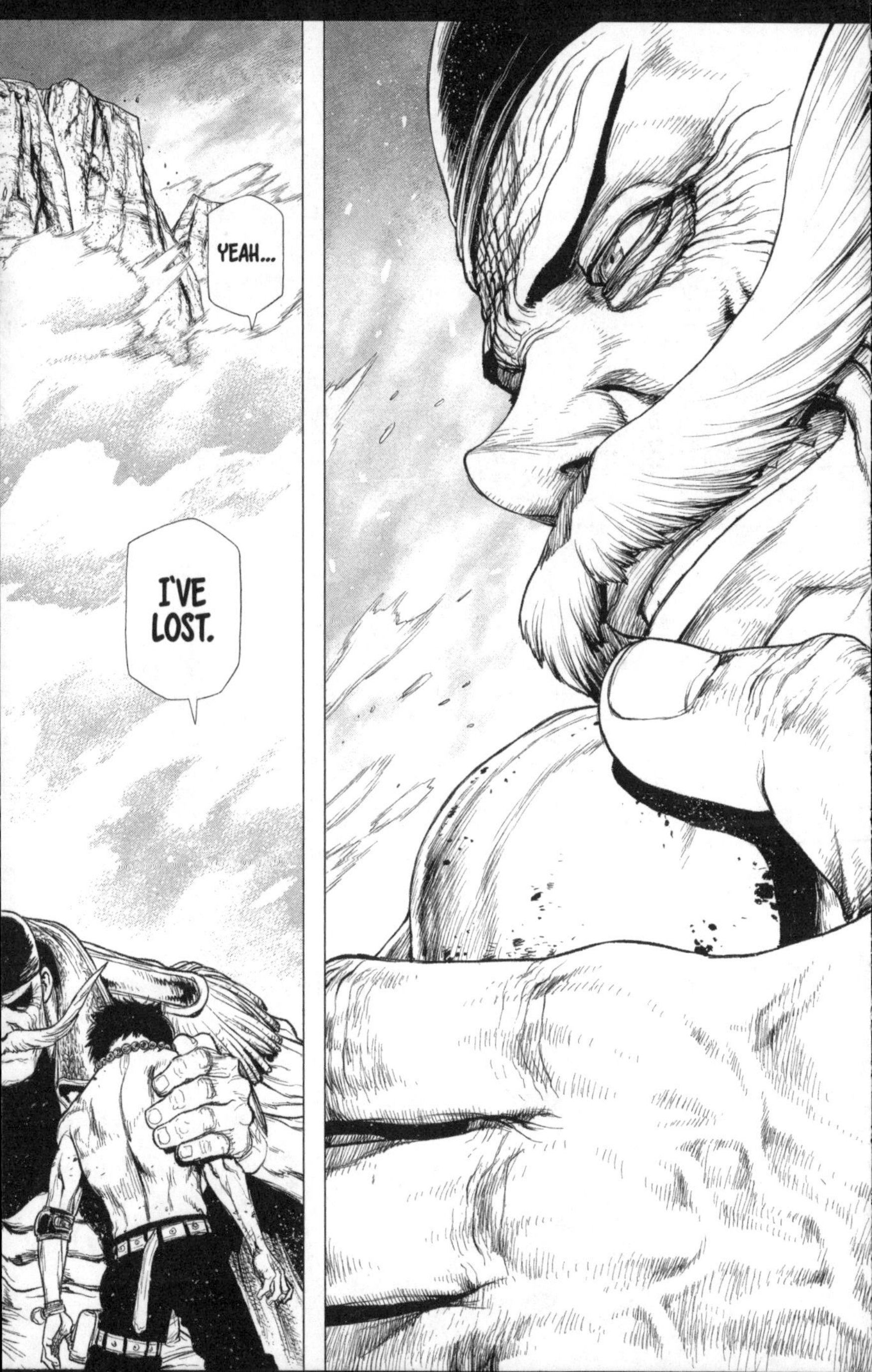
YEAH...
I'VE LOST.

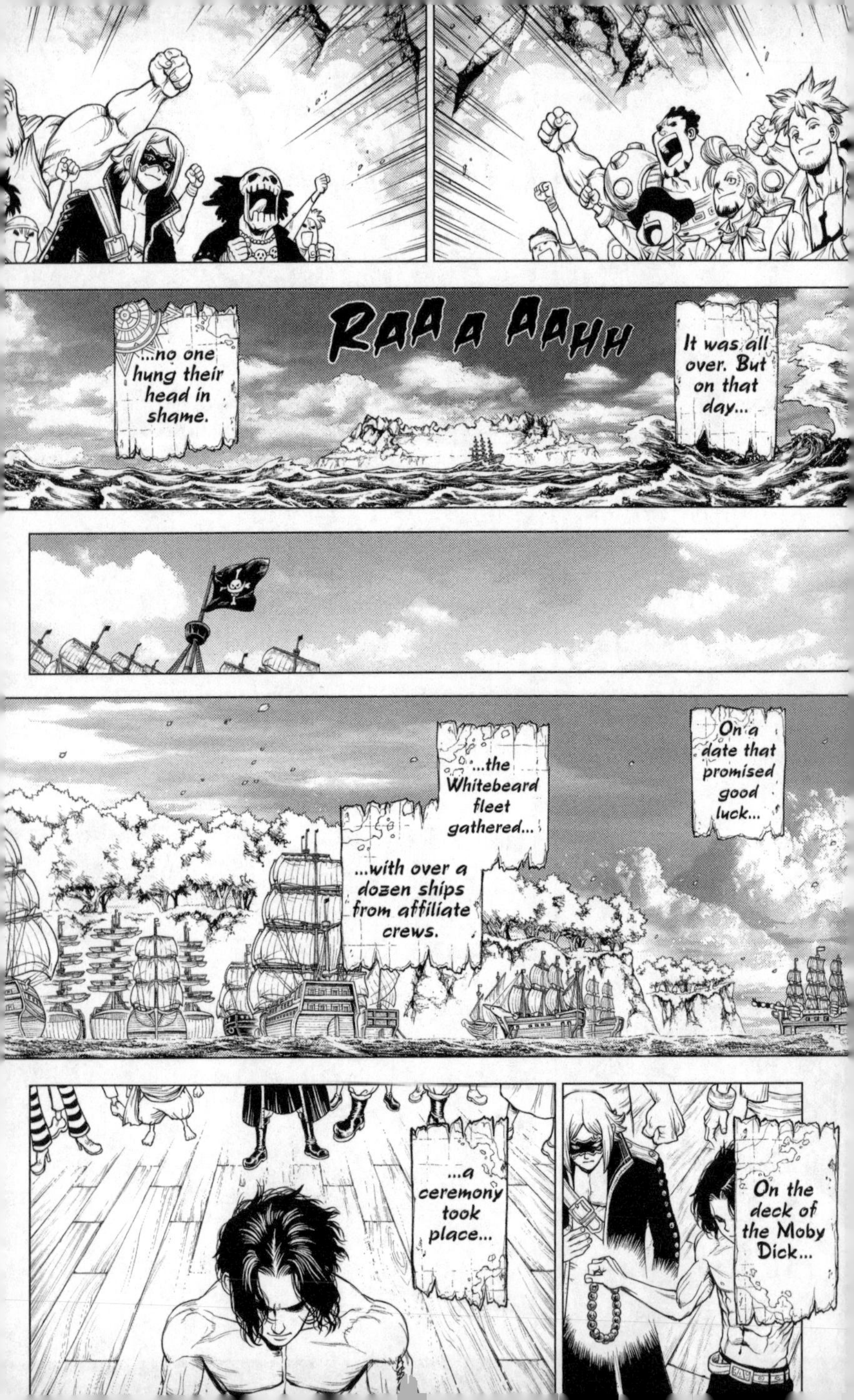
It was all over. But on that day...
RAAAAAHH
...no one hung their head in shame.
On a date that promised good luck...
...the Whitebeard fleet gathered...
...with over a dozen ships from affiliate crews.
On the deck of the Moby Dick...
...a ceremony took place...

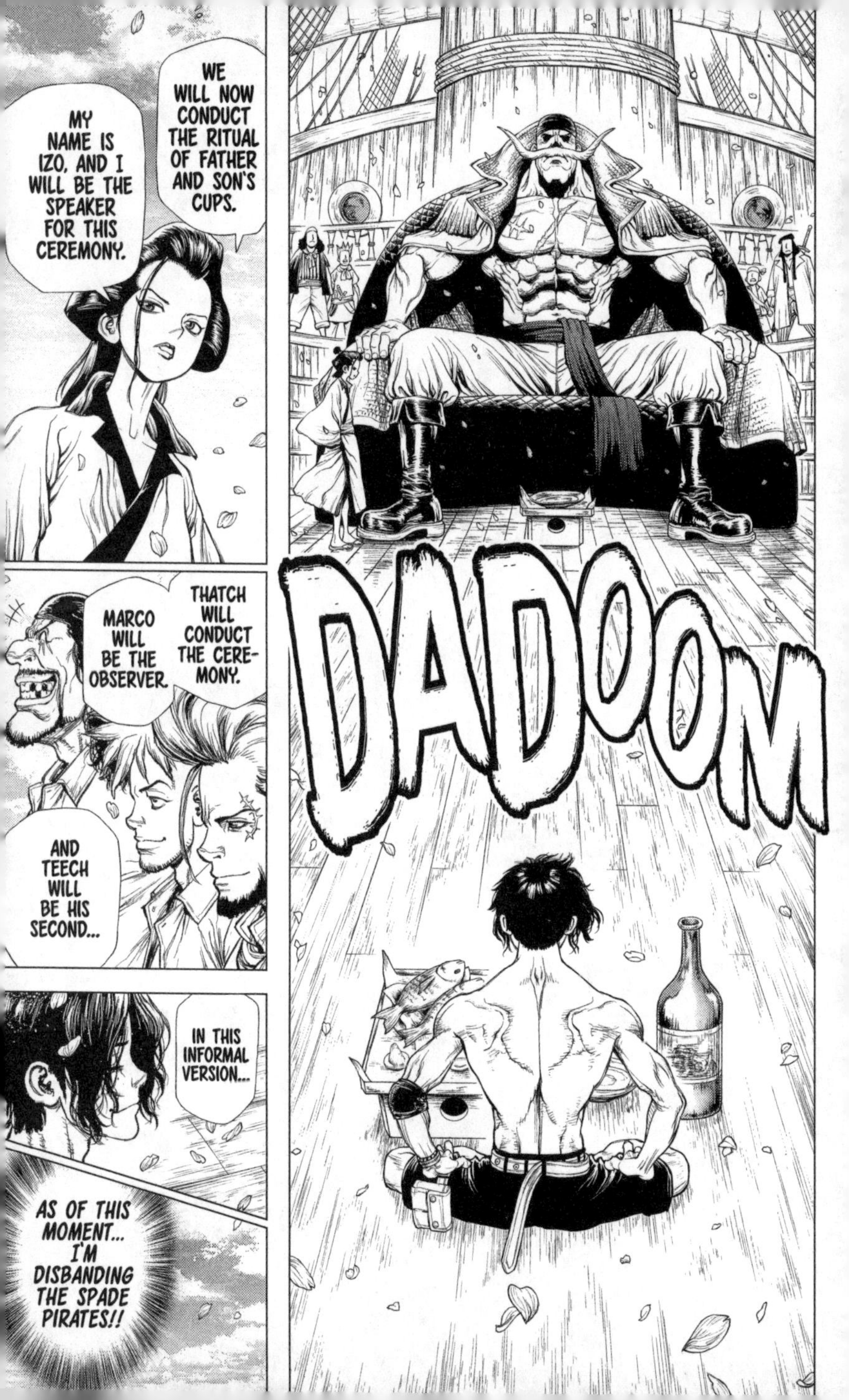
DADOOM
WE WILL NOW CONDUCT THE RITUAL OF FATHER AND SON'S CUPS.
MY NAME IS IZO, AND I WILL BE THE SPEAKER FOR THIS CEREMONY.
THATCH WILL CONDUCT THE CERE-MONY.
MARCO WILL BE THE OBSERVER.
AND TEECH WILL BE HIS SECOND...
IN THIS INFORMAL VERSION...
AS OF THIS MOMENT... I'M DISBANDING THE SPADE PIRATES!!

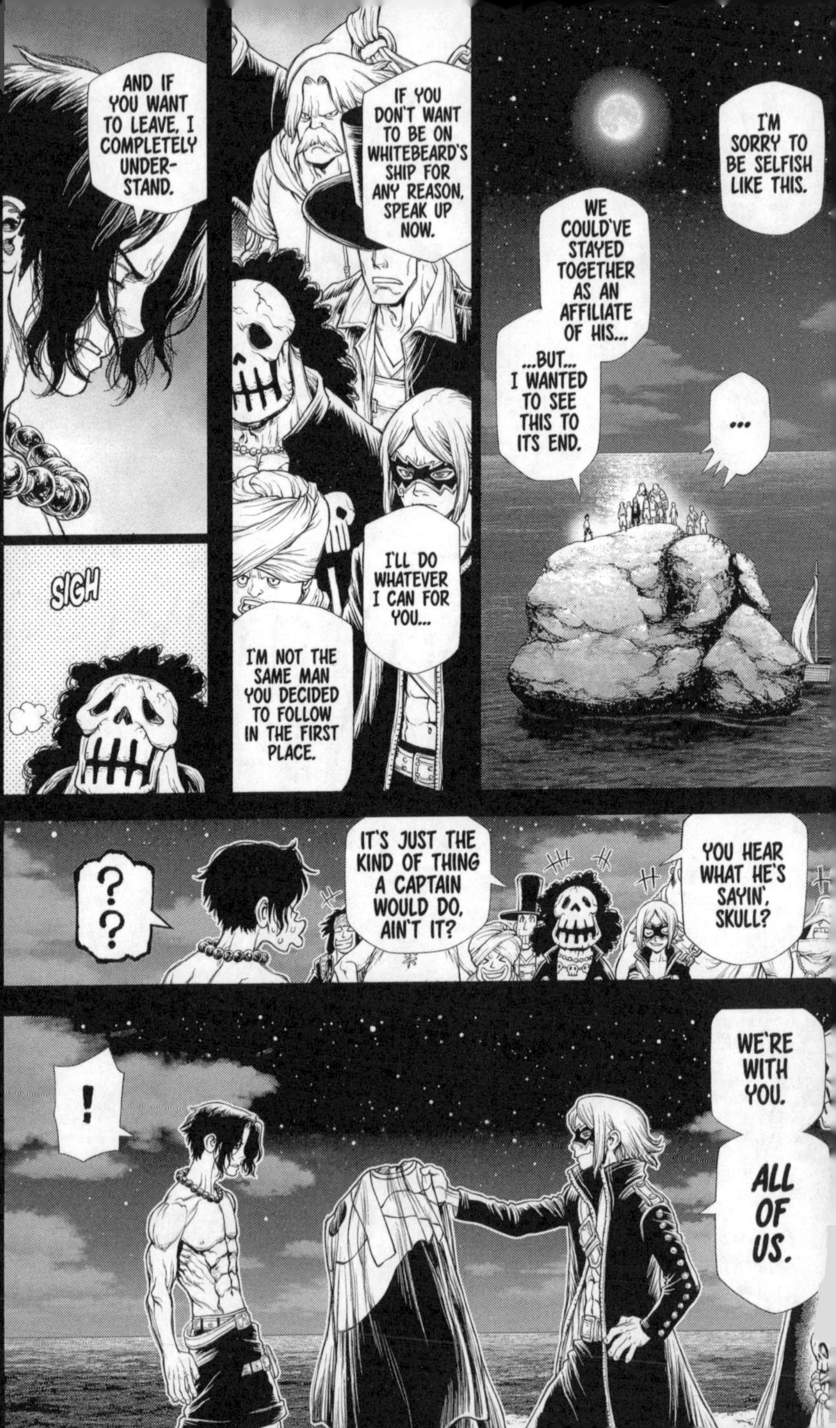
I'M SORRY TO BE SELFISH LIKE THIS.
WE COULD'VE STAYED TOGETHER AS AN AFFILIATE OF HIS...
...BUT... I WANTED TO SEE THIS TO ITS END.
...
IF YOU DON'T WANT TO BE ON WHITEBEARD'S SHIP FOR ANY REASON, SPEAK UP NOW.
I'LL DO WHATEVER I CAN FOR YOU...
I'M NOT THE SAME MAN YOU DECIDED TO FOLLOW IN THE FIRST PLACE.
AND IF YOU WANT TO LEAVE, I COMPLETELY UNDER-STAND.
SIGH
YOU HEAR WHAT HE'S SAYIN', SKULL?
IT'S JUST THE KIND OF THING A CAPTAIN WOULD DO, AIN'T IT?
??
WE'RE WITH YOU.
ALL OF US.
!

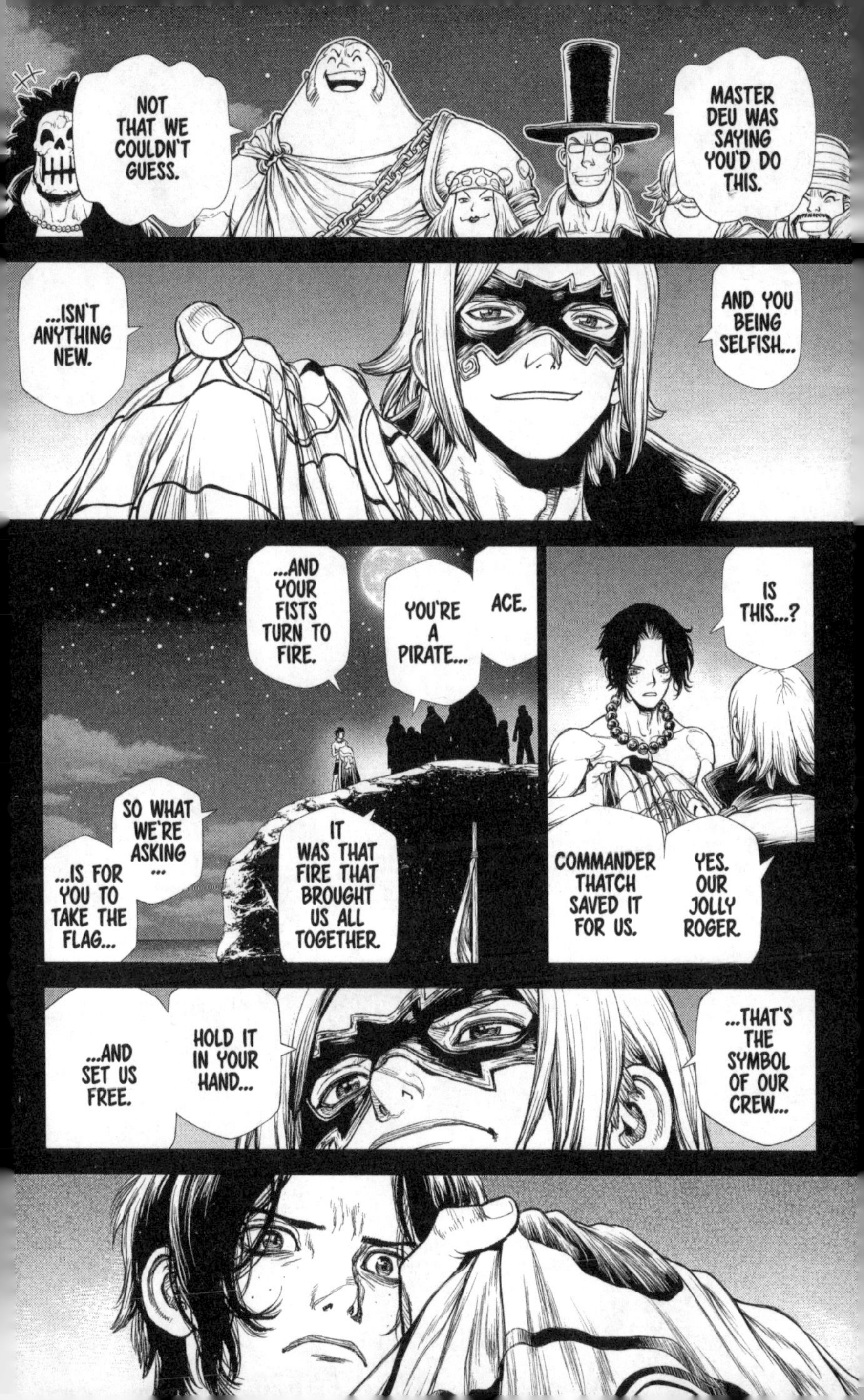
MASTER DEU WAS SAYING YOU'D DO THIS.
NOT THAT WE COULDN'T GUESS.
AND YOU BEING SELFISH...
...ISN'T ANYTHING NEW.
IS THIS...?
YES. OUR JOLLY ROGER.
COMMANDER THATCH SAVED IT FOR US.
ACE.
YOU'RE A PIRATE...
...AND YOUR FISTS TURN TO FIRE.
IT WAS THAT FIRE THAT BROUGHT US ALL TOGETHER.
SO WHAT WE'RE ASKING...
...IS FOR YOU TO TAKE THE FLAG...
...THAT'S THE SYMBOL OF OUR CREW...
HOLD IT IN YOUR HAND...
...AND SET US FREE.

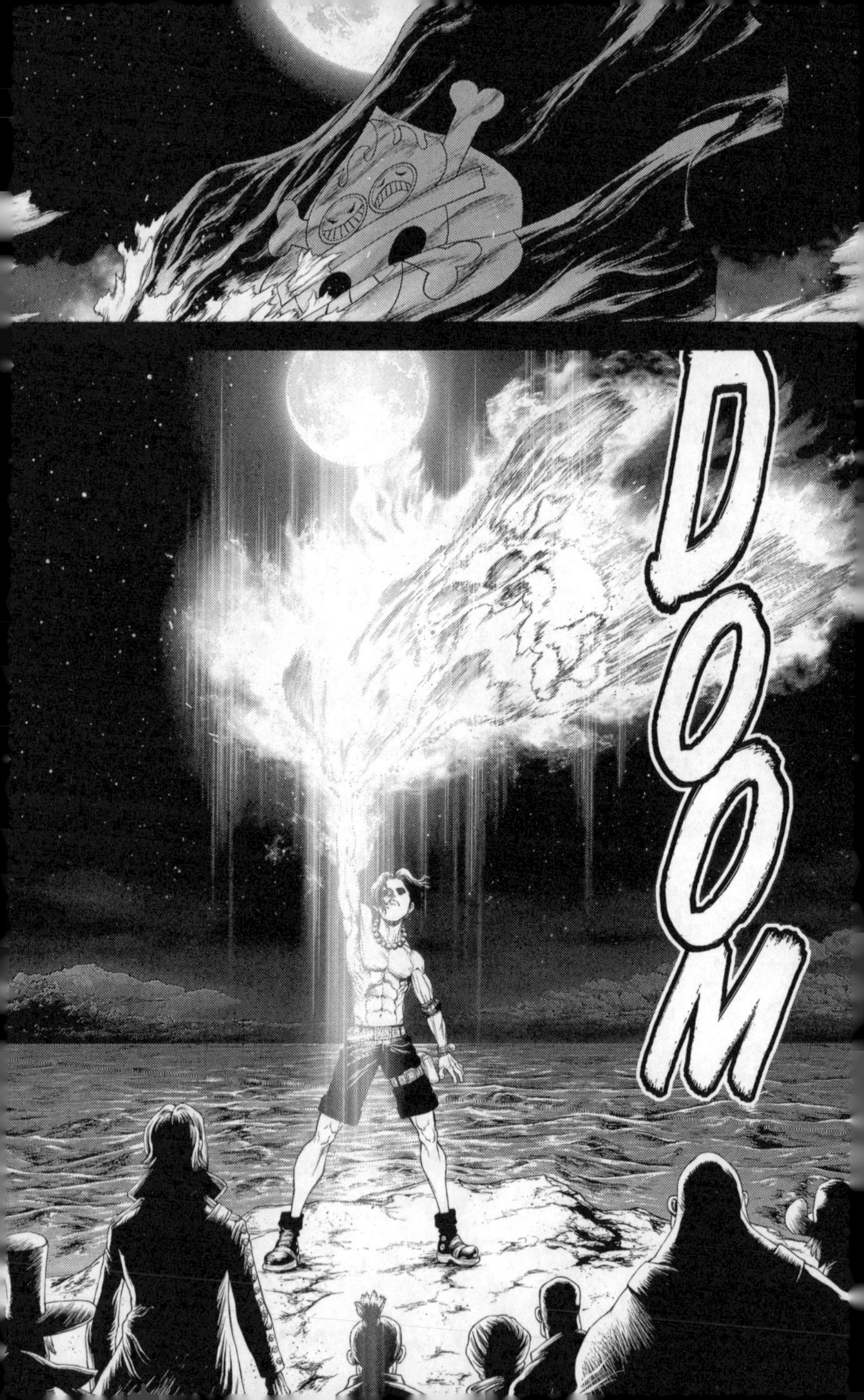
DOOM

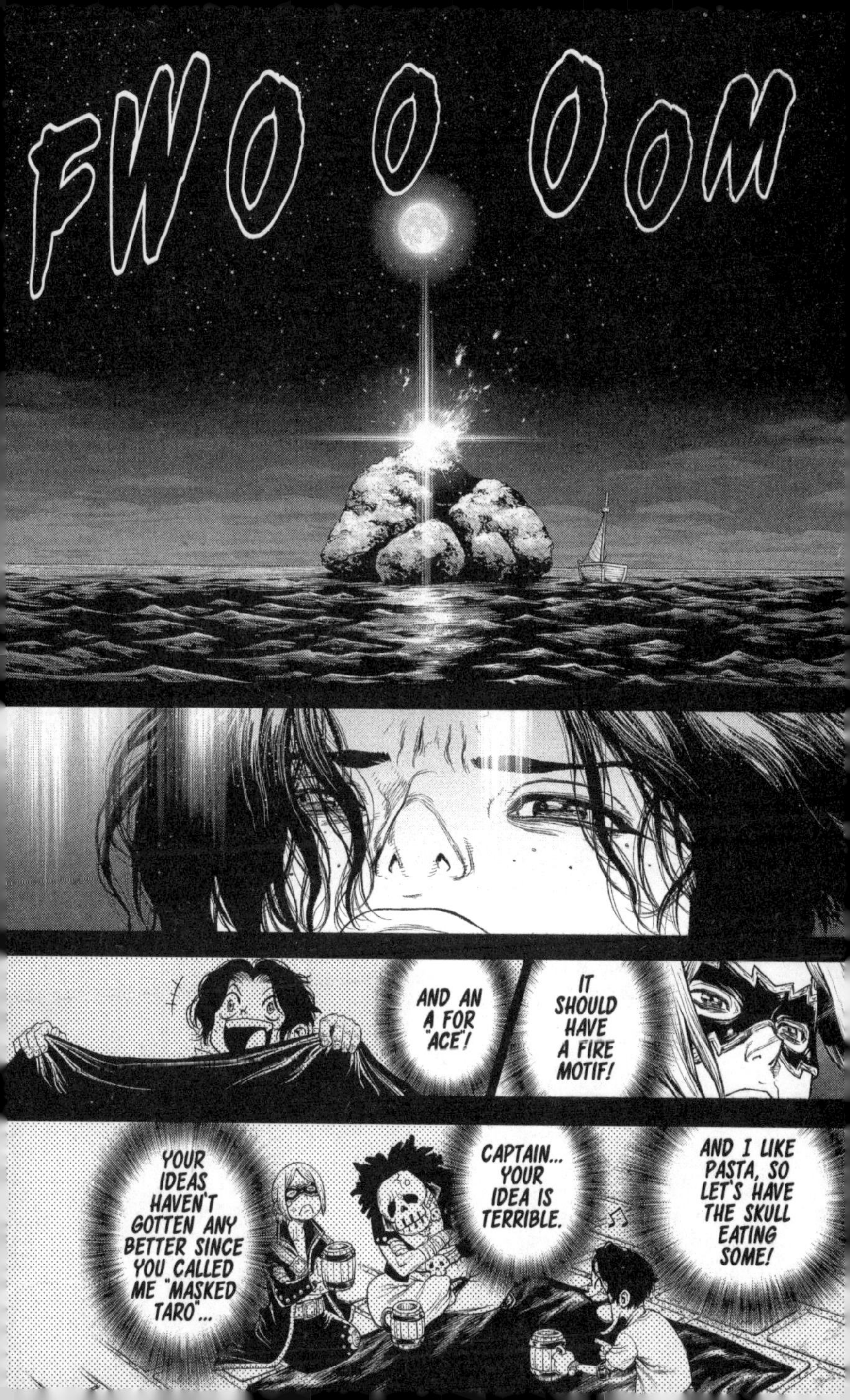
FWOOOOM
IT SHOULD HAVE A FIRE MOTIF!
AND AN A FOR "ACE"!
AND I LIKE PASTA, SO LET'S HAVE THE SKULL EATING SOME!
CAPTAIN... YOUR IDEA IS TERRIBLE.
YOUR IDEAS HAVEN'T GOTTEN ANY BETTER SINCE YOU CALLED ME "MASKED TARO"...

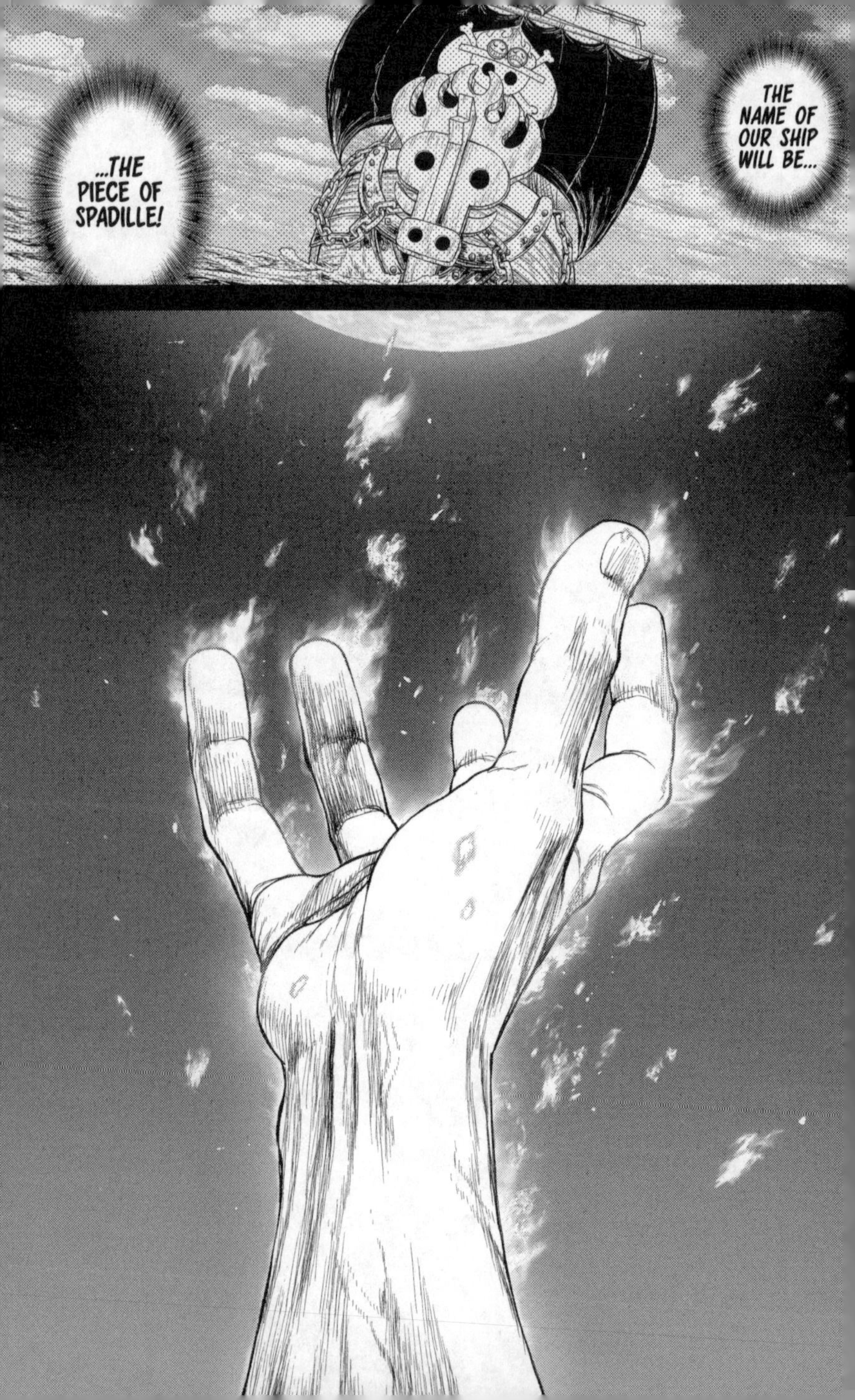
THE NAME OF OUR SHIP WILL BE...
...THE PIECE OF SPADILLE!

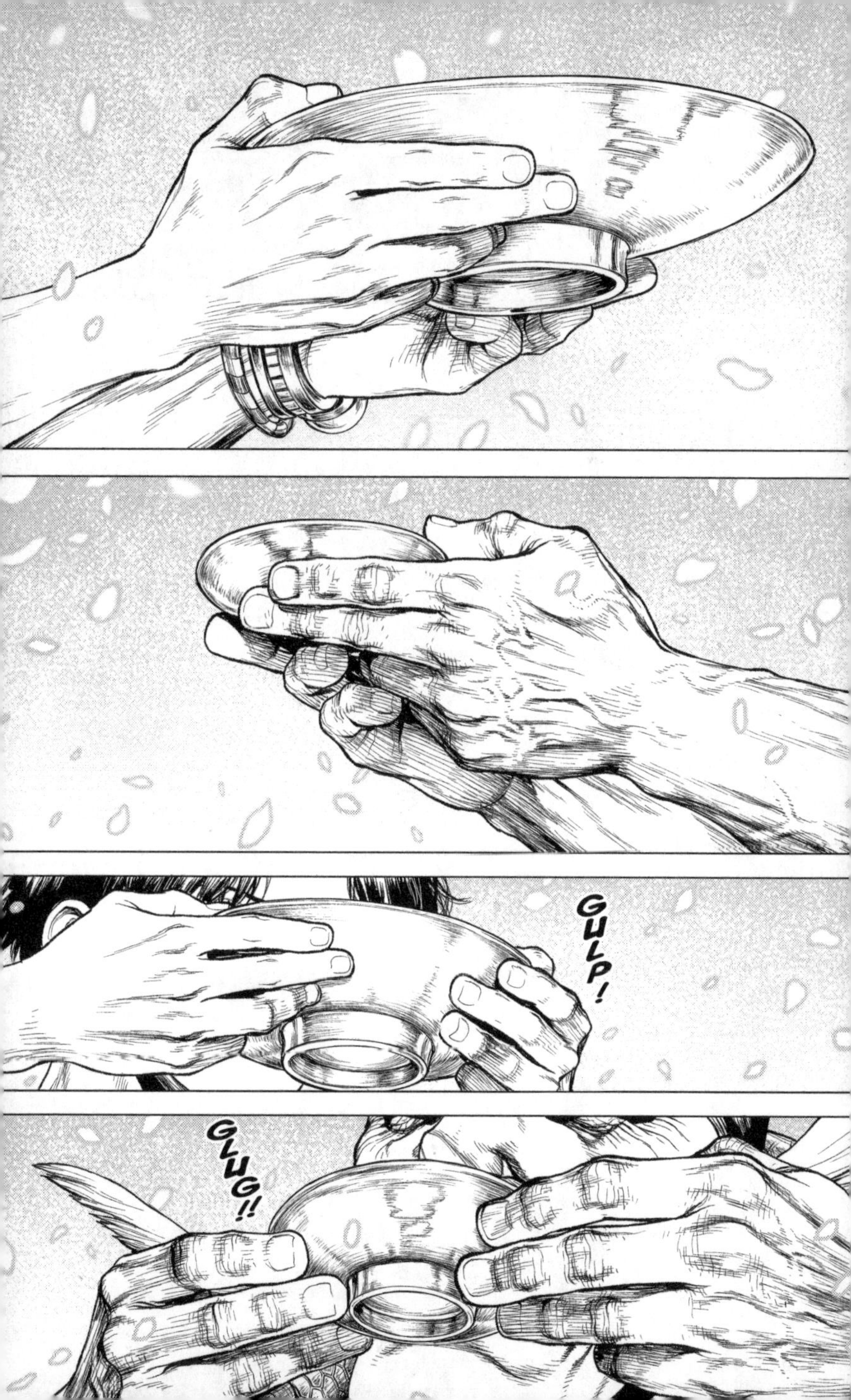
GULP!
GLUG!!

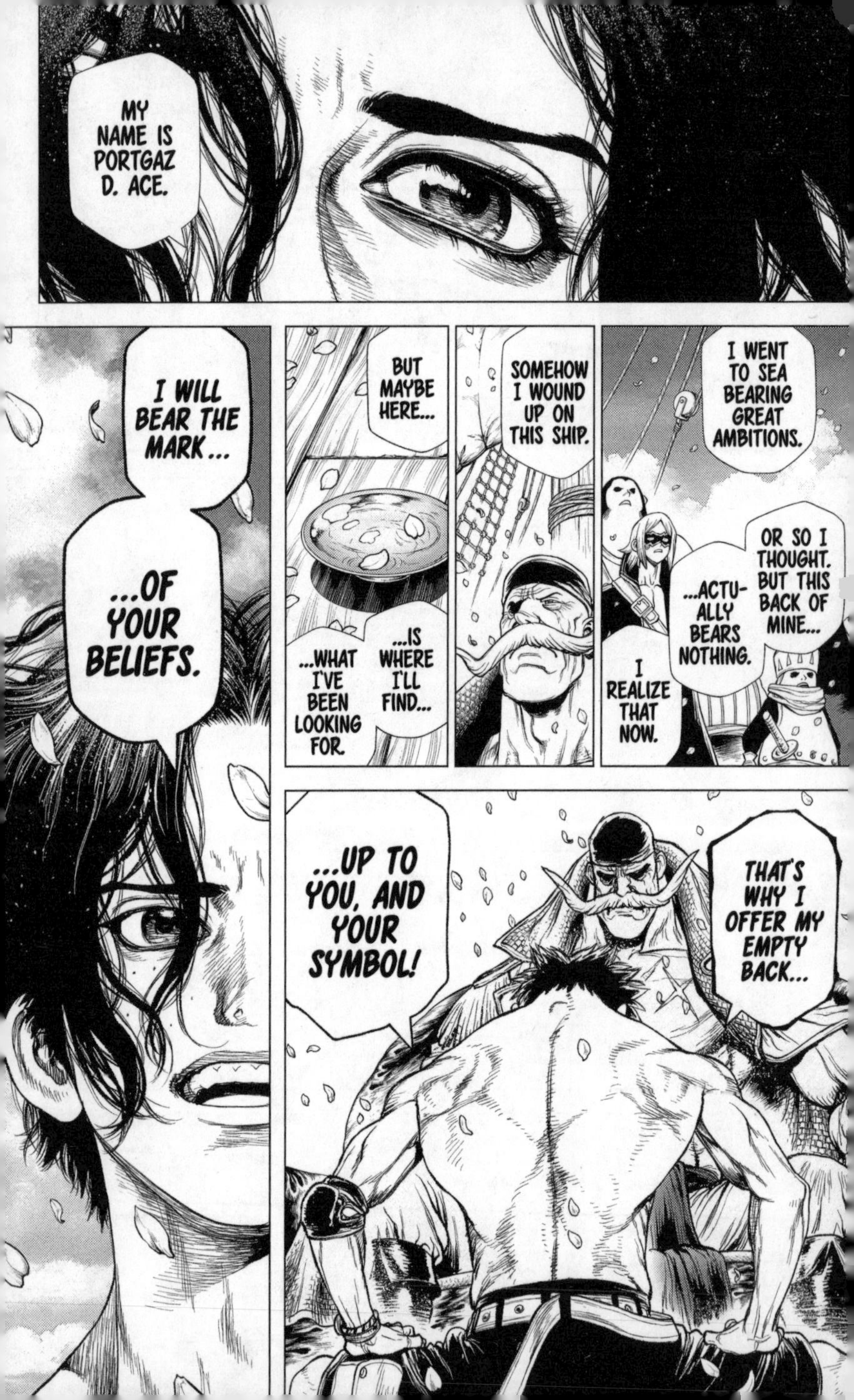
MY NAME IS PORTGAZ D. ACE.
I WENT TO SEA BEARING GREAT AMBITIONS.
OR SO I THOUGHT. BUT THIS BACK OF MINE...
...ACTU-ALLY BEARS NOTHING.
I REALIZE THAT NOW.
SOMEHOW I WOUND UP ON THIS SHIP.
BUT MAYBE HERE...
...IS WHERE I'LL FIND...
...WHAT I'VE BEEN LOOKING FOR.
THAT'S WHY I OFFER MY EMPTY BACK...
...UP TO YOU, AND YOUR SYMBOL!
I WILL BEAR THE MARK...
...OF YOUR BELIEFS.

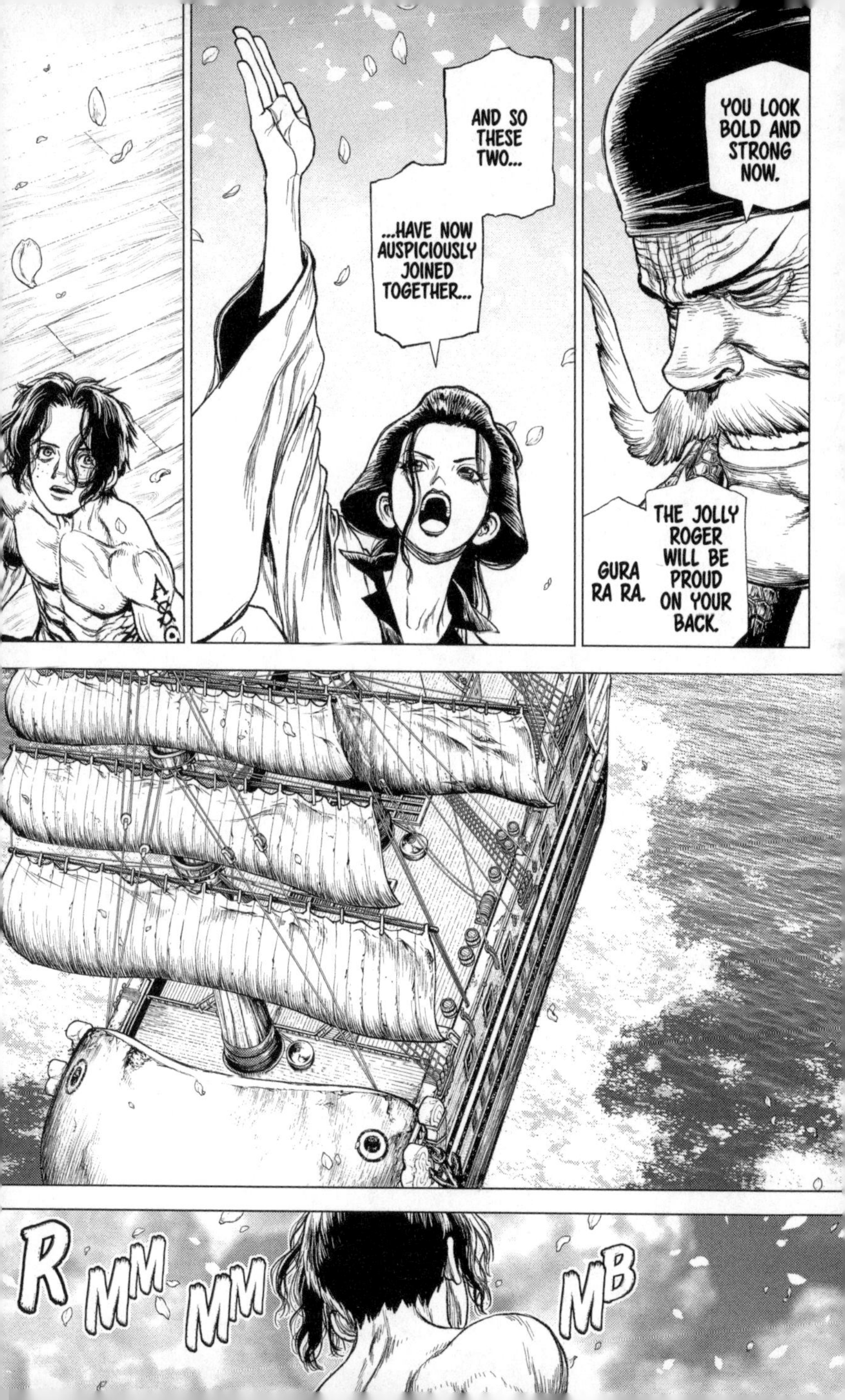
YOU LOOK BOLD AND STRONG NOW.
THE JOLLY ROGER WILL BE PROUD ON YOUR BACK.
GURA RA RA.
AND SO THESE TWO...
...HAVE NOW AUSPICIOUSLY JOINED TOGETHER...
RMMMMMMB

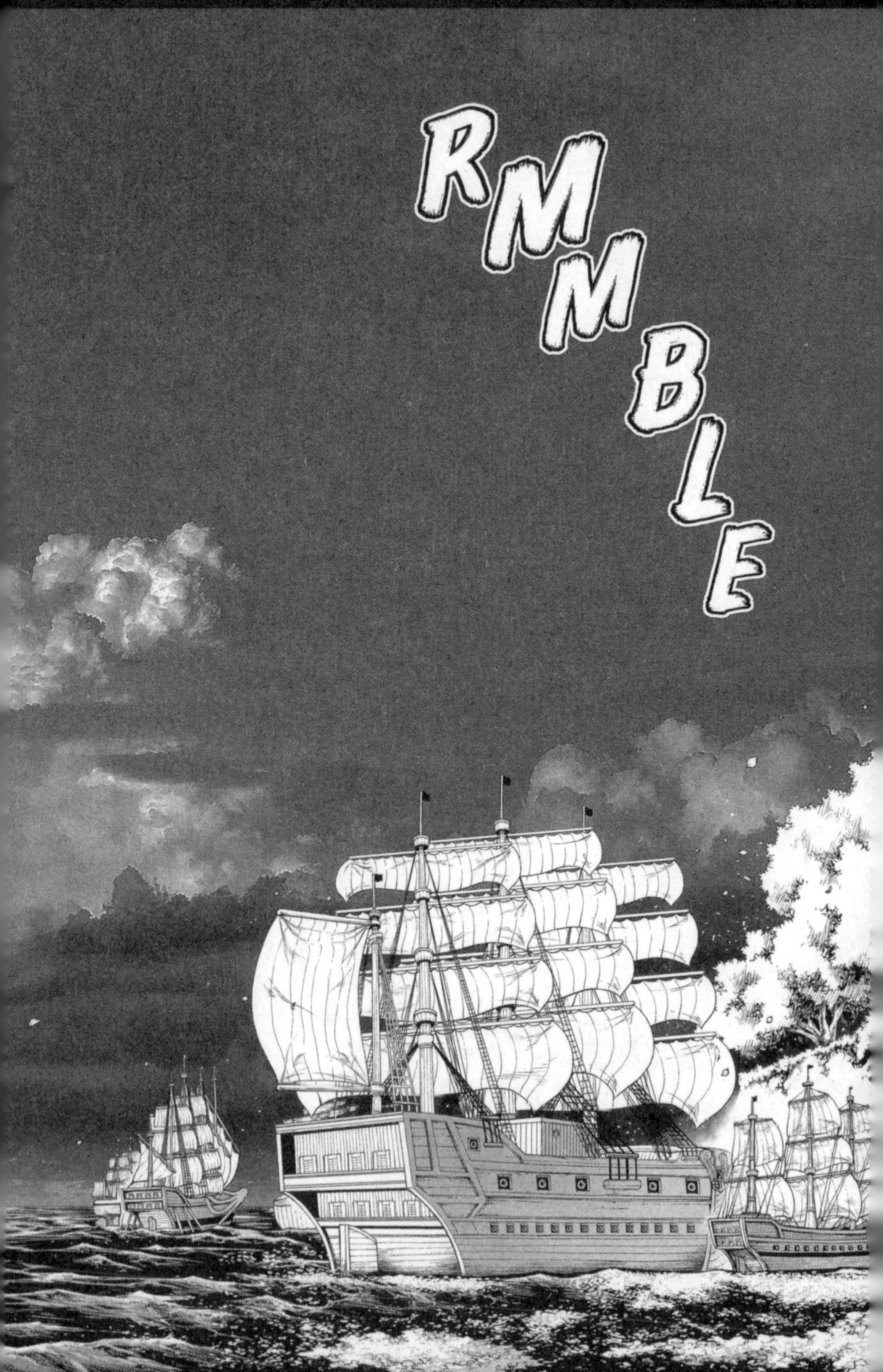
RMMBLE

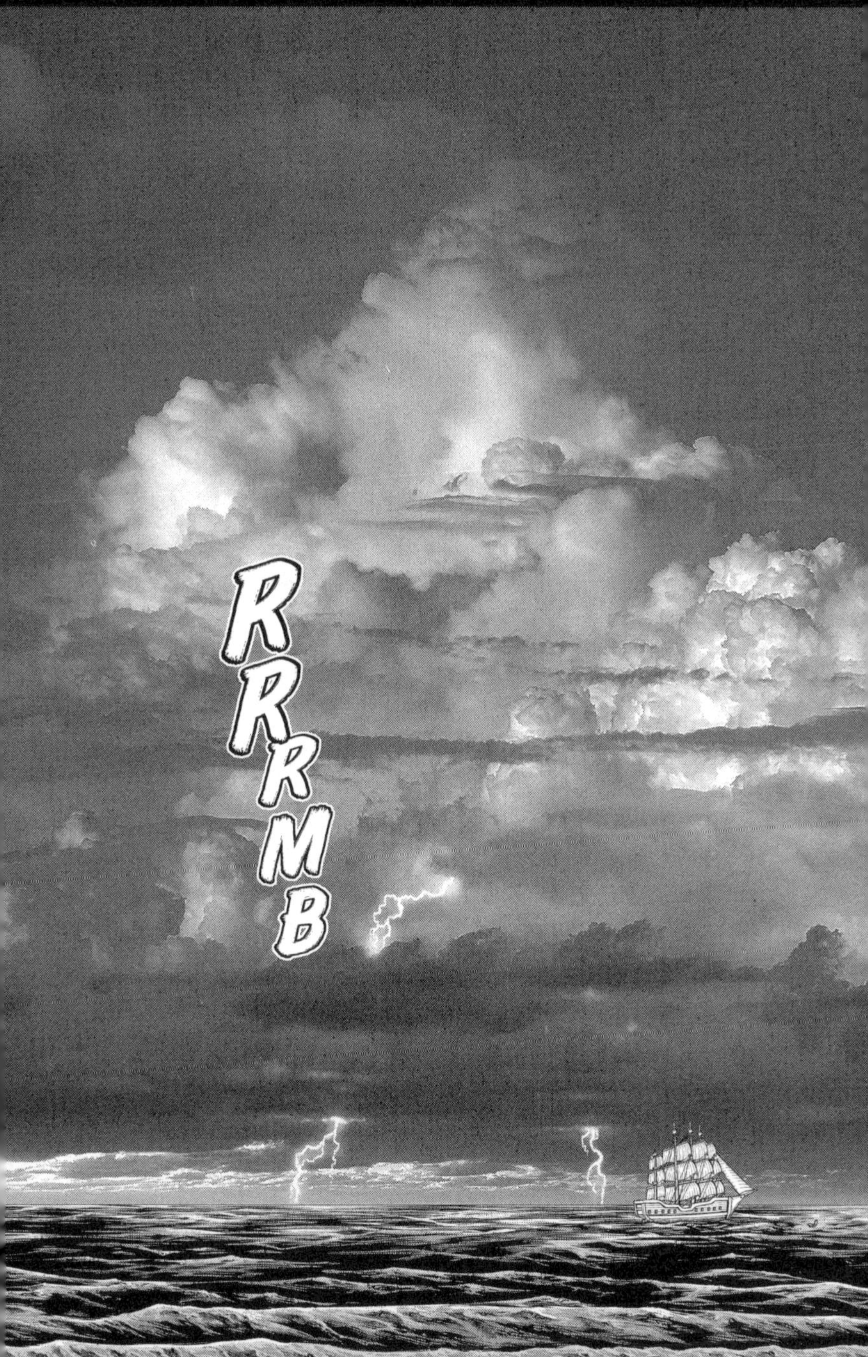
RRRMB

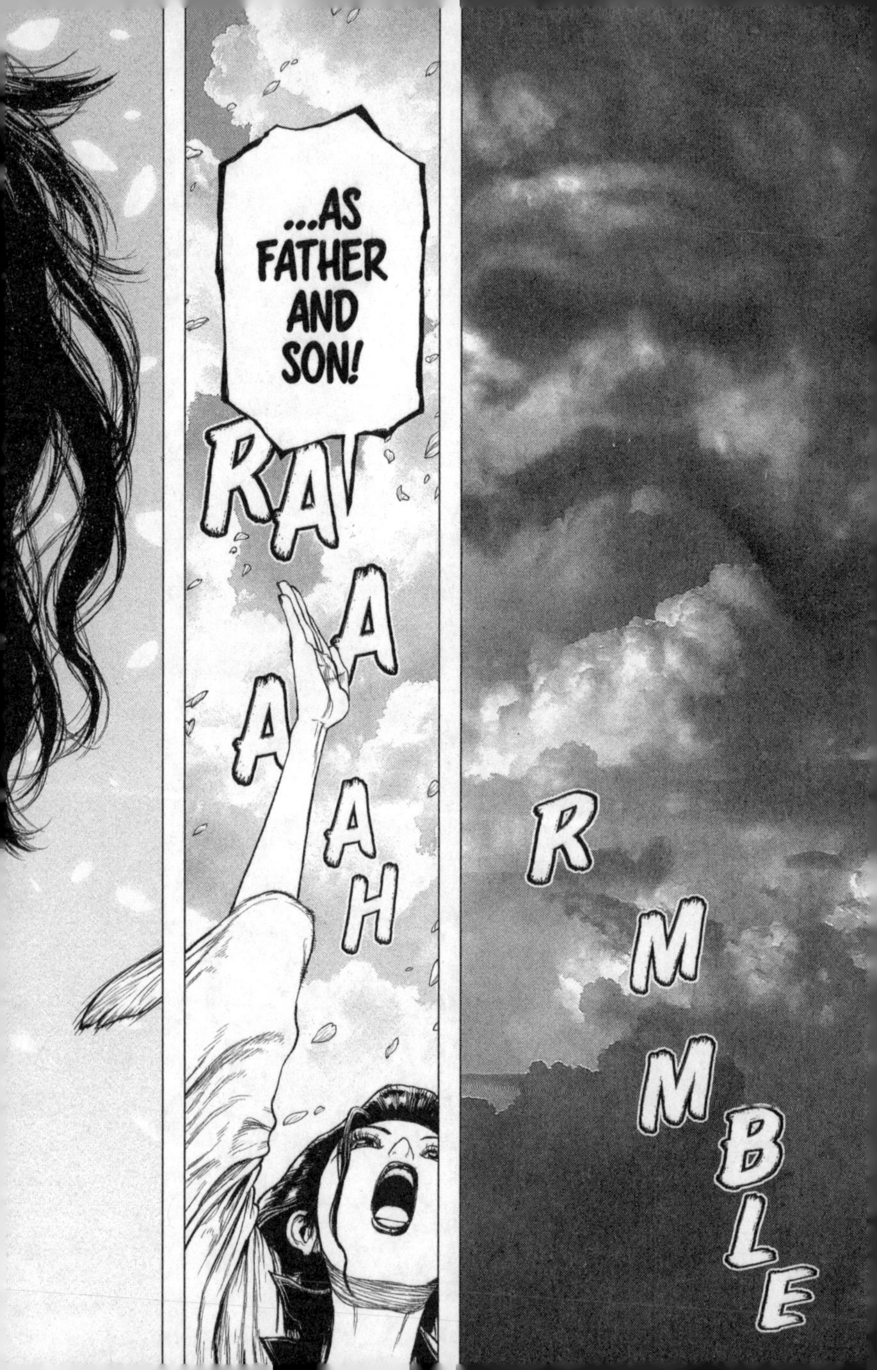
RMMBLE
...AS FATHER AND SON!
RAAAAH

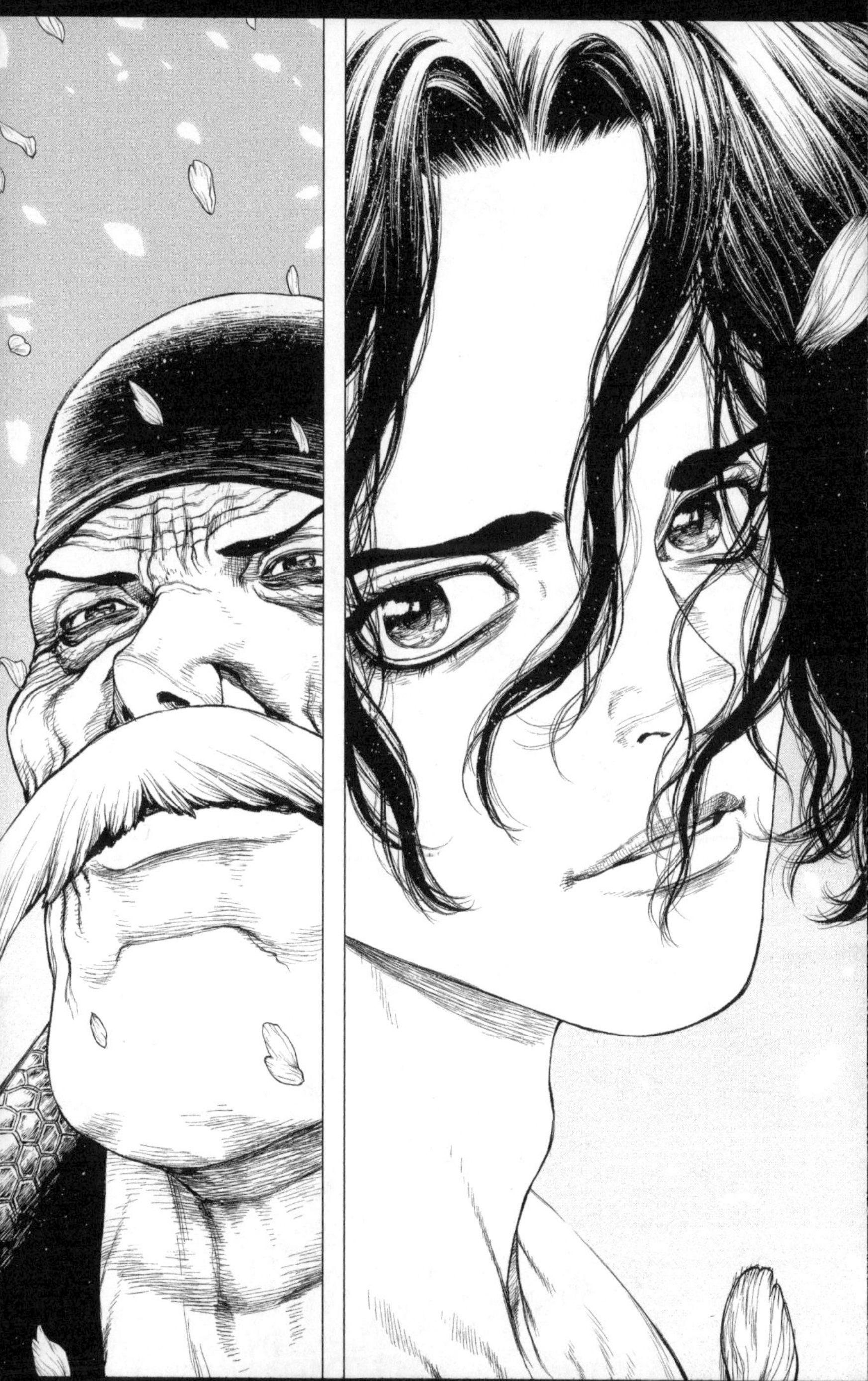

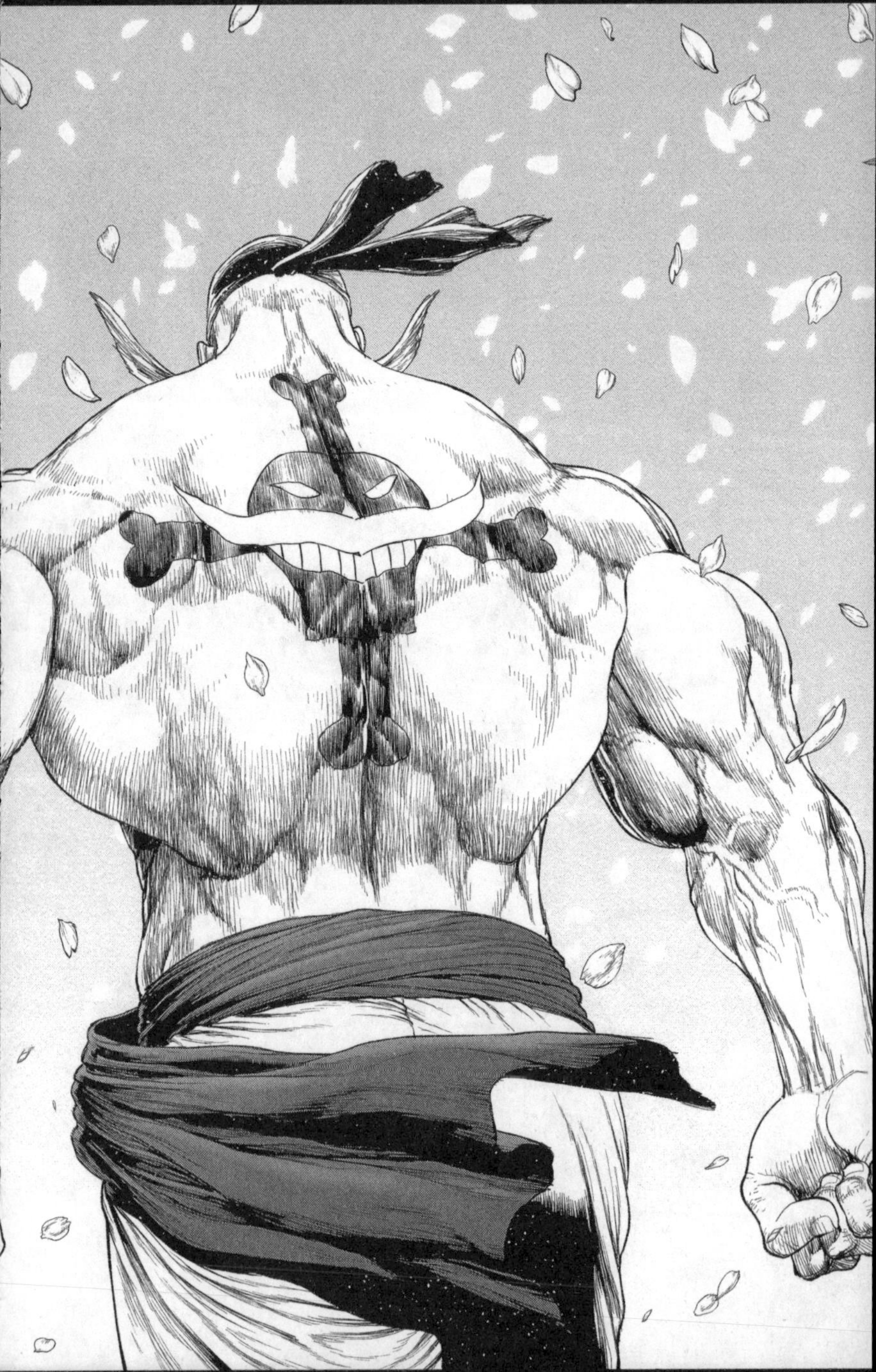

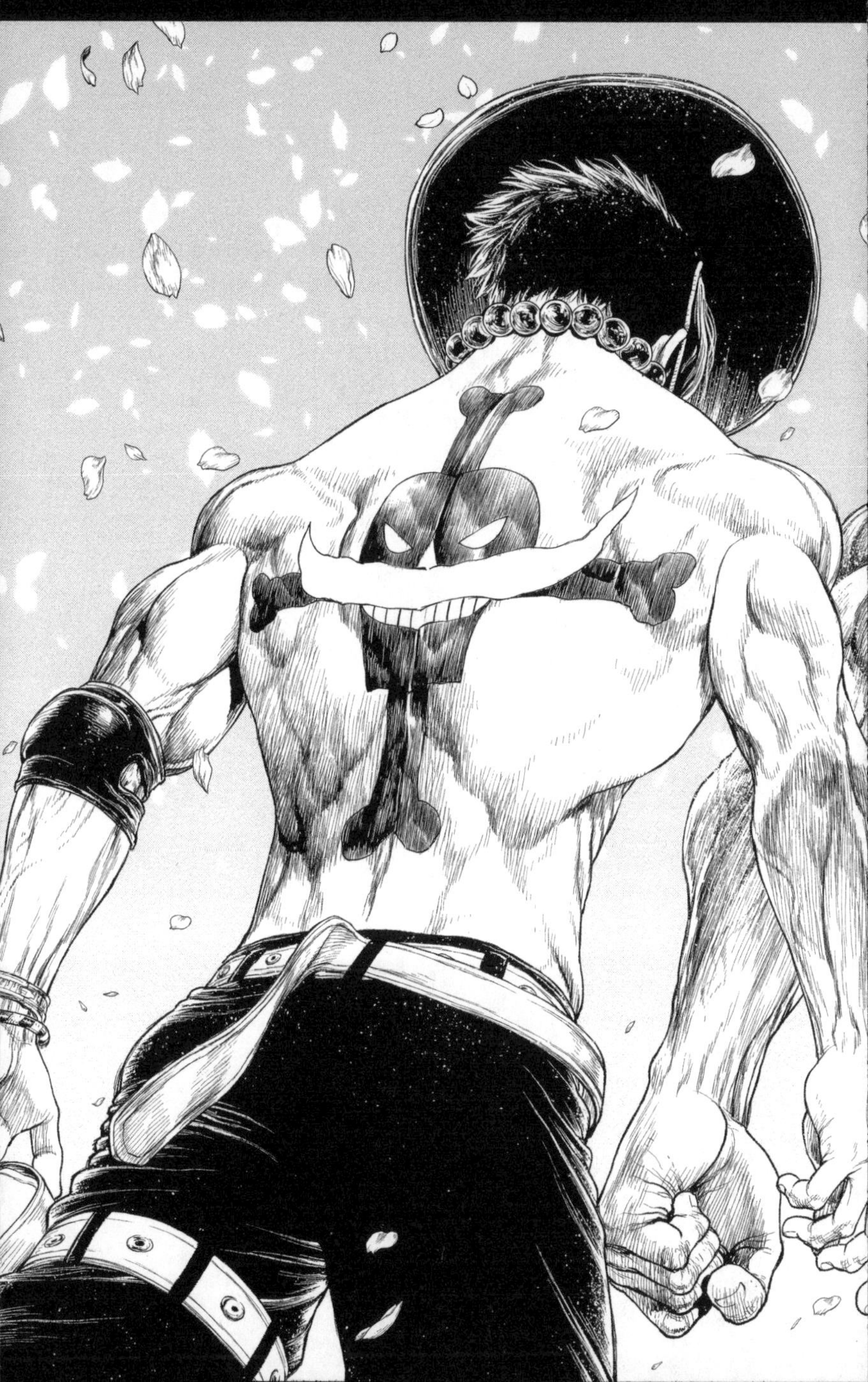

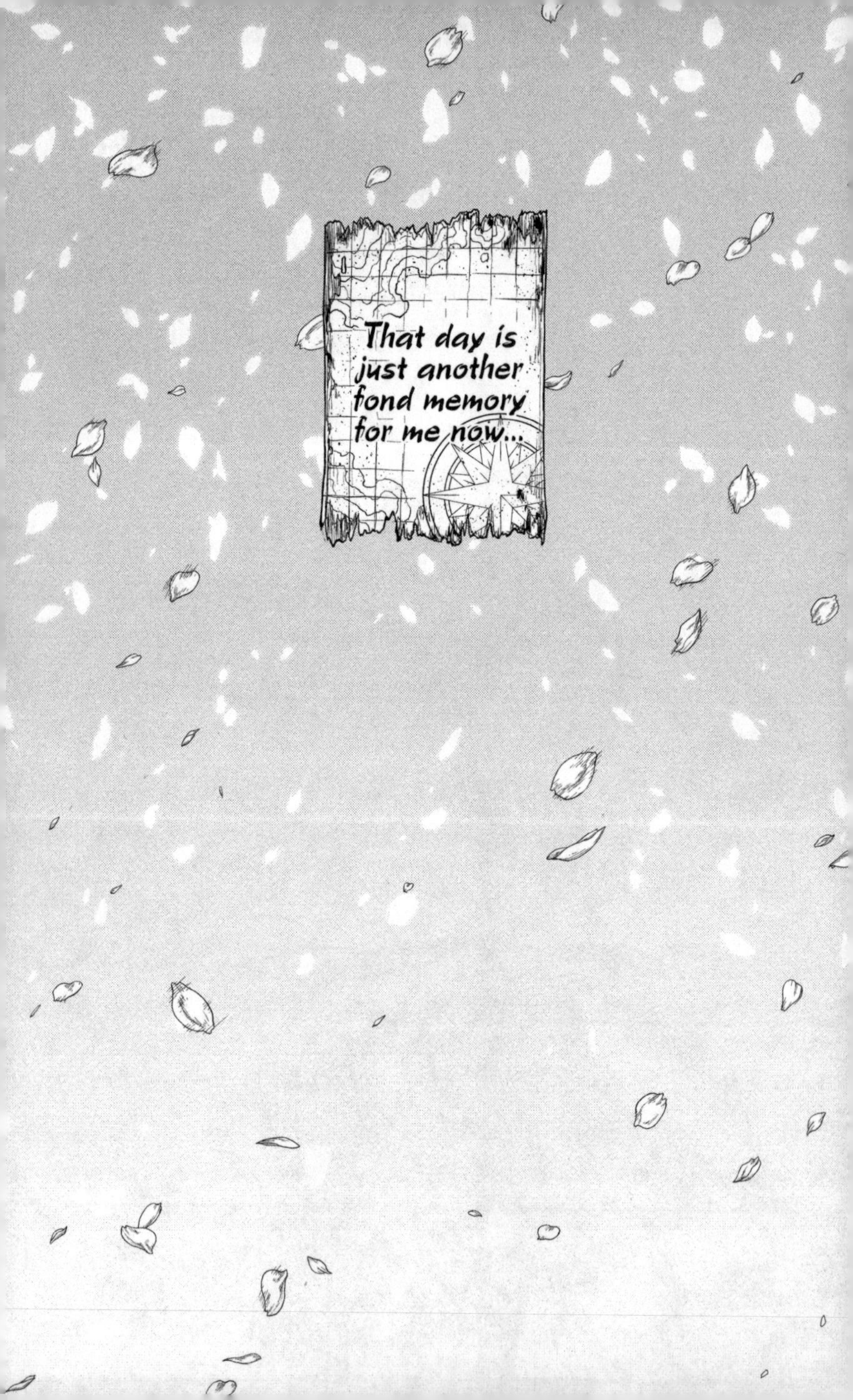
That day is just another fond memory for me now...

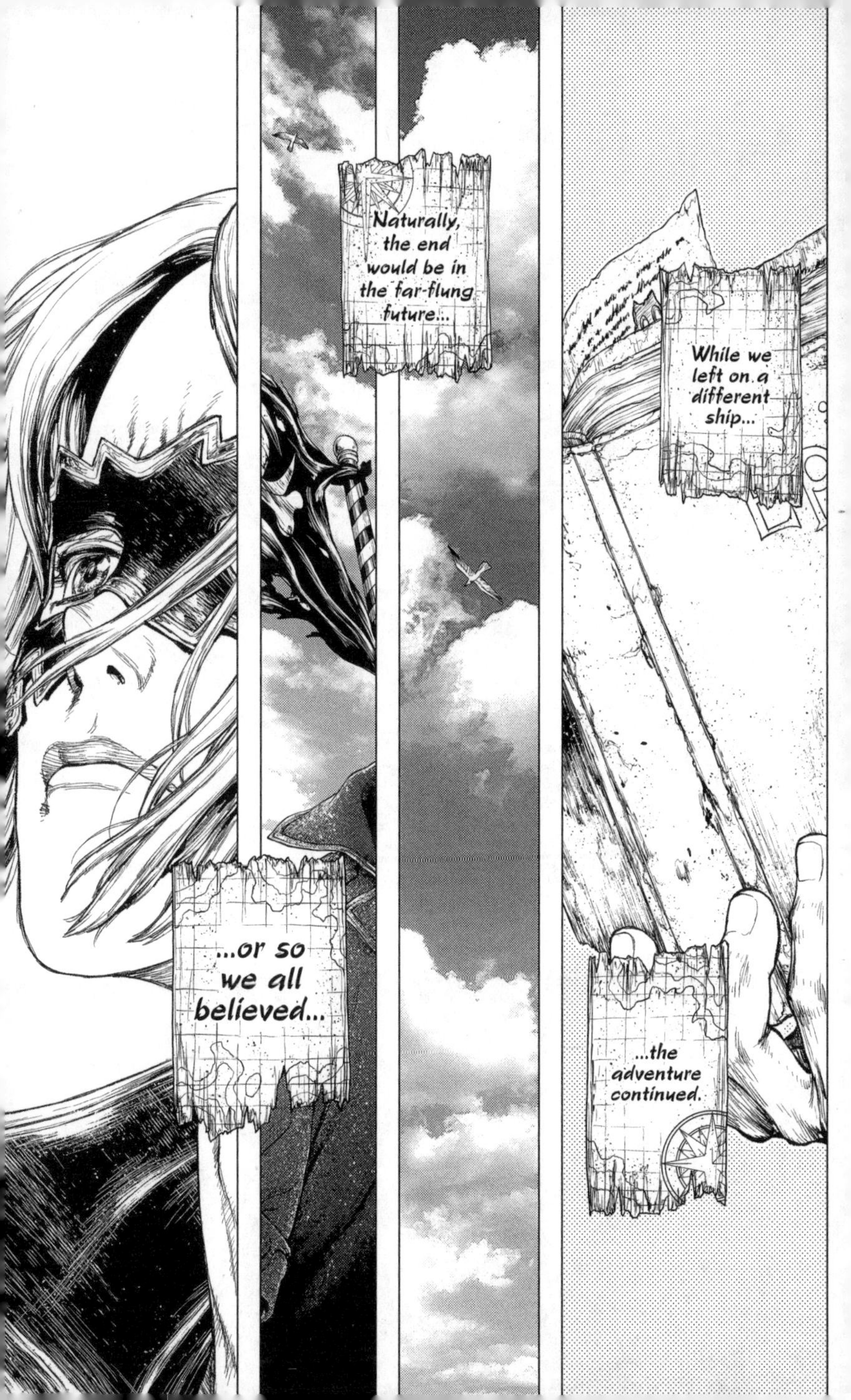
While we left on a different ship...
...the adventure continued.
Naturally, the end would be in the far-flung future...
...or so we all believed...

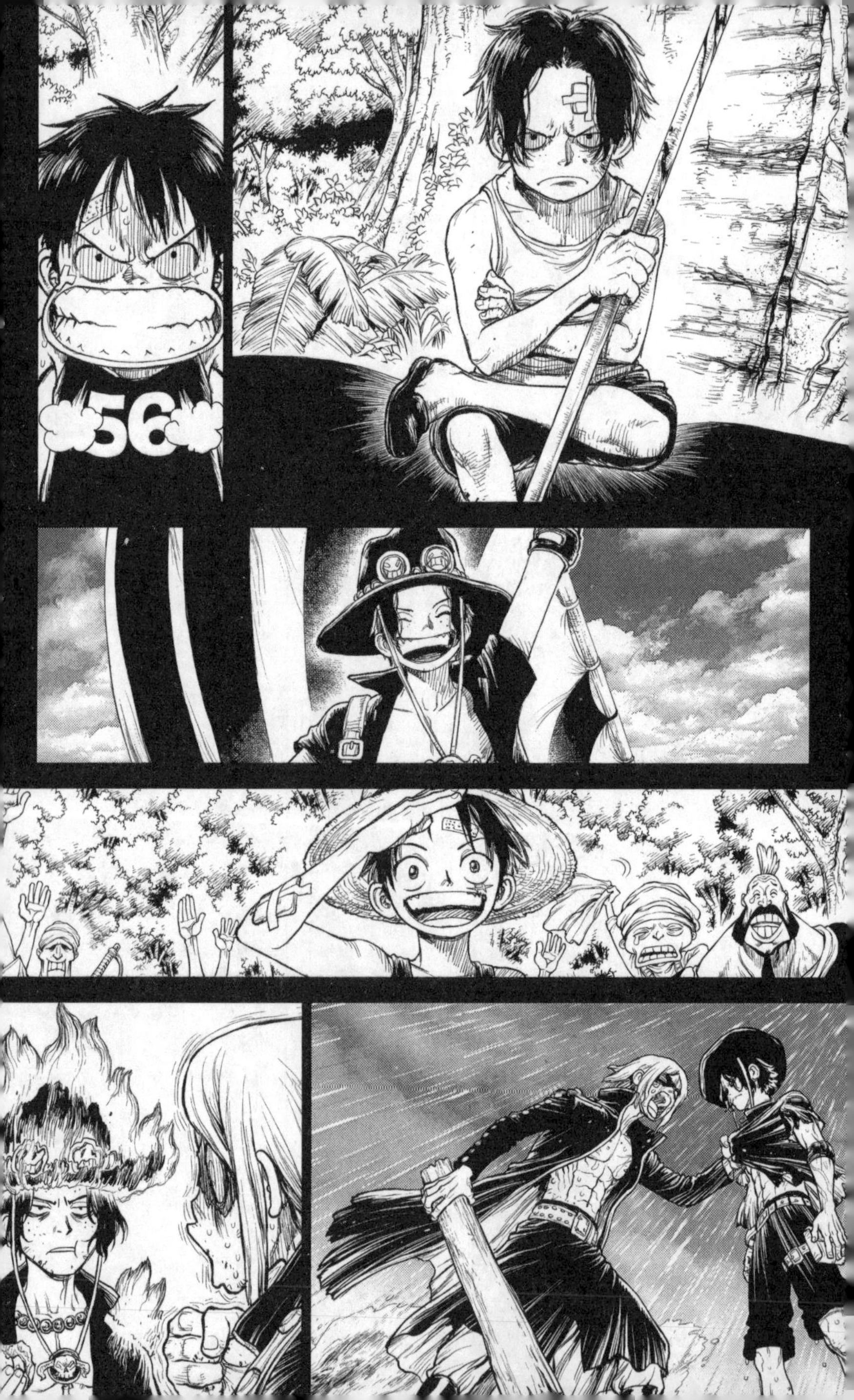
56

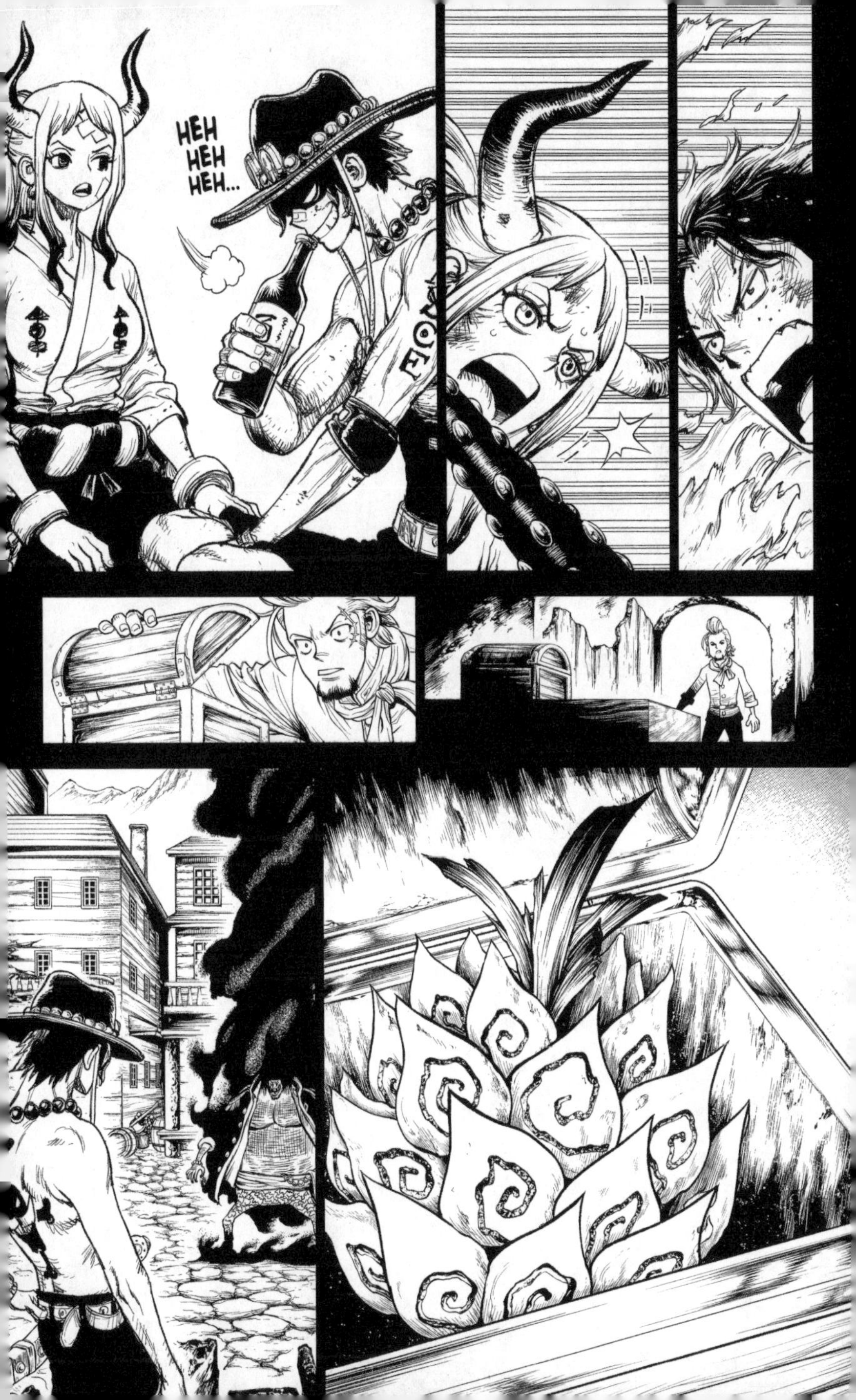
HEH HEH HEH...

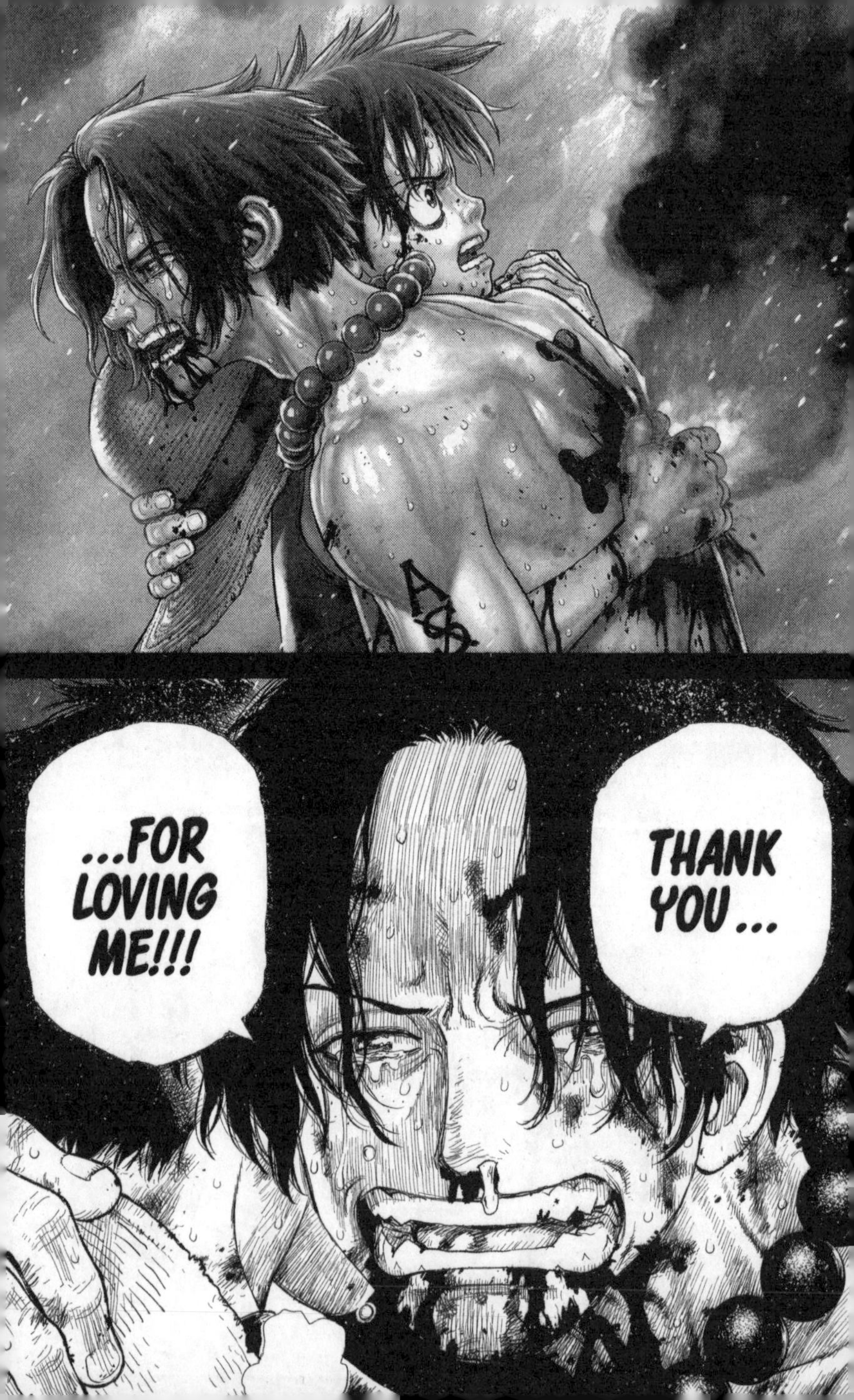
THANK YOU ...
...FOR LOVING ME!!!

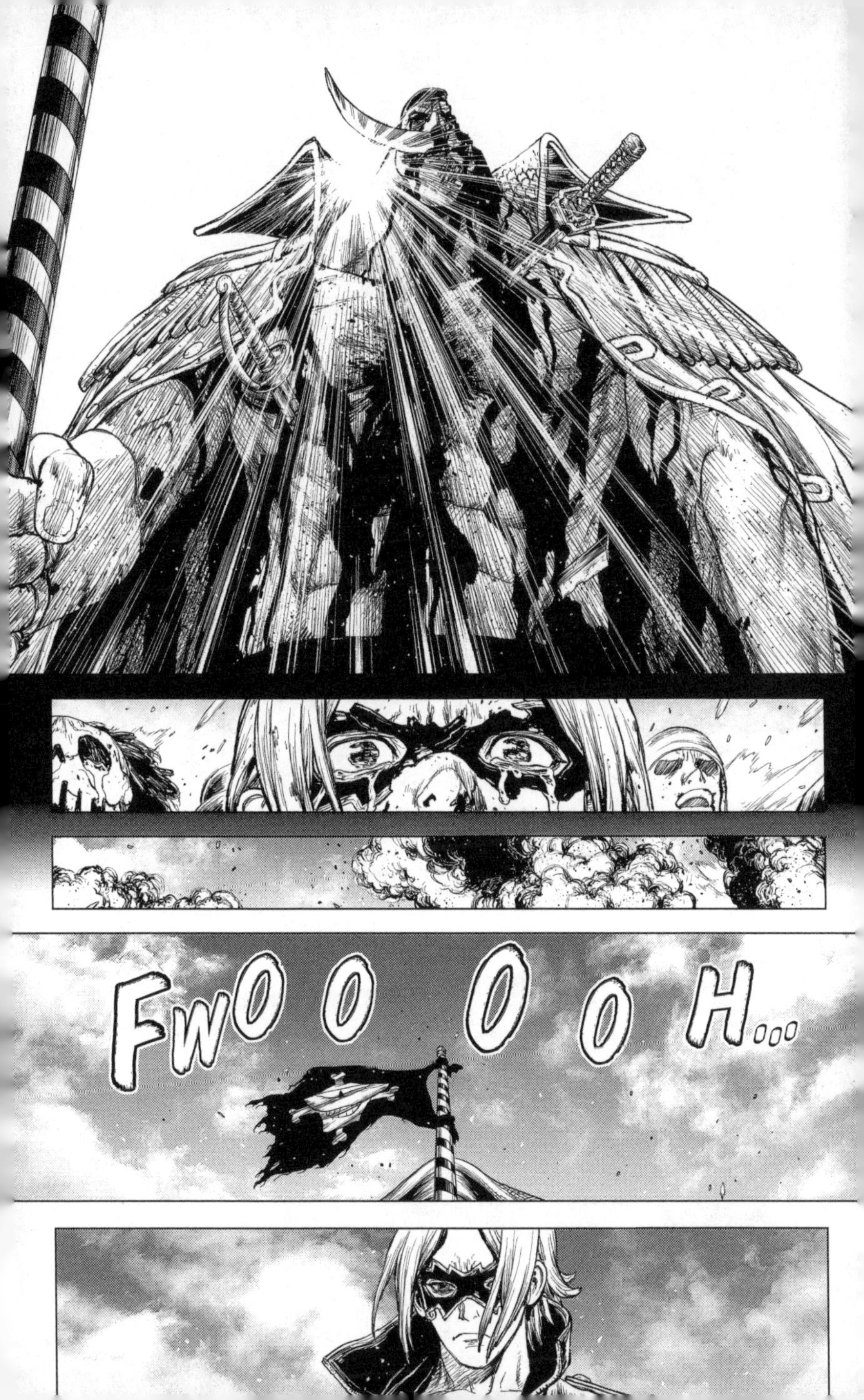
FWOOOOOH...

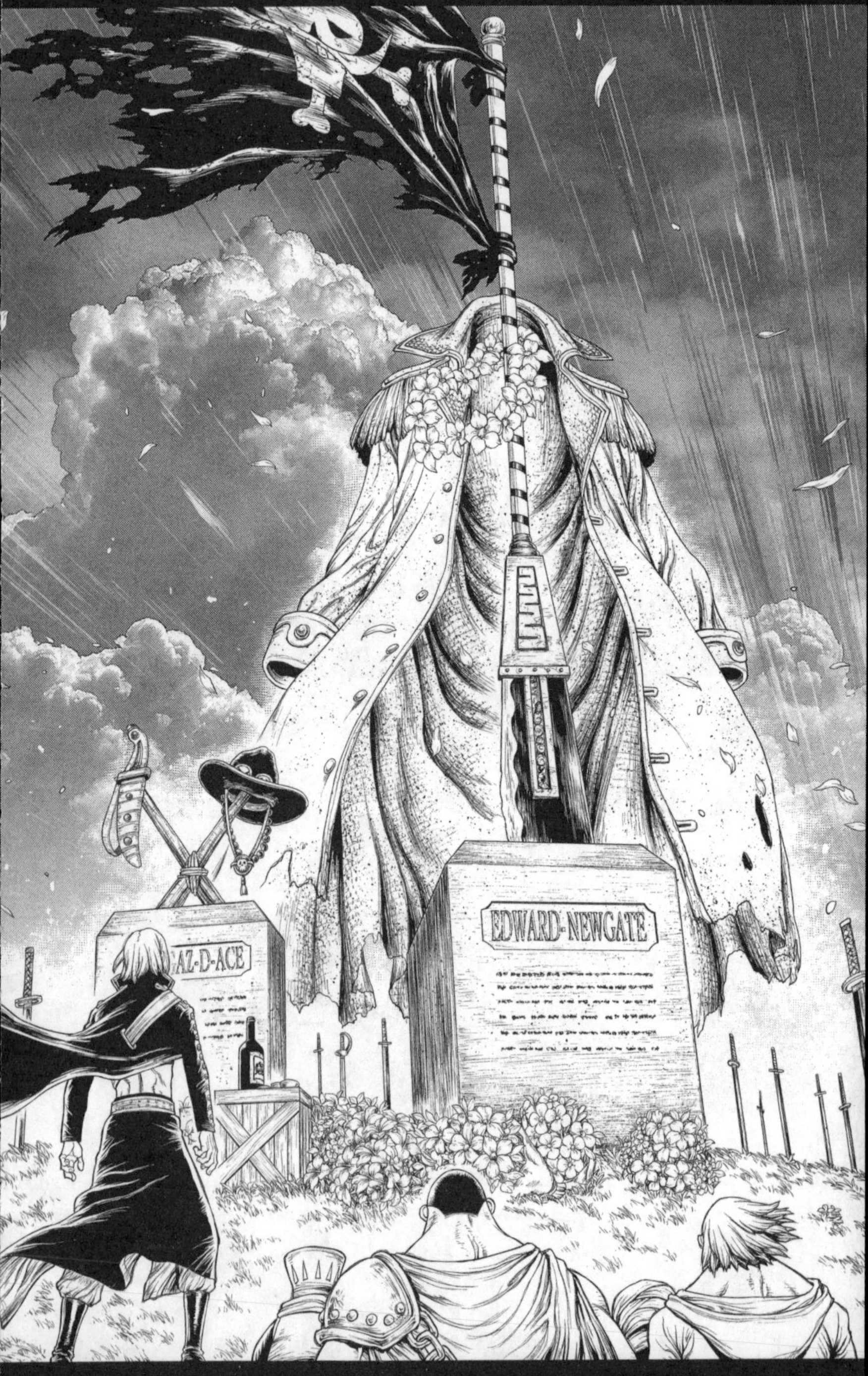
EDWARD-NEWGATE
AZ-D-ACE

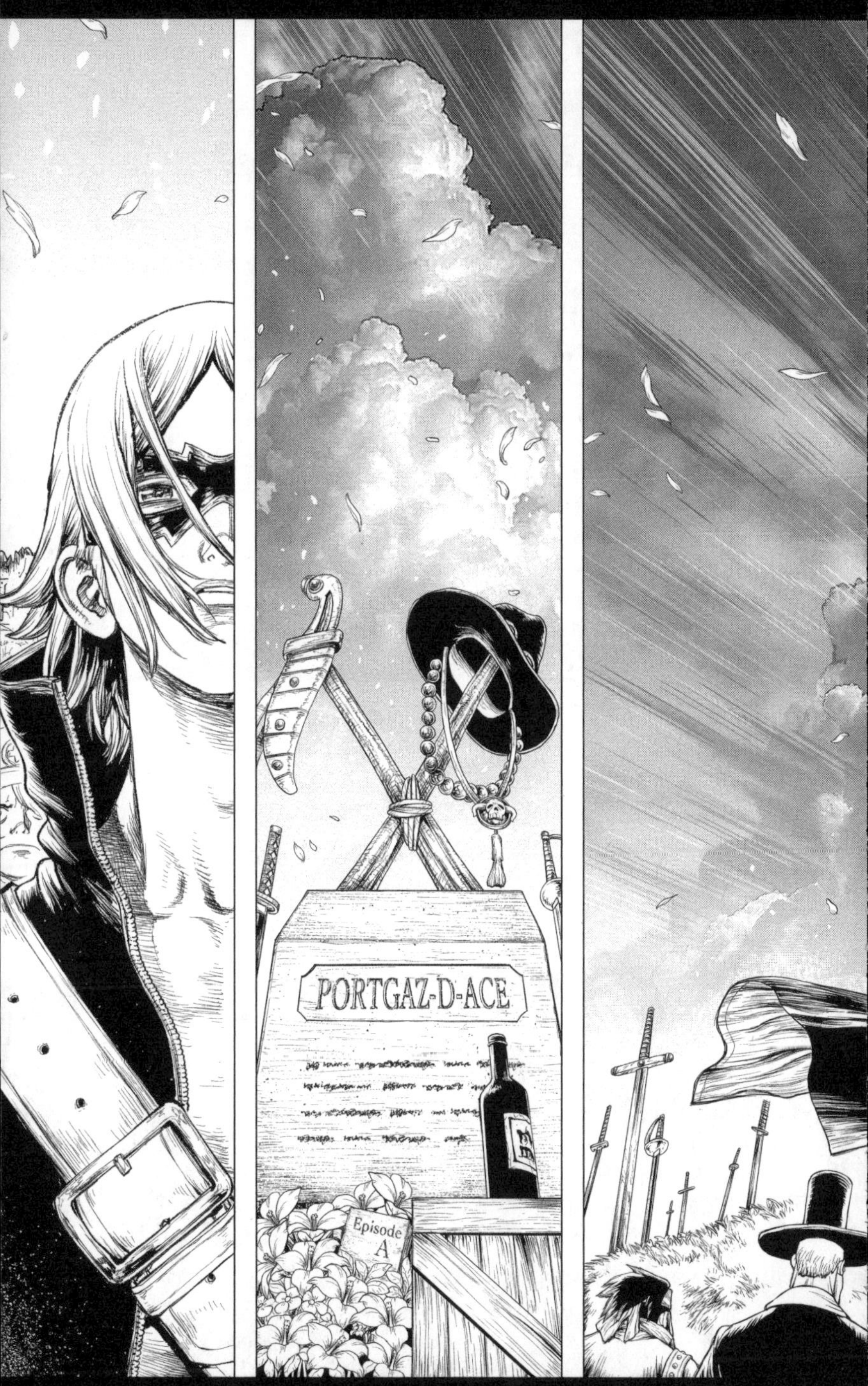
PORTGAZ-D-ACE
Episode A

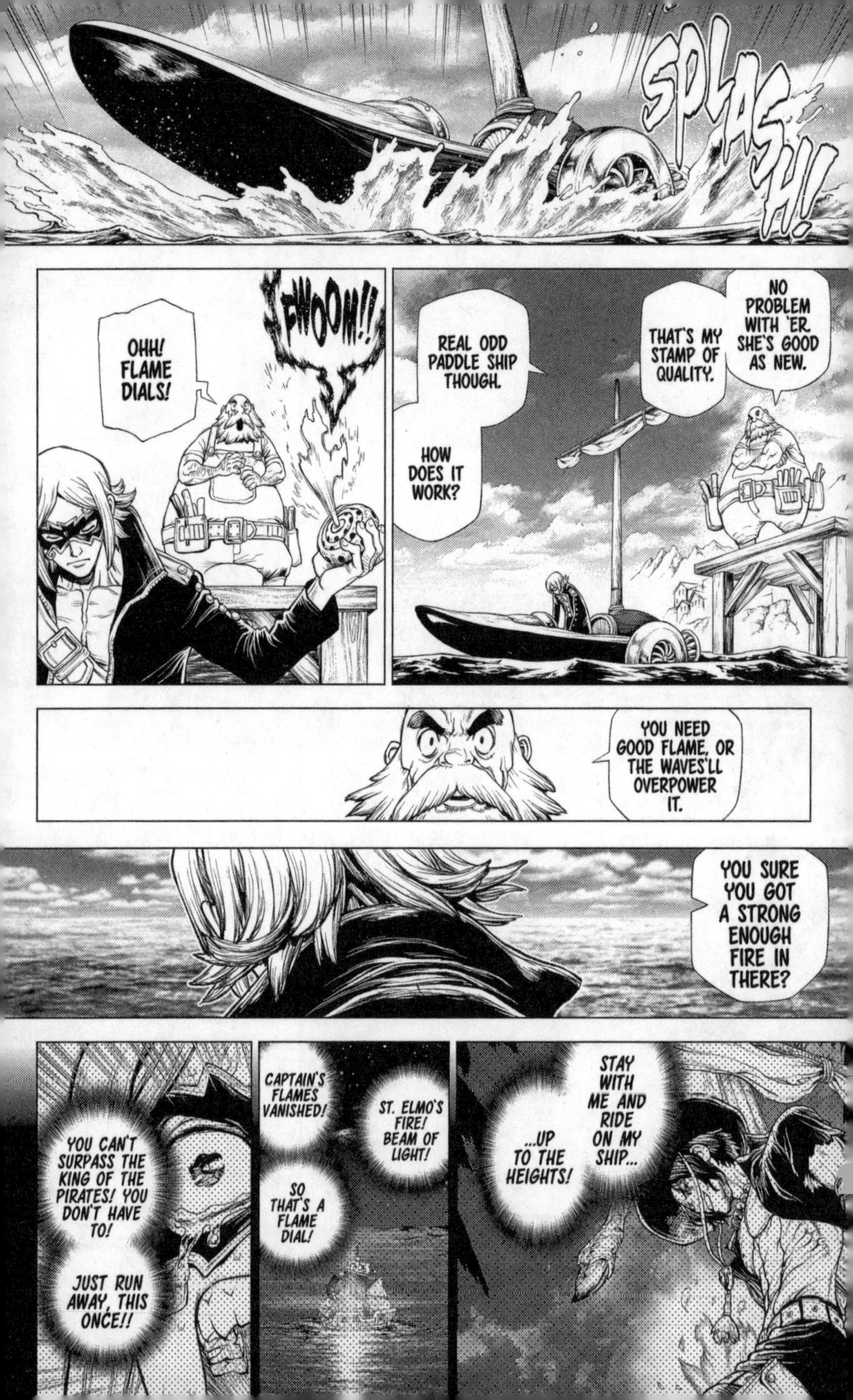
SPLASH!
NO PROBLEM WITH 'ER. SHE'S GOOD AS NEW.
THAT'S MY STAMP OF QUALITY.
REAL ODD PADDLE SHIP THOUGH.
HOW DOES IT WORK?
FWOOM!!
OHH! FLAME DIALS!
YOU NEED GOOD FLAME, OR THE WAVES'LL OVERPOWER IT.
YOU SURE YOU GOT A STRONG ENOUGH FIRE IN THERE?
STAY WITH ME AND RIDE ON MY SHIP...
...UP TO THE HEIGHTS!
ST. ELMO'S FIRE! BEAM OF LIGHT!
CAPTAIN'S FLAMES VANISHED!
SO THAT'S A FLAME DIAL!
YOU CAN'T SURPASS THE KING OF THE PIRATES! YOU DON'T HAVE TO!
JUST RUN AWAY, THIS ONCE!!

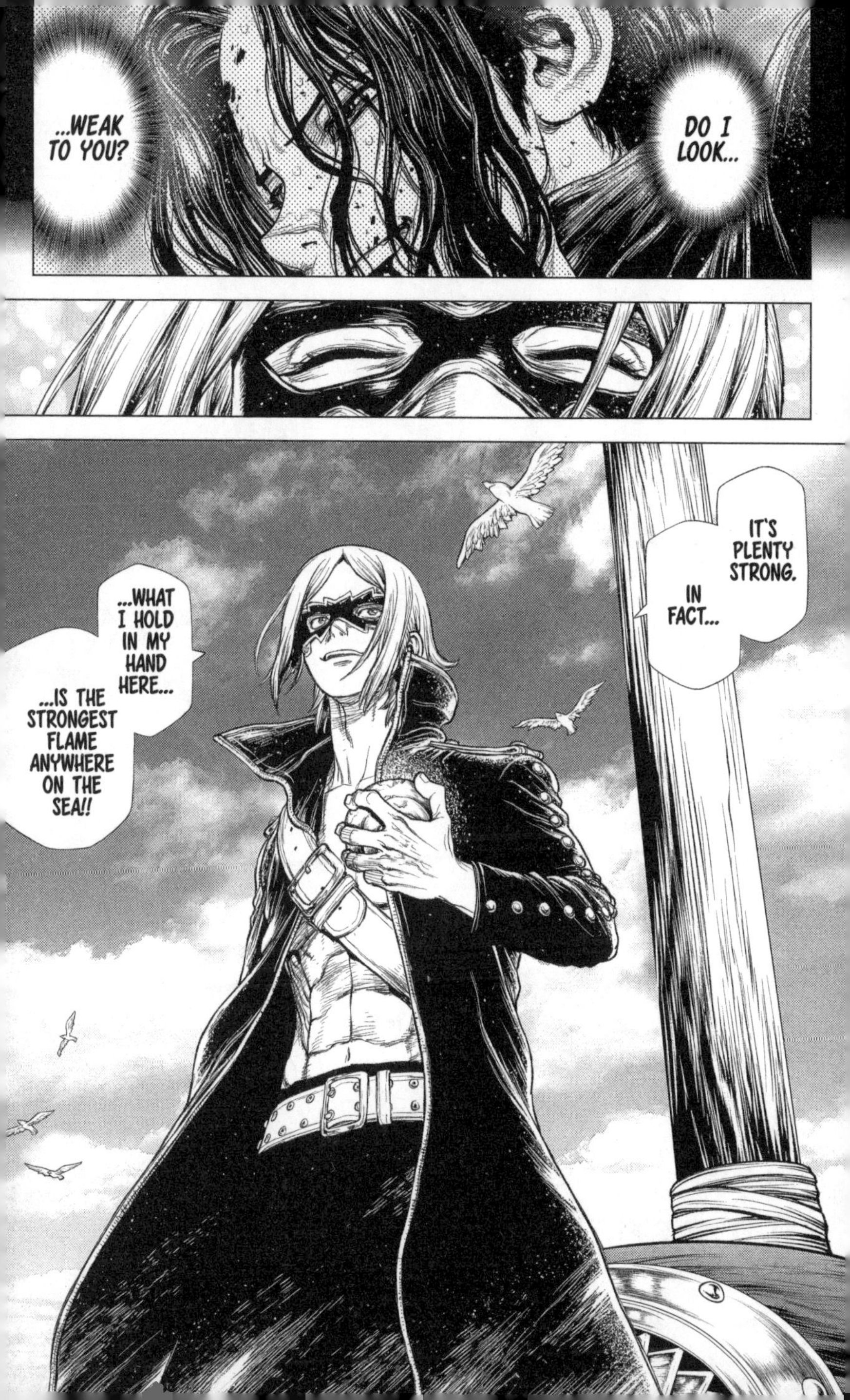
DO I LOOK...
...WEAK TO YOU?
IT'S PLENTY STRONG.
IN FACT...
...WHAT I HOLD IN MY HAND HERE...
...IS THE STRONGEST FLAME ANYWHERE ON THE SEA!!

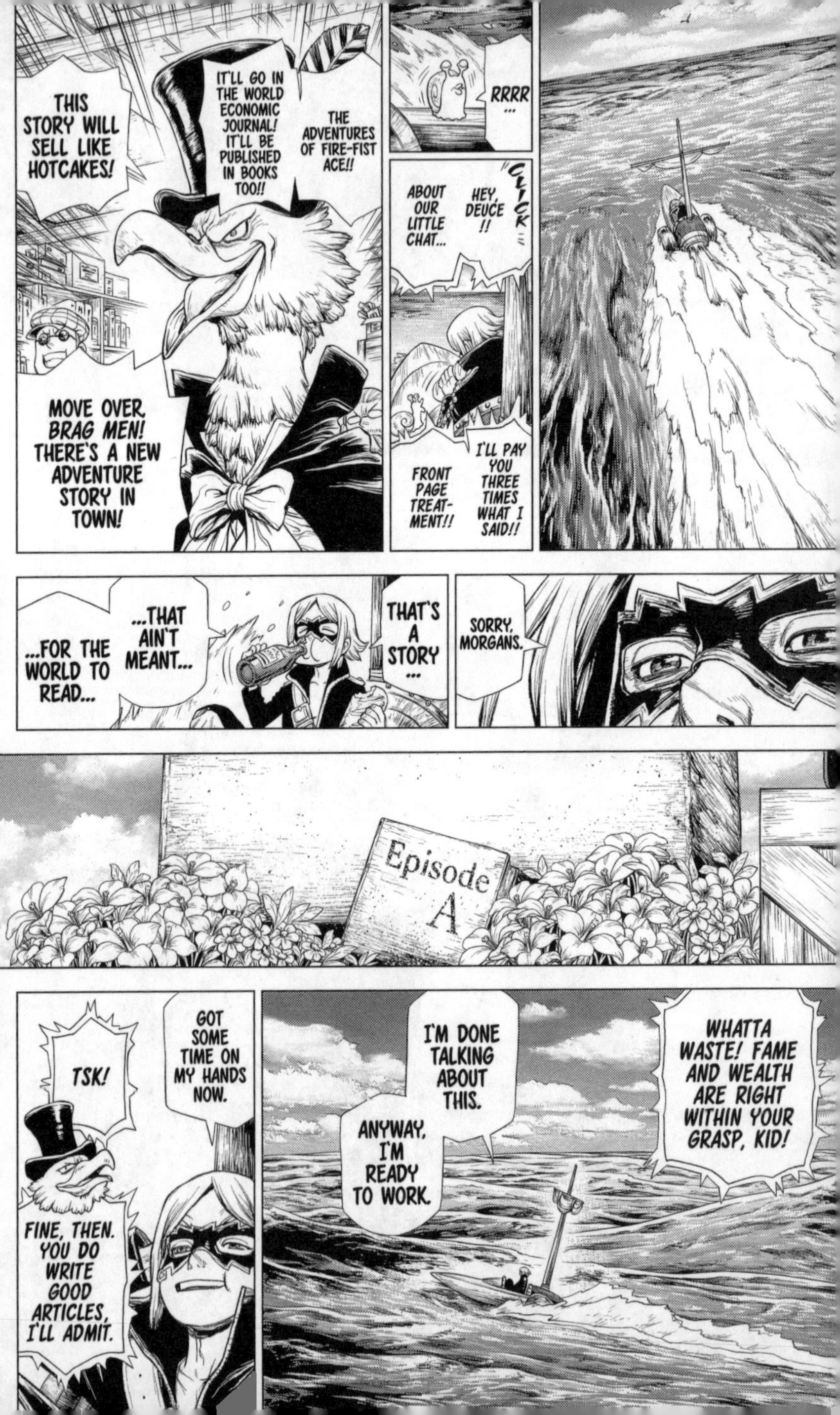
RRRR...
HEY, DEUCE!!
CLICK
ABOUT OUR LITTLE CHAT...
I'LL PAY YOU THREE TIMES WHAT I SAID!!
FRONT PAGE TREATMENT!!
IT'LL GO IN THE WORLD ECONOMIC JOURNAL! IT'LL BE PUBLISHED IN BOOKS TOO!!
THE ADVENTURES OF FIRE-FIST ACE!!
THIS STORY WILL SELL LIKE HOTCAKES!
MOVE OVER, BRAG MEN! THERE'S A NEW ADVENTURE STORY IN TOWN!
SORRY, MORGANS.
THAT'S A STORY...
...THAT AIN'T MEANT...
...FOR THE WORLD TO READ...
Episode A
WHATTA WASTE! FAME AND WEALTH ARE RIGHT WITHIN YOUR GRASP, KID!
I'M DONE TALKING ABOUT THIS.
ANYWAY, I'M READY TO WORK.
GOT SOME TIME ON MY HANDS NOW.
TSK!
FINE, THEN. YOU DO WRITE GOOD ARTICLES, I'LL ADMIT.

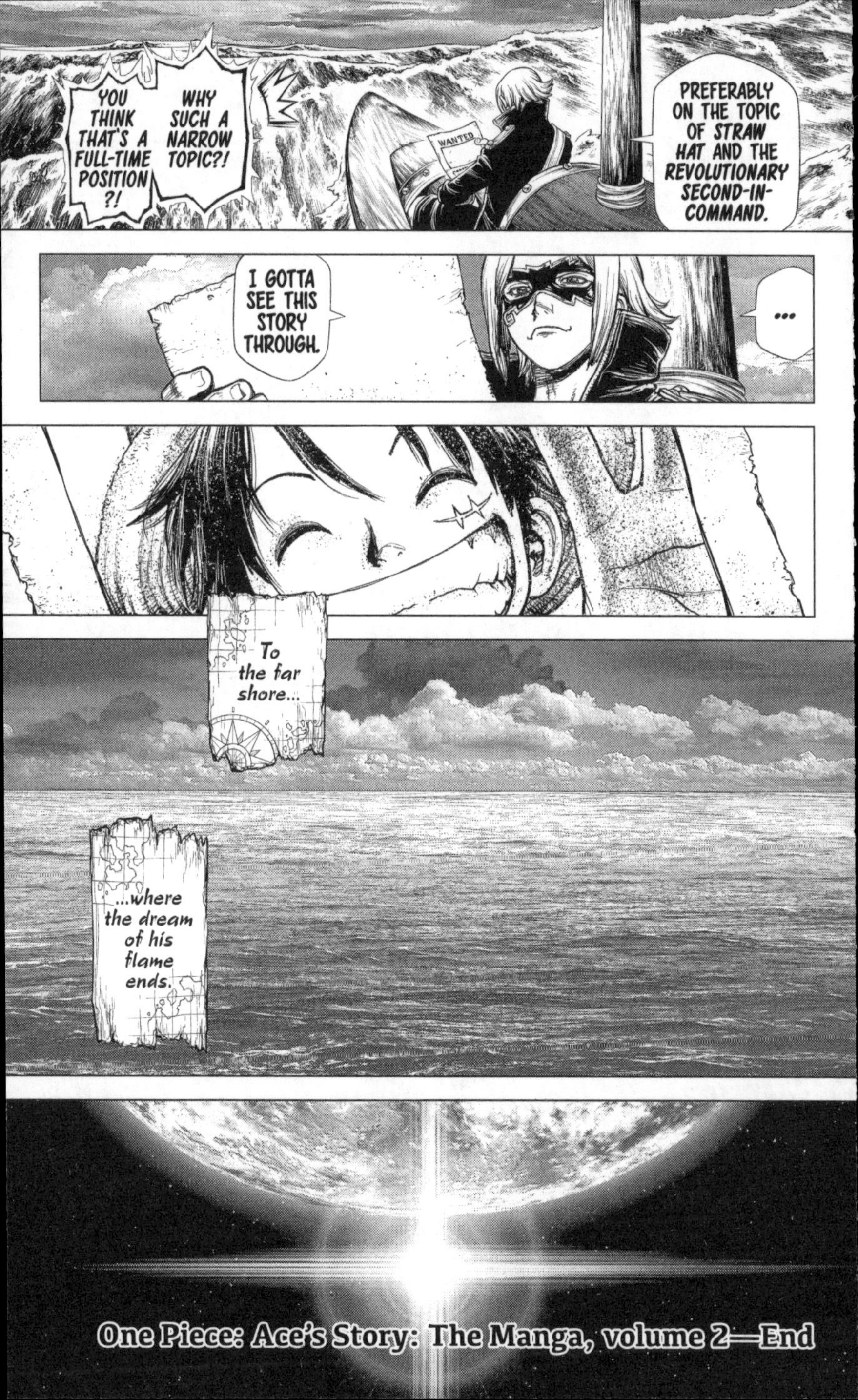
PREFERABLY ON THE TOPIC OF STRAW HAT AND THE REVOLUTIONARY SECOND-IN-COMMAND.
WANTED
WHY SUCH A NARROW TOPIC?!
YOU THINK THAT'S A FULL-TIME POSITION?!
...
I GOTTA SEE THIS STORY THROUGH.
To the far shore...
...where the dream of his flame ends.
One Piece: Ace's Story: The Manga, volume 2—End

Unused page from Ryo Ishiyama's final chapter storyboard

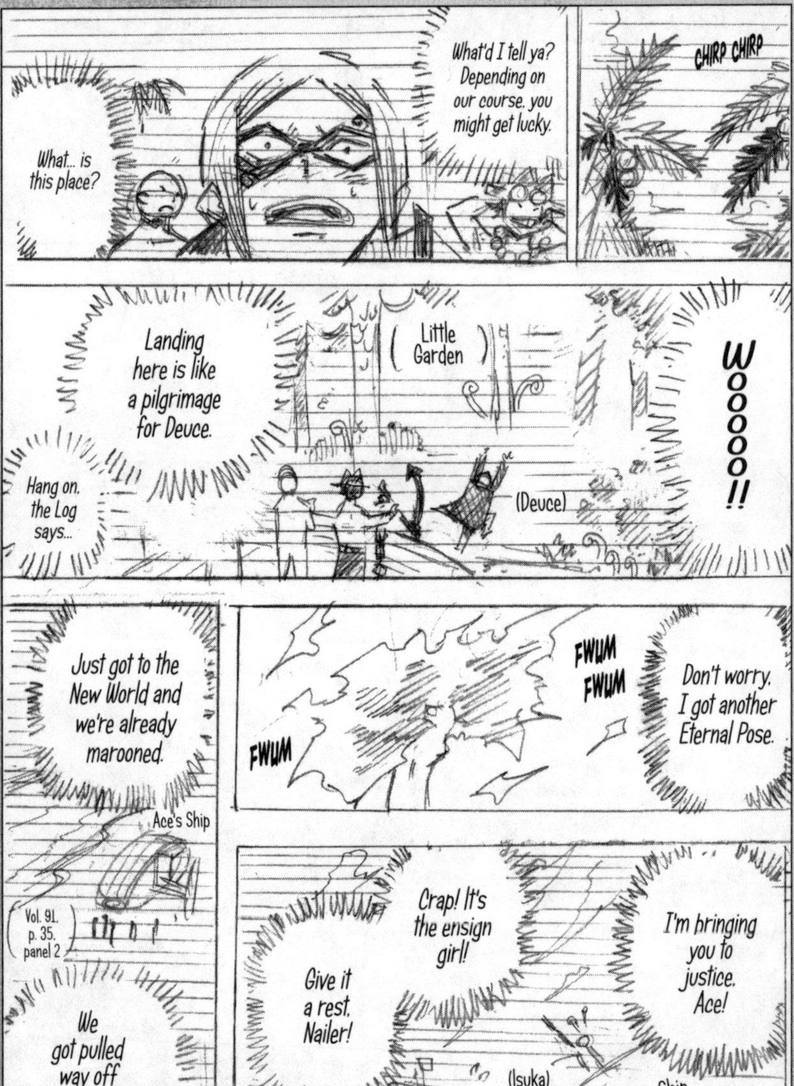

CHIRP CHIRP
What'd I tell ya? Depending on our course, you might get lucky.
What... is this place?
WOOOOOO!!
(Deuce)
(Little Garden)
Landing here is like a pilgrimage for Deuce.
Hang on, the Log says...
Don't worry, I got another Eternal Pose.
FWUM FWUM
FWUM
I'm bringing you to justice, Ace!
Navy Ship
(Isuka)
Crap! It's the ensign girl!
Give it a rest, Nailer!
Just got to the New World and we're already marooned.
Ace's Ship
(Vol. 91, p. 35, panel 2)
We got pulled way off course.

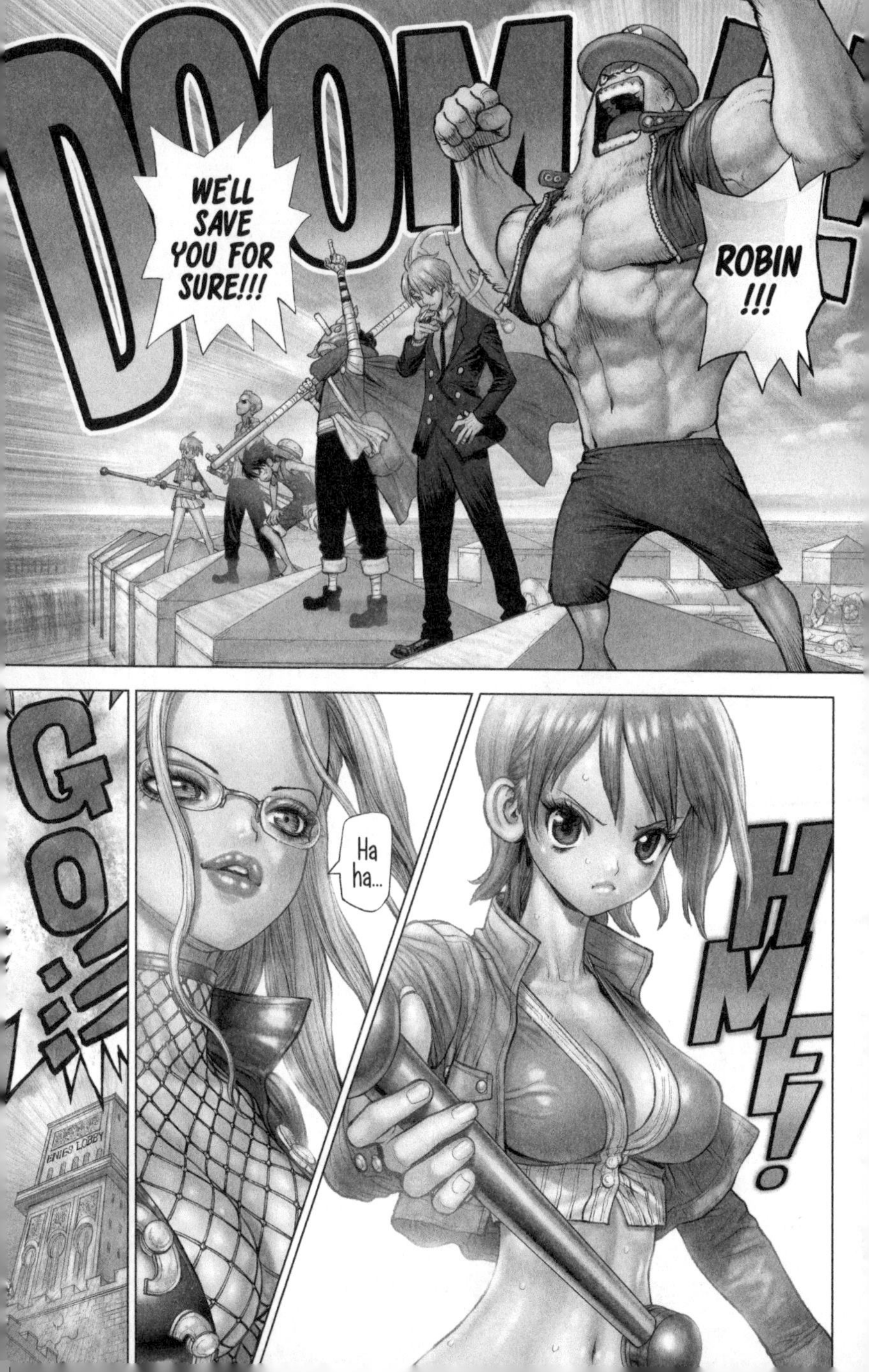
ROBIN!!!
WE'LL SAVE YOU FOR SURE!!!
DOOM
HMF!
Ha ha...
GO

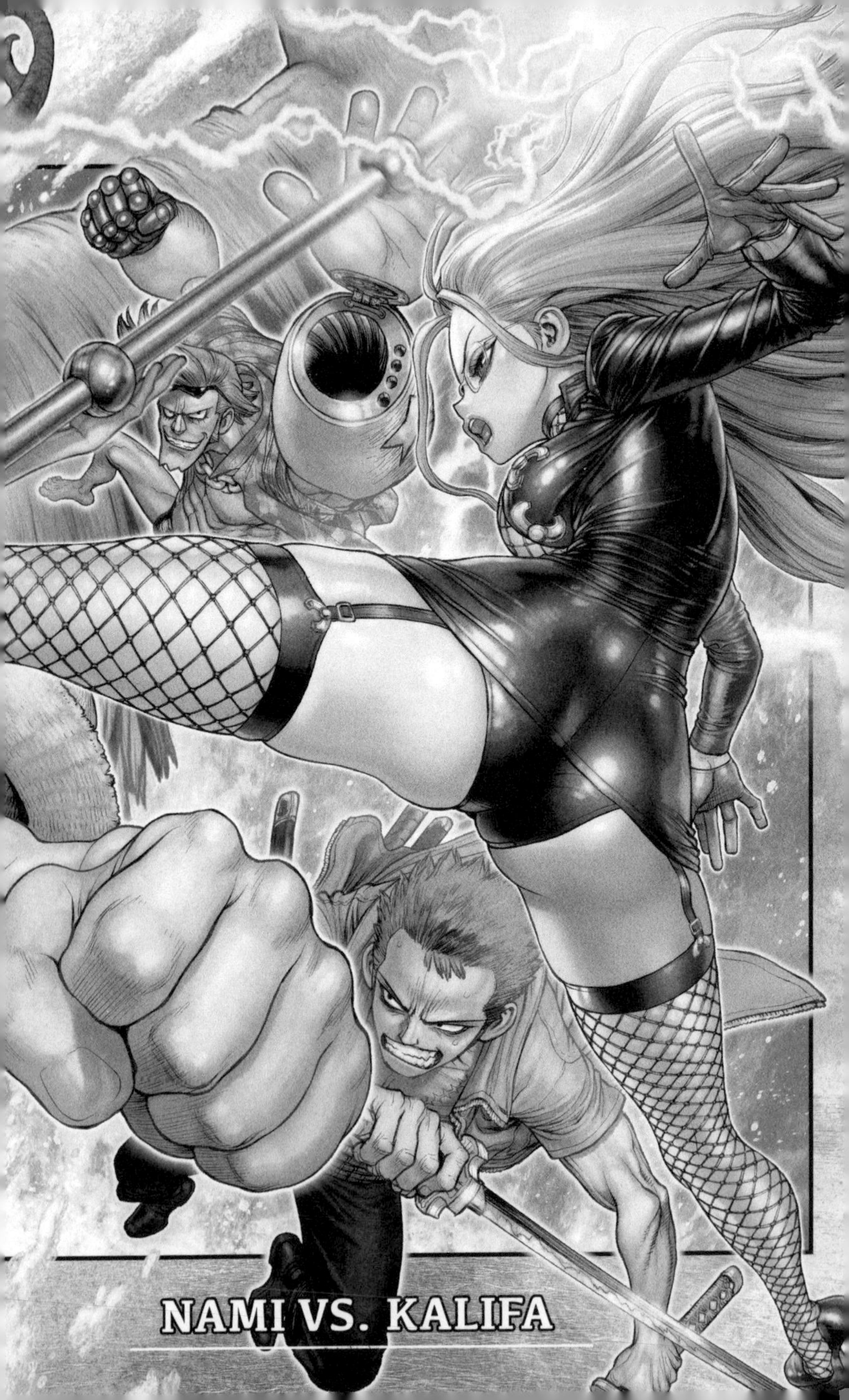
NAMI VS. KALIFA

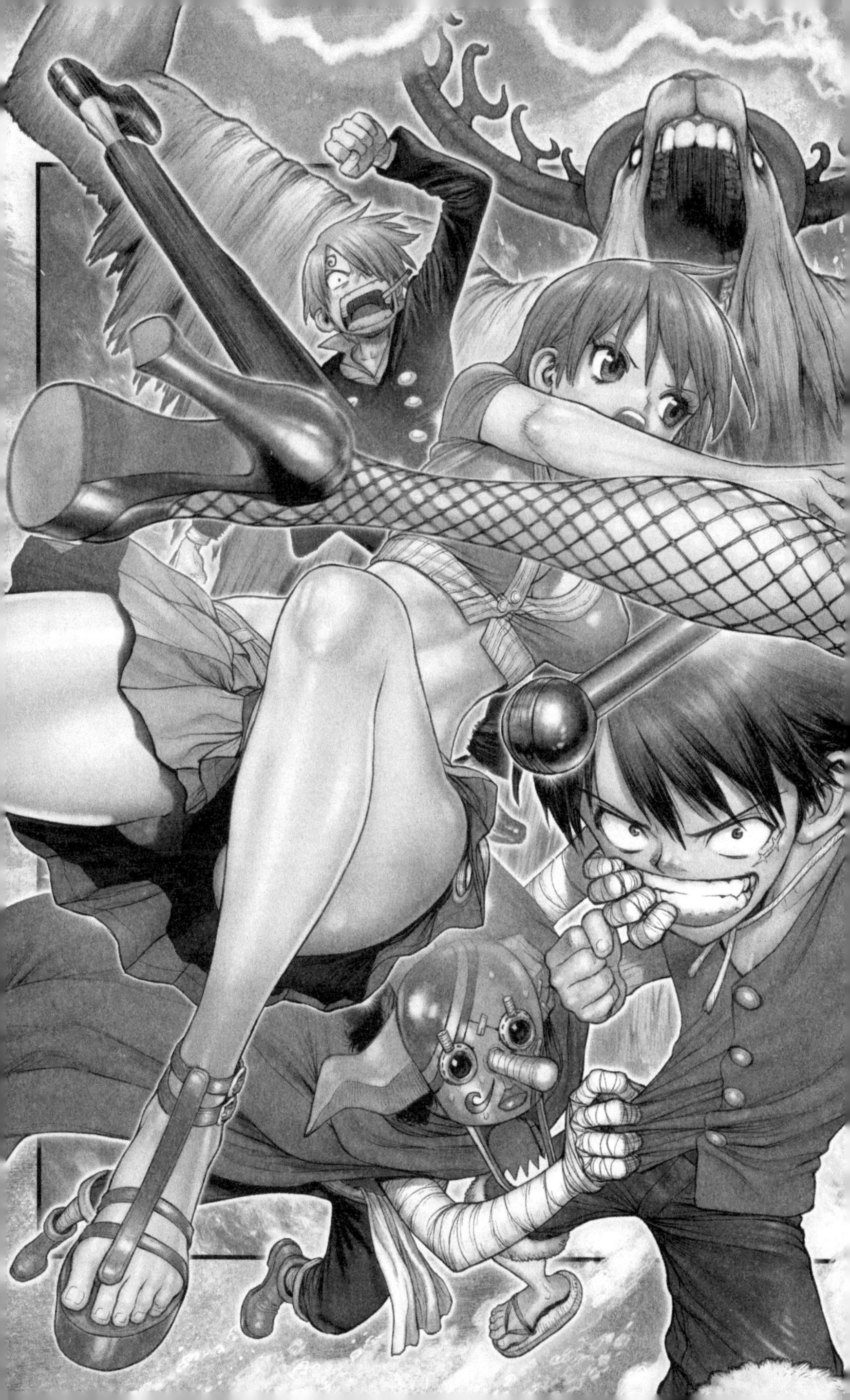

ONE PIECE

Ace's Story

THE MANGA

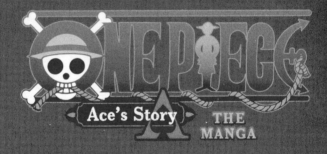

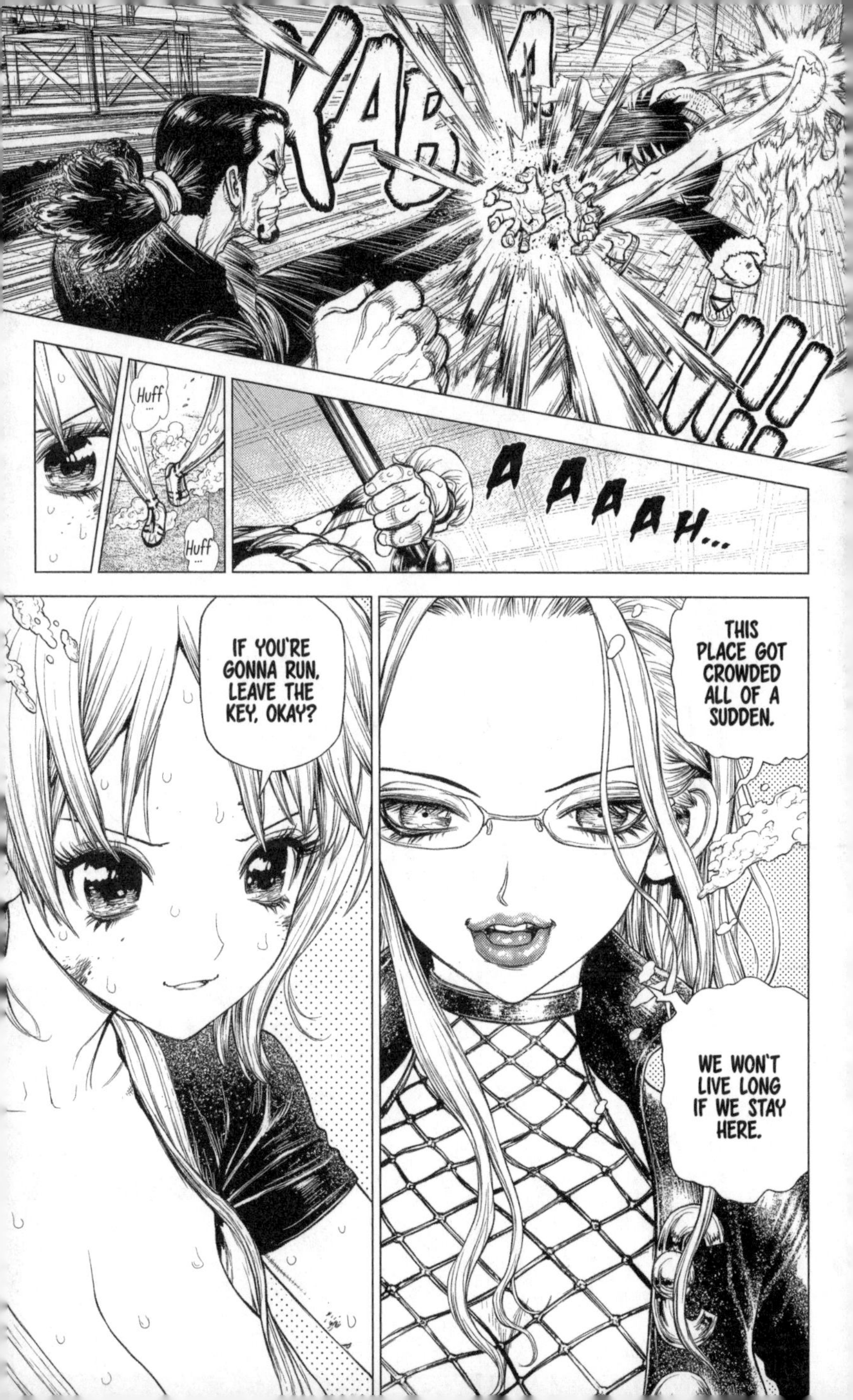
AAAAAH...
Huff...
Huff...
THIS PLACE GOT CROWDED ALL OF A SUDDEN.
WE WON'T LIVE LONG IF WE STAY HERE.
IF YOU'RE GONNA RUN, LEAVE THE KEY, OKAY?

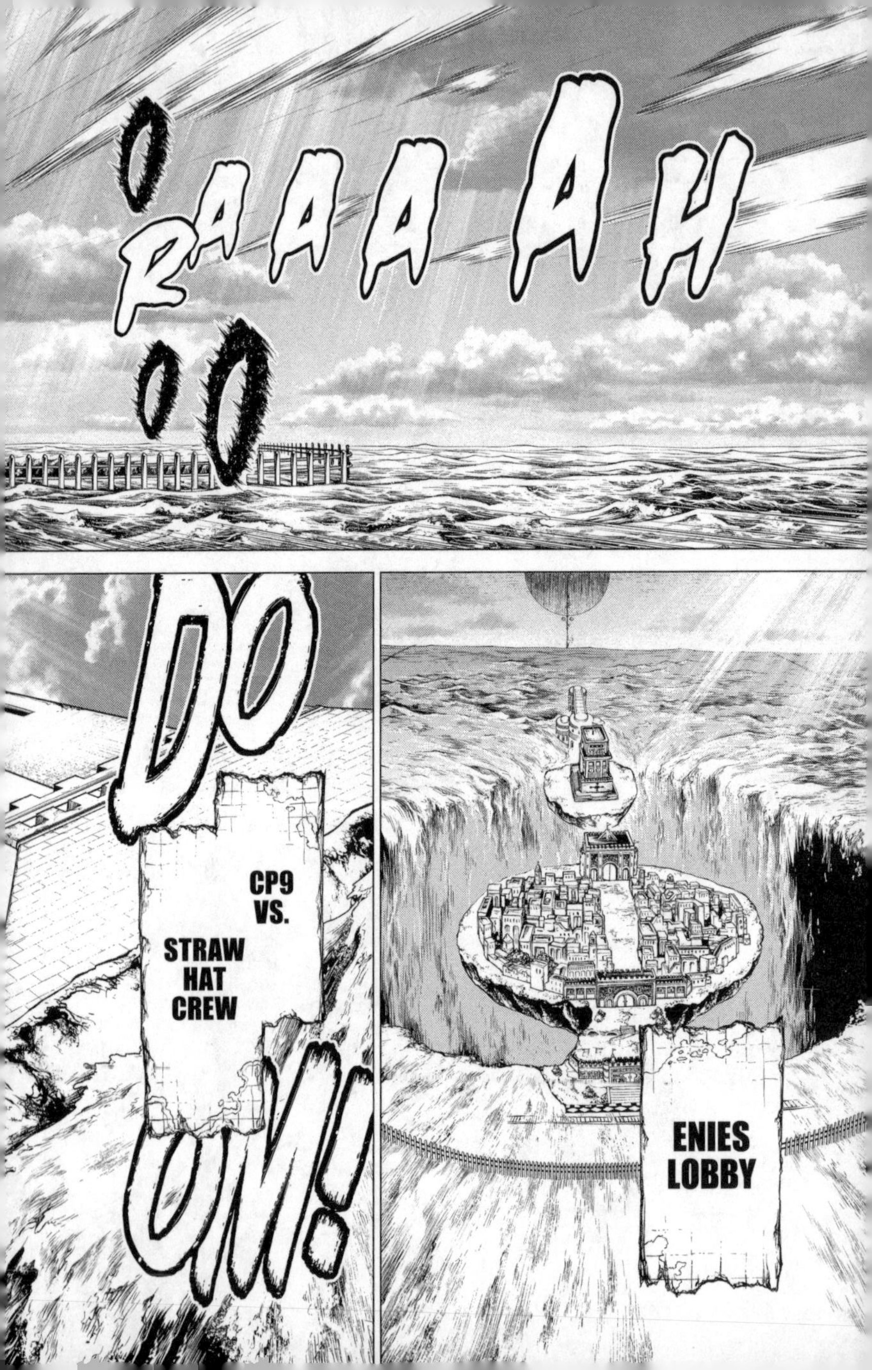

ORAAAAH
OO
ENIES LOBBY
DOON!
CP9 VS. STRAW HAT CREW

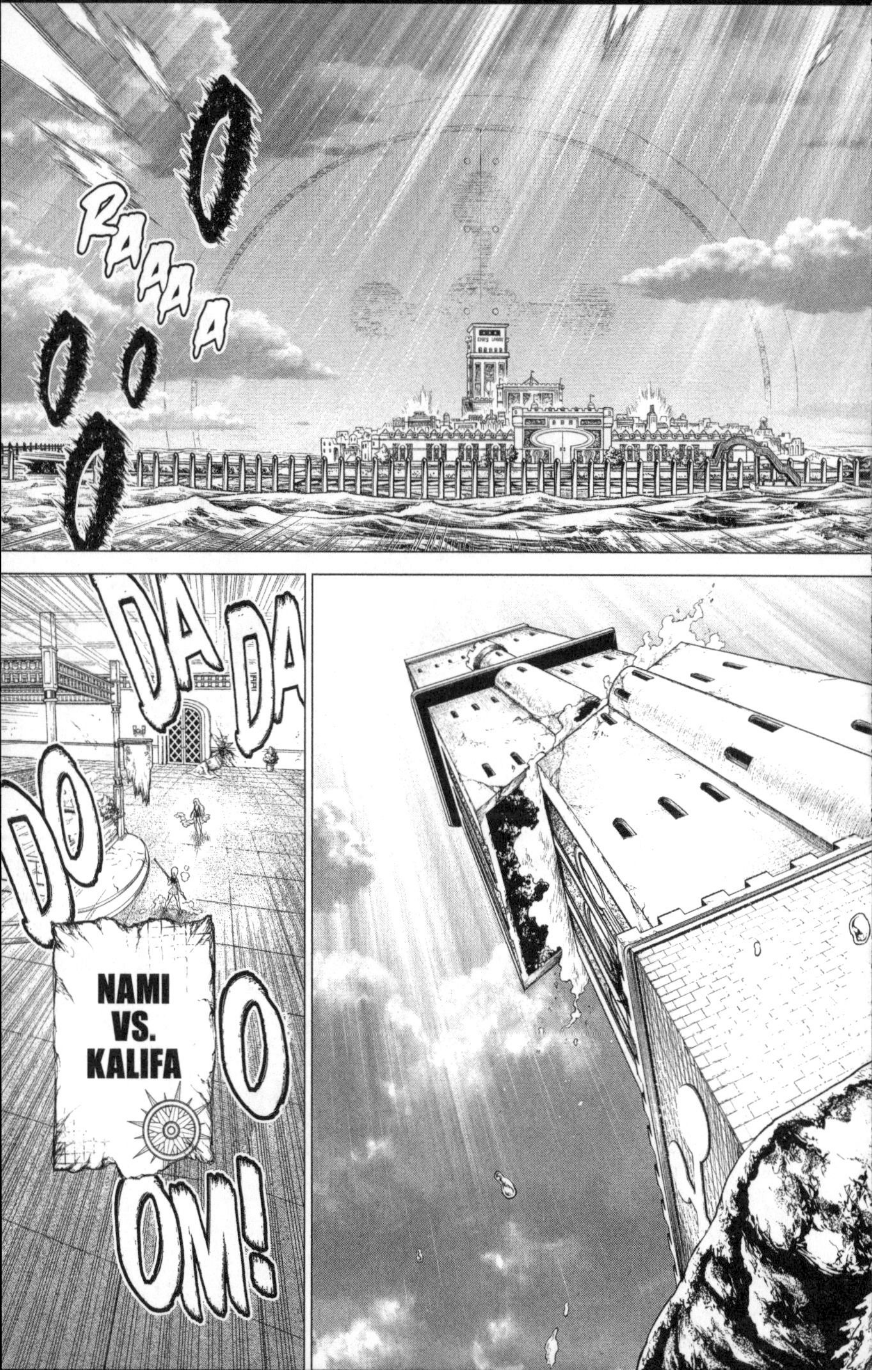
O
RAAAA
OOO
DA DA
DO
NAMI VS. KALIFA
O
OM!

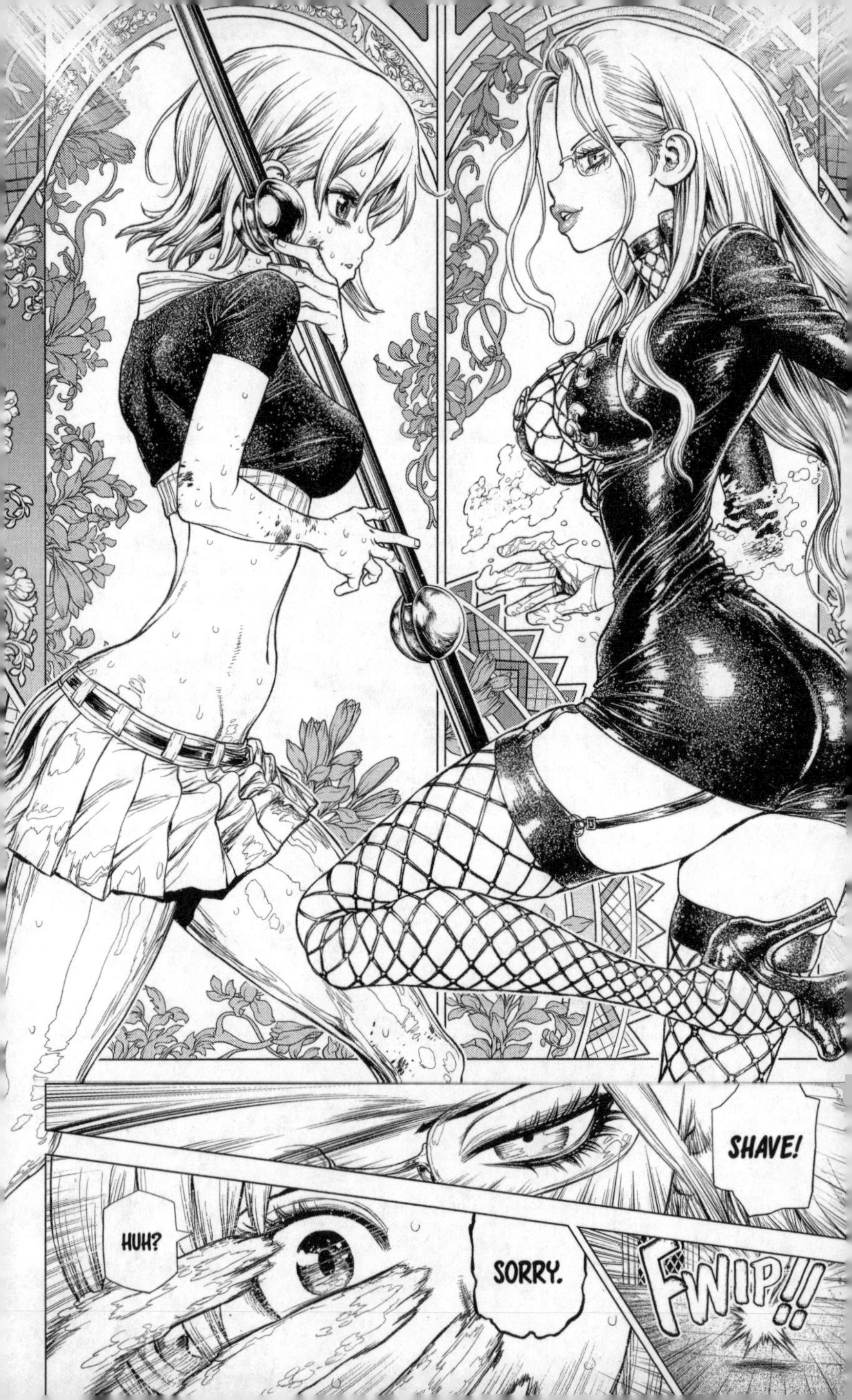
SHAVE!
FWIP!!
SORRY.
HUH?

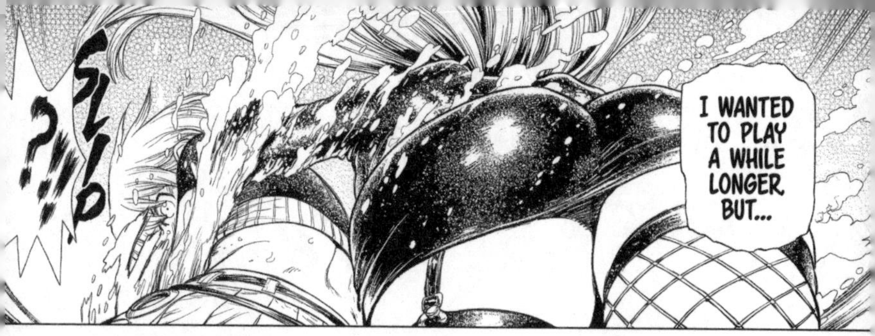
I WANTED TO PLAY A WHILE LONGER, BUT...
SLIP ?!!
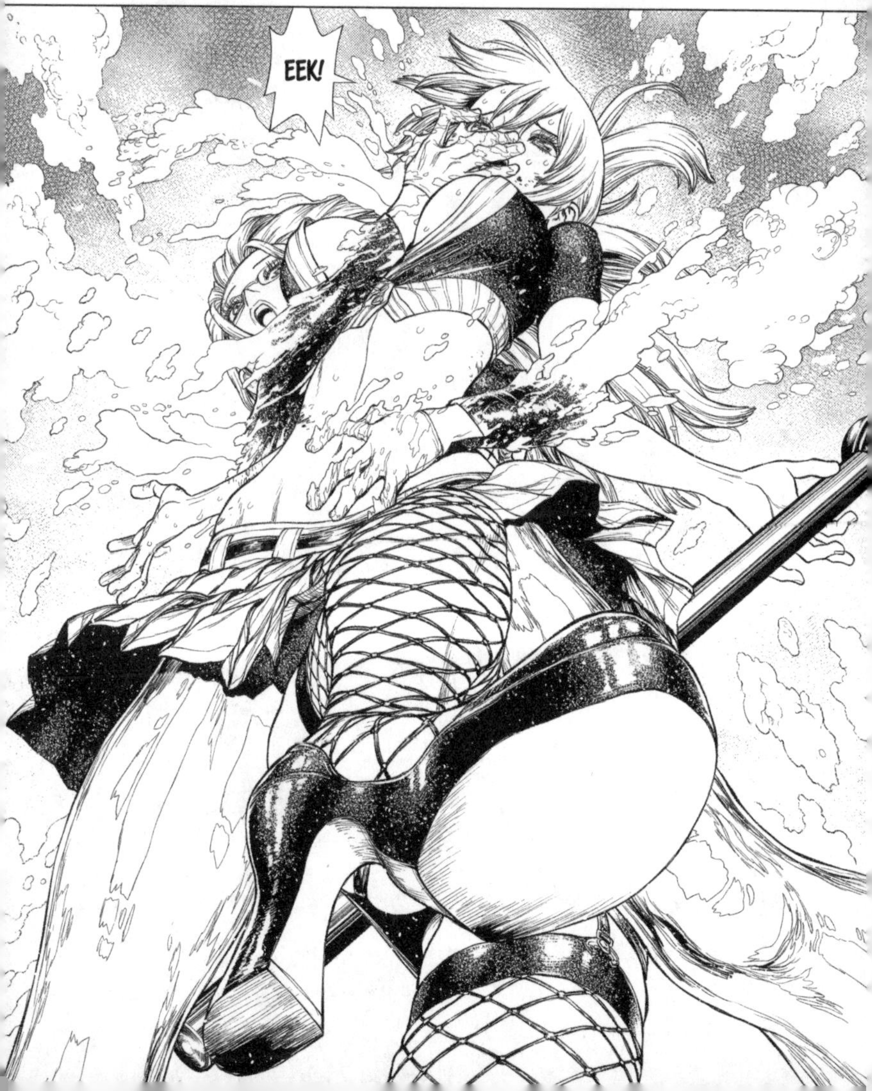
EEK!

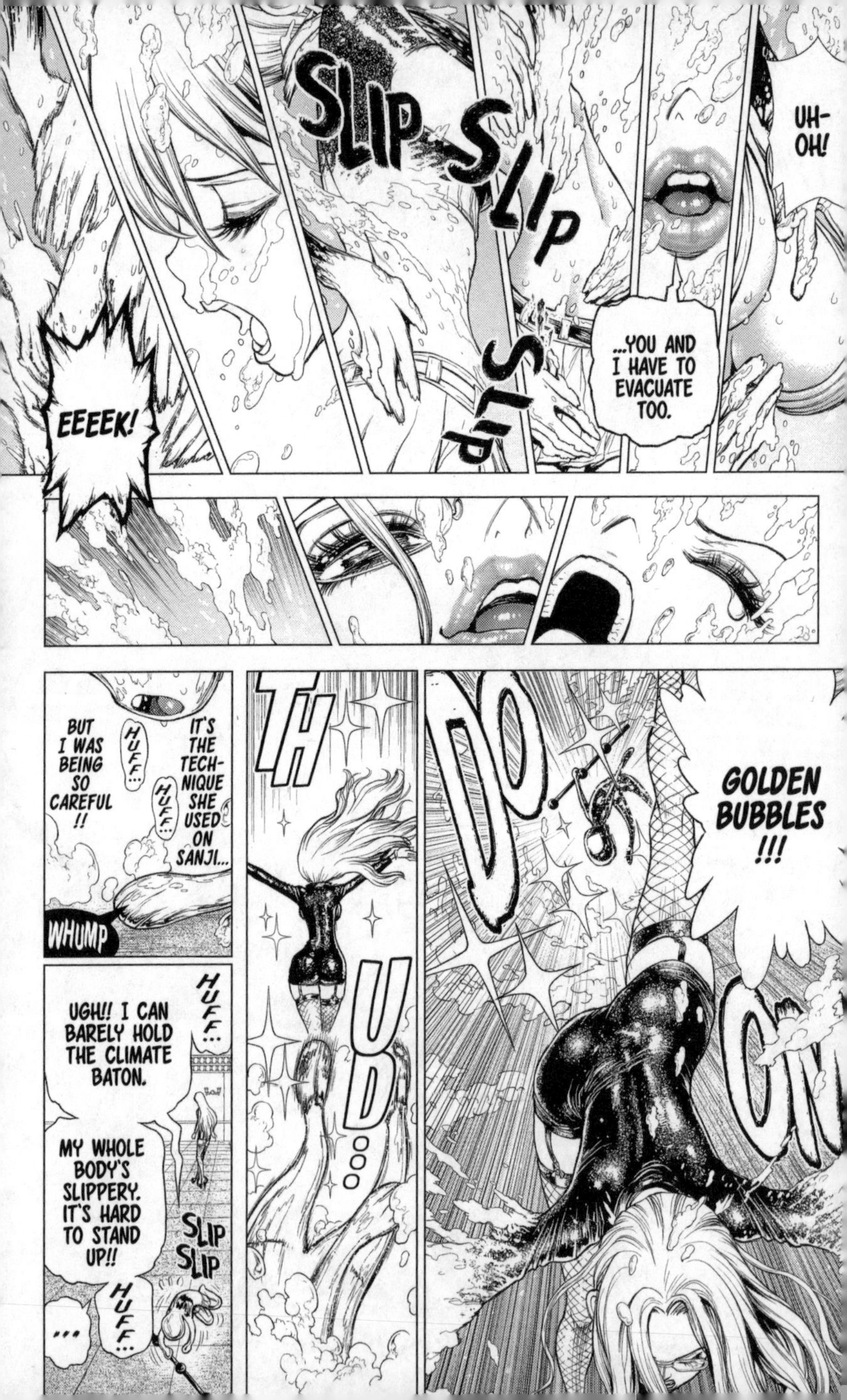
UH-OH!
...YOU AND I HAVE TO EVACUATE TOO.
SLIP SLIP SLIP SLIP
EEEEK!
GOLDEN BUBBLES!!!
DO
ON
THUD...
IT'S THE TECHNIQUE SHE USED ON SANJI...
HUFF... HUFF...
BUT I WAS BEING SO CAREFUL!!
WHUMP
HUFF...
UGH!! I CAN BARELY HOLD THE CLIMATE BATON.
MY WHOLE BODY'S SLIPPERY. IT'S HARD TO STAND UP!!
SLIP SLIP
HUFF...
...

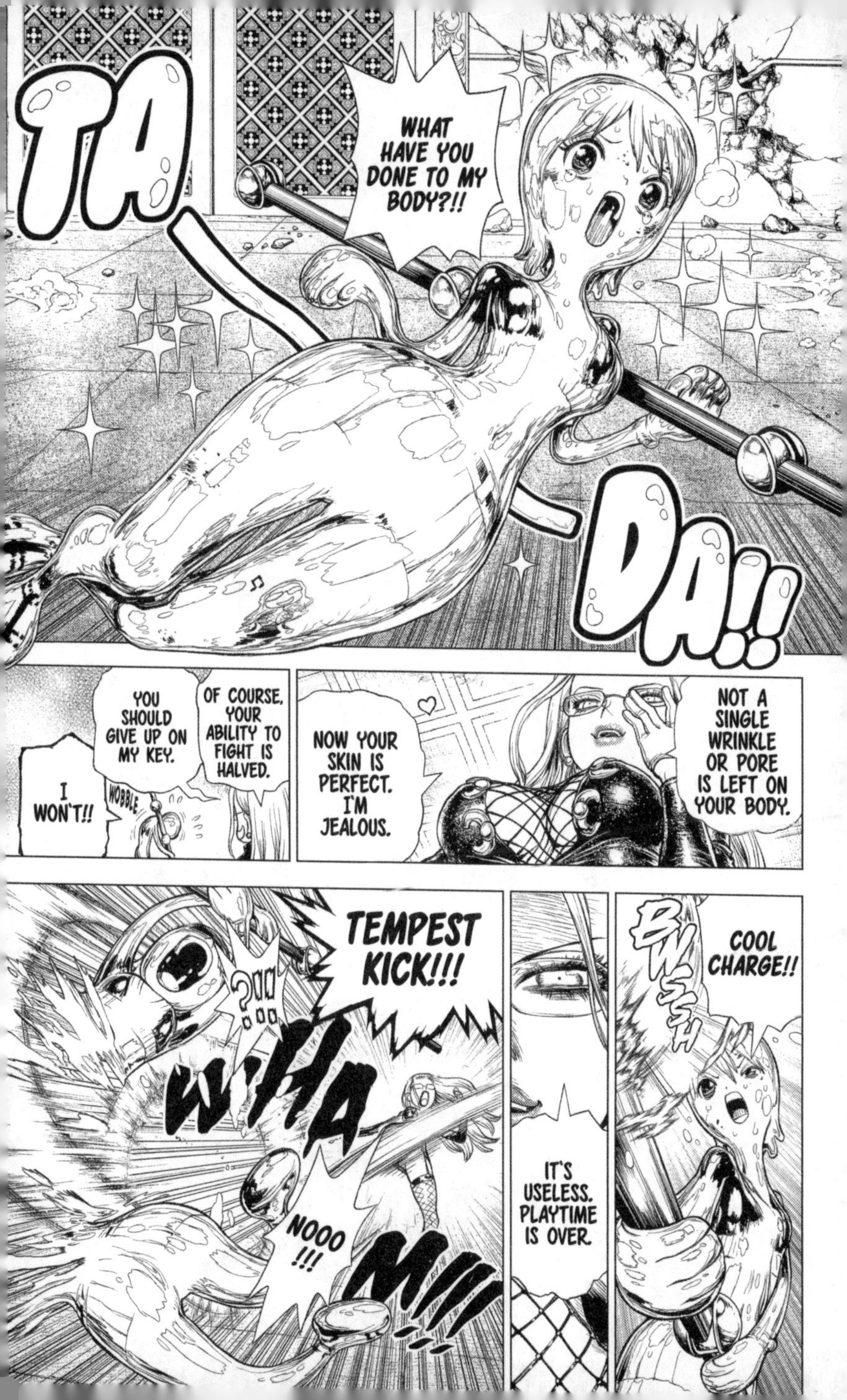
WHAT HAVE YOU DONE TO MY BODY?!!
TA DA!!
NOT A SINGLE WRINKLE OR PORE IS LEFT ON YOUR BODY.
NOW YOUR SKIN IS PERFECT. I'M JEALOUS.
OF COURSE, YOUR ABILITY TO FIGHT IS HALVED.
YOU SHOULD GIVE UP ON MY KEY.
WOBBLE
I WON'T!!
BWSSH
COOL CHARGE!!
IT'S USELESS. PLAYTIME IS OVER.
TEMPEST KICK!!!
?!!
WHAM!!
NOOO !!!

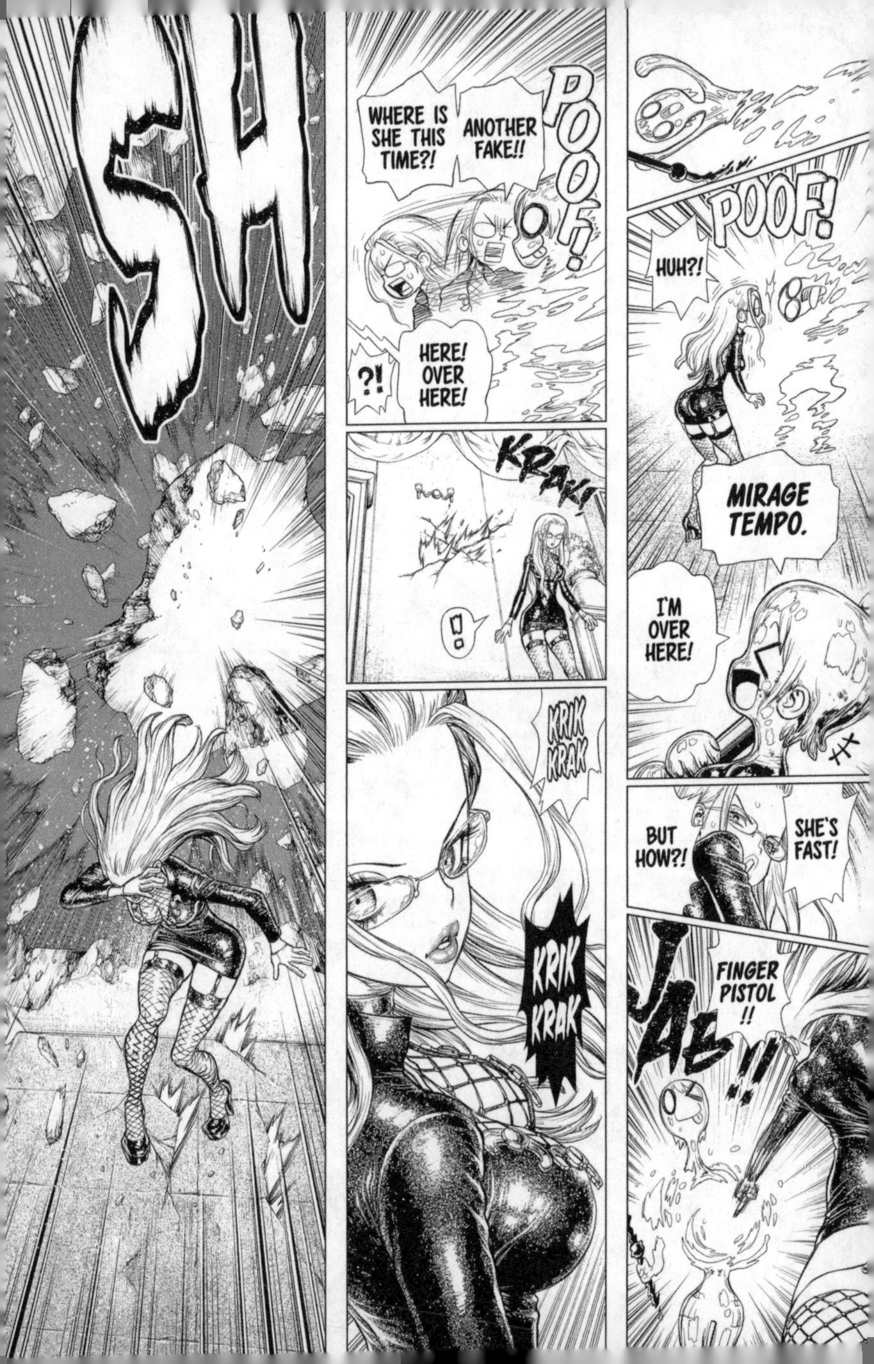

POOF!
HUH?!
MIRAGE TEMPO.
I'M OVER HERE!
SHE'S FAST!
BUT HOW?!
FINGER PISTOL!!
JAB!!
POOF!
ANOTHER FAKE!!
WHERE IS SHE THIS TIME?!
HERE! OVER HERE!
?!
KRAK!
!
KRIK KRAK
KRIK KRAK
SH

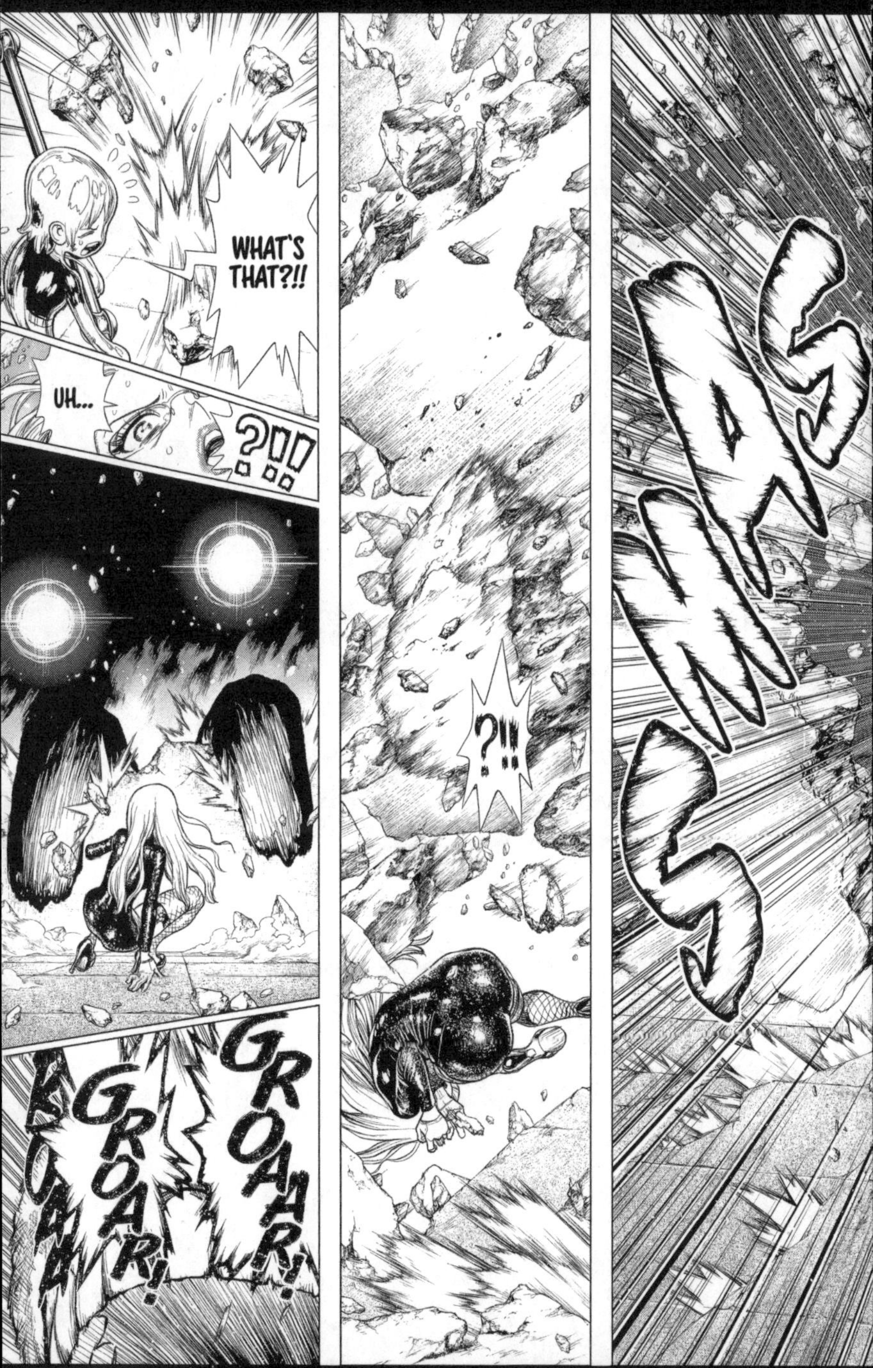
SMASH
?!!
WHAT'S THAT?!!
UH...
?!!
GROAAR!
GROAR!

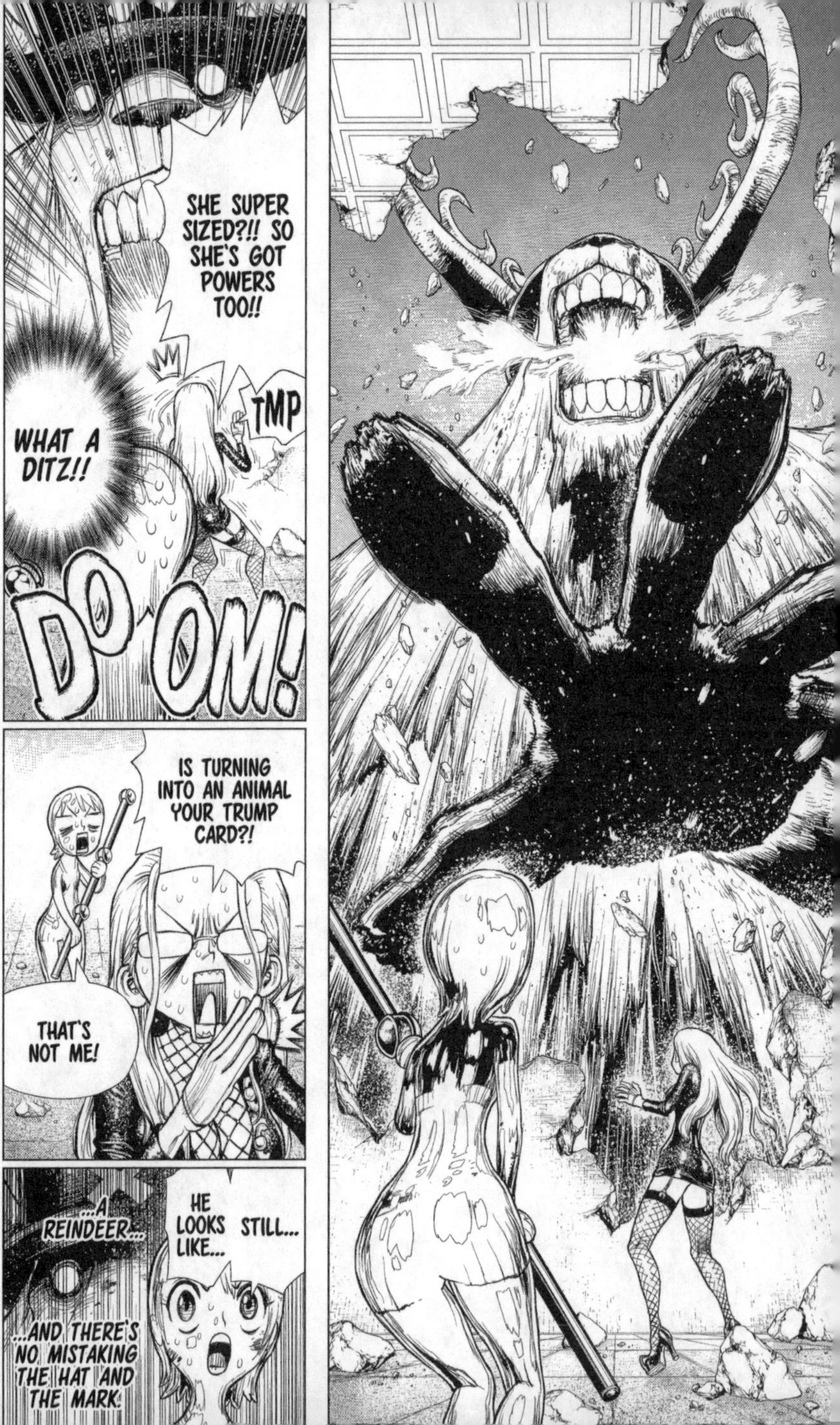
SHE SUPER SIZED?!! SO SHE'S GOT POWERS TOO!!
TMP
WHAT A DITZ!!
DOOM!
IS TURNING INTO AN ANIMAL YOUR TRUMP CARD?!
THAT'S NOT ME!
HE LOOKS STILL... LIKE...
...A REINDEER...
...AND THERE'S NO MISTAKING THE HAT AND THE MARK.

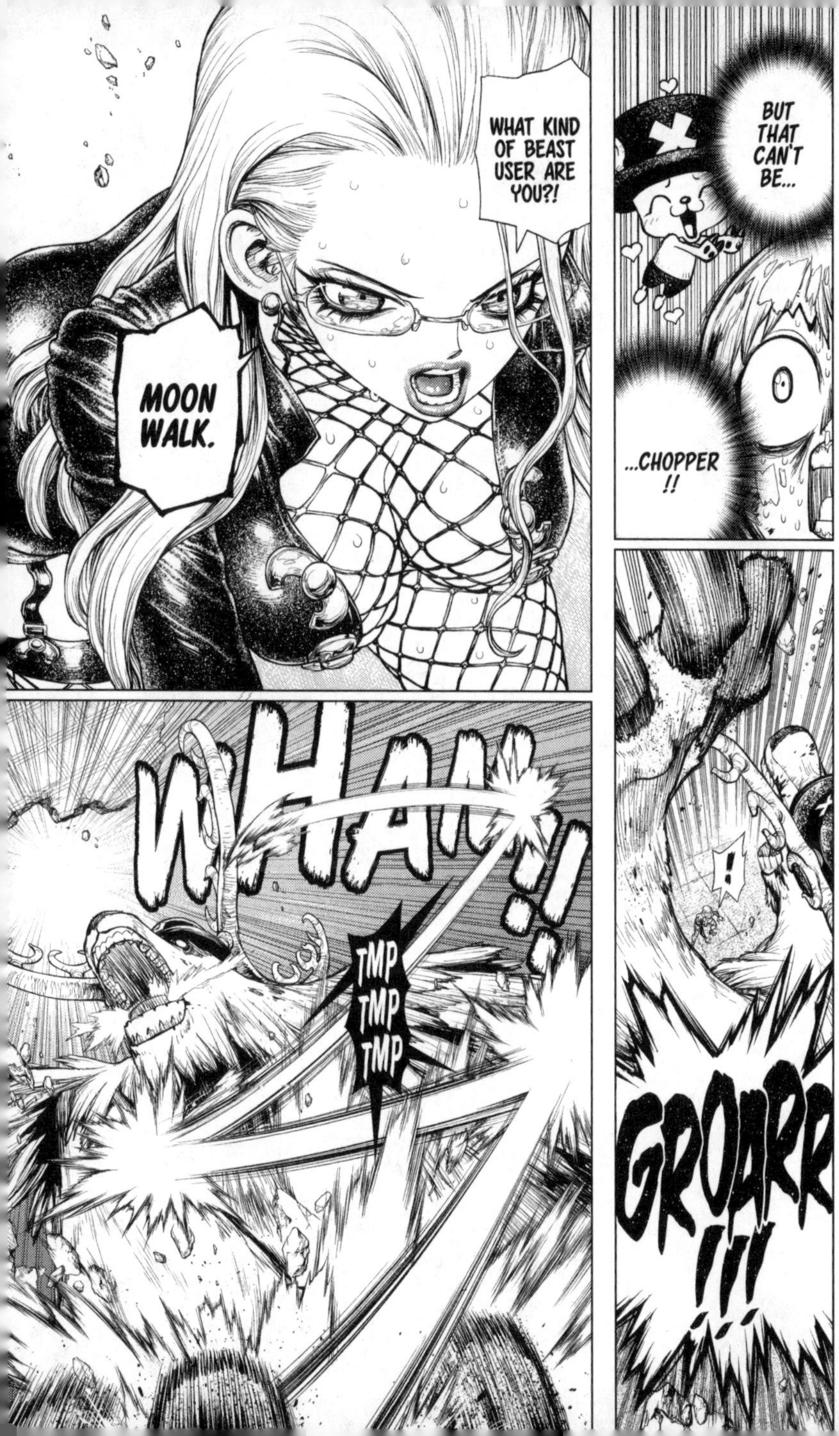
BUT THAT CAN'T BE...
...CHOPPER!!
WHAT KIND OF BEAST USER ARE YOU?!
MOON WALK.
!
GROARR!!!
WHAM!!
TMP TMP TMP

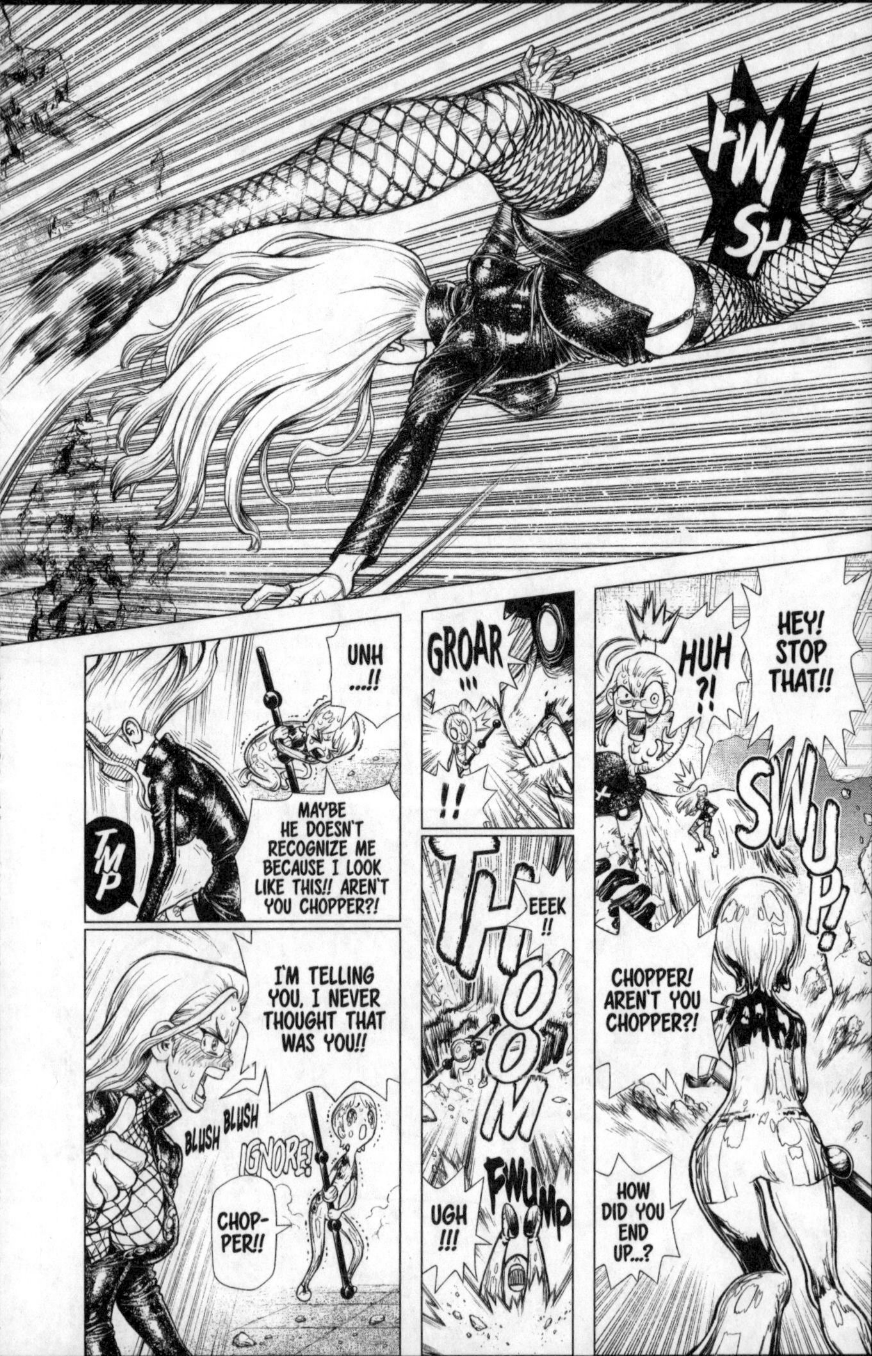
FWISH
HEY! STOP THAT!!
HUH ?!
SNUP!
CHOPPER! AREN'T YOU CHOPPER?!
HOW DID YOU END UP...?
GROAR !!!
!!
THOOM
EEEK !!
FWUMP
UGH !!!
UNH ...!!
MAYBE HE DOESN'T RECOGNIZE ME BECAUSE I LOOK LIKE THIS!! AREN'T YOU CHOPPER?!
TMP
I'M TELLING YOU, I NEVER THOUGHT THAT WAS YOU!!
BLUSH BLUSH
IGNORE!
CHOP-PER!!

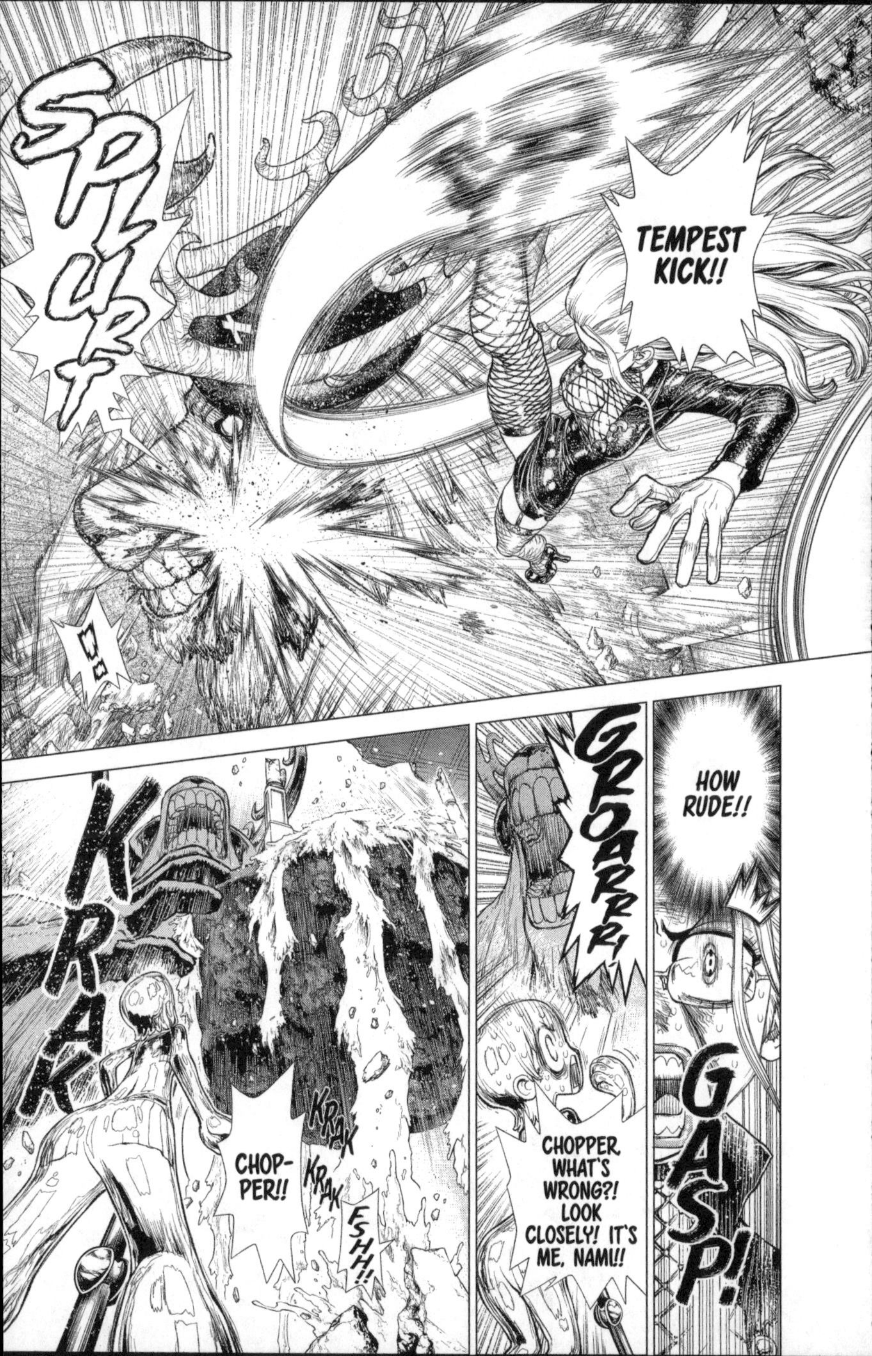
TEMPEST KICK!!
SPLURT
HOW RUDE!!
GASP!
GROARRR!
CHOPPER, WHAT'S WRONG?! LOOK CLOSELY! IT'S ME, NAMI!!
KRAK
CHOP-PER!!
KRAK
KRAK
FSHH!!

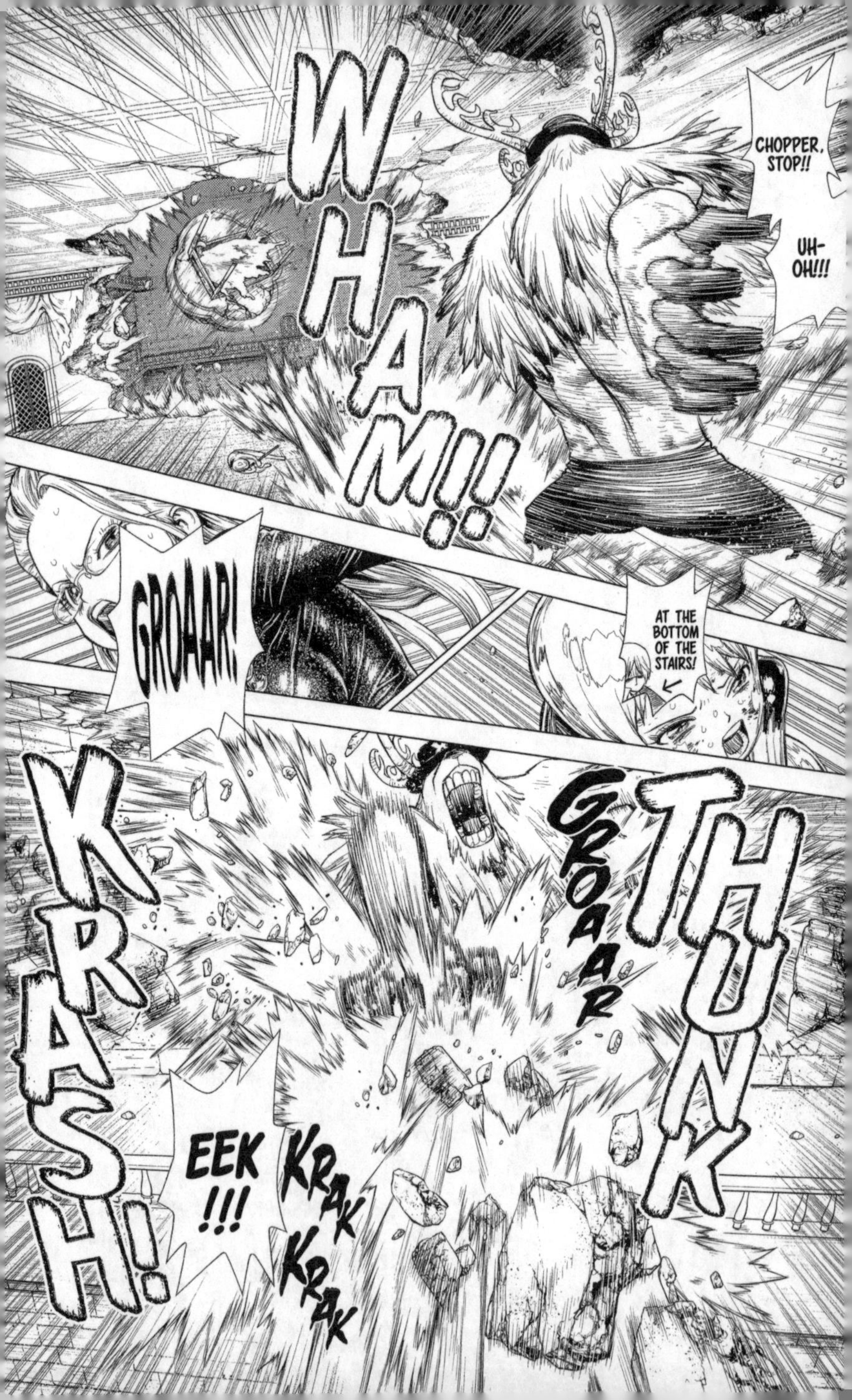
CHOPPER, STOP!!
UH-OH!!!
WHAM!!
AT THE BOTTOM OF THE STAIRS!
GROAAR!
THUNK
GROAAR
KRAK KRAK
EEK!!!
KRASH!

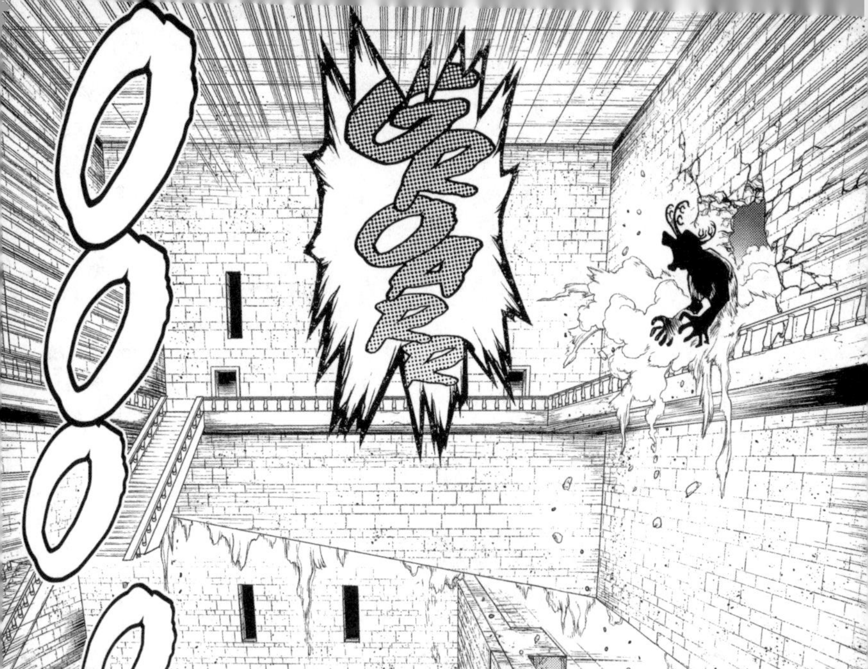
GROARR
OOOOOOOO
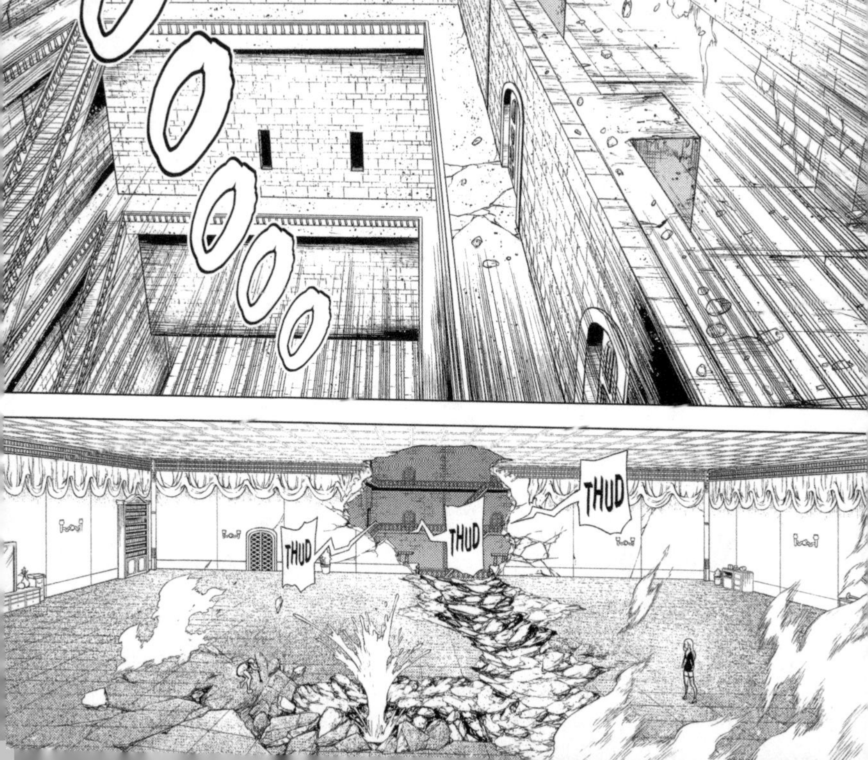
THUD
THUD
THUD

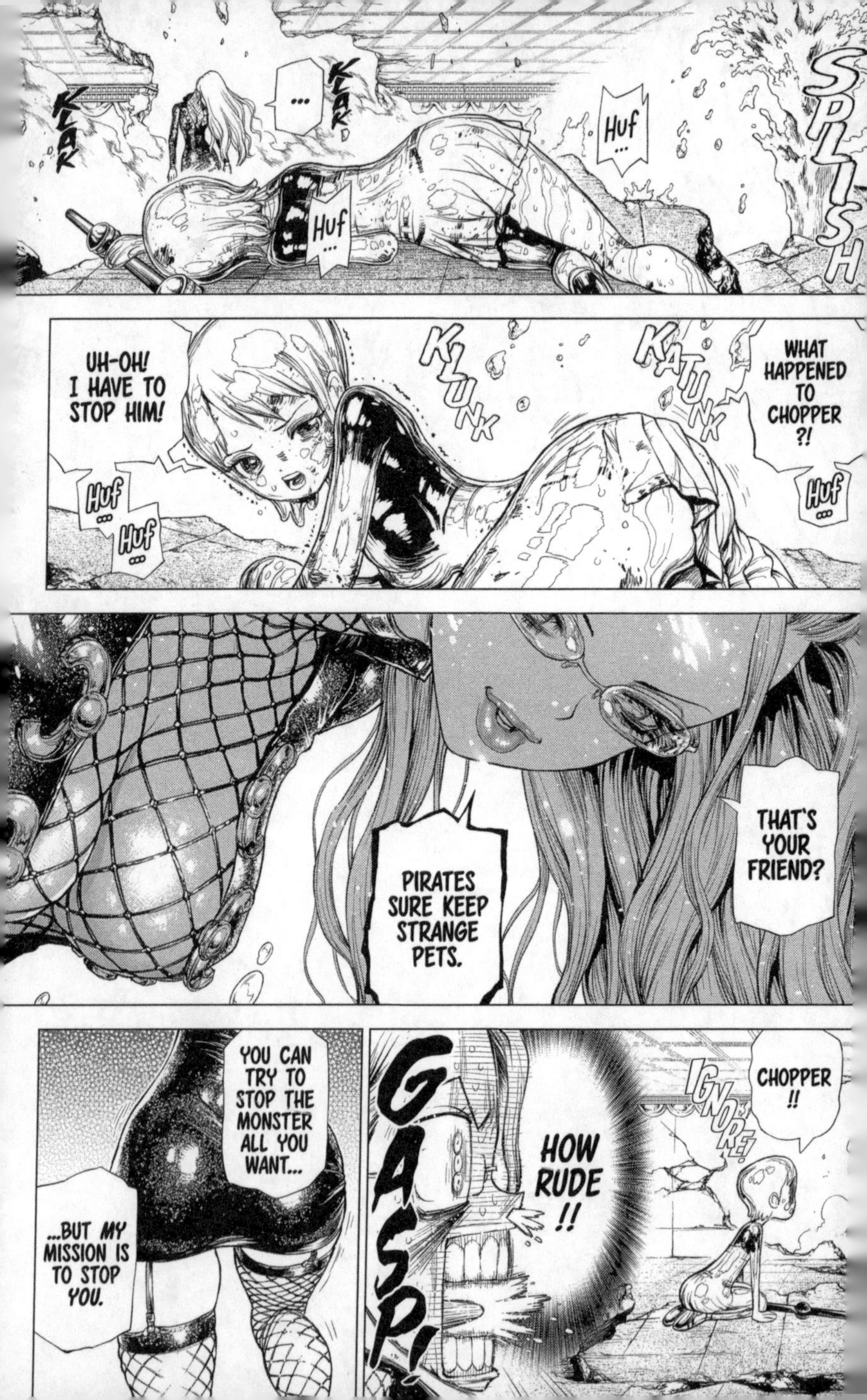
SPLISH
Huf...
KLAK
...
KLAK
Huf...
WHAT HAPPENED TO CHOPPER?!
Huf...
KATUNK
KLUNK
UH-OH! I HAVE TO STOP HIM!
Huf...
Huf...
THAT'S YOUR FRIEND?
PIRATES SURE KEEP STRANGE PETS.
CHOPPER!!
IGNORE!
HOW RUDE!!
GASP!
YOU CAN TRY TO STOP THE MONSTER ALL YOU WANT...
...BUT MY MISSION IS TO STOP YOU.

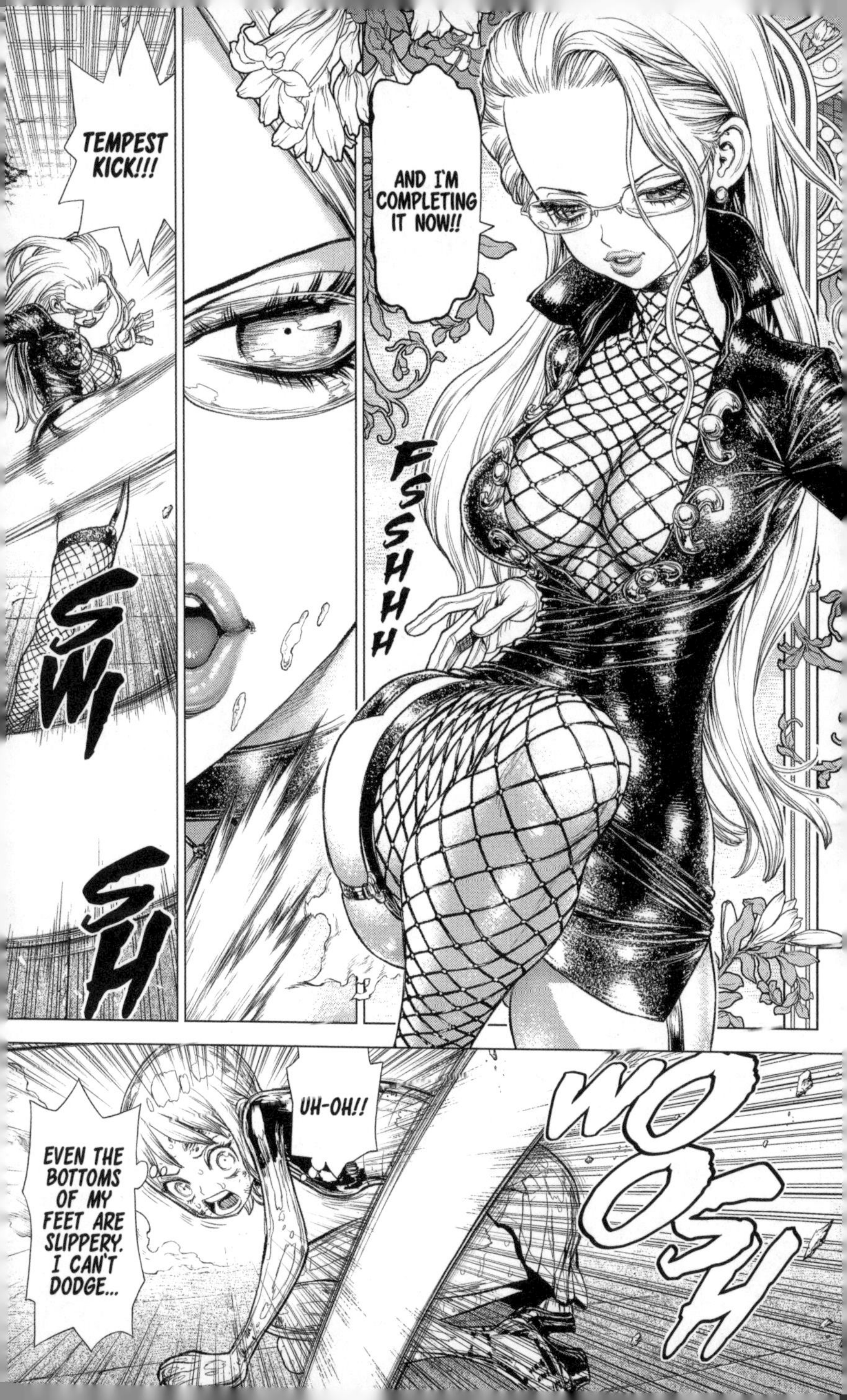
AND I'M COMPLETING IT NOW!!
FSSHHHH
TEMPEST KICK!!!
SWISH
WOOSH
UH-OH!!
EVEN THE BOTTOMS OF MY FEET ARE SLIPPERY. I CAN'T DODGE...

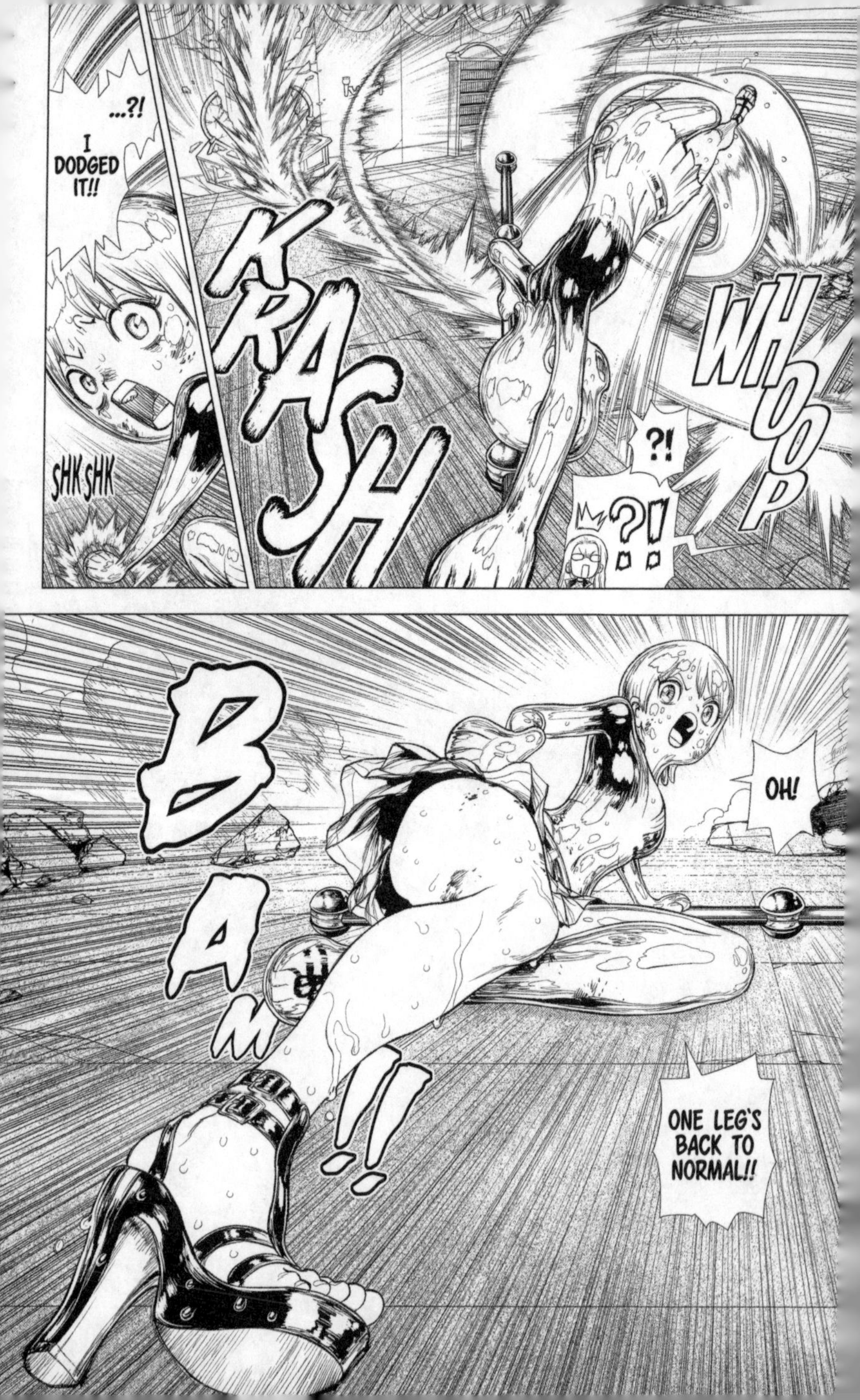
WHOOP
?!
?!!
KRASH
...?!
I DODGED IT!!
SHK SHK
OH!
ONE LEG'S BACK TO NORMAL!!
BAM!!

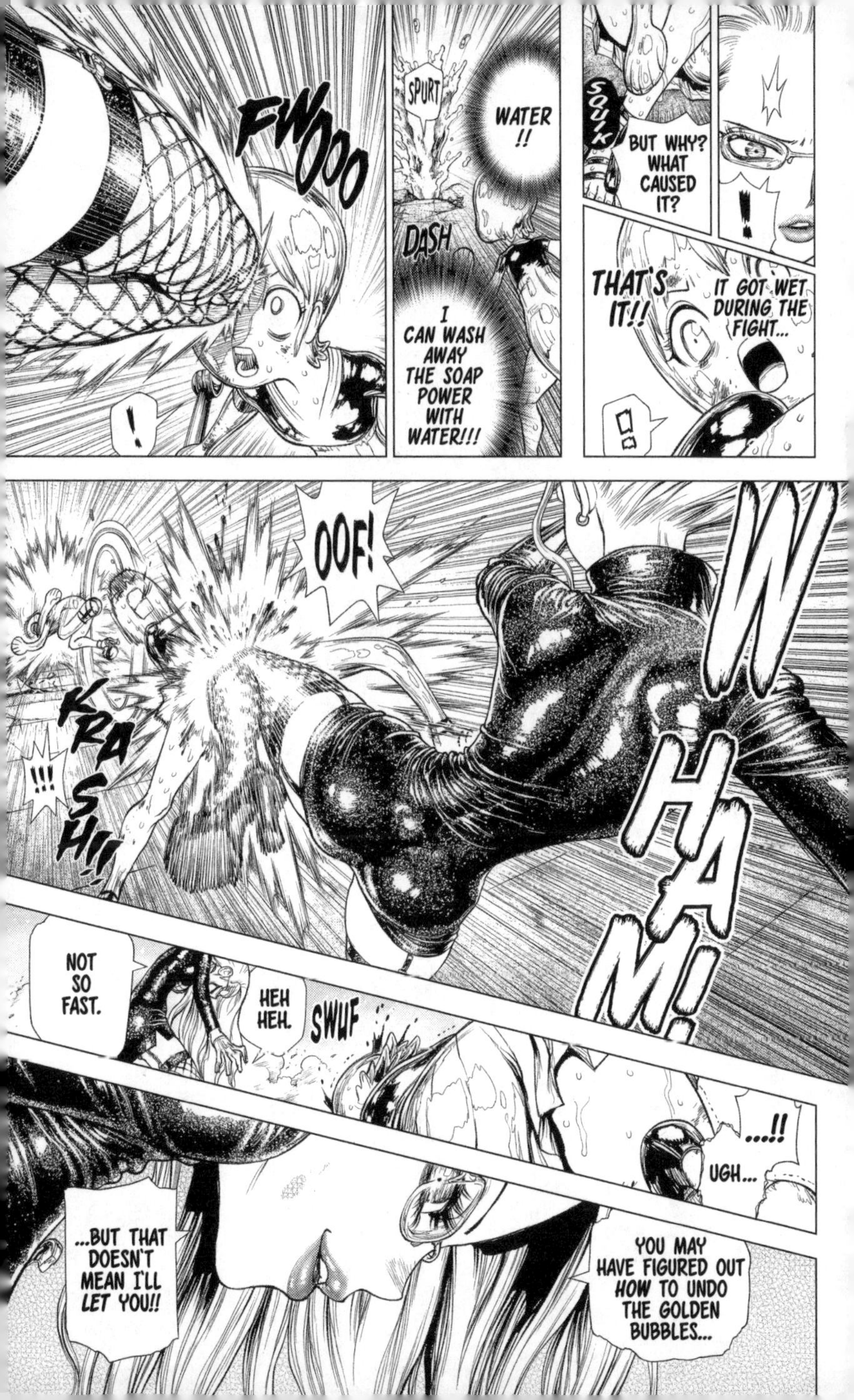
SQUIK
BUT WHY? WHAT CAUSED IT?
!
IT GOT WET DURING THE FIGHT...
THAT'S IT!!
SPURT
WATER!!
I CAN WASH AWAY THE SOAP POWER WITH WATER!!!
DASH
FWOOOO
!
WHAM!
OOF!
KRASH!!
!!!
SWUF
HEH HEH.
NOT SO FAST.
...!!
UGH...
YOU MAY HAVE FIGURED OUT HOW TO UNDO THE GOLDEN BUBBLES...
...BUT THAT DOESN'T MEAN I'LL LET YOU!!

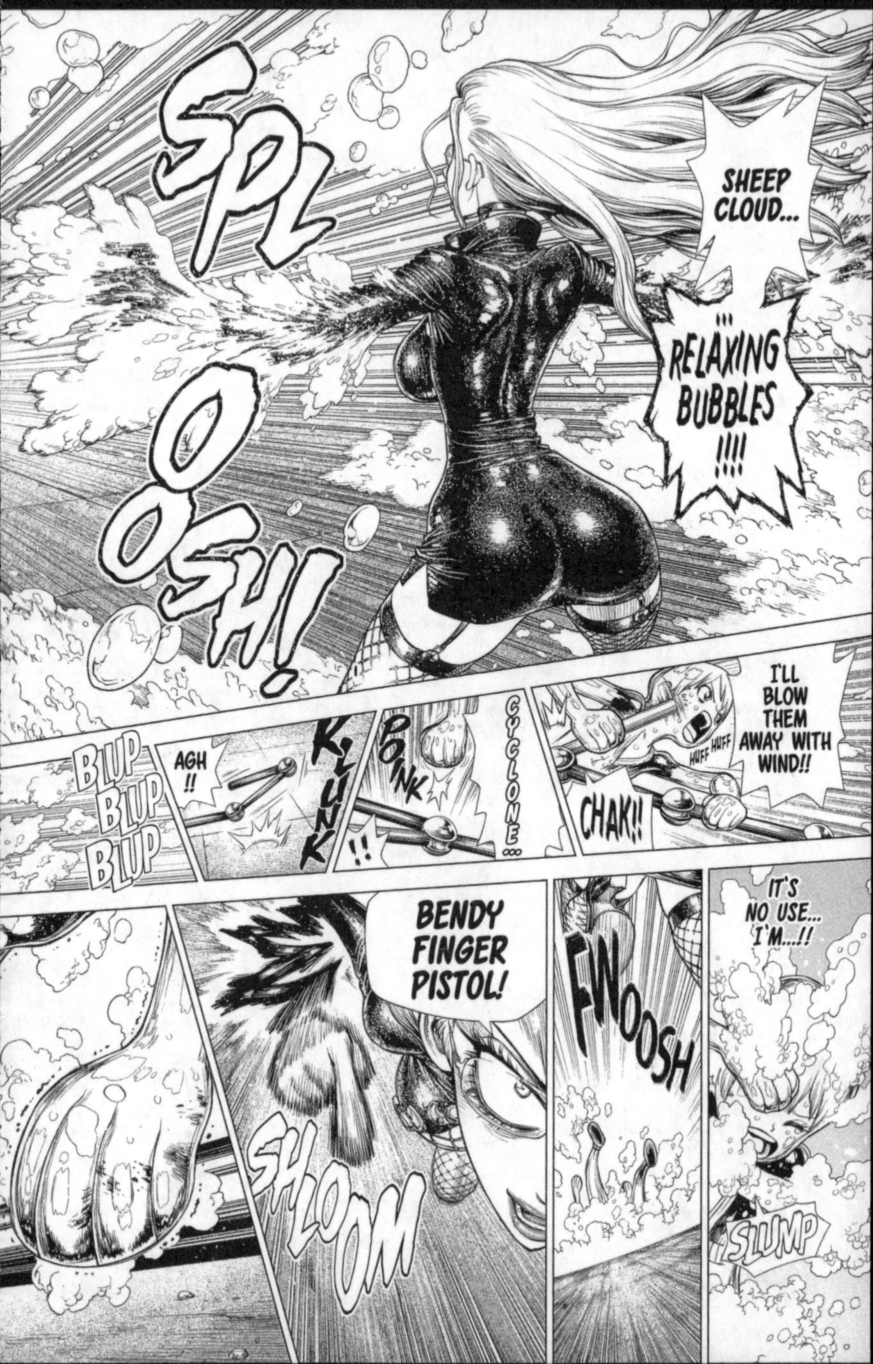
SHEEP CLOUD...
...RELAXING BUBBLES!!!!
SPLOOSH!
I'LL BLOW THEM AWAY WITH WIND!!
HUFF HUFF
CHAK!!
CYCLONE...
BOINK
!!
KLUNK
AGH!!
BLUP BLUP BLUP
IT'S NO USE... I'M...!!
SLUMP
FWOOSH
BENDY FINGER PISTOL!
SHLOOM

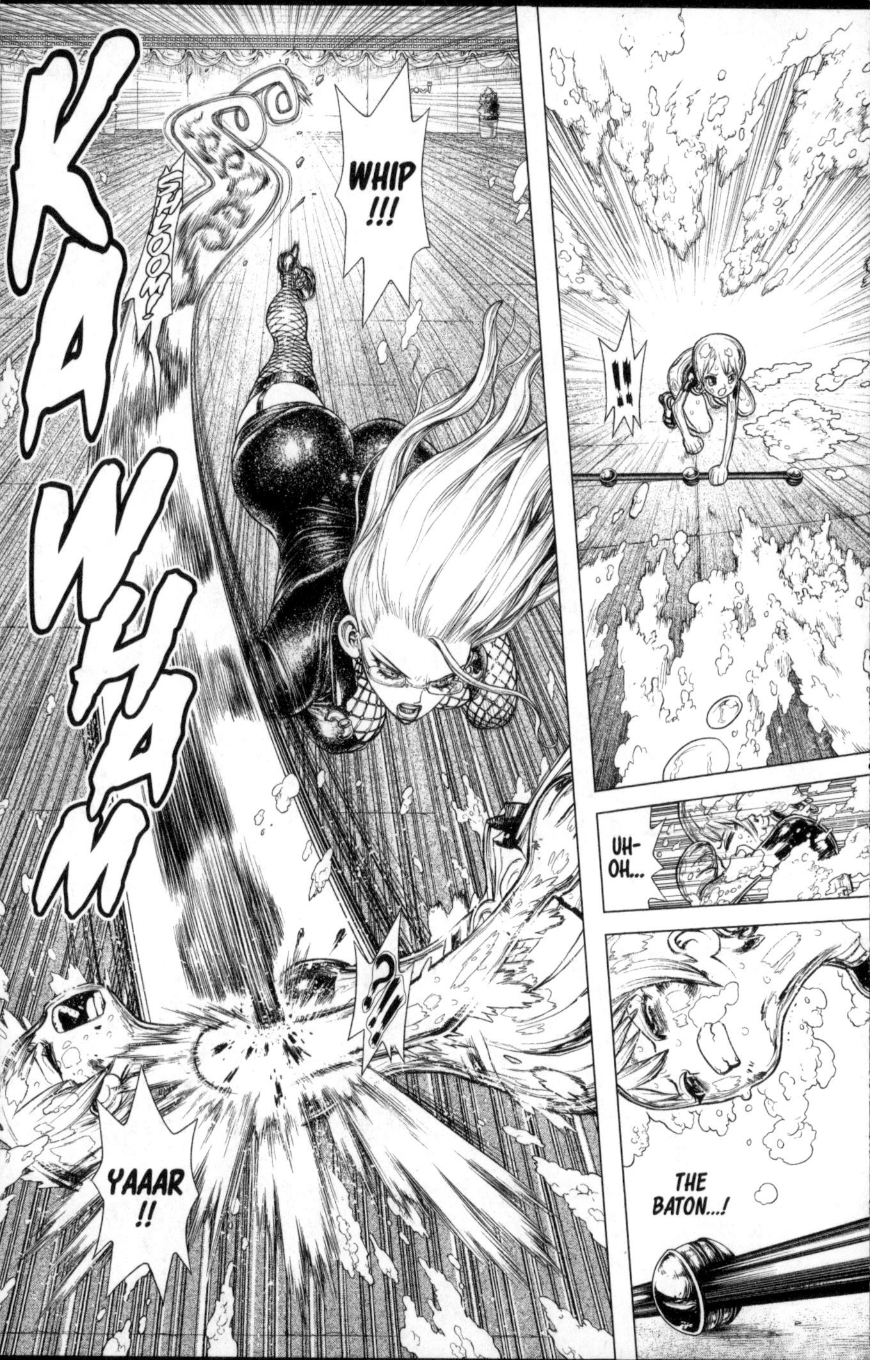
!!
UH-OH...
THE BATON...!
KAWHAM
WHIP !!!
SHLOOM!
?!!
YAAAR !!

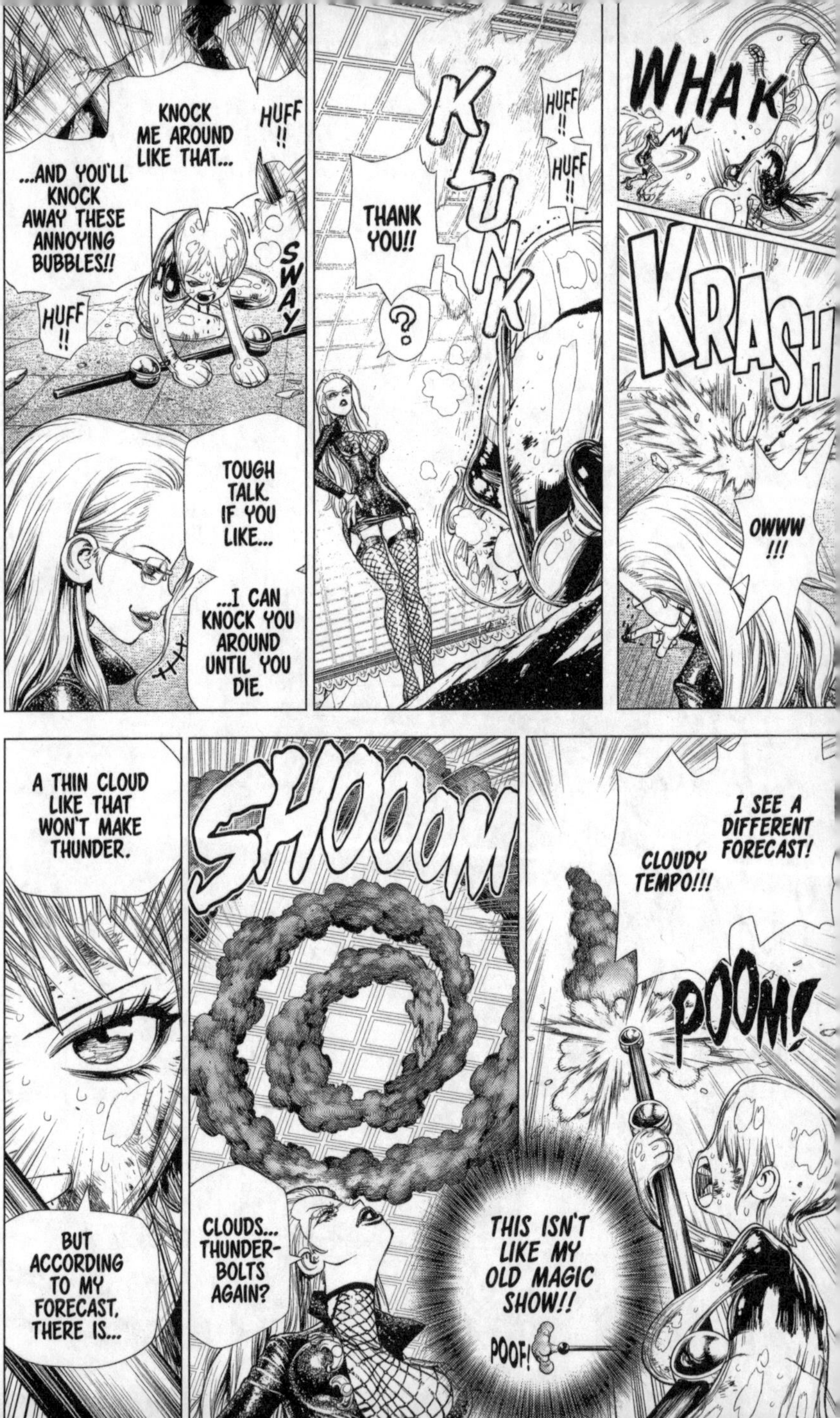
WHAK
KRASH
OWWW!!!
KLUNK
HUFF!!
HUFF!!
THANK YOU!!
?
HUFF!!
KNOCK ME AROUND LIKE THAT...
...AND YOU'LL KNOCK AWAY THESE ANNOYING BUBBLES!!
SWAY
HUFF!!
TOUGH TALK. IF YOU LIKE...
...I CAN KNOCK YOU AROUND UNTIL YOU DIE.
I SEE A DIFFERENT FORECAST!
CLOUDY TEMPO!!!
POOM!
SHOOOM
THIS ISN'T LIKE MY OLD MAGIC SHOW!!
POOF!
CLOUDS... THUNDER-BOLTS AGAIN?
A THIN CLOUD LIKE THAT WON'T MAKE THUNDER.
BUT ACCORDING TO MY FORECAST, THERE IS...

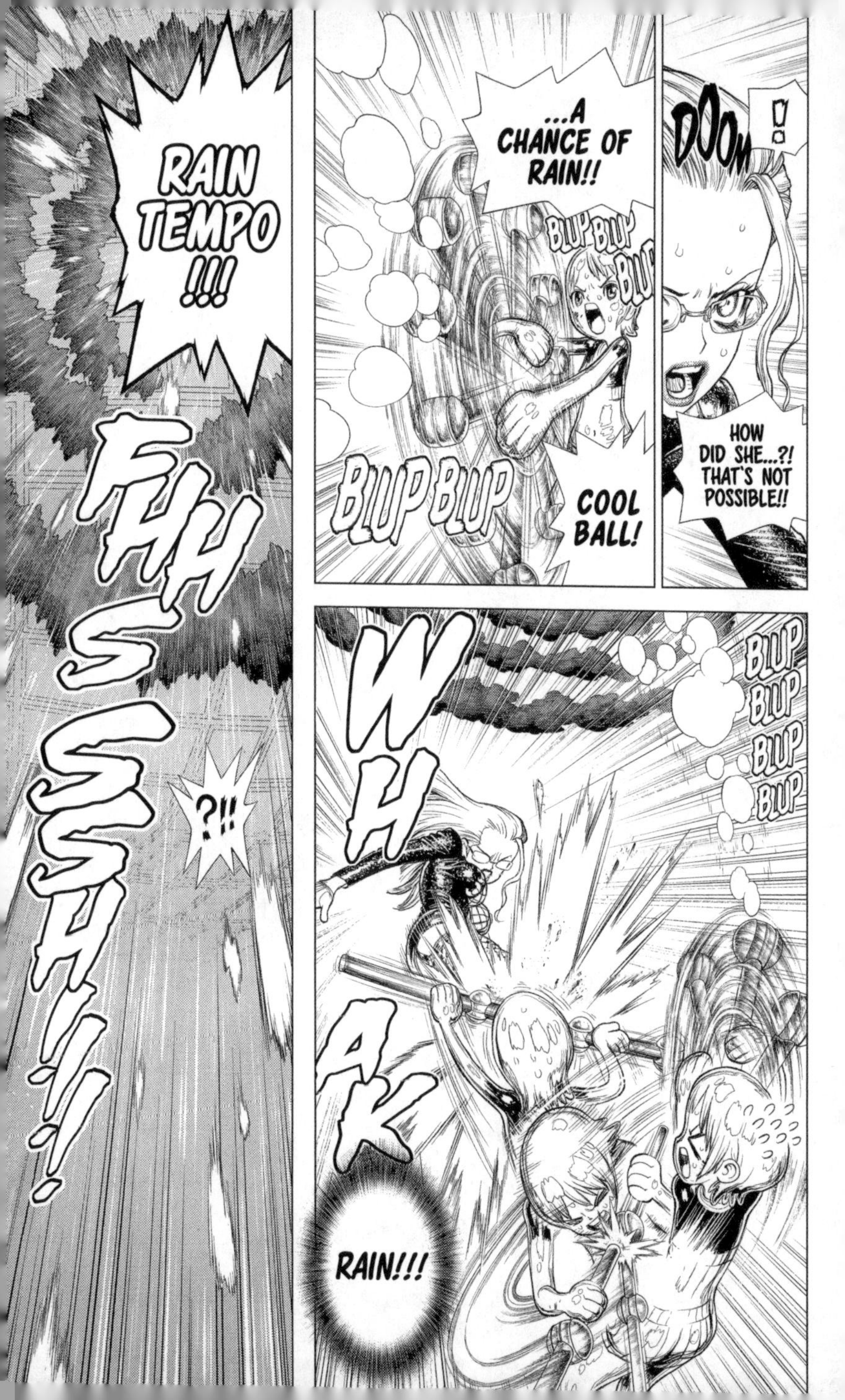
DOOM
!
HOW DID SHE...?! THAT'S NOT POSSIBLE!!
...A CHANCE OF RAIN!!
BLUP BLUP BLUP
BLUP BLUP
COOL BALL!
BLUP BLUP BLUP BLUP
WHAK
RAIN!!!
RAIN TEMPO!!!!
FWHSSSH!!!!
?!!

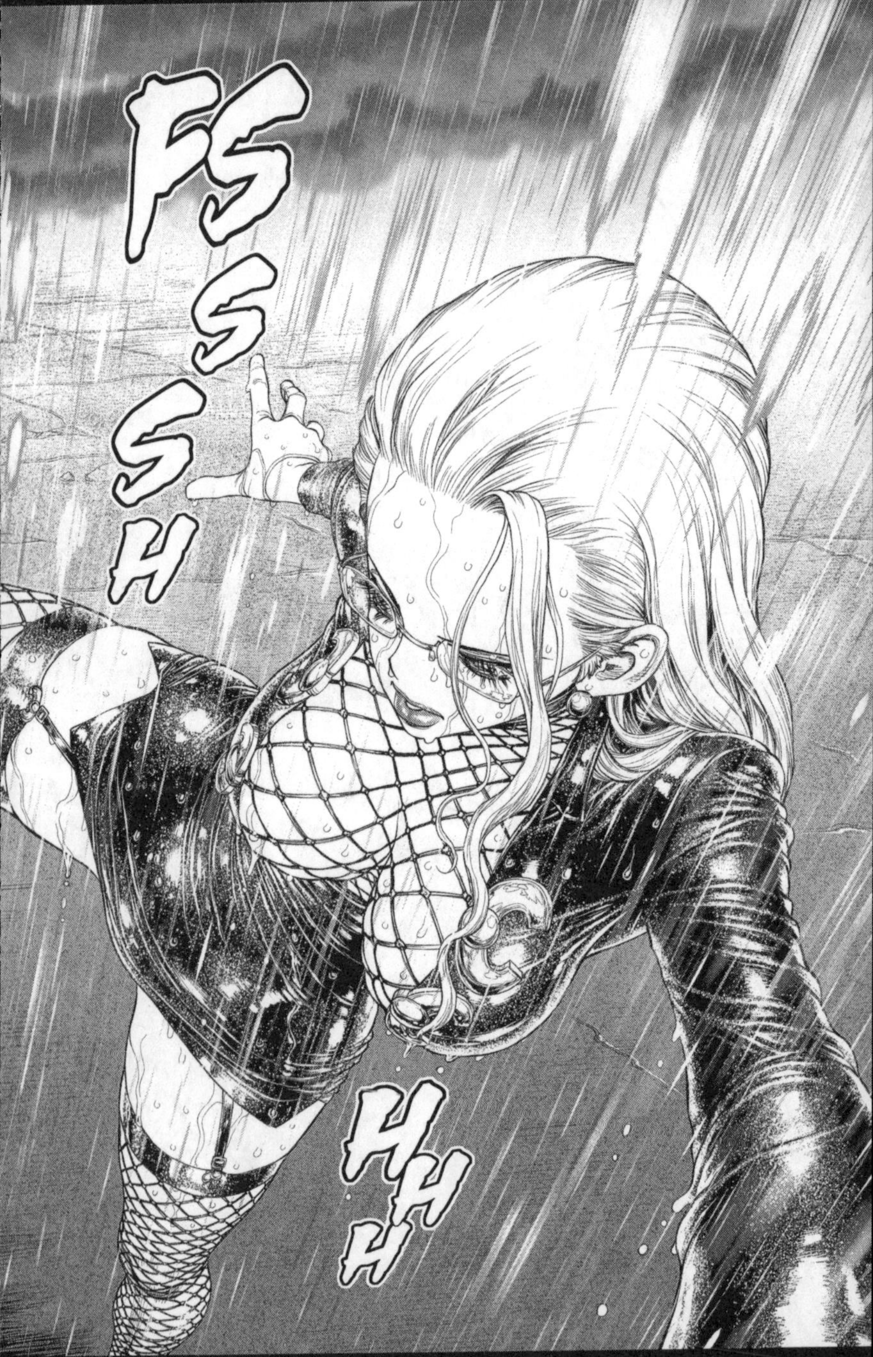
FSSSH
HHH

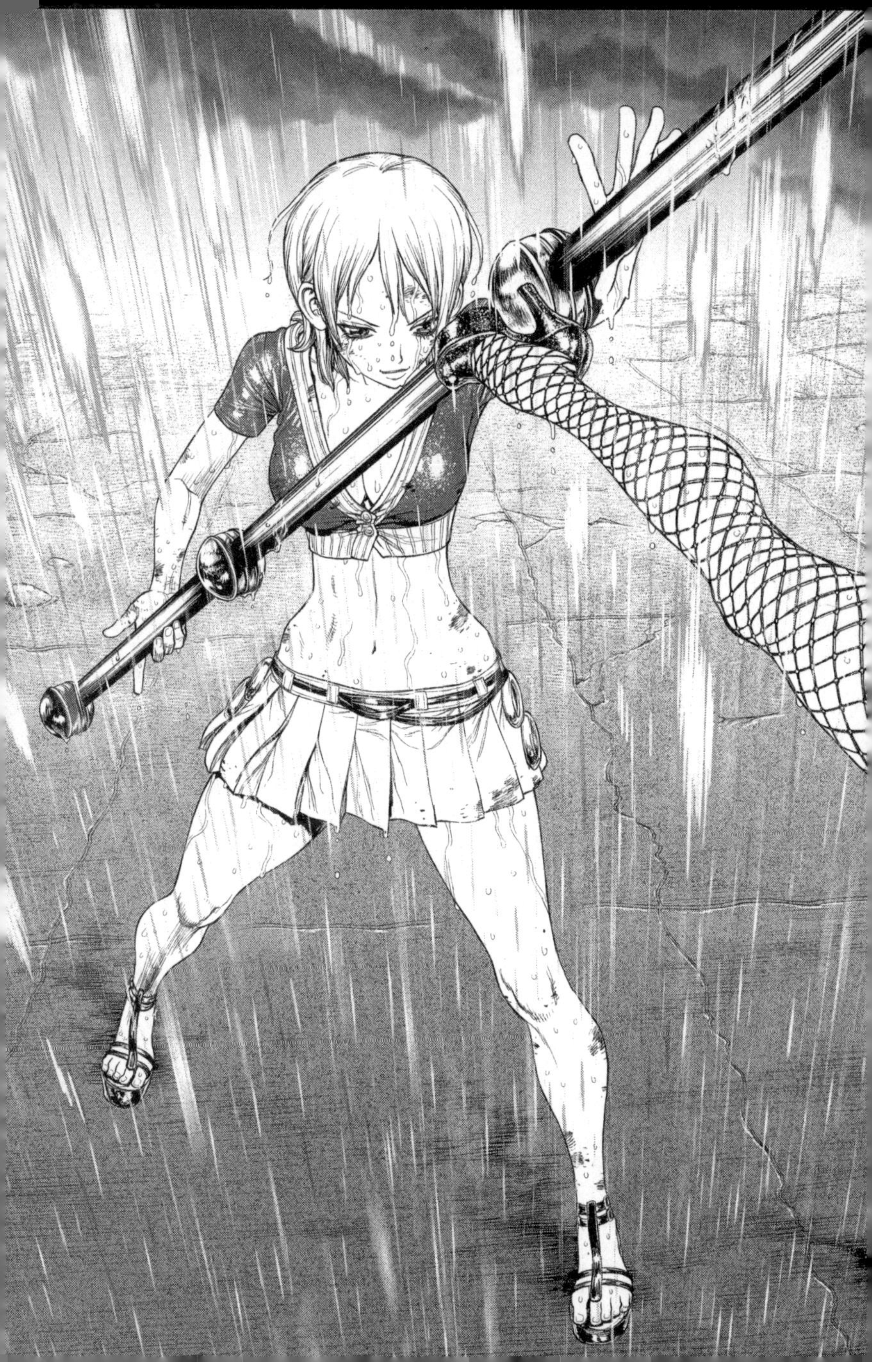

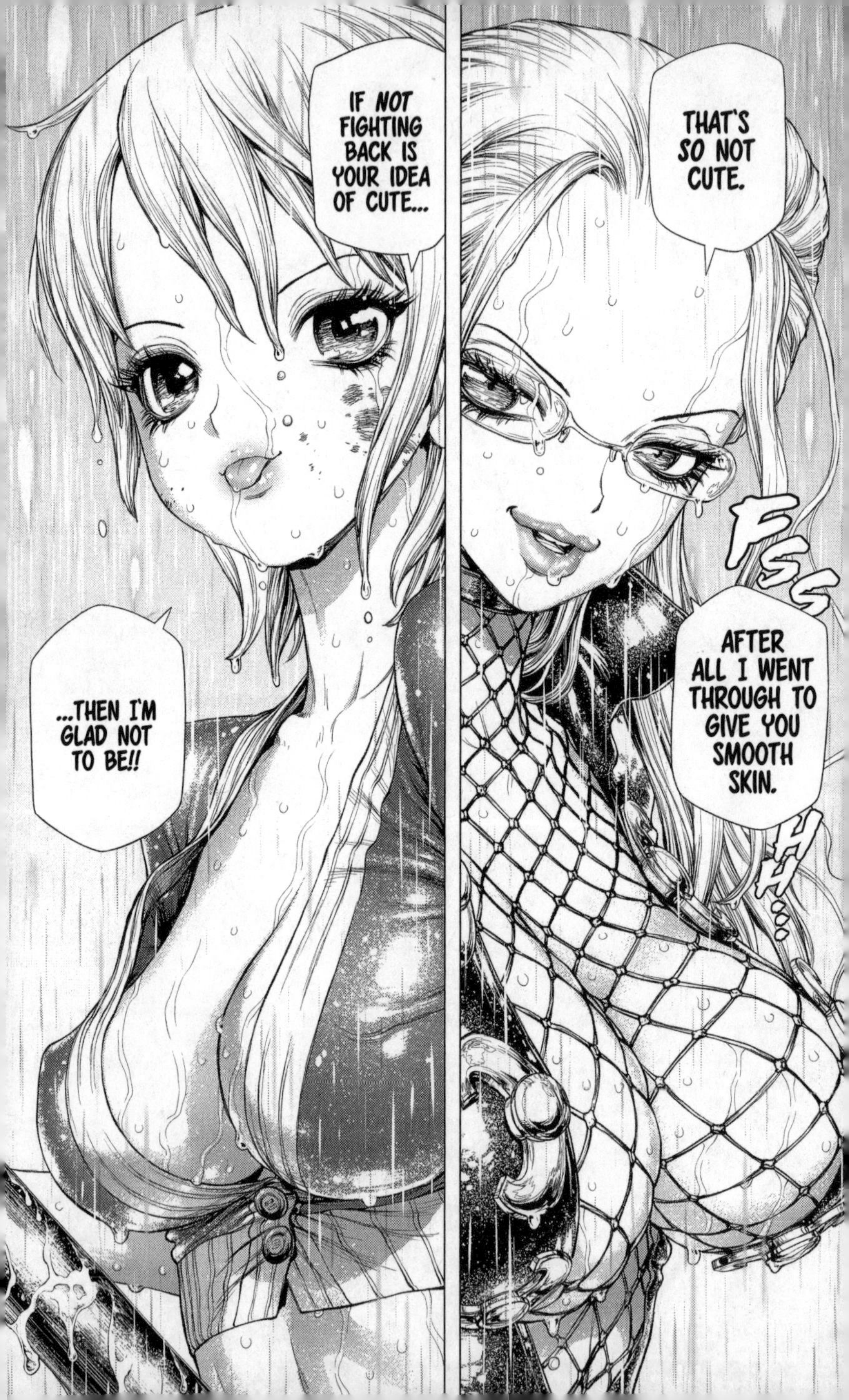
THAT'S SO NOT CUTE.
FSSHH...
AFTER ALL I WENT THROUGH TO GIVE YOU SMOOTH SKIN.
IF NOT FIGHTING BACK IS YOUR IDEA OF CUTE...
...THEN I'M GLAD NOT TO BE!!

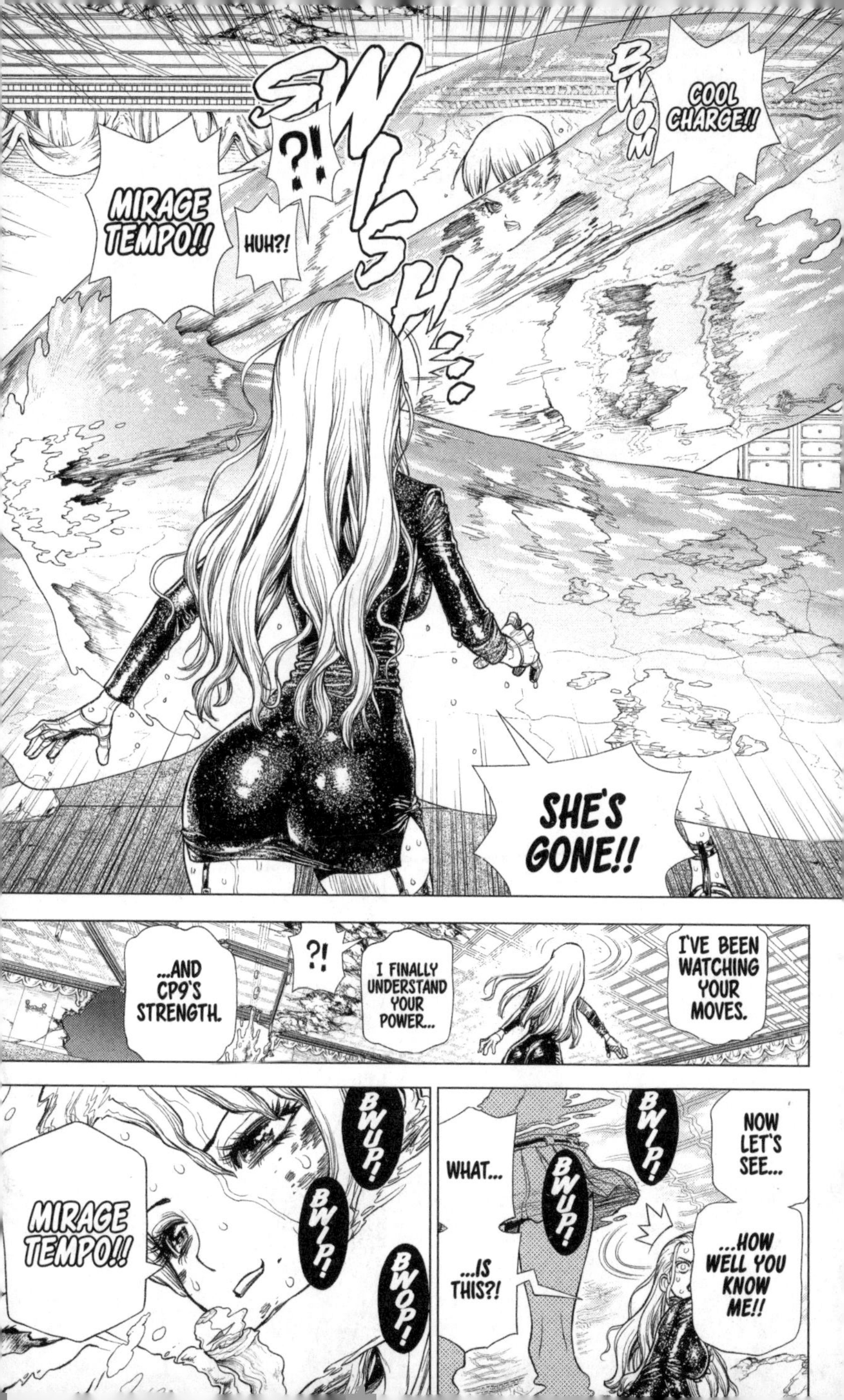
COOL CHARGE!!
BWOM
SWISH...
?!
HUH?!
MIRAGE TEMPO!!
SHE'S GONE!!
I'VE BEEN WATCHING YOUR MOVES.
I FINALLY UNDERSTAND YOUR POWER...
?!
...AND CP9'S STRENGTH.
NOW LET'S SEE...
BWIP!
BWUP!
WHAT...
...HOW WELL YOU KNOW ME!!
...IS THIS?!
BWUP!
BWIP!
BWOP!
MIRAGE TEMPO!!

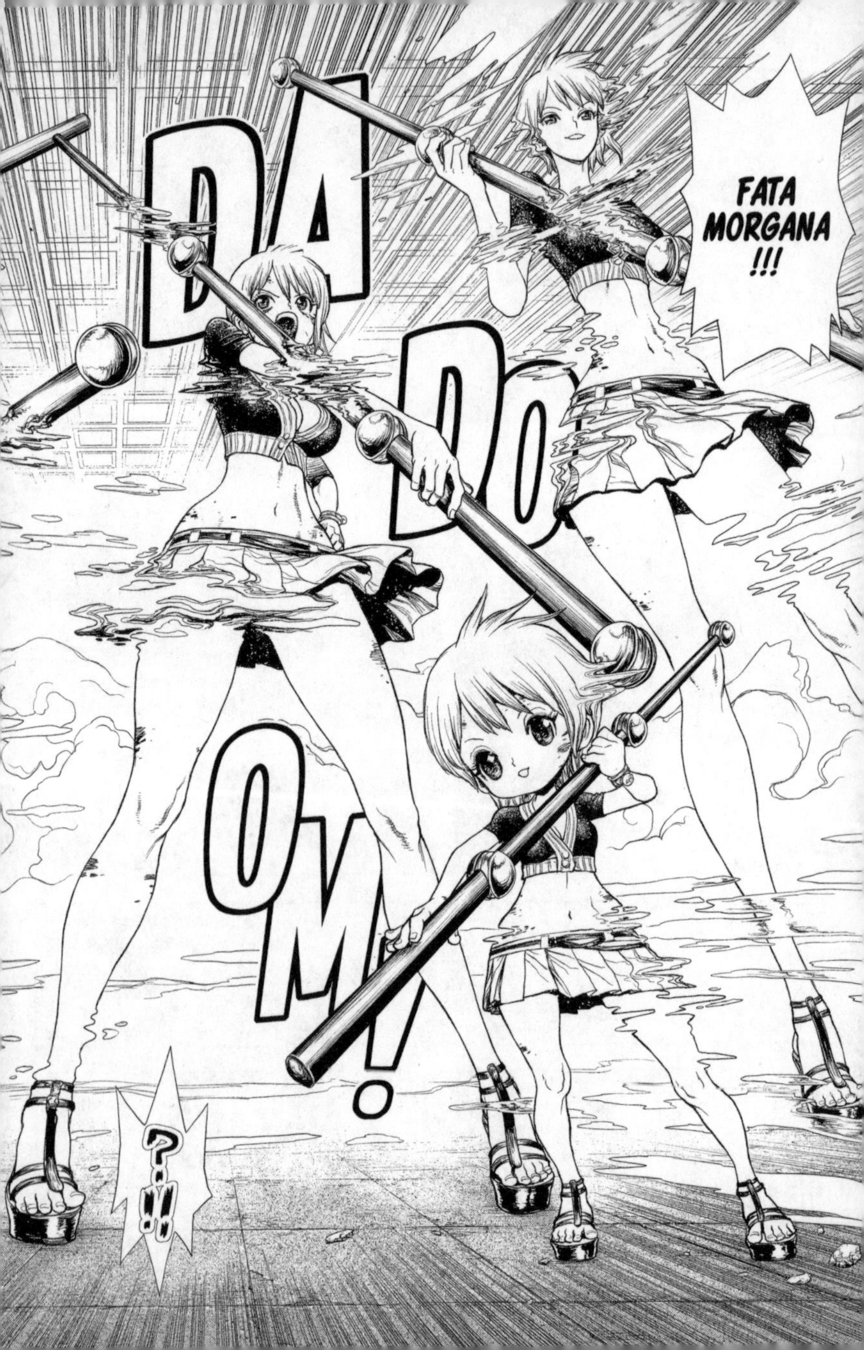
FATA MORGANA !!!
DADOOM!
?!!

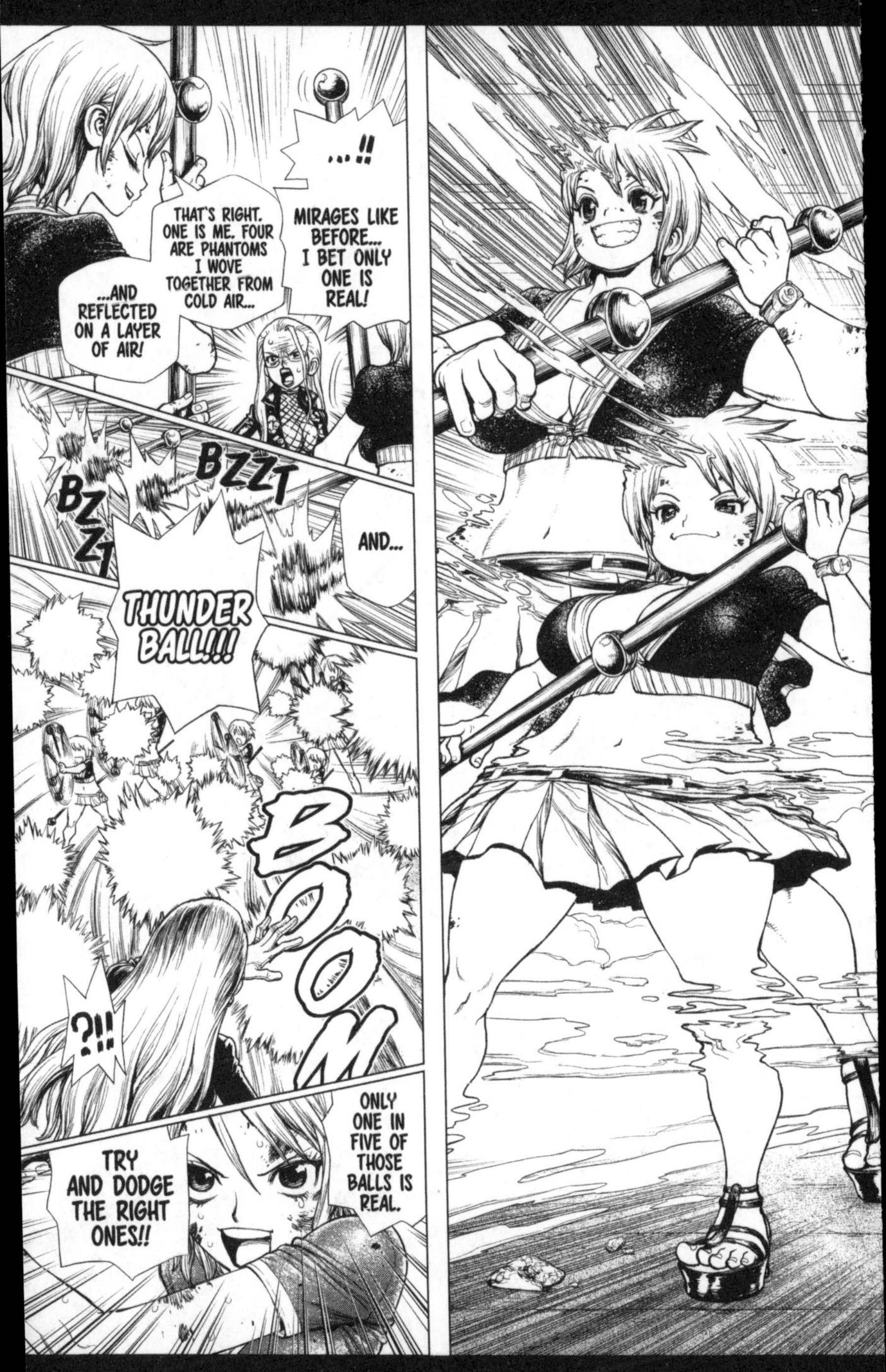
...!!
MIRAGES LIKE BEFORE... I BET ONLY ONE IS REAL!
THAT'S RIGHT. ONE IS ME. FOUR ARE PHANTOMS I WOVE TOGETHER FROM COLD AIR...
...AND REFLECTED ON A LAYER OF AIR!
BZZZT
BZZT
AND...
THUNDER BALL!!!
BOOM
?!!
ONLY ONE IN FIVE OF THOSE BALLS IS REAL.
TRY AND DODGE THE RIGHT ONES!!

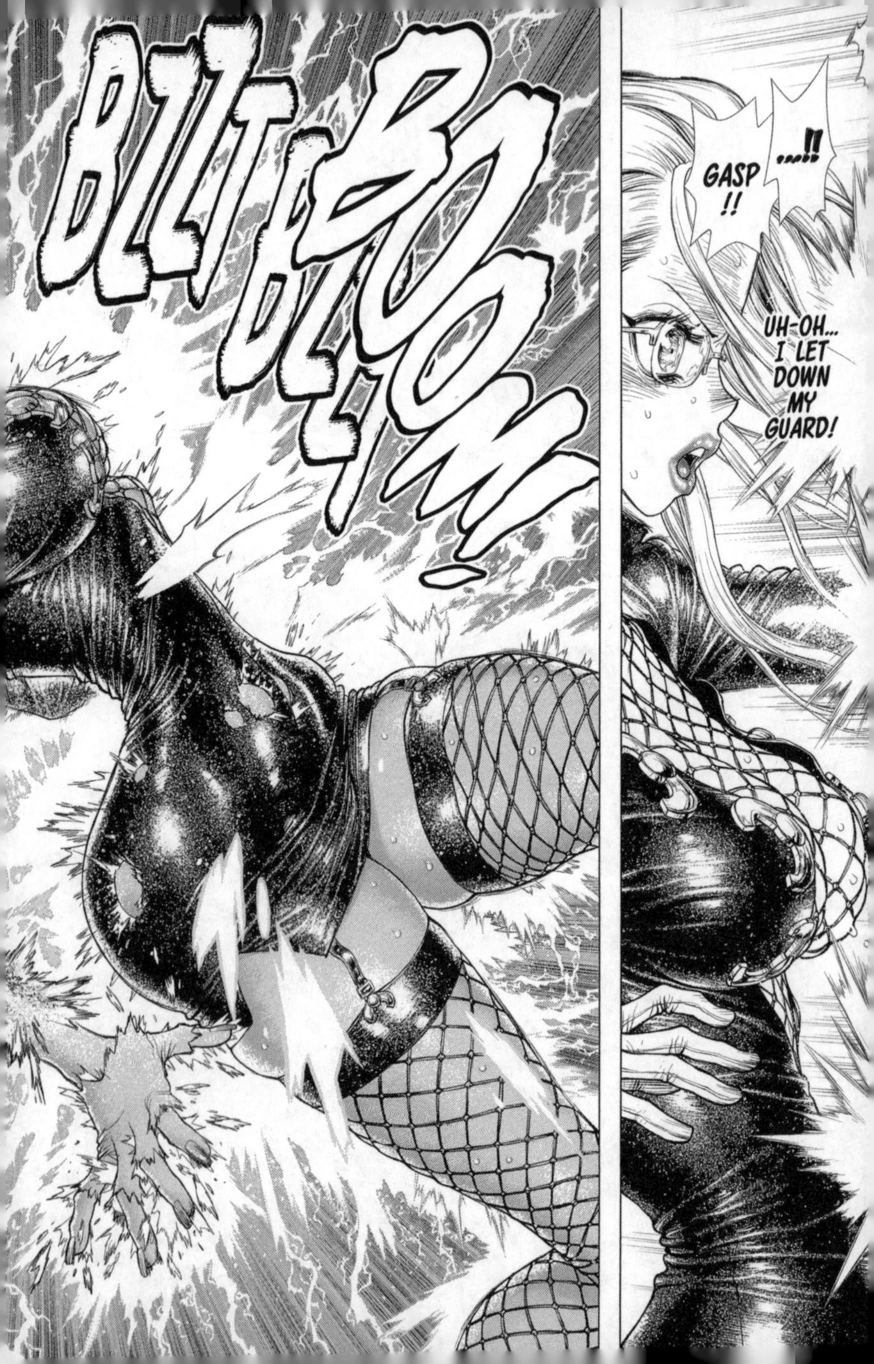
GASP !!
...!!
UH-OH... I LET DOWN MY GUARD!
BZZT-BOOM!

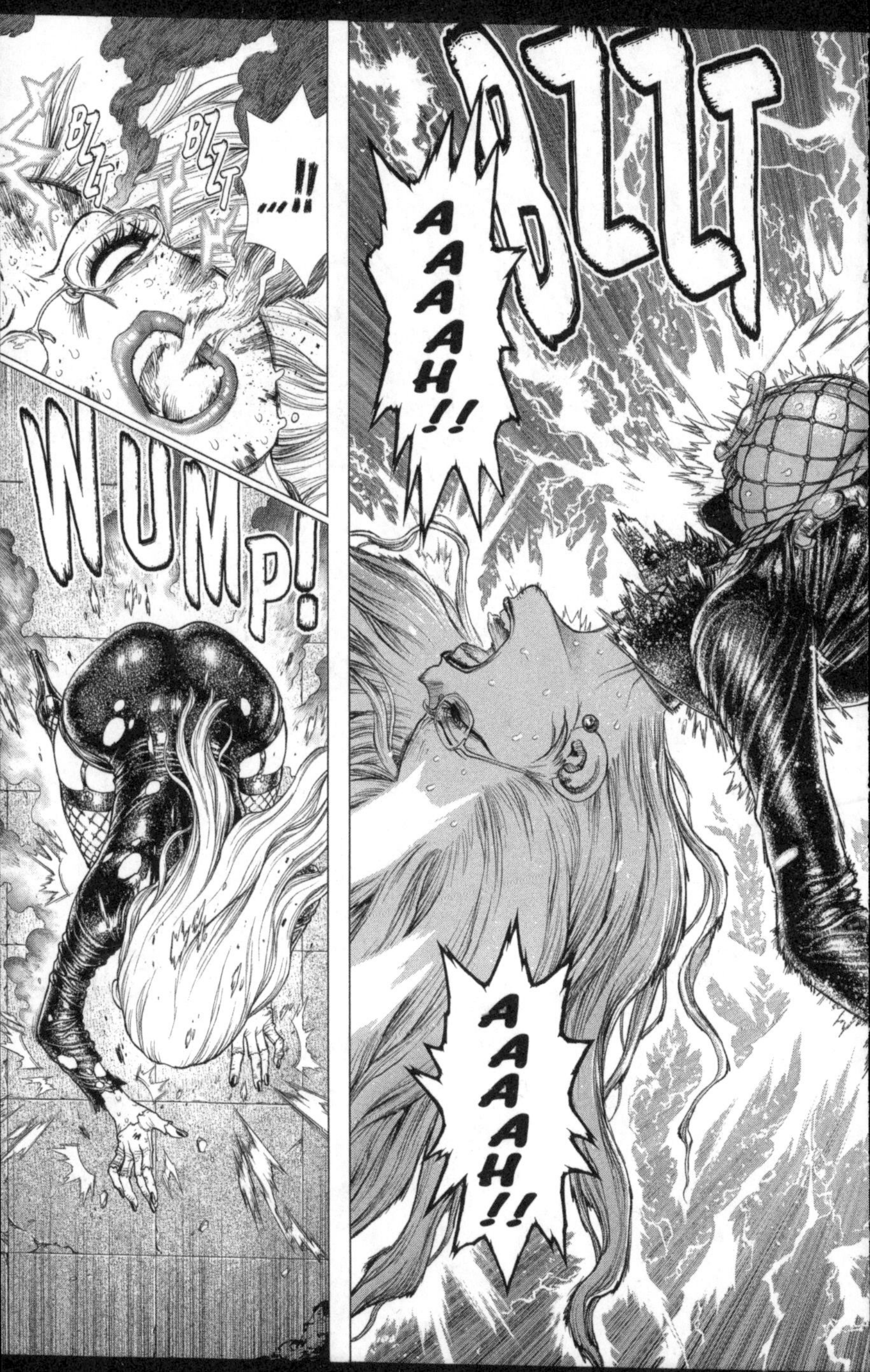
AAAAAH!!
AAAAAH!!
BZZT
BZZT
...!!
WUMP!

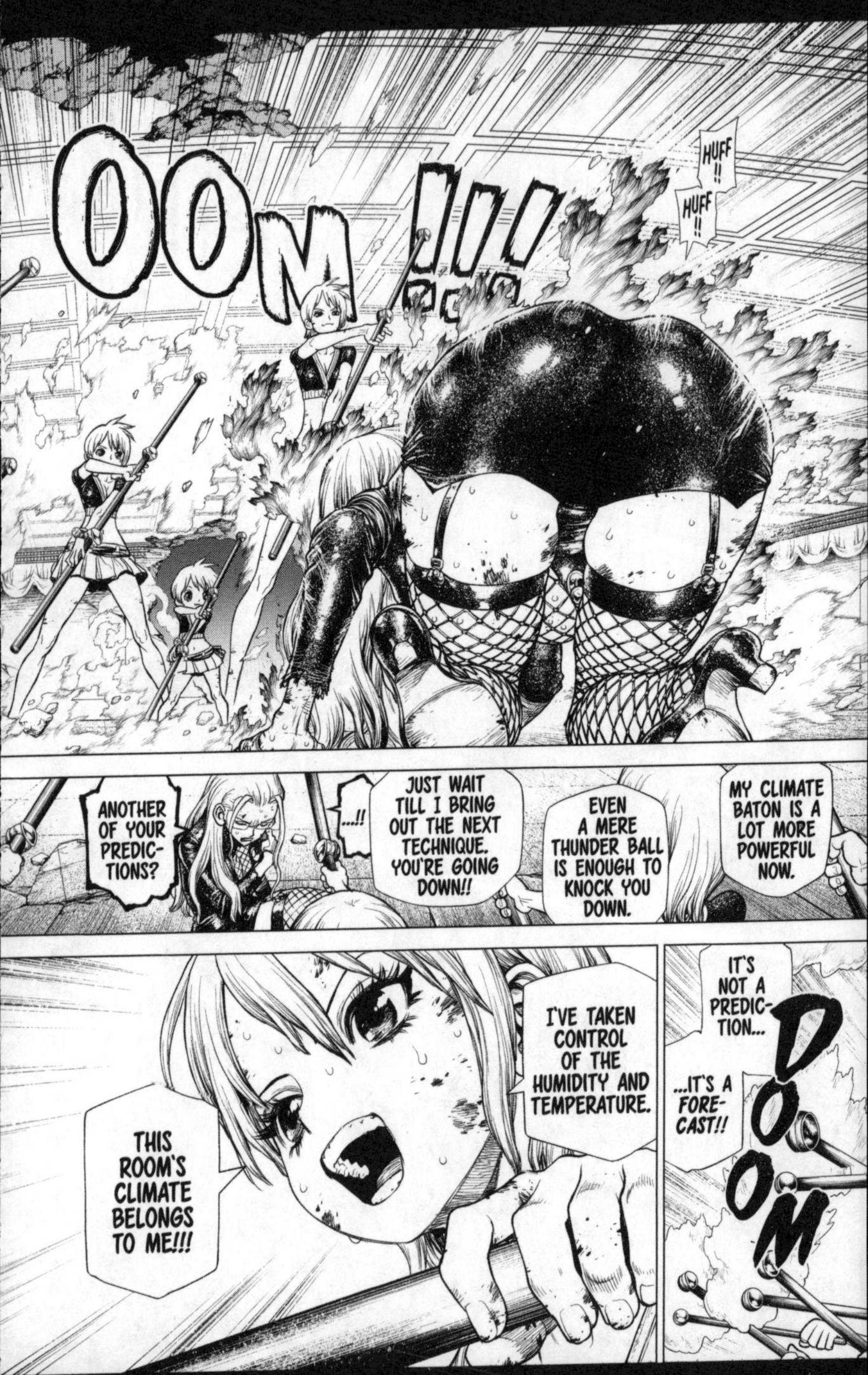
HUFF!!
HUFF!!
OOM!!!
MY CLIMATE BATON IS A LOT MORE POWERFUL NOW.
EVEN A MERE THUNDER BALL IS ENOUGH TO KNOCK YOU DOWN.
JUST WAIT TILL I BRING OUT THE NEXT TECHNIQUE. YOU'RE GOING DOWN!!
...!!
ANOTHER OF YOUR PREDICTIONS?
IT'S NOT A PREDICTION...
...IT'S A FORECAST!!
DOOM
I'VE TAKEN CONTROL OF THE HUMIDITY AND TEMPERATURE.
THIS ROOM'S CLIMATE BELONGS TO ME!!!

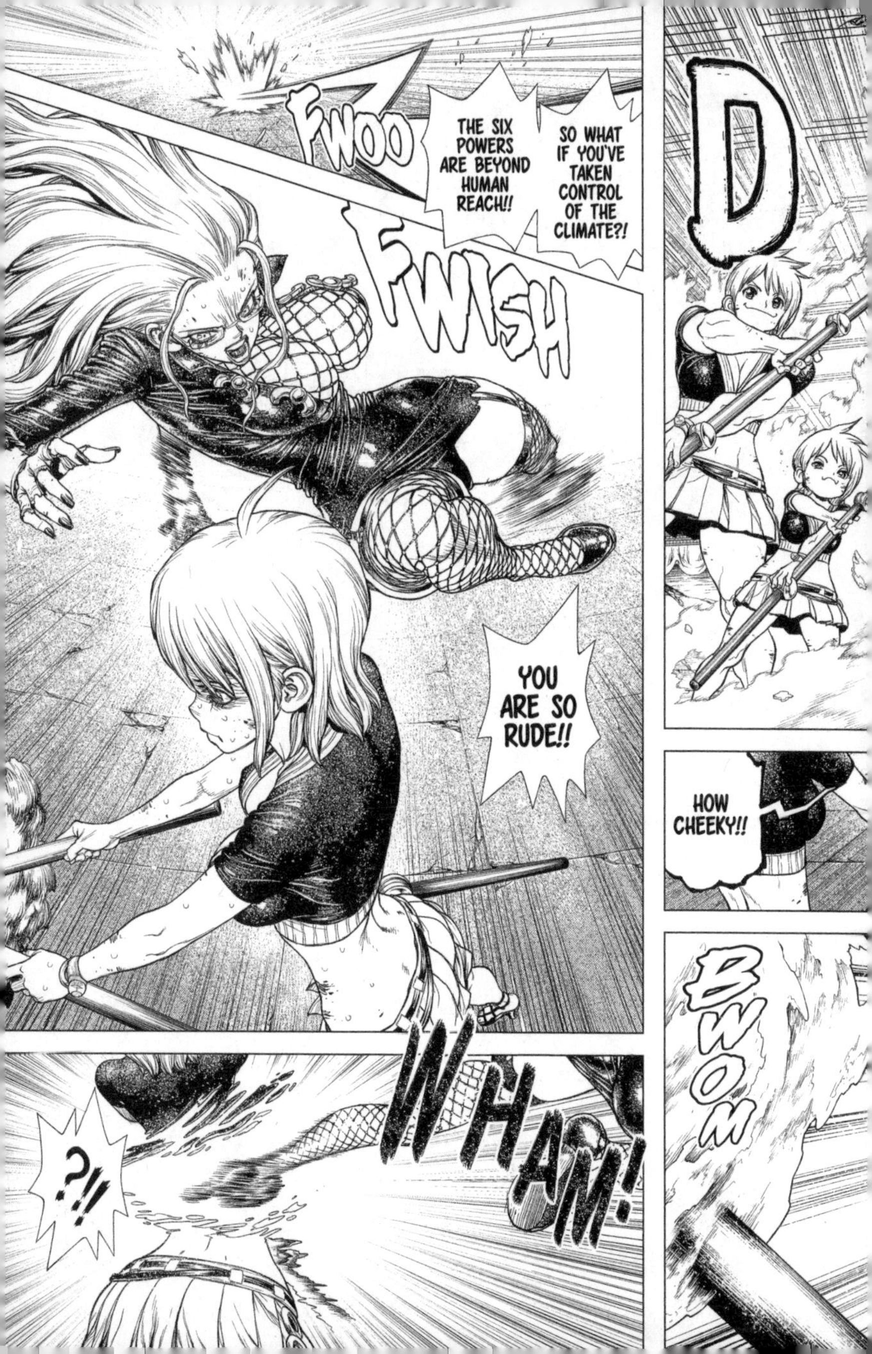
D
HOW CHEEKY!!
BWOM
SO WHAT IF YOU'VE TAKEN CONTROL OF THE CLIMATE?!
THE SIX POWERS ARE BEYOND HUMAN REACH!!
FWOO
FWISH
YOU ARE SO RUDE!!
WHAM!
?!!

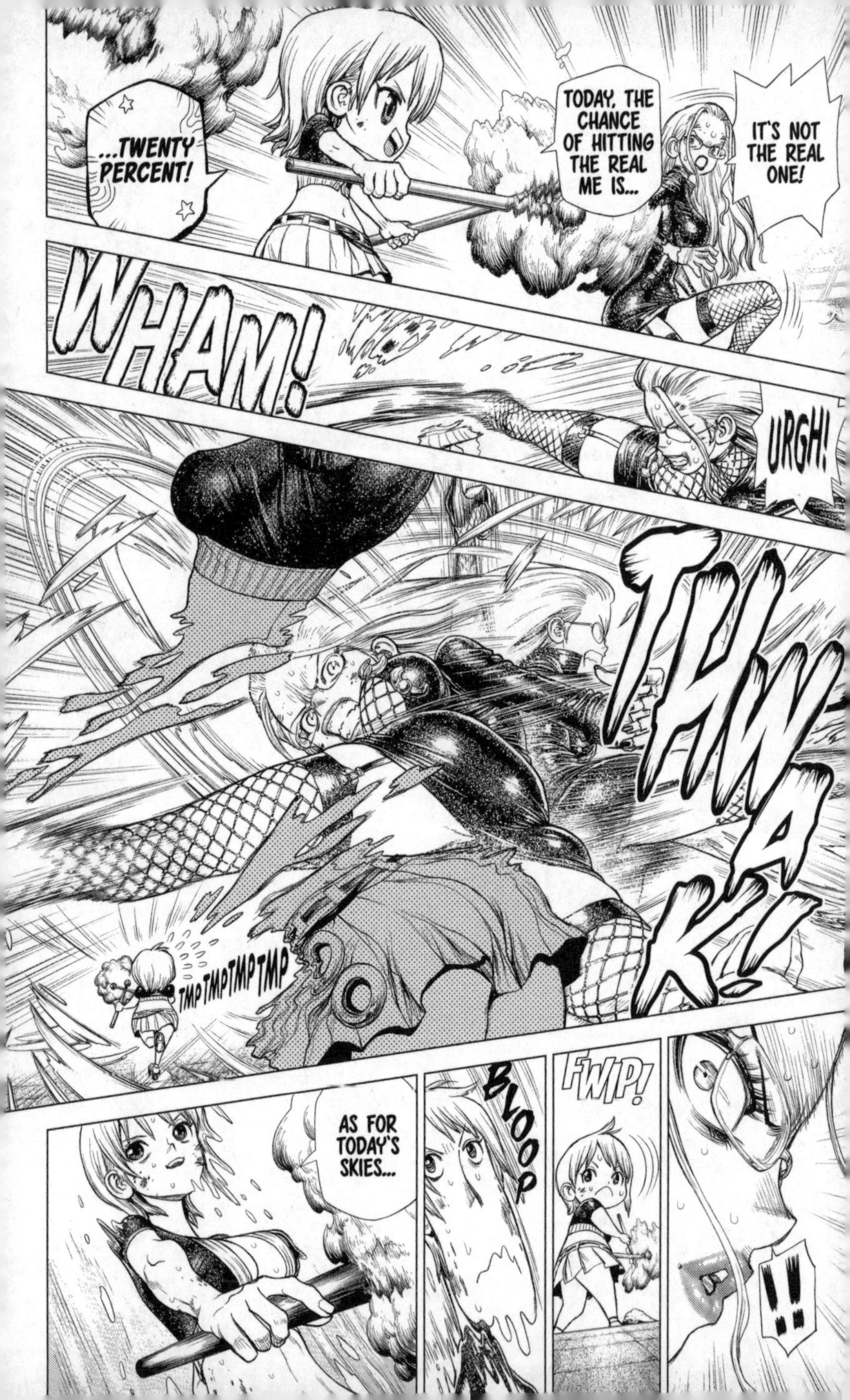
IT'S NOT THE REAL ONE!
TODAY, THE CHANCE OF HITTING THE REAL ME IS...
...TWENTY PERCENT!
WHAM!
URGH!
THWAK!
TMP TMP TMP TMP
!!
FWIP!
BLOOP
AS FOR TODAY'S SKIES...

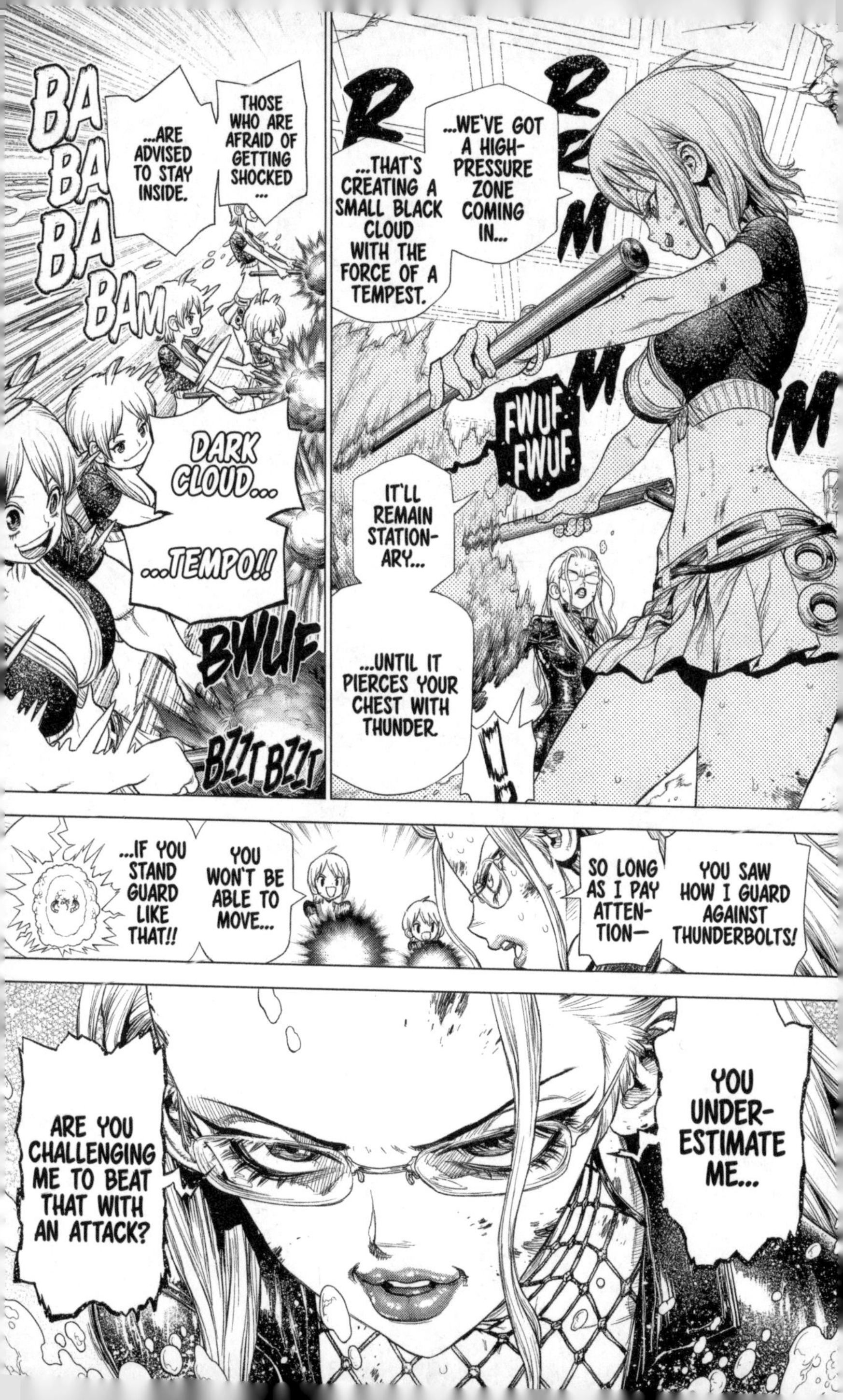
RRRMMMM
...WE'VE GOT A HIGH-PRESSURE ZONE COMING IN...
...THAT'S CREATING A SMALL BLACK CLOUD WITH THE FORCE OF A TEMPEST.
FWUF FWUF
IT'LL REMAIN STATIONARY...
...UNTIL IT PIERCES YOUR CHEST WITH THUNDER.
THOSE WHO ARE AFRAID OF GETTING SHOCKED...
...ARE ADVISED TO STAY INSIDE.
BABABABAM
DARK CLOUD...
...TEMPO!!
BWUF
BZZT BZZT
YOU SAW HOW I GUARD AGAINST THUNDERBOLTS!
SO LONG AS I PAY ATTENTION—
YOU WON'T BE ABLE TO MOVE...
...IF YOU STAND GUARD LIKE THAT!!
YOU UNDERESTIMATE ME...
ARE YOU CHALLENGING ME TO BEAT THAT WITH AN ATTACK?

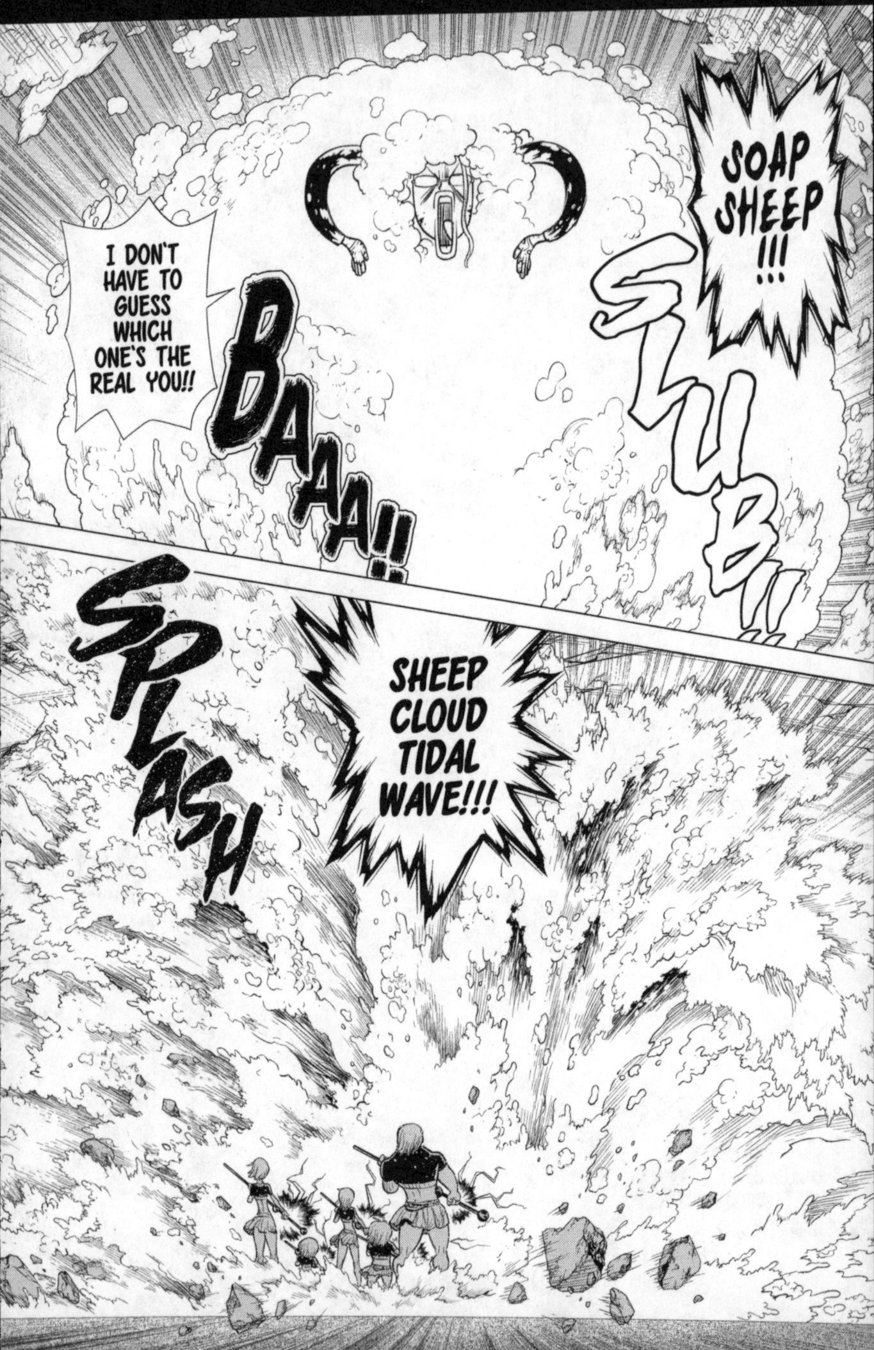
SOAP SHEEP!!!
SLUBB!!
BAAA!!
I DON'T HAVE TO GUESS WHICH ONE'S THE REAL YOU!!
SHEEP CLOUD TIDAL WAVE!!!
SPLASH

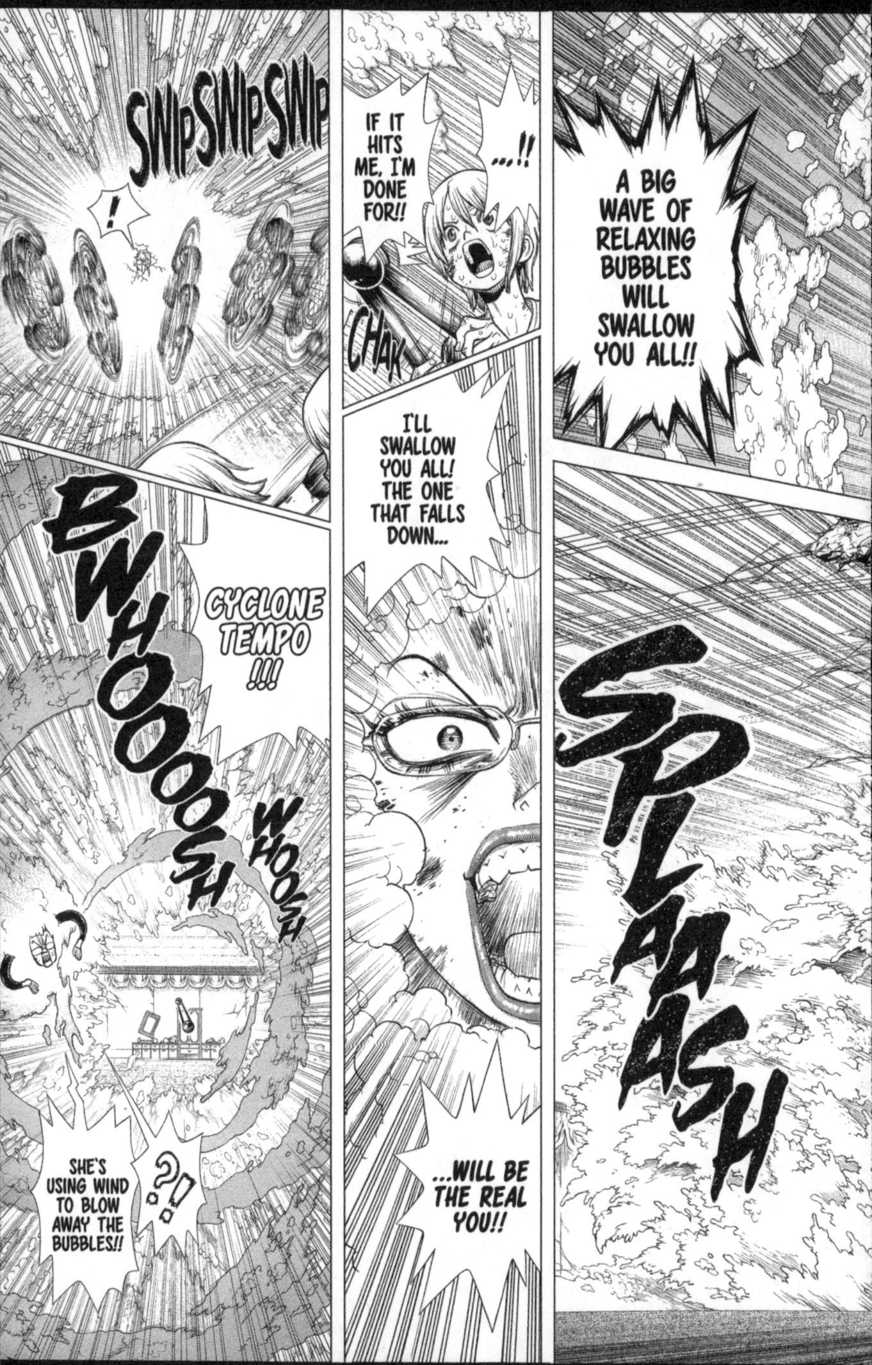

A BIG WAVE OF RELAXING BUBBLES WILL SWALLOW YOU ALL!!
...!!
IF IT HITS ME, I'M DONE FOR!!
CHAK
SWIP SWIP SWIP
!
SPLAAASH
I'LL SWALLOW YOU ALL! THE ONE THAT FALLS DOWN...
...WILL BE THE REAL YOU!!
CYCLONE TEMPO !!!
BWHOOOOSH
WHOOSH
SHE'S USING WIND TO BLOW AWAY THE BUBBLES!!
?!

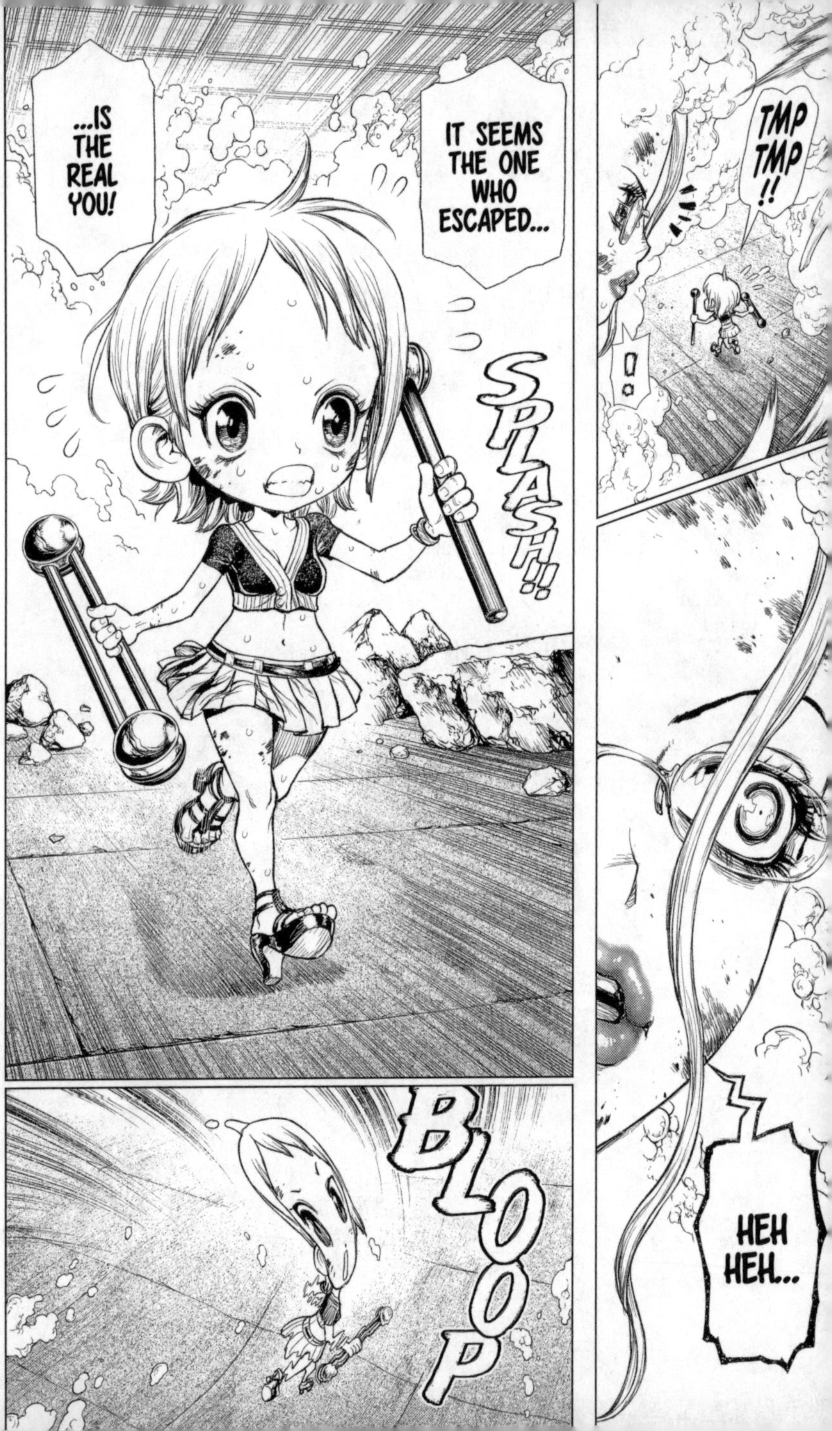
TMP TMP !!
!?
HEH HEH...
IT SEEMS THE ONE WHO ESCAPED...
...IS THE REAL YOU!
SPLASH!!
BLOOP

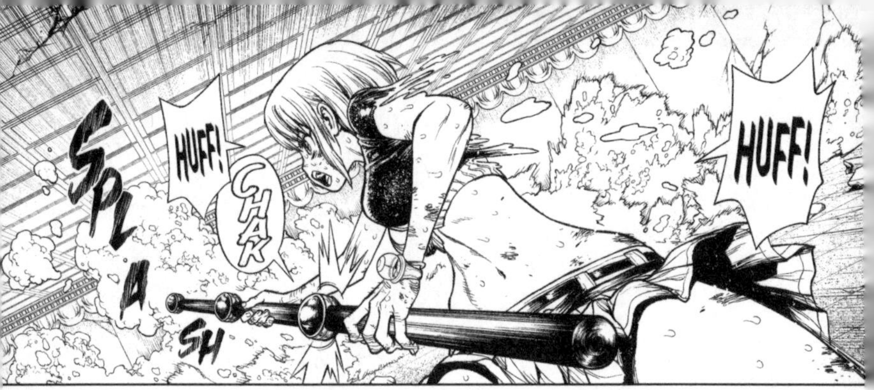
HUFF!
HUFF!
CHAK
SPLASH
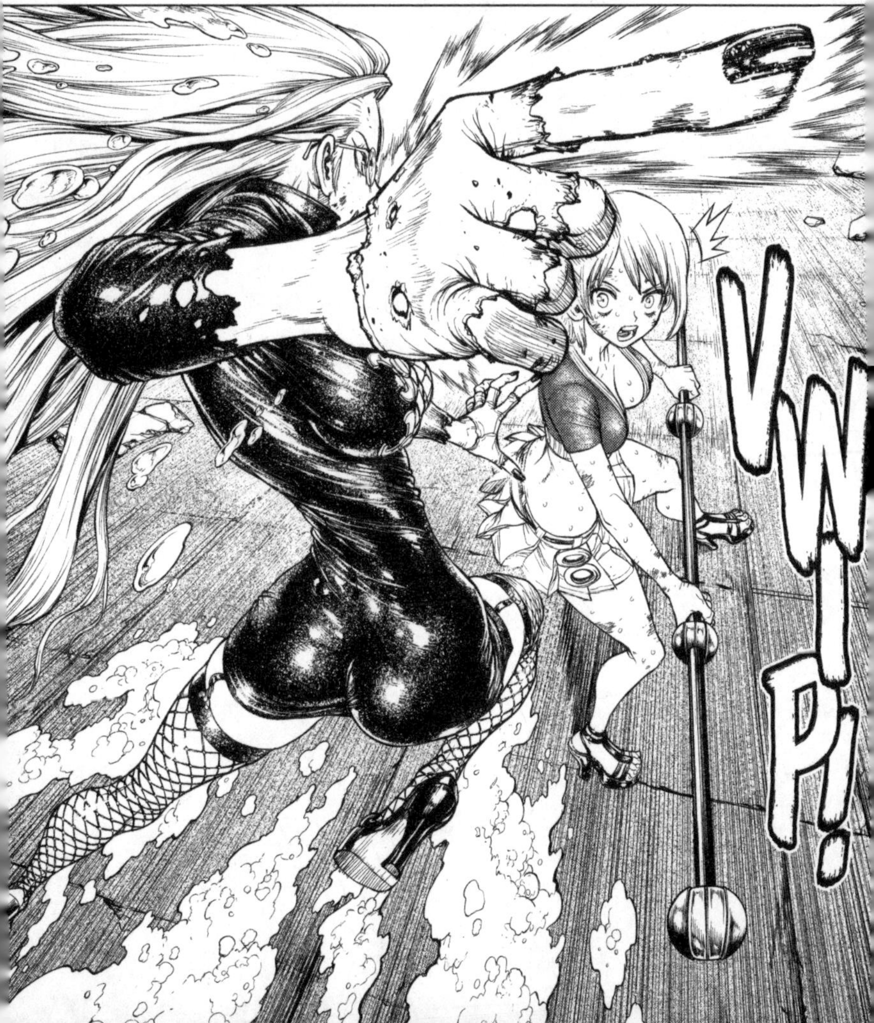
VWIP!

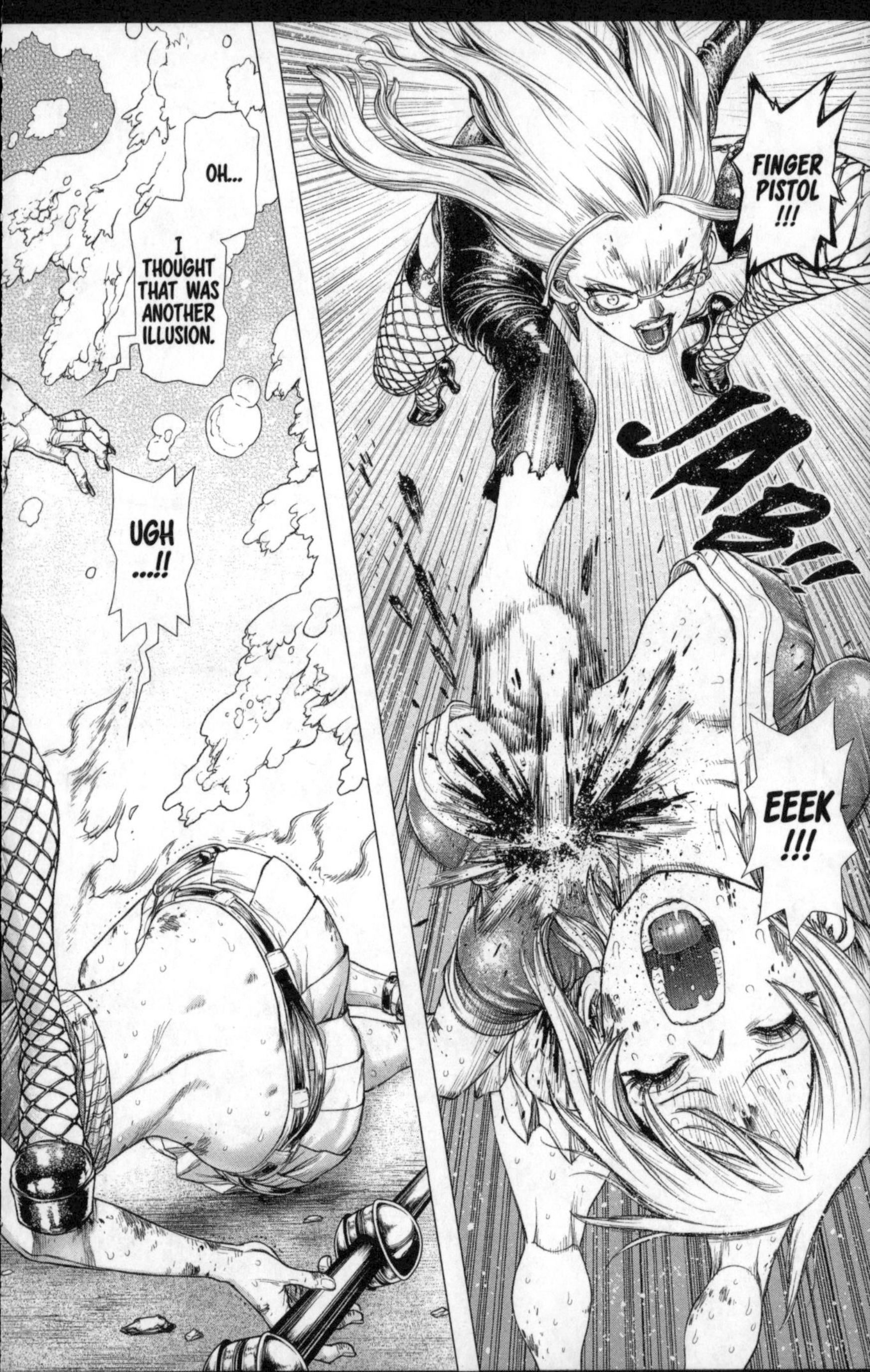
FINGER PISTOL !!!
JAB!!
EEEK !!!
OH...
I THOUGHT THAT WAS ANOTHER ILLUSION.
UGH ...!!

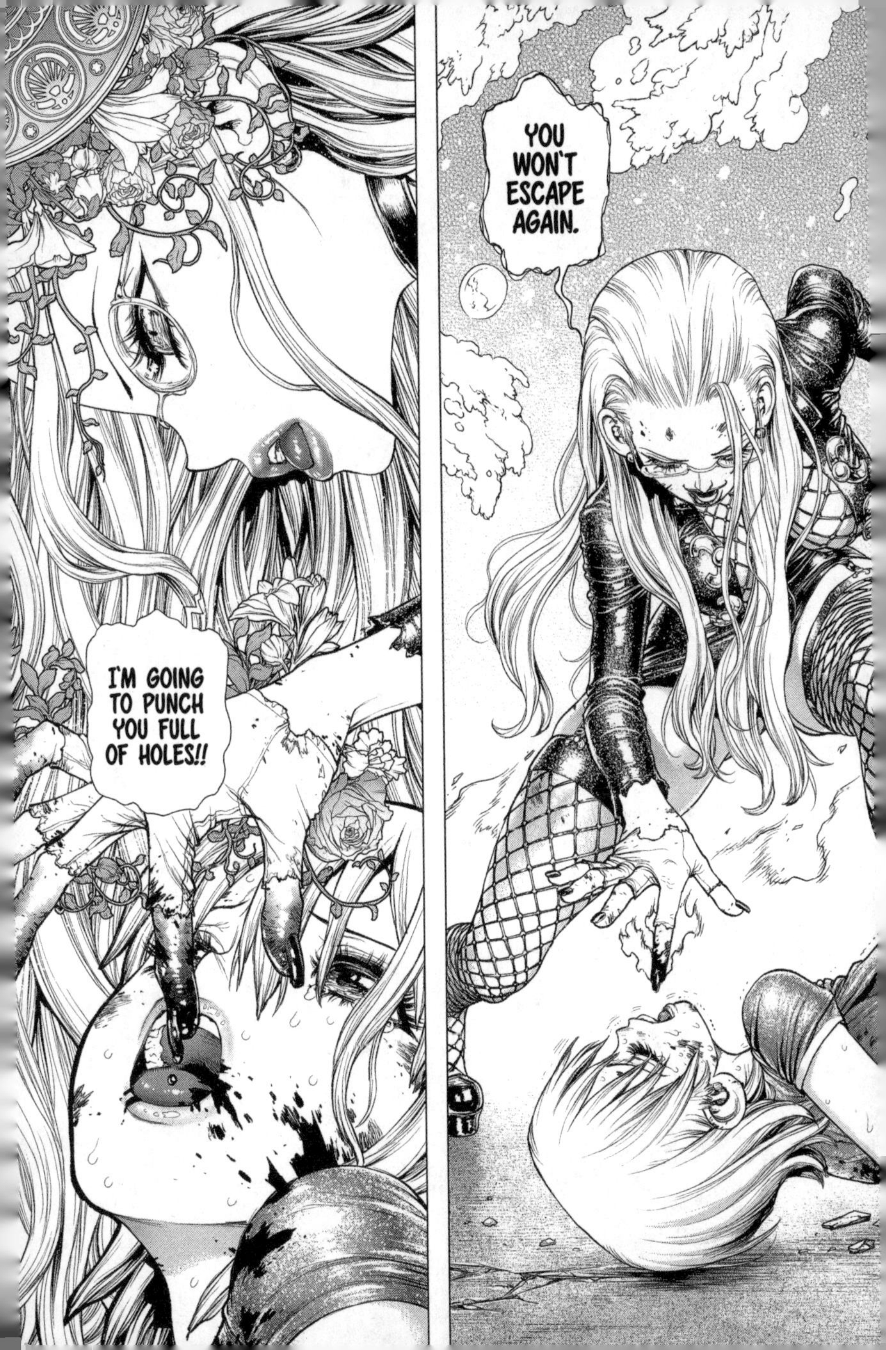
YOU WON'T ESCAPE AGAIN.
I'M GOING TO PUNCH YOU FULL OF HOLES!!

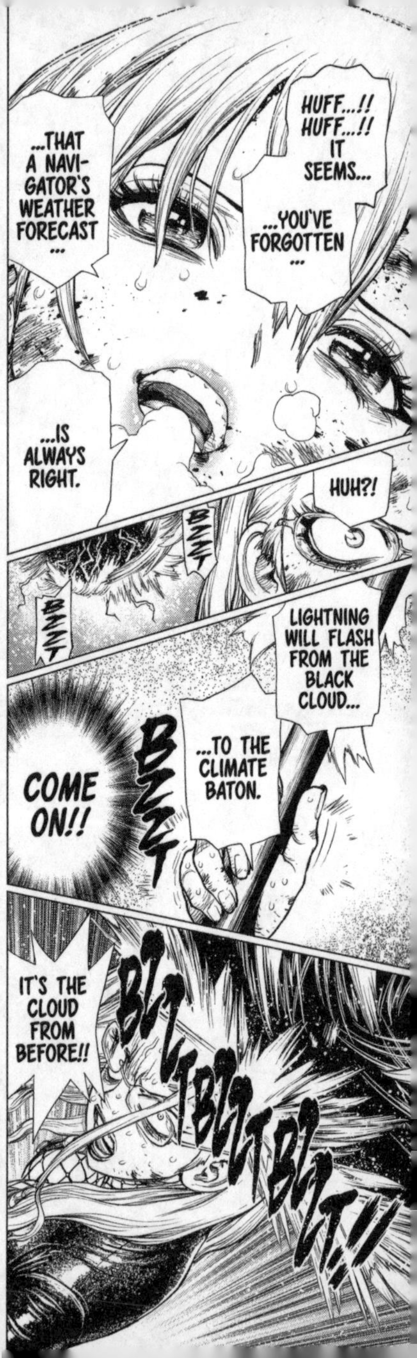
HUFF...!! HUFF...!! IT SEEMS...
...YOU'VE FORGOTTEN ...
...THAT A NAVIGATOR'S WEATHER FORECAST ...
...IS ALWAYS RIGHT.
HUH?!
BZZT
BZZT
LIGHTNING WILL FLASH FROM THE BLACK CLOUD...
...TO THE CLIMATE BATON.
BZZT
COME ON!!
IT'S THE CLOUD FROM BEFORE!!
BZZT BZZT BZZT!!

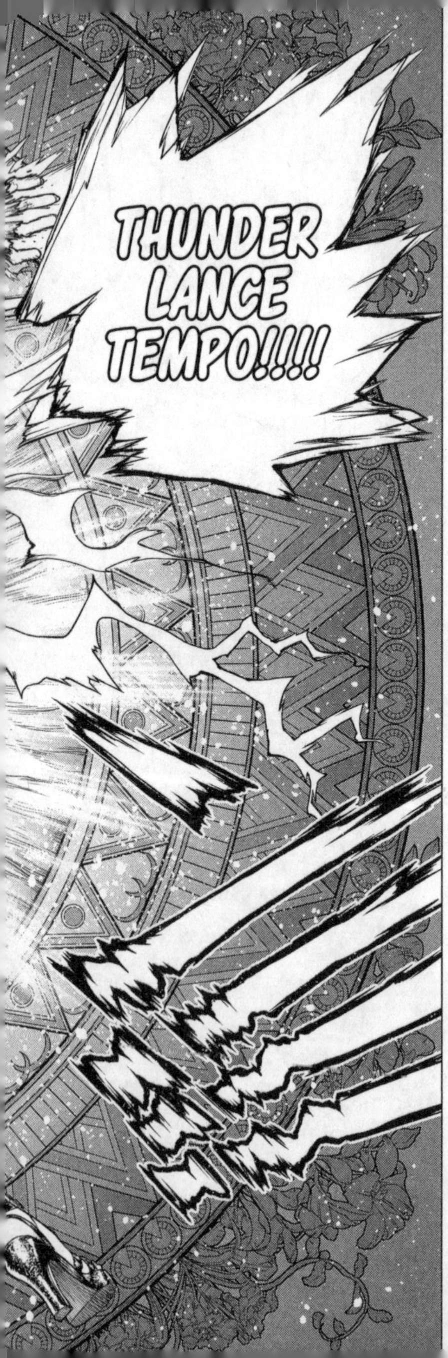
THUNDER LANCE TEMPO!!!!

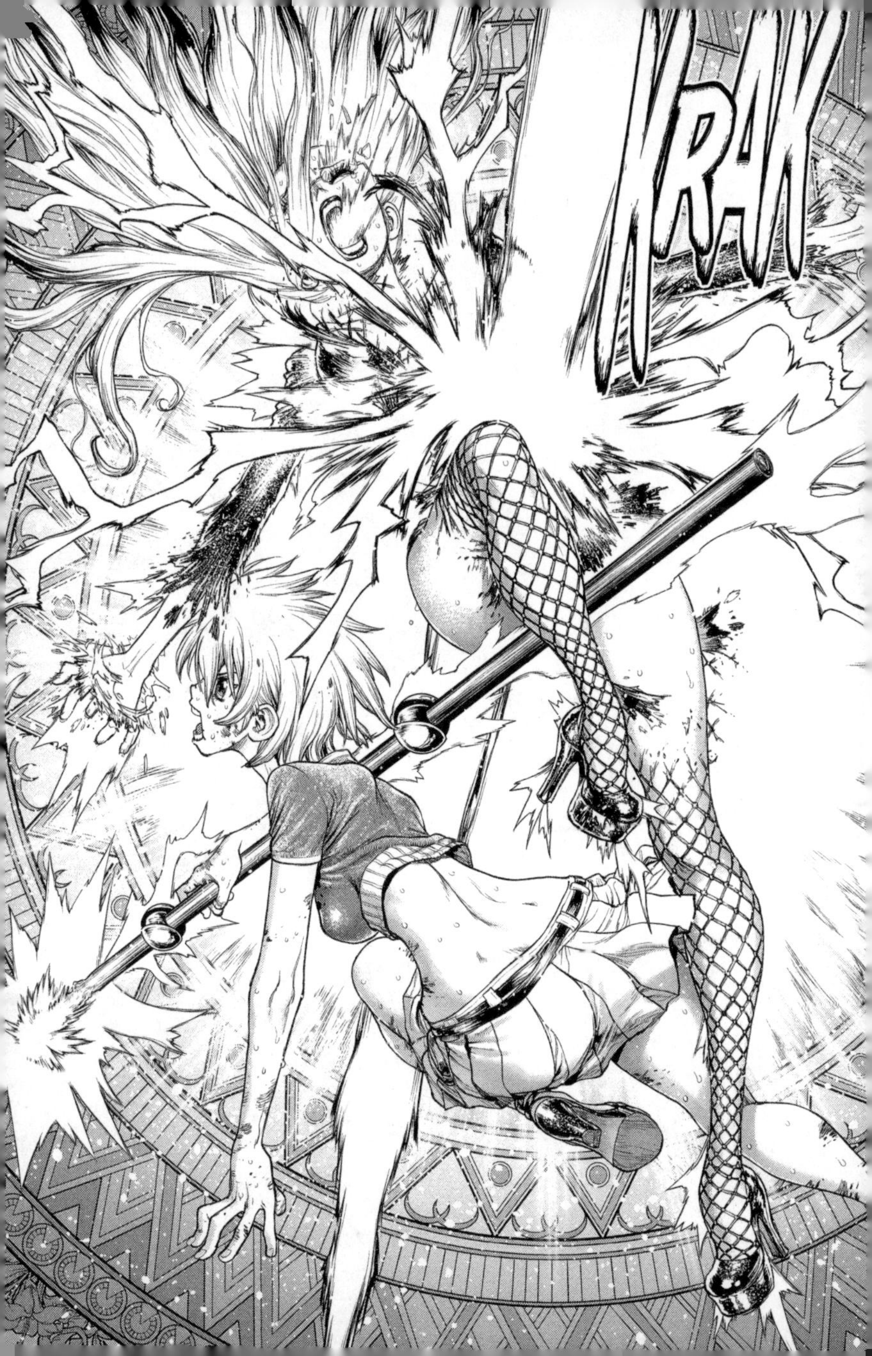
KRAK

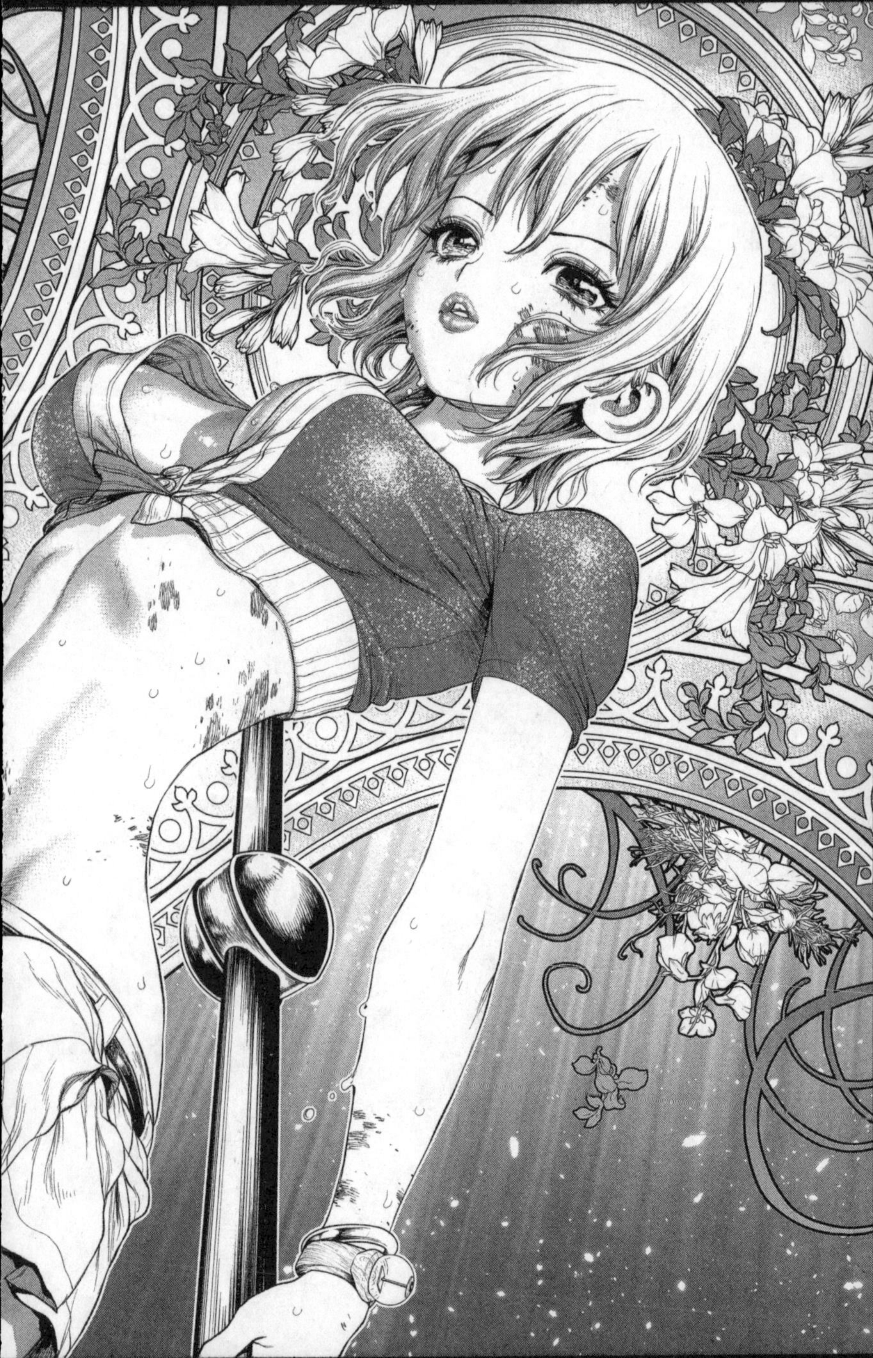

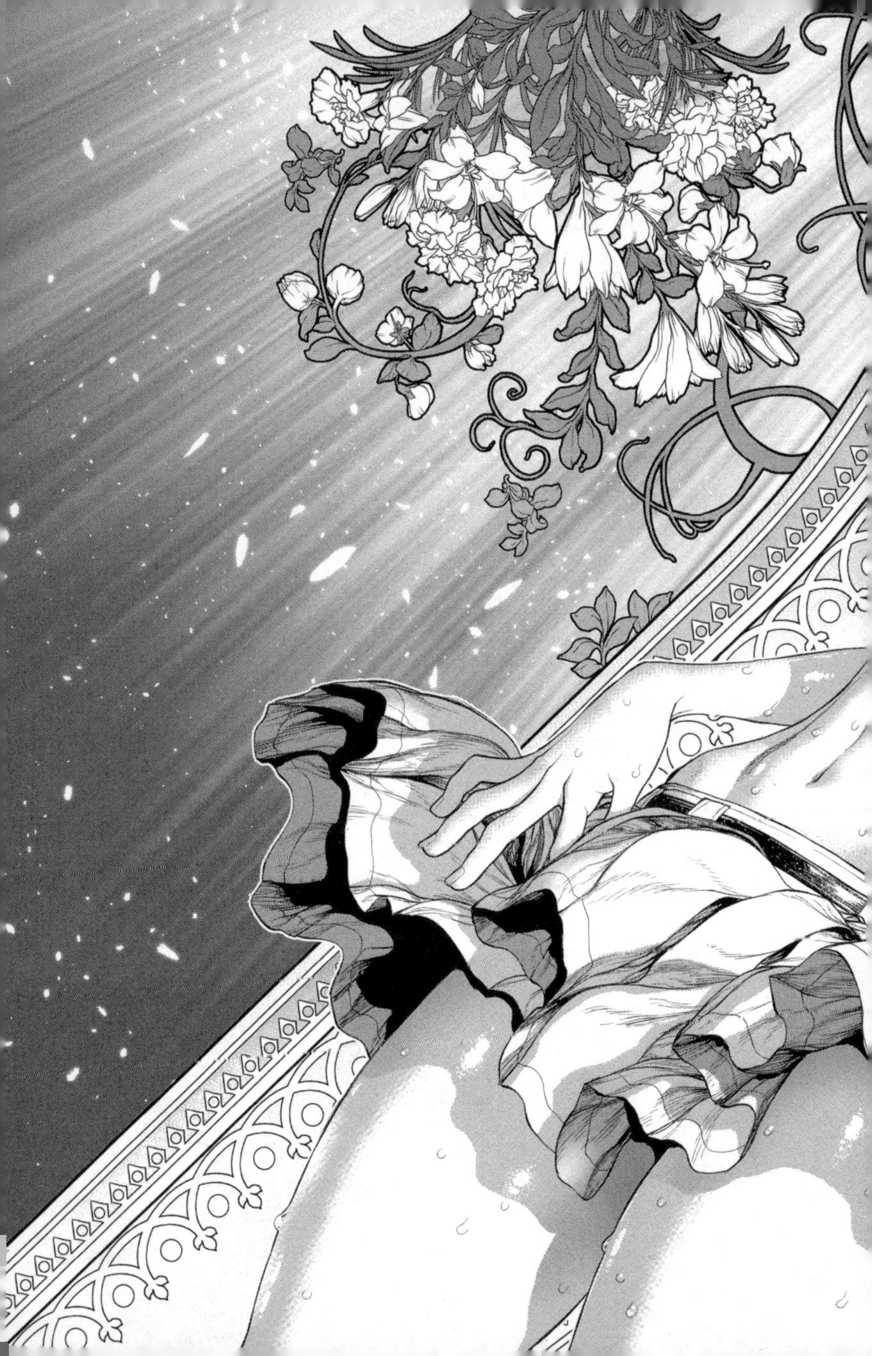

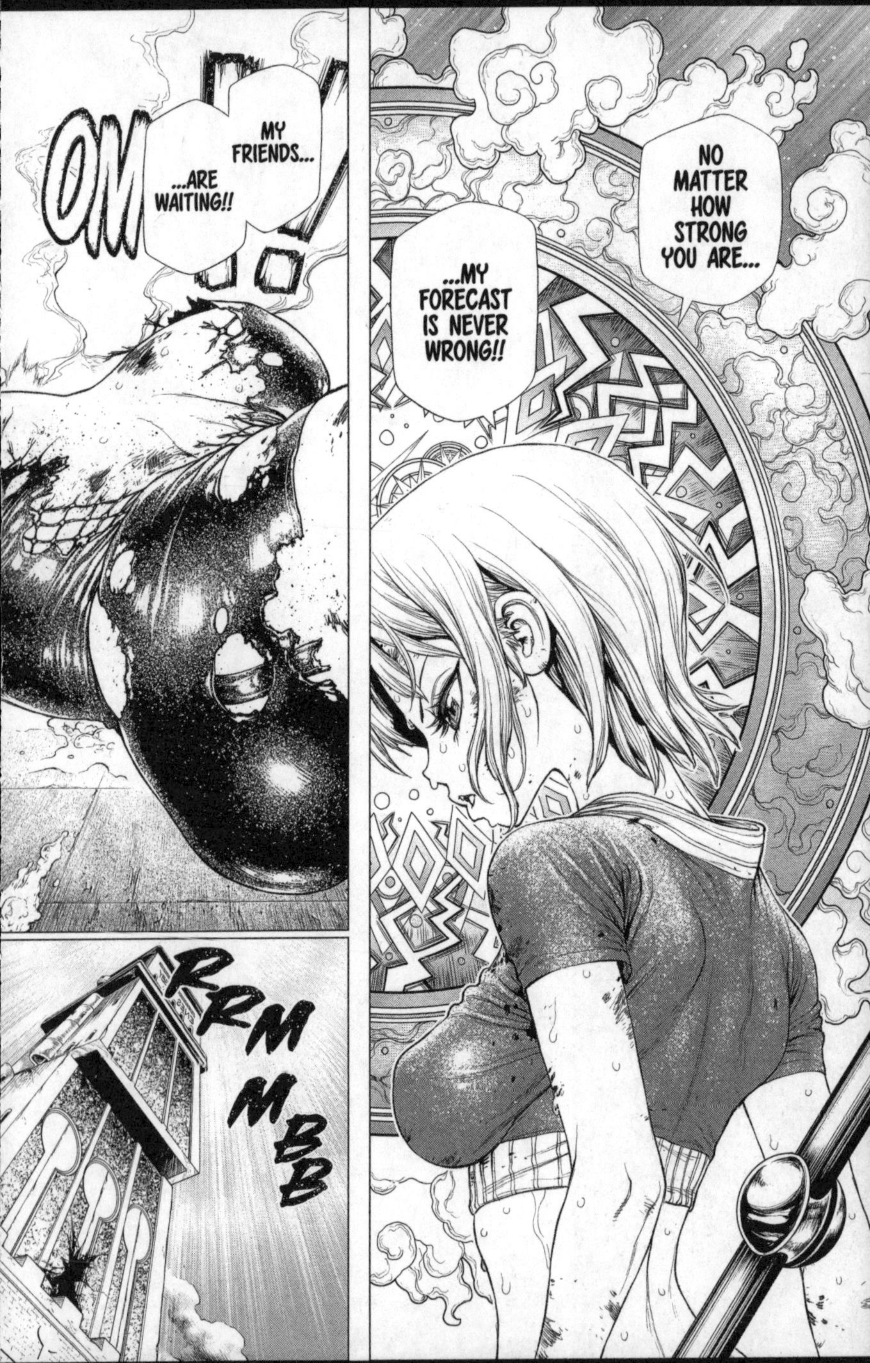
NO MATTER HOW STRONG YOU ARE...
...MY FORECAST IS NEVER WRONG!!
MY FRIENDS...
...ARE WAITING!!
RRMMBB

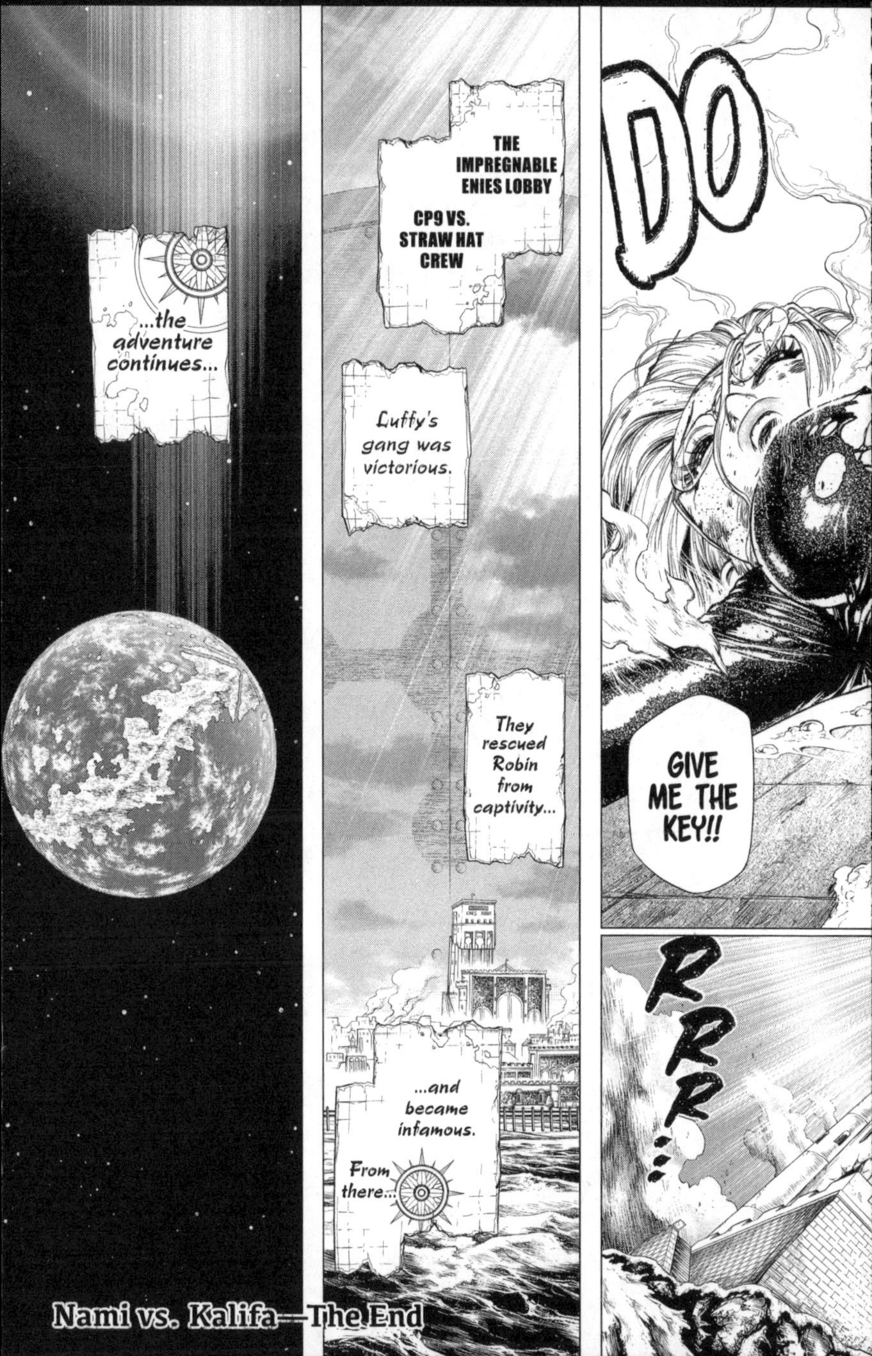
DO
GIVE ME THE KEY!!
RRR...
THE IMPREGNABLE ENIES LOBBY
CP9 VS. STRAW HAT CREW
Luffy's gang was victorious.
They rescued Robin from captivity...
...and became infamous.
From there...
...the adventure continues...
Nami vs. Kalifa—The End

word

Oda Sensei once gave out steakhouse gift cards to all the artists who collaborated on a *One Piece* -themed magazine cover. It was such a delight to me that I thought, "I'll never use this," and I still have it now, sealed in a frame.

But I did want to do right by his generosity, so I took my staff out for steak and paid for the meal instead.

Boichi

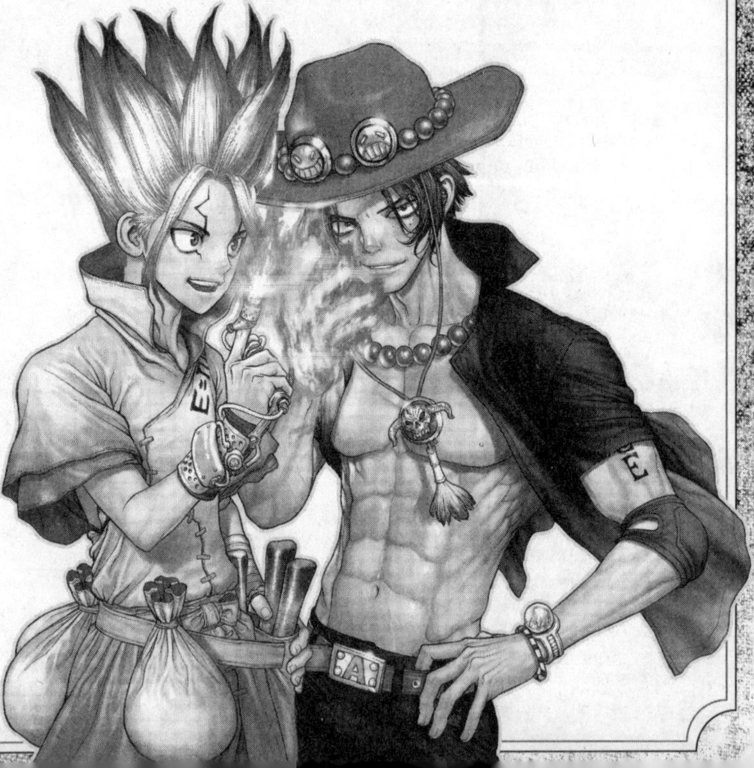

Afte

First of All

If you read the novels of *Ace's Story* before this, you might be surprised by some of the differences in the manga version. I don't blame you. For various reasons, we only had four installments to work with, which meant that it would be impossible to fit all the characters and scenes from the novels into the manga, and sadly I had to cut them out and reformat the story.

I'm very sorry to those readers who might have been looking forward to meeting their favorite characters from the novels again, and didn't get to see them.

If you haven't had the chance to read *Ace's Story* in novel form, I highly recommend it!

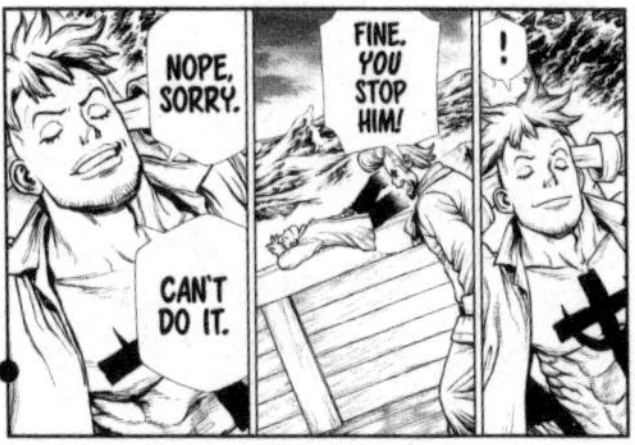
!
FINE. YOU STOP HIM!
NOPE, SORRY.
CAN'T DO IT.

What Filled Me with Joy

This scene in chapter 3 of Thatch and Marco actually came from a storyboard drawn by Oda himself! He was active in doing quality checks on the story-boards already, but in this case he actually submitted his own idea for the scene...

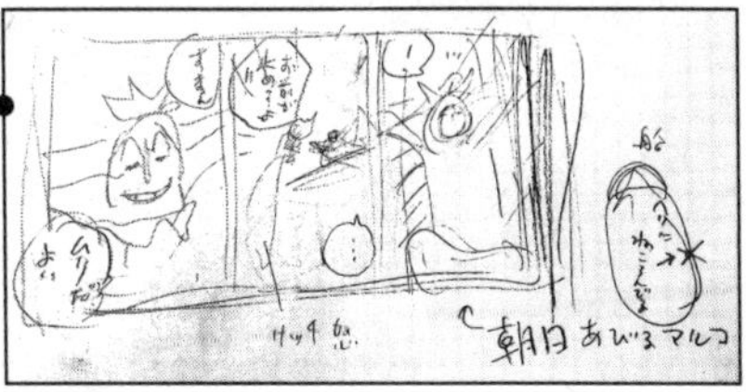
朝日あびるマルコ

He also noted the lines of dialogue he liked when he sent them back. All in all, his care and consideration were incredible! Thank you so much! I was a bit overcome by it all.

What Filled Me with Awe

It's wild that this was drawn while the artist was doing a weekly series! With this level of detail! *Ace's Story* would not have existed if not for Boichi agreeing to do the art.

He did the impossible for me on many occasions, and I have nothing but gratitude for him. He changed layouts and paneling to make the art have greater impact, and every time I got to see the finished product was a true joy and learning experience.

I'm so thankful to these two titans for the opportunity to work with them, and to all the readers whose support made it possible.

Ryo Ishiyama

Boichi

When events were underway for the celebration of chapter 1000, Oda Sensei thanked all the various artists who were involved and said, "Let's do our best for *Shonen Jump*." I swear on volume 2 of *One Piece: Ace's Story*, that, whatever my shortcomings as an artist, I will protect my place in *Jump* as long as the fans support me, and I hope that I get to represent the magazine along with Oda Sensei. I will never willingly leave *Shonen Jump*!

Ryo Ishiyama

This has been a truly wonderful experience. I've been reading *One Piece* since I was a child, and it inspired me to become a manga creator. The experience of getting to be involved with *One Piece* will be a lifelong treasure for me. If anyone who's read this series feels the same way, I would be honored. Enjoy the final volume of *One Piece: Ace's Story*!

Volume 2

Art by Boichi
Storyboards by Ryo Ishiyama
Created by Eiichiro Oda

Based on *One Piece: Ace's Story*
by Sho Hinata & Tatsuya Hamazaki

Translation/Stephen Paul
Lettering/Stephen Dutro
Design/Ian Miller
Editor/Megan Bates

ONE PIECE EPISODE A © 2020 by Eiichiro Oda,
Boichi, Ryo Ishiyama, Sho Hinata, Tatsuya Hamazaki
All rights reserved.
First published in Japan in 2020 by SHUEISHA Inc., Tokyo.
English translation rights arranged by SHUEISHA Inc.

The stories, characters, and incidents mentioned in
this publication are entirely fictional.

Printed in the U.S.A.

Published by VIZ Media, LLC
P.O. Box 77010
San Francisco, CA 94107

10 9 8 7 6 5 4 3 2 1
First printing, June 2024

viz.com

Adventure on the high seas continue in these stories featuring the characters of **One Piece**!

NOVEL

ONE PIECE

Ace's Story

Complete in two volumes!

CREATED BY
Eiichiro Oda

WRITTEN BY
Sho Hinata (Book 1)
Tatsuya Hamazaki (Book 2)

Get the backstory on Luffy's brother Ace! These two volumes contain the origin story of Luffy's adopted brother Ace, and tales of his thrilling quest for the legendary One Piece treasure.

VIZ

Living the life of a pirate requires hearty meals! The master
chef Sanji reveals the recipes that power the Straw Hat crew!

PIRATE RECIPES
ONE PIECE
by Sanji

Monkey D. Luffy has defeated dozens of rival pirates, and that kind of
success takes a whole lot of energy! Fortunately, the pirate cook Sanji
stands by Luffy's side, ready to support his captain with flaming-
hot kicks and piping-hot meals! Hearty and filling, Sanji's recipes
are just what you need to find the strength to achieve your goals!

Over 40 recipes for life on the high seas!

Gorgeous color art from Eiichiro Oda's **ONE PIECE**!
The first three **COLOR WALK** art books collected into one beautiful compendium.

EAST BLUE
TO SKYPIEA COLOR WALK COMPENDIUM

BY EIICHIRO ODA

Color images and special illustrations from the world's most popular manga, *One Piece*! This compendium features **over 300 pages** of beautiful color art as well as interviews between the creator and other famous manga artists, including **Akira Toriyama**, the creator of *Dragon Ball*.

VIZ

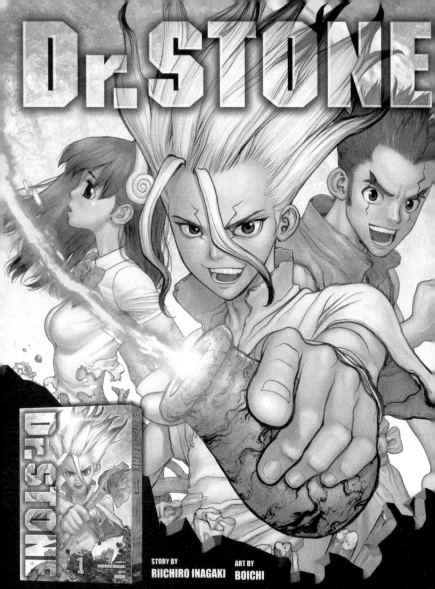

Dr. STONE

STORY BY
RIICHIRO INAGAKI

ART BY
BOICHI

One fateful day, all of humanity turned to stone. Many millennia later, Taiju frees himself from petrification and finds himself surrounded by statues. The situation looks grim—until he runs into his science-loving friend Senku! Together they plan to restart civilization with the power of science!

RATED TEEN

Hey! You're Reading in the Wrong Direction!

This is the *end* of this graphic novel!

To properly enjoy this VIZ graphic novel, please turn it around and begin reading from **right to left.** Unlike English, Japanese is read right to left, so Japanese comics are read in reverse order from the way English comics are typically read.

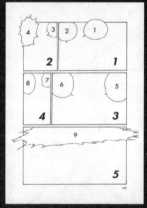

Follow the action this way

This book has been printed in the original Japanese format in order to preserve the orientation of the original artwork. Have fun with it!